RIVER OF FLESH
AND OTHER STORIES

with hope
Ruchira Gupta

D1291539

RIVER OF FLESH
AND OTHER STORIES

THE PROSTITUTED
WOMAN IN
INDIAN
SHORT FICTION

edited by
Ruchira Gupta

SPEAKING
TIGER

SPEAKING TIGER PUBLISHING PVT. LTD
4381/4 Ansari Road, Daryaganj,
New Delhi–110002, India

Anthology copyright © Ruchira Gupta 2016
Introduction copyright © Ruchira Gupta 2016
First published in India in paperback by Speaking Tiger 2016

The copyright for the individual stories and translations
vests with the individual authors.

ISBN: 978-93-85755-58-3
eISBN: 978-93-85755-60-6

10 9 8 7 6 5 4 3 2 1

Typeset in Adobe Caslon Pro by SÜRYA, New Delhi
Printed at Thomson Press India Ltd., New Delhi

All rights reserved.
No part of this publication may be reproduced,
transmitted, or stored in a retrieval system, in any form or
by any means, electronic, mechanical, photocopying,
recording or otherwise, without the prior
permission of the publisher.

This book is sold subject to the condition that it shall not,
by way of trade or otherwise, be lent, resold, hired out,
or otherwise circulated, without the publisher's
prior consent, in any form of binding or cover
other than that in which it is published.

For Saathi Das, who was murdered in Sonagachi,
and for Keya, who bravely continues Saathi's struggle against prostitution

CONTENTS

INTRODUCTION

The idea for *River of Flesh and Other Stories* germinated five years ago over a conversation with my friend Rakhshanda Jalil. I was talking to her about the roadblocks I faced when I tried to make people understand that prostitution was not just a function of women's inequality, but that it actually deepened women's inequality.

~

Wherever I travelled, I came up against the word 'agency'. I was told that some women choose prostitution over marriage, that they find freedom from patriarchal structures in prostitution, that college girls prostitute themselves for the sake of consumerism— to buy shoes, lipstick, bags, clothes, perfume… I was also told that prostitution was a livelihood choice many women make when confronted with sweat-shop work, domestic servitude and oppressive marriages.

As an activist, organizing girls and women suffering from inter-generational prostitution in red-light districts and caste-ghettoes, the reality I saw was vastly different. I witnessed prostituted women struggle to access even their most basic needs— food, clothing, shelter and protection from violence. I saw women live and die in debt bondage. I came to know of the huge profits which pimps and brothel-keepers make. I saw girls and women chewed up and spit out by the brothel system. I met women in their early thirties who had been thrown out of brothels because they were no longer commercially viable—customers constantly demand 'fresh meat'.

The average age of a girl pulled into prostitution is between nine and thirteen years. Ice is used to physically break pre-pubescent girls and make them amenable to exploitation. They are put through a process known as 'seasoning', in which they are beaten,

starved, drugged, told to call their pimp 'Papa' and their brothel-
manager 'Ma' or 'Masi', and made to believe that they are repaying
the small loans of five or ten thousand rupees which their fathers
have taken. These girls are raped by eight to ten customers every
night. They are made forcibly available to customers at any time,
day or night. They have to stand on the streets for long hours to
attract customers for themselves or for older women. They suffer
from sleep deprivation, insomnia and aching legs.

I saw mutilated bodies, bottles shoved up vaginas, scars of
cigarette butts on breasts, repeated fractures, suicides and murders.
I saw pimps and brothel-managers beat women black and blue for
talking to other girls or for simply crying. Many suffered from
Stockholm Syndrome, and were grateful for small acts of kindness
by their kidnappers.

Almost everyone had normalized the violence to such an extent
that, if asked, they denied having faced any. For the women, the
violence inflicted by the customers upon them was paid for, and
thus couldn't be defined as such. However, according to current
research, the physical and mental consequences of the repeated
body invasion that prostituted women face is so extreme that these
girls and women suffer from higher rates of psycho-social trauma
than even war veterans.

I saw little 'agency' in their lives.

Yet, I have heard smart men—and smart women, too—say
that prostitution is empowering and not de-humanizing; that it is
one livelihood choice among the other unequal choices available
to women. Some even say it should be defined as work like any
other and prostituted women should be called 'sex-workers'.

I cannot tell whether these men and women are protecting the
status quo or just have no faith in anyone's ability to change it. Do
they, by accepting prostitution as inevitable, accept women's
inequality as inevitable? When they said that women prostitute
themselves, did they mean that these women have sex with
themselves? Why do they negate the role of men? Perhaps the
problem is that they do not want to address the issues of male

power and privilege. So, as long as men hold on to power and entitlement, my friends are happy to let women settle for 'agency' within deeply exploitative systems.

~

It was in this context that Rakhshanda suggested an anthology of stories by progressive writers from undivided India which provides insights into the link between women's inequality and prostitution. And while she set the ball rolling by finding some stories and commissioning their translations, the book soon acquired a mind of its own. It decided that it would represent more of India. We began by including Bengali and Hindustani stories. Then heard about a fantastic story in Hindi, a sensitive one in English, a despairing one in Marathi, a searing one in Malayalam, a heart-breaking one in Tamil, a soul-wrenching one in Kannada, a gentle one in Konkani, a moving one in Assamese, a brave one in Punjabi, a challenging one in Odia... Now the book has stories in twelve languages.

All the stories reveal the commonalities among the inequalities of women across our sub-continent. All reveal the low self-esteem, incompleteness, emptiness, self-doubt and self-hatred that comes from being the oppressed. All the stories show the limitations of 'agency'. Women attempt to equalize power by exercising the only 'agency' they have, the power to destroy the self—and others who resemble the self. Premchand's heroine prostitutes herself to shame her husband, Manto's heroine murders her pimp knowing that she will be caught and punished, Indira Goswami's heroine walks out naked from her lover's coffin, and Amrita's Pritam's concubine sings at her lover's son's wedding in the presence of his wife and family.

Every story reveals the absence of choices prostituted women and their un-prostituted sisters face in and outside marriage. While the trauma and brutality of prostitution is exposed, so is the subordination of women through marriage as a cultural caste system.

Not surprisingly, caste inequality, too, is revealed in subtle ways. Dalit writer Baburao Bagul describes the dehumanizing way in which a shopkeeper treats a low-caste prostituted woman who tries to earn money to visit her sick son, Goswami's heroine lives in abject poverty to honour the promise of marriage made by her high-caste lover, Amrita Pritam's heroine comes from the Kanjar tribe—known officially as a 'Denotified Criminal Tribe', Bibhutibhushan Bandyopadhyay describes the friendship between a low-caste prostituted woman and a Brahmin child, and Kamleshwar's protagonist is a low-caste woman, whose very body begins to smell from her illnesses, yet continues to be exploited.

And then, there are the men. They are predatory, self-willed, entitled, judgmental, and preoccupied with the notions of shame and honour. Some live off the earnings of prostituted women, like the men in 'River of Flesh', 'The Hundred-Candle-Power Bulb', 'Woman of the Street' and 'God Forsaken' while the men in the stories 'Ponnagaram', 'Market Price' and 'Kalindi' depend on women for their very existence.

Over the twenty-one stories in this collection, a system of abuse by customers, pimps, brothel-keepers, lovers, husbands and recruiters is delicately uncovered.

The term 'sex-worker' cannot erase the trauma of body-invasion. Nor can any kind of legislation do away with the shock of body-penetration. There is no glossing over the fact that prostitution is an inherently exploitative practice, more akin to slavery that to occupation. As a feminist and campaigner for social justice, these stories, as well as the lived experiences of the women I meet, have only strengthened my belief that women do not choose prostitution, they are prostituted. *River of Flesh and Other Stories: The Prostituted Woman in Indian Short Fiction* is our attempt to de-normalize the efforts to legitimize the exploitation of women.

17 December 2015

RUCHIRA GUPTA

RIVER OF FLESH
AND OTHER STORIES

A DOLL FOR THE CHILD PROSTITUTE

Kamala Das

It was the same old story. The stepfather was raping the minor girl while her mother was out visiting her relatives. The fat woman called Ayee by the inmates of the house threw back her head and laughed aloud, displaying two rows of brown teeth like rusty nails. 'Anasuya, what did you expect from a bum like your Govind?' she asked the thin visitor who had brought her twelve-year-old daughter for sale. 'Anyway, let bygones be bygones. Stop worrying about this nice-looking girl of yours. She will be all right here. You will hardly recognize her after a couple of months. What she needs is good food. Look at my girls, Anasuya. Do you see any one of them looking unhealthy? I feed them eggs with their parathas in the morning.' The little girl looked around. There were seven young women seated on the floor and all of them did look healthy. But peeping out of a window was a frail girl who wore orange bangles on her thin wrists. She could not have been more than fifteen. Perhaps she will be my friend, thought the little girl.

'Rukmani, come closer to me,' said Ayee, drawing the child to her swollen bosom. 'Take leave of your poor mother. She has a long way to go, and it is already late. The postman is returning home...'

'Any letter for me?' asked Ayee and the postman, slowing his bike, smiled good-humouredly at her. 'I am always hoping to hear from my beloved son, that good-for-nothing fellow who ran away from home ten years ago,' said Ayee.

'You will hear from him,' said the visitor, wiping a reddened nose on the corner of her saree. 'Your heart is pure. God will not make you suffer long.'

The child Rukmani looked at her mother with dry eyes. She was not unhappy about leaving her home. The man who had moved into her home some months ago, after her father had

1

disappeared, was a monster. He not only beat up her mother every night, but squeezed her own little breasts, hurting her dreadfully when she was alone in the house. And, last week he had pierced her body until she bled all over the floor.

'You ought not to have sent away the good man I married you off to, Anasuya,' said Ayee. 'He was a steady fellow and he never drank. But you lusted for a younger one. Are you satisfied now?'

'Do not taunt me so, Ayee,' pleaded Anasuya. 'I have been a sinner. But please look after my child. She is innocent.'

Anasuya rolled the dirty currency notes inside a paper and tucked the roll into her waist. 'I would not have taken any money from you, Ayee,' she said, a sob rising in her throat, 'but we are practically starving at home. The baby is given nothing but tea and maybe a banana at noon.'

When she left the place and walked towards the bus stop, the child Rukmani watched her, leaning against the bars of the porch. Finally, when her mother resembled a tiny green spot and dissolved with the other colours in the distance, she turned back to look at her new mother. Ayee was kneading lime and tobacco in the palm of her left hand. The thin girl emerged from the interior and smiled at Rukmani, crinkling her eyes. She was wearing a blue skirt and a torn white blouse. The bangles on her wrists had a frosted look.

'Do you wish to have some of these?' asked the thin girl. 'They are nylon bangles, not plastic. Ayee bought them for me at the fair last month.'

'Sita, you must teach Rukmani the customs of this place,' said Ayee. 'She is two years younger than you.'

Sita held Rukmani by her waist. 'You can have my bangles,' she said, looking at the child's wrists. Then she gave a laugh. 'Oh, you are big-made, aren't you?' Sita asked Rukmani. Rukmani's hands were large compared to Sita's pale ones. She felt clumsy all of a sudden.

'Orange will not suit a dark skin,' said Rukmani. 'You are not dark,' said Ayee. 'You have been walking to your school in the hot sun and that is why you have such a tan. We shall make you fair-skinned in a month's time.'

A dark woman lying curled up on the floor, got up and glared at the child. 'What is wrong in being dark?' she asked Ayee. 'I am dark, but every client asks for me…'

Sita dragged Rukmani into the corridor of the house, which was dark and had a steamy smell. Then she was taken to a hall where some young women were sleeping on reed-mats. One of them was wearing only a short skirt which had slipped up to reveal the cheeks of her buttocks. Rukmani looked away in disgust. 'Oh this one, she is utterly shameless,' said Sita, throwing a towel over the sleeping woman's legs. 'She is Radha. She has a bad temper. So be careful when you deal with her.' Sita pointed to a mat in the corner of the hall. 'That is where I sleep in the day,' she said. 'You may share the mat with me.'

'I cannot sleep in the day,' said Rukmani.

Sita laughed loudly and held on to her stomach as though it was about to burst. 'You are a baby,' she said. 'You are so innocent. Do you think we can sleep at night in this house? We shall all be so busy entertaining the visitors.'

'Visitors at night?' asked Rukmani. 'Who will come at night?'

Sita could not control her laughter. 'Oho ho,' she laughed, 'you are too funny, you will make me piss in my skirt…'

Rukmani kept her satchel of books on the mat meant for her and Sita. 'Men come to do things here,' said Sita.

'What things?' asked Rukmani. She was thinking of her stepfather and the pain she had experienced when he climbed atop her on the floor.

'You will find out soon enough,' said Sita. 'Obey them or else Ayee will starve you to death. Do whatever they want you to do. Men are real dogs.'

Then they tiptoed out into the corridor, while a soft voice asked them from inside a room, 'Who is it?' 'It is me, Sita,' said the pale girl. 'Don't make too much noise,' chided the soft voice.

'That is Mirathai, the favourite of this house,' said Sita in a whisper. 'Ayee has given her a room all to herself. She is a beautiful woman. And she is a matriculate, not like the rest of the gang who are all uneducated. How far have you studied, Rukmani?'

'I am in the sixth standard,' said Rukmani.

'That is good enough,' said Sita. 'You must be able to read English, just a little?'

'Not English,' said Rukmani. 'English is tough. We started it only this year. I can read Marathi and Hindi.'

'Then you must read out a book a client left for me to read. It contains dirty pictures of naked men and women. I pretended that I was educated, and so he gave that book to me.' Saying this, Sita laughed again.

'Why do you hold your stomach when you laugh?' asked Rukmani.

'When I laugh I get a queasy feeling inside my belly,' Sita said. 'I am not too well these days. I have even lost my appetite.'

From the porch rose a strident voice in protest. 'No, no, that is not true, Lachmi,' it said. 'I will never speak against your girls. You are like a younger sister to me. Besides, what can I say against your girls? Everybody knows that you keep a disciplined house and that your girls are plump and healthy. The Inspector Saheb told me that your Mira resembled a film-star who has become of late very famous. I cannot recollect the name. It is a lengthy fashionable name.'

Ayee spread out her fat legs and leaned against the wall. She chewed the tobacco pensively for a minute. 'Where did you meet the Inspector Saheb, Sindhuthai?' she asked the visitor. The old woman took a pinch of tobacco from Ayee's betel-box and pretended not to hear. Ayee repeated the question. Sindhuthai knew what a loaded question it was. 'I met him at Koushalya's place yesterday,' said Sindhuthai.

'The ingrate,' shouted Ayee. 'Here I give him expensive gifts and every week his hafta of fifty rupees and all the girls free, and he has the audacity to go to my rival's house for his quota of fun. What is wrong with my children? Are Koushalya's girls as clean as mine? Filthy five-rupeewalis.'

'Don't get upset, younger sister,' said Sindhuthai. 'Inspector Saheb said he was tired of women. He wanted little girls.'

'We don't have little girls?' asked Ayee. 'What about Sita? Is she not lovely with her white skin and petite figure?'

'Sita is not cooperative any longer, he said,' whispered the hag.

'Have you seen the child I have bought today?' asked Ayee. 'Rukmani, come here and let Sindhuthai see you.'

Sita pushed Rukmani into the porch. The old woman pinched the child's calves and stroked her posterior. 'Yes, she is firm and sweet,' said Sindhuthai. 'How much did you pay for her? She must have cost you a lot of money.'

Ayee whispered something into the old woman's ear. 'Oh, she is our Anasuya's child,' Sindhuthai said, 'that is why she has such beautiful legs.'

'Will you tell the Inspector Saheb that we have this little goddess in our house?' asked Ayee.

'Yes, I shall do so this very evening,' said Sindhuthai. She took some betel from the brass box and turned to go. Her gnarled hands with their dirty talons frightened the little girl. When the hag was staring at her, she had felt that a woodpecker was pecking at her skin. 'What an odious creature,' she murmured to Sita.

'Yes,' said Sita, 'she is a scandalmonger. I hate her.'

II

All the street lights were on but the sky was still grey when Mirathai's client, the college student, walked in with a swagger, calling out imperiously, 'Mira, Mira.' Ayee was still in the bathroom having her legs massaged with mustard oil but she heard his voice and frowned. 'It is that talkative swain again,' she remarked to the girl who was at her feet. 'If he does not pay this time, I shall get the police to throw him out,' continued Ayee. 'Radha, has he been to you any time?'

'No,' said Radha, 'he wants only Mira. He behaves as if he is her husband. He talks to her half the night, and even quarrels.'

'Half the night?' asked Ayee. 'Does he pay for such a long session?'

'Don't ask me,' said Radha. 'After all Mira is your pet. None can question her in this house. She has begun to be fastidious of late. She refused even the Inspector Saheb yesterday, complaining that she had a headache. She does not behave like a prostitute. She wants to be faithful to her college student...'

'Don't use such coarse terms, Radha,' said Ayee.

'You do not like the word *prostitute*,' muttered Radha, 'but you know well that all of us are prostitutes. I believe in being frank and truthful.'

'Rub my knee harder,' said Ayee.

From Mira's closed room rose the rumble of a male voice.

Mira laughed once.

Ayee was disturbed. 'What is he always talking about?' asked Ayee.

'He is teaching her politics,' said Radha.

'He is impotent, is he?' asked Ayee.

'I do not know, Ayee,' said the girl. 'He does not touch any of us. All I know is that he always leaves Mira with a headache. After he has visited her, she refuses to entertain any client. She sits on her bed humming strange tunes.' Ayee got up and walked towards the closed door. The young man was still talking briskly and Ayee could only pick out certain words which were familiar. Once or twice, he mentioned the word 'revolution'. Ayee knocked on the door. 'Who is it?' asked Mira. 'Open the door,' said Ayee. Mira opened the door. She was wearing her green saree and on the bed which still had an uncrumpled sheet, sat the student, smoking.

'Do you come all the way here to tell her of a revolution?' asked Ayee.

The youth coloured. 'I have paid the money,' he said.

Ayee looked at him with contempt. 'This is a brothel,' she said, 'not a conference hall. Get on with your job and get out.' Then she added, 'Other clients will be coming in a few minutes' time.'

The door was shut again. Ayee went up to the porch and surveyed the scene. The girls were wearing clothes sparkling with jari and sequins. They had make-up on their faces and flowers in their hair. The two young ones were playing with bits of tiles on a large diagram chalked out on the floor. 'Stop this childish game, Sita,' ordered Ayee. 'The clients are about to arrive.'

At that precise moment, the Inspector, who was a burly man, entered the porch and pointing to Rukmani asked: 'Is this your new recruit?' Ayee nodded. 'Come in,' said the man, dragging the child into the interior.

'Go, child, he is our friend,' said Ayee.

The Inspector threw the child on a charpoy and lifted her frock. 'You wear underpants like girls of the upper classes,' said the man, laughing. Rukmani felt his hands on her and struggled to get free. 'Let me go,' she cried, 'if you don't, I shall scratch your eyes out.'

'What did you say, you wild cat?' asked the angry man. His voice underwent a change, and became very hoarse. 'You will scratch me, will you, little whore...'

'I am not a whore,' cried Rukmani. But the man did not care to listen. He was panting as though he had run a race and there was froth at the corners of his wide mouth. Later, he turned over and closed his eyes. 'I shall buy you a red frock,' he whispered, 'and panties with lace on them.'

Rukmani rose from the bed and ran back to the porch. Her hair was tousled and sweat beaded her brow. But she began once again to hop in the squares of the diagram while Sita watched animatedly. 'I have won,' cried Rukmani a little while later in triumph. Just then, the Inspector came out of the room and gave Ayee a slow smile.

'She is a vixen, all right. Knows the tricks of the trade. I liked her immensely.'

Rukmani glanced at the man whose face was red with the scratches inflicted by her own nails. He looked complacent.

'Who is prattling away in Mira's room?' asked the Inspector.

Ayee beat her head in mock anguish: 'It is that student again, come to teach her politics.'

'I can drive him out of this place,' said the Inspector, 'only give me a day's notice. I can even get him arrested and sent to jail.'

'I know you can,' said Ayee. 'But let us wait until Mira tires of him. Mira is like my daughter. I love her dearly. I don't wish to hurt her feelings.'

'You have spoilt her already, Lachmi bai,' said the Inspector. 'She behaves as if she is well-born.'

'Who can say for certain that she is not well-born?' asked Ayee. 'When I found her at my doorstep, she was wrapped in an expensive silk saree, not the kind worn by people of our station.'

'Her mother must have been a maid working for a rich woman who gave that saree to her for Diwali or some such function,' said the man reaching for Ayee's betel box.

'She certainly does not look like a poor woman's child,' said Ayee. 'Whenever I take the girls out to the town for shopping, people stare at her with hungry eyes. If my lost son were to return, I shall certainly marry her off to him. They will make a fine couple. Both are fair-skinned, and both have light eyes.'

'Is your son's father a Chitpavan Brahmin?' asked the Inspector, and both he and the old woman laughed in mirth. 'I must get going,' said the man.

'Is it true that you have started to visit Koushalya's place?' asked Ayee. 'Do not leave my place without giving me a truthful answer.'

'I shall get that witch Sindhuthai arrested and sent to jail,' said the man. 'She must have seen me walk past that house yesterday towards the bus stop, and she did not waste time in passing the information to you. Why should I go to that house, Lachmi bai?'

Ayee blew out her nose and looked as if she was about to cry. 'That Koushalya, she spreads such horrible tales about my innocent girls,' said Ayee. 'Sindhuthai said that she was telling people that my girls were diseased. What will happen to our business if such stories are circulated…My poor girls will starve to death.'

'Don't cry,' said the Inspector, sheepishly stroking the woman's plump hand. 'I shall protect your reputation. I am your friend. I shall never let you down.'

Ayee brightened up a little. She even attempted a smile. 'Take some paan, Inspector Saheb,' she whispered.

After the Inspector had left, Ayee slipped into a sullen mood. She began to taunt her girls who were looking out through the bars. 'What is wrong with all of you?' she asked. 'Have you forgotten how to attract men? I waste my money buying eggs and dalda and fish for all of you but not one of you know how to hold on to a man except that Mira, and now she has latched on to a good-for-nothing fellow who teaches her politics. How many important people pass this way in their cars, slowing down as they pass this way to be able to see you, and yet you do not do a thing to lure them in. What a bunch of pigs, I have reared here. Koushalya is far more fortunate than I am. She whips her girls, but that has only done them good. Look at the cars that have stopped near her place. Two already and it is not yet eight o'clock. I am going to throw you all out and go to Benares. Let me at least die in peace...'

The dark girl called Saraswati climbed down the porch and gestured to a young man who was watching out from a bus. Within a few minutes the young man was at her side, having got off at the next bus stop. She took him into the corridor, swinging her full hips and walking ahead of him. Ayee rubbed her eyes with the edge of her saree.

'I don't do these things because it is crude,' said the girl called Radha. 'I hate to stand out and solicit like a common streetwalker.' Then someone came asking for Sita. 'Ayee, not tonight,' begged Sita, wanting to be let off.

'Go with him, child,' said Ayee, pushing Sita gently beyond the doorway.

'Rukmani, do not remove my piece from that square,' cried Sita. 'I shall be back to finish the game.'

'He is a kind man, although a Madrasi,' said Ayee. 'He is working in a school. Comes during the first week of every month and only selects Sita. He has three grown-up daughters studying in college. His wife is stricken with arthritis. He tells me all about his life. He does not hide anything. He is not secretive like the others...'

Ayee heard the sound of a woman's weeping from inside the

house. She listened in silence for a moment or two. 'Is that our Mira weeping?' she asked. 'Go and see what is happening inside her room. Men are odd creatures. One cannot predict their actions. When I was young, a rich man came to me and whipped me for half an hour and went his way paying me thirty rupees. In those days, thirty was a large sum of money. I was too astonished to cry. I used to wait for him but he never turned up again.'

'What was your son's father like, Ayee?' asked Radha.

Ayee got up and gave a friendly slap on her cheek. 'Don't you dare talk about the father of my son,' said Ayee. 'He was a Brahmin. He was not like any of the men who come here to see all of you. He was a wise man. He used to recite the scriptures while dressing up to go.'

'He sounds so much like our Mirathai's friend,' said Radha. 'He sings the *Gitagovinda* to her on some nights. I have heard her trying to sing the songs that he has taught her.'

'Mira has a sweet voice,' said Ayee. 'She is a gem of a girl. I wonder who left her on my doorstep nineteen years ago. Perhaps it was some high-born woman who had conceived while her husband was away.'

'Perhaps it was some harlot who did not want to be saddled with a baby,' said Radha.

'All of you are jealous of Mira,' said Ayee.

Just then, Mira's client walked out without looking back even once. Ayee sat up in surprise. He looked as if he had been weeping too. What was wrong with the young man? Was he mentally unbalanced? She decided to speak to Mira about him. It would not do to encourage such an eccentric. Mira ought to try and bait a man of substance, a businessman who is tired of his wife or a politician who craves for relaxation off and on, someone who can bring her expensive gifts and bestow on the house a certain prestige.

'Mira,' Ayee called out to the weeping girl, 'come out this minute.' Mira came out and stood under the neon lamp, moon-coloured and slender. Only her eyes, made large by collyrium, looked red. 'What has he done to you, my daughter?' asked Ayee.

'He did nothing, Ayee,' said Mira. 'He is always kind to me.'

'What made you weep?' asked the old woman. 'He must have said something to upset you.' Mira looked down at her feet. She did not reply.

'Did he call you names?' asked Ayee.

'No, Ayee,' said Mira, 'he said that he had to sell his pen to visit me. He has no income of his own. He comes here saving his lunch allowance and his bus fare. He loves me...' Mira's eyes filled with tears.

III

When Sita vomited all over the floor of the room and scared her client away, Ayee was very angry with her. The man had asked for a refund of the money he had paid Ayee and, as a parting shot, had exclaimed that the house was full of diseased whores. Ayee entered the room to find Sita seated on the floor with vomit all round her and making a loud sound while she struggled to bring out more from her stomach. Her eyes were wide with fear. Ayee pulled her by her long braid and slapped her hard on her face. 'You have ruined the reputation of this house,' said Ayee. 'You eat all kinds of dirty things sold by the street vendors and throw up into the faces of our clients. How many times have I told you never to eat pani-puri or bhel? Ungrateful girl. I will see that you starve for three days.'

Sita began to weep: 'Ayee, it is not my fault,' she whimpered. 'I have not been feeling well for the past few days. I cannot eat anything. I feel a heart-burn in the evenings...'

'You have lost some weight,' said Ayee. Then she lifted the girl's white blouse and peered at her tiny breasts. 'It is not possible,' murmured Ayee. 'You have not even attained puberty.'

Sita was given three days' leave. She was overjoyed. 'I do not have to attend to any man for three days,' she cried out in a voice thickened with happiness. 'We shall play hopscotch with bits of tiles, Rukmani, for hours and hours.'

Leaning against the bars of the porch, Sita said to her friend:

'Look at the sky this afternoon, it is like a whitewashed wall. Once upon a time I lived in a house with white walls. Every year during Diwali, my father whitewashed our walls with lime and powdered sand.'

'Where is your father?' asked Rukmani. Sita shrugged her shoulders. 'He is dead. All are dead. Cholera got them all four years ago. There were five deaths in my family. My father, my mother, my three brothers...'

'But what happened to that house with the white walls?' asked Rukmani.

'That must have died too,' said Sita laughing. 'Everything dies, Rukmani. Even the sky.' Rukmani looked up at the blanched brilliance of the sky. It hurt her eyes.

Ayee called the young girls to her side in the afternoon. 'Come, let me do your hair for you,' she said. First, it was Rukmani's turn. Ayee removed the snarls from her curly hair and plaited it tight. Rukmani wrinkled her face in discomfort. 'I shall get you Brahmani oil for your hair,' said Ayee. 'Then in two months' time, it will have more body. Your hair is too soft and silky. Sita's is thick enough. In fact, she is too weak to carry the burden of her hair.'

While their hair was being done, Sindhuthai climbed up the steps beside the porch, rubbing her rough feet gratingly on the stone. She cleared her throat and said: 'How are you today, my younger sister, you look happy today.'

Ayee grew pale at the thought of the hag's evil eye. 'We are pulling on, thanks to the blessings of Lord Ganesh,' said Ayee. 'Sita here is not too well. She has lost her appetite for food.'

'Has she attained puberty?' asked Sindhuthai.

'No,' said Ayee. 'Otherwise, I would not have been so thoroughly upset. I am wondering if I should take her to the Doctor Saheb today.'

'Don't you take your girls to the Doctor Saheb every week?' asked Sindhuthai. It was another of her loaded questions.

Ayee squirmed in embarrassment. 'Why do you ask such a question?' she asked the old woman. 'Has that bitch Koushalya been telling you that I do not get my girls medically checked up every week?'

'Yes, that was what she told me yesterday,' said Sindhuthai. 'I was passing by her house on my way to the ration shop when she stopped me. She insisted on my going in, to take a glass of tea with her. How could I refuse the offer and incur her displeasure? You know well what a lot of mischief she is capable of, when her ire is aroused. Koushalya will make a deadly foe for anyone who irritates her. She has of late become very influential too. I saw the car of a high government official parked near her place.'

'How does she manage it?' asked Ayee, 'with her scummy bunch of girls?'

'They are well-trained,' said the hag.

'I am taking my girls this very minute to the Doctor Saheb's dispensary,' said Ayee. 'I am sorry I cannot sit here talking to you, Sindhuthai.'

'I understand, sister,' said the hag, picking up shreds of tobacco from the box. 'I am feeling weak and dizzy today,' said Sindhuthai. 'Younger sister, have you any money you can spare for a soda? Soda settles my stomach each time I feel ill.'

'Sindhuthai, you don't mean soda, do you?' asked Ayee. 'You drink country liquor whenever you can lay your hands on it. The Inspector Saheb himself told me that he saw you buy a bottle of moosambi.'

'Scandalmongers all over the place,' cried out the hag. 'Everybody hates me nowadays. In my time, I have helped all of you in many ways. Now nobody loves me. All make fun of me. When youth goes away, every woman becomes an object of ridicule. Lachmi, you have a house now, but watch my words, after another ten years you will be thrown out from here like a rind and another will become the Ayee of this place. Most probably Mira. Or that dark one, Saraswati.'

'Don't say such things with your accursed tongue, Sindhuthai,' cried out Ayee. 'My girls will always love me. I have never ill-treated them. Ask Rukmani here. Ask them all how I have fed them, and how I have nursed them with my own hands during illness. They will not throw me out as your girls once threw you out, Sindhuthai. I will be their Ayee until my death.'

Sindhuthai chortled sarcastically: 'This is what I too thought once upon a time, Lachmi,' she said, 'but see what happened. My favourite girls threw me out calling me names. What could I do? I was past the age for attracting any man. All I could do was roam around looking for a hut to live in, a shelter over my head. I begged at street corners for a year. Then I became a useful member of this locality. I could perform abortions for as little as twenty rupees. So you invited me into your houses. I was lucky. But how can you be sure that you will be as lucky as I have been?'

Ayee hid her round dark face in the folds of her saree and wept unashamedly. Sita remembered the gurgling sound the buffaloes made while they wallowed in the muddy pools of her village. How funny Ayee's sobs sounded. She nudged Rukmani with an elbow. She wanted suddenly to giggle. But Rukmani was watching the fat woman cry, intently and with a sympathetic expression on her face.

Mira called out from inside: 'Rukmani, come here for a minute. I cannot hook my choli which is open at the back.'

Rukmani went inside to help Mira who was standing, dressed only in a satin petticoat of black and an open choli. She looked radiantly happy. She had a red spot of sindoor on her brow and kajal in her eyes. 'Mirathai, are you going out anywhere?' asked the little girl.

'Oh, no, I am dressing to meet my friend who is coming this evening,' said Mira.

'You look like a married woman,' said the girl and Mira embraced her with a sudden laugh.

'I am married,' said Mira, 'but don't tell anybody about it...'

'Are you married to the student who visits you?' asked Rukmani. 'The one who sold his fountain pen to come to you?'

'Yes, he is my husband. He is called Krishna. Is that not strange, Rukmani?' Mira asked the little girl. 'Is it not strange that I am Mira and he is Krishna?'

Rukmani remained silent. She felt Mirathai was behaving peculiarly that evening. It was like the delirium of those who have high fever. There was a red flush on her high cheekbones and a glitter in her eyes. Mira decorated her hair with a string of mogra flowers and bit her lips to make them redder. 'Why don't you use some lipstick?' asked Rukmani.

'He does not like lipstick,' said Mira.

When Rukmani had finished hooking her choli, Mira hugged her with passion and kissed her forehead. 'God bless you, my child,' said Mira.

When she went out in the porch, Ayee had stopped her crying and Sindhuthai had vanished. Rukmani sat on the steps near Sita who was watching the buses go by. 'One day, Ayee took us in a double-decker bus,' said Sita. 'Then I put out my hand and plucked a guava from a tree.'

'You are a liar,' said Rukmani.

'Ask Ayee,' whispered Sita. 'I plucked a ripe guava from the tree. I ate it on the bus. It was full of seeds. I liked the seeds the best of all. Ayee said that the guava seeds produce worms in the stomach. Long wriggly worms.'

'Maybe you have such worms in your stomach,' said Rukmani. 'That is why you threw up last night...'

'I threw up because I cannot any longer stand being messed up by men. I hate all of them.'

'Don't you want to get married?' asked Rukmani. 'Don't you want a home of your own and a few children?'

'Yes, I would love to have a home of my own and a few children. I want a plump baby to dandle on my knee. I want him to smile at me and call me Ma. But I don't want to have any man in my house.'

A client entered, hiding his face from the passers-by. 'You are very early,' said Ayee, 'it is not yet evening.'

'I am busy in the evening,' said the man. He wore a white bush-shirt and terylene trousers which looked dirty. He looked around him nervously and bit his nails.

'All right, make your choice,' said Ayee, gesturing towards the group of girls. Except for Mira, all were seated on the porch. Radha was as usual showing a lot of her things, sitting in a careless posture. The man signalled to her and she rose obediently to escort him indoors.

From Mira's room rose the lilting tune of Jayadeva's *Gitagovinda*. 'Mira sings beautifully,' said Ayee.

The girls listened in silence.

'Ratisukha sare gathamabhi sare madana manohara vesham. Nakuru nithabini gamanavilambhana manusarathum hridayesham Radhe!'

IV

It was only towards the morning that Ayee discovered that Mira had eloped with the college student. Mira's room was shut and the other girls knocked on the door casually while passing, calling out, 'Mirathai, did he leave you so exhausted that you cannot even get up from your bed?' There was no angry answer, no light laughter. 'Come and eat your breakfast,' cried Radha, knocking hard at the door. Breakfast was served at six every morning, a heavy meal of parathas dripping with vanaspati and an egg curry. There was a glass of milk to top the meal. After partaking of this, the girls normally curled up on their mats and fell asleep until it was time again for the next meal, which was at two. It was only after five that they stirred themselves to attend to their toilet. The bath was elaborate and afterwards their hair was decked with strings of flowers and rouge was rubbed into the skin of their cheeks, to make them look healthy. Beneath the pink powder, the bare skin was ashen and seemed to have aged prematurely. Using their bodies as rinds had killed their spirits. Only the young children, Rukmani and Sita, laughed normally. But they hardly knew the significance of the sexual act. For them, it came as an occasional punishment meted out for some obscure reason.

Perhaps the mistake they committed was that they got born as girls in a society that regarded the female as a burden, a liability.

The two girls resented the frequent interruptions during their game of squares and even while the coarse men, old enough to be their grandfathers, took their pleasure off their young bodies, the children's minds were far away, hopping in the large squares of the chalked diagram on the floor of the porch.

When Radha pushed open the door, she found Mira's room empty except for the bed which was not slept in. Her tin trunk, containing the coloured sarees she was fond of wearing, had disappeared. On the window-sill lay a cracked mirror, as small as Mira's palm, and some sindoor, spilt on the edge. 'Where has our Mirathai gone?' asked Radha clutching at her own brow. 'Has she run away with that crazy student of hers?' Ayee sat on Mira's bed and wept with a great deal of emotion. 'My golden bird has flown out of her cage' she wailed while, from outside the window, a crow cawed rapidly as though it had also heard the shocking news and was perturbed. Radha smoothed Ayee's hair and spoke soothing words. 'She is sure to return,' she said. 'That fellow has no money with him. After they have sold Mirathai's gold chain and have lived off its price, they will come back to beg for food.' Still Ayee continued with her wailing which rose higher, higher, until the neighbours rushed in to seek the cause of her grief. Koushalya was the first to arrive. 'What has happened, elder sister?' she asked Ayee.

'My Mira has been kidnapped by my enemies,' said Ayee. 'All were jealous of her beauty. All the high government officials came asking for her. And rich businessmen. Now I am lost. There is no girl here who can lure in men the way my Mira could. What a golden skin she had. What a body. I shall go to Benares this week and die there.'

'Mira must have gone willingly,' said Koushalya. 'Such things have happened before, and in the best of houses. Didn't that Nepali girl fly the coop last year from Marine Drive? Let her go and perish. You must not upset yourself about an ungrateful girl.'

'You know how I looked after the girls here, Koushalya?' asked Ayee. 'I used to give them parathas made in ghee, eggs, milk, and cod-liver-oil tablets. I used to take them to all the melas and the exhibitions going on in the city. I loved them deeply...'

'Elder sister, you are too kind,' said Koushalya. 'I have been wanting to warn you about being overkind to these girls. Kindness does not beget kindness. I whip them whenever they make a mistake and so they fear me. My girls are docile. They will not play hopscotch on the porch all through the afternoon like your young ones. You know that it is illegal to subject minors to a life of prostitution, don't you? People are beginning to talk about your house. People who are your so-called friends. I shall not mention their names.'

'Who talked about my girls?' asked Ayee, rising from Mira's bed with red eyes. 'Was it that witch Sindhuthai? Was it the Inspector Saheb?'

Koushalya shook her head enigmatically and smiled. 'I did not come here to gossip,' she said. 'I wanted only to comfort you.'

Ayee embraced Koushalya with a new-found affection. 'You are kind to me,' she said.

'We should stick together,' said Koushalya. 'We have common enemies. If we are united none can harm us, not even the police...'

The dark girl, Saraswati, immediately moved her things into Mira's room. 'I get more clients than anyone else,' she said in explanation. 'I have always had an eye on this room. This looks out on the wide street. I can sit at the window-sill and charm the men who go about in motor cars.'

Radha sulked. But she could not afford to argue with Saraswati who brought in an income higher than hers. 'She is common,' she murmured in another's ear, 'have you seen how she swings her fleshy hips, this way, that way, when any man is looking at her...?'

Ayee kept whining about the ingratitude of Mira, seated on the charpoy in the porch while the labourers and mill-hands walked past nonchalantly. When the Inspector came in, it was past noon, and he asked her incredulously, 'Lachmi bai, why did you not inform me earlier?' Ayee beat a slow tattoo on her dark forehead and continued wailing monotonously. 'If I had known of this earlier, I would have brought back the erring wench by now,' the Inspector said. 'I would have had my men comb the railway platform and the bus stops and would have by now sent that rogue to our jail. Now they must be far away from the city, probably in some village trying to find work.'

'What is the use trying to jail the boy?' asked Ayee. 'Mira went willingly. She is not a minor either. Rukmani told me that Mira had secretly married the boy.'

'Marriage,' shouted the Inspector. 'Why would a decent boy marry a prostitute? He will set up practice as a pimp and earn money from her. Lachmi bai, you are much too innocent to guess the ways of this shrewd world. That hussy refused to let me touch her, do you know that? One day, I offered her thirty rupees and yet she said "No Inspector Saheb, I cannot be unfaithful to the man I love." Is that the way a girl from a decent brothel like yours talks to an influential man like me? I could have thrashed her then and there with my cane but I did not want to create a ruckus in your house. You are like my elder sister, Lachmi bai.'

'You speak the truth, Inspector Saheb,' cried Ayee. 'You are my brother. In times of distress, I look to you for guidance. Without your help, I would not have flourished in this locality. I often wonder why I cannot take my girls and move to a better locality, the Grant Road or Colaba for instance. My girls have class, don't they? My little moppet Rukmani has charmed every client who has come here. She has such a supple body, such a clean smell. Inspector Saheb, she was telling me yesterday that she liked you immensely. She called you a handsome man.'

'Where is the girl?' asked the man, trying to peer into the darkness of the corridor. 'She must be lying asleep in the hall,' said Ayee. 'She wept the most when Mira disappeared. Mira used to bathe her in the mornings and sing songs to her.'

'May I see Rukmani for a few minutes?' asked the man.

Ayee went inside to call the little girl and found her playing with two plastic dolls, dressing them up to look like a wedded pair. Sita lay on the floor, sideways, watching her.

'The Inspector Saheb wishes to see you child,' whispered Ayee to Rukmani. 'Leave your dolls and go to the little room next to mine. I shall send him there...'

'Ayee, not now,' protested the child. 'We are playing a game just now. We are about to marry our doll off to the new doll bought yesterday. We have named them Mira and Krishna. Please ask that horrid man to go away.'

Ayee bent down and tweaked her ear. 'Get up this very minute,' she said. 'You cannot afford to displease the Inspector Saheb. He is a very important man. If he wants you now, you must go and please him. I do not want disobedience from you.'

'All right, Ayee,' said the girl, rising slowly from the floor. 'Wait for me, Sita, I shall be back in a short while to complete the wedding ceremony.' Sita smiled wanly, still lying on the floor.

The Inspector Saheb was very gentle with the young girl. 'Do you want me to buy you a doll that opens and closes its eyes?' he asked her, fondling her chubby arms. 'Yes,' said Rukmani. 'There is such a doll in a shop at Churchgate,' said the man. 'It cries "Mummy" when you press it on its stomach. It is a foreign doll. It costs about hundred rupees. But I do not mind spending the money on you if you are kind to me off and on. I love you more than I love anyone else in this world.'

'What about your wife and children?' asked the child.

'I do not love them the way I love you, Rukmani,' he said. 'I have a granddaughter of your age, but even her I cannot love the way I love you. I will get you toys every month if you promise to remain kind to me. I am not good-looking like that student who carried Mira away but I have a soft heart inside me. I am ugly. I am like a monkey, am I not? Do you feel an urge to laugh at me when you see my face?'

Rukmani felt moved by the man's humility. 'You are not ugly,' she said. 'You are a little bit like my father who left us and went away. Whenever I see you I remember him.'

'You will never be unhappy again in your life, my darling,' cried the Inspector. 'I shall protect you. I shall ask Lachmi bai to keep you away from all clients except myself. You can be my keep. I shall pay her a fixed sum of money so that she will not complain. Will you like that arrangement?'

'But what will happen when some young man comes forward and asks me to marry him?' asked the girl.

'I shall be that young man, my mogra flower,' whispered the man hoarsely, holding her tight.

Rukmani felt a slight nausea when she was assailed by the mouldy smell of his scalp where white hair grew in untidy patches. But she closed her eyes immediately and lay passive, thinking of the foreign doll that cost a hundred rupees.

V

When Rukmani saw Sindhuthai go into the little room next to Ayee's with a lump of green paste, resembling ground mehndi leaves and a sharp stick, she had a sense of foreboding. Sita had already been taken to the room, Ayee dragging her by her thin arms, while the child cried out, 'No, no Ayee, I do not want that hag to touch me.' The door was locked from within but Rukmani stood near the door, trying to listen to the sounds from inside. She could hear Sindhuthai's shrill voice chiding Sita and then the girl's slow whimper. Later, there was a shriek which was muffled midway by somebody's rough hands. Rukmani felt her legs weaken. What were they doing to her friend Sita?

Rukmani walked over to the bars of the porch and looked out. A double-decker bus rumbled along the road, carrying in it men who stared at her. The sky was once again like a newly whitewashed wall. She remembered what Sita had told her of the little house in the village where five deaths took place in a month. Then at that precise moment she heard the scream which did not sound like a human voice at all. Was it some kind of a beast that had escaped from the zoo, she wondered. After a few minutes, Sindhuthai came out and quietly sat herself down on Ayee's charpoy. She picked up a drying leaf from the betel box and began to chew. 'Our Sita is in a grave condition,' she said. 'I think she may even die.'

Rukmani ran into the house. The door of the small room was half-open. Ayee and Radha were tucking old sarees between Sita's thighs. Blood was soaking through the clothes rapidly. Sita lay insensate like a doll. How pale she looked with the rash of the midday sun mottling her narrow face. She resembled a foreign doll. Only her belly seemed alive, protruding from her flat body like a growth. Would she utter 'Mummy' when she was pressed on her tummy, like that expensive doll? 'Rukmani, our Sita is going away,' sighed Ayee, speaking in a soft voice. 'She is going to paradise where all the good people go after death.' 'Is Sita dying?' asked Rukmani. No one answered.

The Inspector was very helpful during the next few hours. He brought the doctor to write down the medical report, and after another hour, the body was taken to the electric crematorium and burnt down to ash in the presence of Ayee and three of the older girls. What remained of Sita was only a plastic doll bought from a street hawker, a light-green male doll, which was named Krishna by Rukmani and was married to the other doll. Rukmani lay between the two dolls in the evening, shedding tears in silence. When a client knocked at the door, Radha whispered to him: 'Please go away today, we have had a tragedy at the house this morning,' and he left without much protest.

That night, Rukmani woke up to hear a male voice coming from Saraswati's room. Saraswati's period of mourning did not last long. Rukmani felt all of a sudden a need for emotional security. If only Ayee put an arm around her shoulders and comforted her, she would sleep well again. She felt the presence of Sita in the room. If only the Inspector Saheb could come and take her to the little room and tell her that he loved her more than all...

The next morning, Ayee called an astrologer to the house. He drew a diagram on the floor and spread out some cowries in each of the squares. 'You are certainly passing through an unfavourable dasa in your life,' he said. 'You said that a girl eloped from here with a client and that another girl died. More calamities will follow, if you do not do a puja to control the evil stars who are your enemies.'

'Stars are my enemies?' asked Ayee. 'Even stars have turned against me. I have several enemies in this locality. All are jealous of me. I shall not, of course, mention names. I was planning to move to a better place, Marine Drive or Pasta Lane in Colaba. Would that give me peace of mind?'

'Getting a new place will cost you a fortune. The pugree itself will be a lakh,' said the astrologer. 'This place is well-located. All you need to do is a havan which will cost you only a thousand at the most. All your foes will be wiped out. Your business will thrive.'

'Can you find someone to do it for me?' asked Ayee.

The astrologer glanced with lewd eyes at the girls lounging around on the porch. 'I shall myself perform it,' he said. 'But it has to be done in secret. Is there a back verandah in this house?'

After the astrologer left, Sindhuthai arrived to comfort Ayee. 'It is God's will, younger sister,' she said. 'Otherwise why would such a young girl become pregnant? She had not even attained her puberty. Such a thing is unheard of. Sita was not destined to live long. She had all the signs of one who is to die early in life. Don't you remember her pale lips? Her frail wrists?'

Ayee began to weep. 'She was such an affectionate girl,' said Ayee. 'She used to prepare my paan for me in the afternoons. A village procurer sold her to me for three hundred rupees when she was only ten. Her parents had died of cholera. I gave her cod-liver-oil every winter but she did not put on any weight. Then one day, the Inspector Saheb told me that I should stop trying to make her fat. "She has the lithe body of a dancer," he told me. "Teach her to dance. She will charm your rich clients." I was planning to send her to a school to teach her some Bharatanatyam. But God has taken away my sweet child. Sindhuthai, please don't tell anyone what really happened. The Doctor Saheb wrote in the certificate that her appendix burst.'

'What is this appendix you are talking about? Is it the womb?' asked the old hag. 'No, no, it is something else,' said Ayee.

'Be more careful in the future, Lachmi,' said Sindhuthai, 'don't take chances. Rukmani should not be left to her fate. She too, can become pregnant. She is well-developed.'

'Ah, Rukmani, she is not going to be in trouble,' said Ayee. 'The Inspector Saheb has taken a great fancy to her. She is to be his keep. He is too old to have children. He must be quite old.'

'No man is too old to procreate, Lachmi bai,' said Sindhuthai. 'I have known of a case when an eighty-year-old man married a twenty-year-old girl and gave her two sons. The Inspector Saheb is a lion among men. He is virile enough to populate one whole planet.'

Ayee laughed and together with her laugh rose the dissonant cackle of the old hag.

'Do you want bangles?' asked a bangle-seller who stopped at their front door. He held strapped to his shoulders a heavy case of wood and glass which contained bangles of myriad hues. Rukmani rushed forward to look at them. He sat down on the floor and took out a few cardboard rolls.

Each such roll bore on it about three dozens of plastic bangles. 'May I have a look at the orange ones?' asked Saraswati, thrusting forward her dimpled arm. 'Are they nylon ones?' she asked the bangle-seller. 'Yes, they are expensive,' he said. 'Do you think I cannot afford your nylon bangles, my good man?' asked the dark girl with mocking eyes. The man gave her a knowing smile. 'You can afford even gold ones, lady,' he whispered. She laughed, and her laugh was like the tinkle of silver bells.

'Don't you want to buy some bangles for yourself, Rukmani?' asked Ayee. 'The red ones of nylon will look good on your arms.'

Rukmani shook her head. The bangles suddenly reminded her of Sita and then the desire to wear them on her own wrists went away. 'No, Ayee, I do not want any,' she said.

Saraswati coaxed the man to put around her wrists, squeezing her palms, a dozen of the orange-coloured bangles. 'What if I don't pay you?' she asked coquettishly. The man grinned sheepishly.

'You do not have to pay me,' he said. 'What kind of a businessman are you?' asked Saraswati, taunting him. He smiled at her, noting for the first time her full breasts straining at the thin red voile of her choli and her wide haunches. 'I am not much of a businessman,' he retorted, 'but I am a man all right. Do you want me to prove it to you?' Saraswati laughed aloud. She went inside the house to bring out the money.

'Where are you from?' asked Ayee. 'I am from Varanasi,' said the man. 'My brother has a paan-shop near Dadar and we stay together at Koliwada.' 'Are you making a lot of money selling paan?' asked Ayee. 'No, Mother. We are just pulling on…' Just then the Inspector Saheb entered the house. He was perspiring profusely. 'Everything is taken care of,' he said. 'I want now to lie down and relax for an hour. Where is Rukmani? Ah here she is…'

Ayee thrust the little girl into the room with the Inspector Saheb. Rukmani leaned against the shut door and stared at the fat man on the bed. He had already taken off most of his clothes. His baton lay near the pillow. 'Come to me, my moppet,' he pleaded, his voice thickening with lust. Rukmani did not move.

'Are you angry with me, darling?' asked the man. 'Are you angry because I did not get you the foreign doll from Churchgate today? You know how busy I was today with that girl's death and her cremation and all the technicalities connected with the events? Give me time. In three days' time the doll will be yours. You can call her Sita in honour of your playmate…'

Then Rukmani for the first time after her friend's death, broke down. She rushed towards the man and hid her sobbing face in the bushy growth of hair on his deep chest. 'Papa, papa,' she called out, sobbing, while the man, stupefied beyond words, kept stroking her curly hair. 'Oh papa, take me away from here,' she said, 'Otherwise I too, will die…'

The man kissed her forehead. Lust had suddenly retreated. 'Papa. Is that what you called your father?' he asked.

'Yes,' said Rukmani. 'Papa was very fond of me. But he quarrelled with my mother, and left our home without even telling me that he was going away. He did not ever return. Before Diwali, I used to wait for him near our house, hoping that he would bring me a new frock, but he did not come. He will never come to see me again, will he? He has forgotten me, hasn't he?'

'Don't cry, my child,' said the Inspector, 'you have me as your papa. I shall from now on treat you like my daughter. Is that enough, Rukmani?'

Rukmani lay cradled in his arms and fell asleep. She dreamt that Sita and she were travelling by a double-decker bus and that they were plucking ripe guavas from tall trees and eating them, seeds and all...

VI

When Mirathai returned, her clothes dishevelled and herself very hysterical, Ayee was taking a short nap in the afternoon, open-mouthed like a crocodile lying in wait for the dragonflies that might settle on its tongue. She looked hideous in sleep. Rukmani was seated on the floor watching Ayee sleep.

Mirathai fell on the ample bosom of the old woman and began to weep. 'Help me Ayee,' she cried, 'the Inspector Saheb has ordered his constables to thrash him to death. They are torturing him at the police chowki. At this rate, he will fall down dead in an hour's time and I shall be a widow. Please go and tell them to stop beating him.'

Ayee stared at the young woman. No emotion showed on her dark face. 'What has happened, Mira?' she asked slowly. 'You have decided to return...'

'They are thrashing him to death,' cried Mira. 'Get up, Ayee, and tell the Inspector Saheb that he is not at fault. I was not kidnapped from here. I coaxed him to take me away. Then why should he bear the punishment while I am let off free?'

'Where is this boy, Mira?' asked Ayee.

'He is at the police station,' said Mirathai. 'Please let him go free. I shall remain here for the rest of my life.'

Ayee got up from her charpoy and ate a paan. 'All right, I shall go there and speak to the Inspector Saheb. You go inside and take a bath. Ask Radha to give you a good meal. You look as if you have been starving for a week.' Mirathai kissed Ayee's hands in gratitude and went into the interior of the house. So our Mira has come back, said Ayee to herself. She walked towards the police station, escorted by Rukmani. 'Falling in love with men is a dangerous thing,' she told the little girl. 'It is like tying oneself with a rope. If you do not love any man, you remain free. Please remember that.'

The young man had been beaten black and blue by the time Ayee reached the police station to plead with the Inspector for mercy. But soon, she was carrying him back to her house in a tonga, triumphantly, while he sat with his face bent and tears streaming from his eyes. 'It is not my fault,' he mumbled once. But Ayee did not bother to converse with him.

When the tonga stopped near their house, Ayee asked the young man to alight. He was helped down by Rukmani. 'All my bones are broken,' said the boy.

'There is a letter for you today, mother of the house,' exclaimed the postman stopping his cycle. 'Open it and read it out to me, Rukmani,' cried Ayee. 'Can it be that my son has finally forgiven his sinner of a mother?'

The groaning young man limped into the house and sat down. The postman was lingering on to hear the contents of the long-awaited missive. Rukmani read: 'Dear Ayee, I have remained silent for ten years but today my master who is a learned man showed me what true love means. He scolded me for having hurt you and for having abandoned you for years. He said that every profession has its own code of honour and that I ought not to have felt ashamed of you. He is a rich man owning a motor garage but he says that he will gladly give all his possessions if he were to be given back his mother who has been dead for ten years. You can earn money, you can get wives and children, but a mother lost is a mother lost forever, he said. Therefore, at his persuasion, I am writing to inform you that I shall be coming over to visit you this Saturday in the afternoon. Your loving son, Sadashiv Mane.'

Ayee burst into tears. Rukmani felt tears filling her own eyes. Even the postman was turning emotional. 'This is happy news,' he said. Ayee took out of her waistband a rupee note and handed it to the postman. 'See, how wise he has become, my son, my little son Sadashiv,' said Ayee blowing her nose violently. Just then, Mira came out and saw the young man seated, still as a statue, on the floor. 'Forgive me,' she said, falling on the floor and clutching at his feet. 'If I had not forced you to take me away from here nobody would have beaten you. Are you hurt badly? May I bring you some warm milk? Come and lie down for an hour.'

'Mira, let him be,' said Ayee. 'Give him some peace. He has suffered all this because of you. Now leave him alone to find his own peace.'

'What peace can he find without me?' asked Mira. 'Is he not in love with me?'

The boy stretched himself on the floor and closed his eyes.

'Don't you love me still?' asked Mira.

'I don't know,' said the boy.

'You go home to your mother now,' said Ayee. 'She must be so upset about your absence from home.'

'She could not have been upset,' said the young man, 'because both she and my father were away visiting a relative in Poona. Today she is expected back at seven in the evening. I shall get home before she comes...'

'Was this to be merely a week's holiday, a short idyll?' asked Mira, a sob rising in her throat. 'Were you lying to me when you said that we were going to live as husband and wife?'

The boy was silent.

'How old are you, son?' asked Ayee, chewing betel leaves. 'I am nineteen,' said the boy. 'Go home to your mother and forget all about Mira,' said Ayee. 'Come to us after you get yourself a job and can afford to visit prostitutes.'

Mira flinched at the words. The boy rose, and folding his hands in a salute, he walked away.

'The ungrateful swine,' hissed Mira. 'He told me that he was twenty-four and that he had found a job at a mill. A liar. A stinking liar.'

Mira threw out Saraswati's things from her former room. There was a lot of trouble then. Saraswati scratched Mira's fair face. 'You slut,' she called out to Mira, 'you think you own this place? You run wild with a schoolboy for a week and return home as though nothing has happened. I shall not let you have this room. It belongs rightfully to me.'

It was a question of seniority. Ayee could not take Mira's side this time. Mira had erred. Of that, there was no doubt at all. Saraswati was the most qualified of the lot, the one who was totally devoid of emotion and was the most professional of all. She deserved the best room.

Mira gave in and took a corner of the common hall where the juniors slept. She had to start rehabilitating herself again.

When the Inspector Saheb came, Ayee brought forth for him a plate of ladoos. He smiled at her. 'What are you celebrating today?' he asked her. Then the letter was once again read out and once again tears flowed copiously from several pairs of eyes. 'Your luck is changing, Lachmi bai,' he said. Then he called Rukmani, gesturing with hand and held out the large parcel which was with him. 'Open it and see what I have brought for you, my daughter,' he said.

Of course, it was the foreign doll. It did resemble Sita to some extent. Its vinyl-skin was very pale and its tummy had a bulge. Rukmani pressed it and made it squeak out the word 'Mummy'. Rukmani kissed the doll all over its face and on its half-opened hands. 'No kiss for your papa?' asked the Inspector. She embraced him with her free hand and rubbed her nose on his shirt-front. 'You are getting very sentimental,' said Ayee to the Inspector. He nodded and gave another of his wide smiles. 'Lachmi bai, I am an old man now,' he said. 'This child reminds me of my granddaughter who is staying with her parents at Nagpur. She is sweet and affectionate like this one. Sends me a sweet letter every year at Diwali time.'

'There is nothing like affection, Inspector Saheb,' said Ayee. She kneaded the tobacco shreds with lime in the hollow of her left palm. 'I am also not as young as I used to be. I wonder why I cannot leave this house in Saraswati's hands and go to Benares to die. I have enough money saved up to live in comfort until the last day of my life. Perhaps I shall carry someone with me, an old woman for company, perhaps our Sindhuthai. She has no relatives. I shall make up my mind after seeing my son this Saturday.'

'We will miss you, Lachmi bai,' said the Inspector. 'This house will not be the same without you. And, Rukmani. Where will she go? She will have to be at the mercy of the new Ayee of the house…'

'I shall marry her off to my son,' said Ayee. 'Surely, he can now support a wife.'

'Am I too early?' asked a client walking in, furtively glancing around. 'You can never be too early in this house,' said Saraswati coming forward to lead him into the room inside. He eyed her with appreciation.

'Would you like to spend some time with our Mira?' asked Ayee to Inspector. 'You have always liked her.'

'No, Lachmi bai, I do not feel like playing with a woman today,' said the man, applying lime on the leaves of the betel carefully. 'Something has died in me today.'

'Perhaps something has been born inside you today,' said Ayee with a tender grin. Rukmani's doll kept crying out: 'Mummy, Mummy, Mummy…'

WOMAN OF THE STREET

Baburao Bagul

Girija had visited Haji Malang at night. In the morning, as soon as she woke up, she distributed Baba's prasad to all in the shanty town who would accept it. Then she left for her breakfast. She was still carrying some prasad to give to people she would meet. After breakfast she was going to go up the hill to wash her soiled clothes, to scrub down her body with coir and soap. In the evening she would set off for business, chewing paan. She was going to rake in the money. She was no longer afraid of the new girl. She had asked Baba to ensure her success and made him responsible for bringing ruin upon her rival. Everything was going to turn out according to her wishes. She had the support of so many fakirs' blessings. She had fed one of them for two days. Done charity with an open hand. Offered a chaddar to Baba. She had done all that was demanded of the faithful. She was certain that her faith would guarantee good business for her.

Knowing this, she went tripping up the steps of the restaurant, laughing, glittering and calling out, 'Kassam, come get your prasad'. The owner, fed up of giving her credit, told her to come to him. But she didn't budge from her chair and instead called out her order loudly. The owner was enraged to see the flurry she was in. He shouted, 'There's a telegram for you.'

When she heard this, she shoved her chair back with a bang and shouted, 'Telegram!' The restaurant owner calmly explained the telegram to her in Marathi. She heard him and howled. She fell at his feet instantly, begging him to lend her money to go to the village. Not in the least bit moved by her pleading, he said, 'I kept your telegram for two days. I didn't throw it with the waste paper. Another thing. I gave a woman like you an address. I've given you a lot of credit. A lot of credit. Go now. I've done enough for you.'

She left without a word. There was a surging lava of grief in

31

her. Every cell in her body was numb. Even then, she began to get ready. She rubbed soap into her face and scrubbed it. She wiped it dry with a used choli. She brought a mirror up to her face. Then the sob that had been heaving in her body, repressed, now broke loose. The mirror fell from her hand. She wept till she grew calm. Once again, she sat down to adorn herself. She oiled her hair and parted it. She made a loose bun on the nape of her neck to make her face look attractive. She pulled out a tendril of hair and let it hang down against her cheek. She etched a kumkum spot on her forehead. She took off her choli, pulled the edging and stretched and knotted it halfway up her breasts. She turned the sari she was wearing inside out and arranged the border to show off her back. Then she stepped out of her shanty, trying to walk mincingly on her toes. She got herself some paan and betel nut on credit after a lot of pleading. But her fingers would not move quickly enough to fold it. Nor did she feel like eating it. She forced herself, only because she had to make her lips red. But her lips would not take the colour and her face would not glow. Her body had no energy. Her walk had no spring. Her heart was despondent. Inside her, sorrow simmered. She tried hard to lessen it, but it only grew. She had lost her mind with the telegram and nothing would bring it back.

Although grief had torn her to pieces, she still walked to the garden and stationed herself there. She had been coming here for many years to do business. So far, nobody she knew had turned up. She continued to chew paan to bring colour to her lips, but her mouth was dry. She kept going to the garden tap to wash her face, to see if she could rid it of its sadness. But the sadness would not go. Men paid no attention to her and the tears in her heart did not have permission to spill.

She smiled at men. She tried hard to muster all the art in her body to arouse them, but none of them approached her. Nobody asked her her price. Time and men passed her by. They felt no concern for her grief. It seemed to her that the day had turned into a dungeon in which all men were locked up.

Then suddenly she saw him. He had talked to the old woman and was coming towards her. As he came nearer, her heart began to thump. Her body broke out into a sweat at the memory of the terrible atrocities he had committed on her body. He was quite close to her now. He was about to speak to her. Once he spoke, she would not be able to say no. She would have to go with him. She would have to do all that he demanded of her. She would have to pretend to enjoy his abuse. She did not know what to do. Did not know how to escape. She was terrified.

He came but went past her. She stood rooted to the spot. For a long time afterwards, the white expanse of his back stayed stubbornly in her eyes. When she came to herself, she thought she should have smiled at him, talked to him. She would have been able to meet her son soon. She hurried forward to call him but the call stuck in her throat. The memory of that outrage sat upon her like a spirit come back from the dead. She ran back and said to the old woman, 'You old witch. Don't send that monster to the girl.'

'Why?' asked the old woman, not even looking at Girija.

'Because I'm saying so,' Girija shouted.

'Leave us to look after ourselves,' the old woman said, kicking at Girija's boundless sympathy. Girija shuddered, cursed with rage and went to sit under a tree, her limbs limp. The shadow of the tree, angry with the earth, kept speeding away. But the earth would not let it go. Girija lay under the tree. There was hunger in her stomach, grief in her heart. Her mind was like the shadow of the tree, dumb, but wanting to run.

'Girija!' When she saw Narayan Shetty standing before her, she quickly rearranged her face, repaired her heart, and rose. He was a guarantee of money. He was going to take her with him and put an end to her grief and anxiety. He was going to bring along two others and he was going to treat her like a human being, leaving her sorrow untouched. She was determined not to let go of a customer like Narayan. She was not going to allow her grief to show itself. She was not going to allow herself to cry. In a moment she was the beautiful seductive heroine of a Saganbhau lavani. She circled his face with her palms and cracked her knuckles against her temples.

'Where were you all these days?'

The mother in her was eager to share her grief and lessen it. She wanted to say, 'The child is ill. I got a telegram. I don't have a paisa.' But she was instantly on her guard. She killed that cry for human sympathy. It would have made the ready customer flee and she would not be able to see her child. She gathered her skills together. She stood up. She blushed. Began to demur. Then stammered with a coy smile, 'I was not to be touched.' A customer loses his wisdom when he hears something like that. He does not haggle over money but takes a woman at her price. This she knew. That is why she lied. And a dagger plunged into her heart.

'Oh really!' he said.

'Five rupees,' she said hiking the price of her body when she thought he had become reckless.

'Five?'

She was going to entice a few customers at five rupees apiece and catch the night train to the village. To arouse him further she began to playfully extract a five-rupee note from his pocket. She pretended coyness, blushed and said softly, 'You're the first one. The first after the...'

Then she showed her eagerness to surrender herself to him by falling against his chest. He hugged her, helped her to steady herself and said, 'Really?' But he would not agree to her price. She used artful movements of her body to convince him. But to no avail. Sad as she was, she still felt some satisfaction at having cuddled up to him and advertised her profession explicitly. Many men had seen her do it. She was certain that at least three or four customers would now approach her. But nobody did. Time was passing. Her hunger was growing. Her sadness increased. She was being ignored. She wanted to cry. She wanted to rage. She was at her wit's end. She was ready to throw up her business. She came out of the garden. But she went back in. Her mind trembled like a flame in a tempest. Trying to calm herself, she went in search of

Narayan Shetty. She had little time now. She was willing to do business at any price to be free by midnight. She went back into the garden to seduce Narayan Shetty and make a naked advertisement of herself.

She walked everywhere but did not see him. Nobody else bothered to talk to her. She spotted two pehlwans coming her way. She winked at them and walked a few steps. Then she stopped and turned around to see the effect. She brought the loose end of her sari forward to wipe her face of sweat and fan herself. But she really did it to reveal the curves of her waist and buttocks. The pair said, 'Fuck! The old mother winked.' They looked at her, spat, laughed, cursed and walked away.

Raging at the humiliation, consumed by grief, exhausted with trying, weakened by hunger, going berserk, she inclined her head at the man in glasses who was looking at her. He came, asked her her price. 'Five rupees.' The strength had drained out of her body. Her voice had become faint. It trembled. He took her weariness to be a sign of her timidity. Her inexperience.

'Two rupees!' He fixed her price looking to her lack of inexperience and her clothes. Girija shook her head hesitantly.

'Come on.' He was impatient. He also knew that showing impatience was a way to get a woman going. Seeing his impatience, she concluded he was in her net and aroused him further with seductive body movements.

'How many years have you been doing business?' He was now fully aroused.

She knew why he was asking her. So she told him a lie. 'For two months.'

'And before that?' He had no wish to continue talking. Her intention was to fool him and make more money. So she told another lie. 'I was a dancer.'

She said this with such a fetching movement that he was lost. The only word he could utter was, 'Come.'

'Give me the money first. Bombay people...' She was now fully into the role of the innocent. The mother inside her dropped her head meekly like a cow.

'I'm not going to run away.'

'And I won't be able to get up to catch you.' She raised her sari-end to her eyes and skillfully mopped up an errant tear that had broken through all barriers. She pushed her sari-end aside. Her face was distressed. He was so taken by what she had said and the expression on her face that he quickly thrust a five-rupee note into her hand. Then they took a tram to Foras Road.

Girija played a respectable woman to squeeze more money out of him. She suppressed her old habit of signalling to prospective customers as she walked. She did not look at anybody. She did not allow her sari to slip from her breasts. She constantly pulled the sari-end, covering her head down to her nose. Her eyes were filled with the fearfulness of an innocent. She had turned into his very own respectable woman. She clung to him while her urgent wish to hug her child inflicted wounds on her like a sharp sword. No amount of trying would blunt its edge or destroy it.

And he was planning to rob her. A woman who is new to the business is not wary. She does not have the skill to take on several customers without feeling fatigue. Her behaviour is straightforward, good. It is possible to take all you can get out of her and cheat her. He made up his mind to dupe her.

They got off at the corner of Foras Road and entered a room. She sat on the bed like a wilted flower. He locked the door. 'Stand up.'

It was part of her role as the timid newcomer to the business to not get up. But she genuinely had no strength to do so.

'Stand up,' he urged her again. She shook her head. He kept on insisting. She kept on refusing. He loved this stubborn, bashful bride. He stuffed a two-rupee note in her hand and, thrusting his hands under her armpits, hauled her up. Urgently insistent, fobbing off her refusals, putting money in her hand as he went, he undressed her, garment by garment. When there was not a stitch on her, her fist was bulging with money. After that, he did with her all that he wished. With every act he gave her money. She began to feel the effect of Haji Malang Baba's powers. She accepted the money with devotion. She told herself her body was a stone and endured unspeakable horrors. She now had enough money to take her to the village and back and pay for medicines and liquor. She gave up her entire body to his perverted lust.

Her strength ebbed away. Her endurance left her at zero. She lost consciousness. Her fist, which had been locked tight, loosened. The wad of notes in it fell down. Suddenly she came awake, as though scorched by fire. The drowsiness flew out of her eyes. She raised her hand and looked at her fist. It was empty. Still in bed, she trailed her hand feverishly on the ground, but it touched nothing. Her eyes went to the door. The man in the glasses was getting dressed. In a flash, she saw his cunning.

She had borne unlimited horrors. Her endurance had ebbed. But now it was transformed into fury. It danced in her exhausted body like lightning. It consolidated the strength in her muscles giving them power. Snake-like steeliness flashed in her eyes. Her face grew red with rage. Her upper lip rode up to her nose and became a straight line. Somehow, she pulled her sari around her and exploded like dynamite. 'You fucking pimp! Where do you think you're going, you bastard? Throw down my money first.' For a moment, the sight of her altered face stunned him. But then he came to his senses, and waited for Girija to reach him. When she lunged at him, he squeezed her throat and pushed her away. Then he picked her up by the scruff of her neck like a kitten and flung her down.

She, a woman who had gone berserk with mother love, who had been on fire with grief, lay where she fell, never to get up. The hand that had held her sari tight around her body, grew rigid. The tongue that had shot up like a flame from the sacrificial fire, was imprisoned behind the gates of her teeth.

And yes…

The restaurant owner who had explained the telegram to her had told her a lie. Her son had died.

Yes, he had died.

Translated from the Marathi by Shanta Gokhale

THE LAST CUSTOMER

Niranjana

No one was willing to go beyond the intersection. The ceaseless expanse of buildings and the cool breeze over the plains brought along a foul odour. A few stood there, creating a busy hum of gossip, a confusing medley of sounds.

As the sun came up, the weather turned warm. Those who could not avoid the intersection walked past in a hurry, glancing to their left for an instant and then not raising their heads at all. Everyone was busy while walking past. No one seemed to have any time for this. Eventually, the news reached the municipal offices.

~

Kani woke up in the middle of the night to see that her partner, who had been sleeping beside her, was missing. This girl of sixteen had come running after the boy just ten days earlier, to the capital of Karnataka from some place in Tamil Nadu. He was a rag picker, with a blunt stump in the place of an arm. One of those nights, he pulled her into an embrace using his other arm. She looked at him with a shudder in her heart. She looked at his arm, an arm which had the strength of two.

That night, they eloped.

She had had a house, a small hut. Her parents had worked on a piece of land as tenants. The same year they lost everything. The patriot that he was, the landlord had asked for a higher tenancy, failing which, he said, he would give away the tilling rights to someone else. And just that did happen. Kani's parents lost their piece of land. The family migrated with their remaining pots and pans. The elder son decided to become a coolie and went away to Madras. The younger one fought with the parents and left home. With a mute girl hanging at their breast, the parents flitted from one town to another.

They would not find any employment in the city. After

begging for work and failing, they got used to the task of begging for alms.

The mute girl, we must say, was sad at leaving her parents' side. The stump-armed beggar, who rolled all over her in the dark, under the shadow cast by a house, was now her only support, a support feeble and falling apart by the minute.

It was just ten days since they had eloped. Today, the eleventh day, she discovered that she was alone. She felt like she was desperately shouting for help in a bottomless pit where there was not a blade of grass for her to clutch at.

Her eyes kept flowing the entire day. She squeezed her stomach in grief, banged her forehead against a wall. She walked aimlessly but could not find him. By now he would have got on to a train and left for another place, without a ticket, of course.

Kani walked to the lake by the side of the railway station. She sat there with her feet in the water. She pulled a comb from her blouse and combed her hair, wetting it with the waters of the lake. After taking a gulp of water from the lake she started walking past the bund.

She had a frail body—and no one would call her good-looking, exactly—but she was buxom for her age. For people who craved flesh, she was a sumptuous meal.

Walking, she turned askance to check behind her. Someone was following her with a cigarette dangling from his mouth. Just then the street lamps lit up. She looked at those lights in wonder, as if a new world had opened up in front of her. A cyclist went past her. A policeman's whistle shrilled in the distance. She turned again to see. He was still following her.

She stood below the deodar tree on the footpath. He, too, came close and held out a packet of snacks. Her throat chuckled some noises. She opened the packet and gobbled the food he had brought. He lit another cigarette.

He said, 'I have been watching you since morning.'

She understood him by the quiver of his lips. A cackling sound fell on her eardrums, but made no sense.

She answered him in her monosyllabic noises. Tears started welling up within her. He made some noises of sympathy and gestured her to follow him. She followed him with her head bent faithfully like a dog.

Thus, under some unknown shelter, that night gave way to day.

~

Some four days went by like this. He braided her hair and decked her up. Using a mix of phrases and gestures, he explained to her slowly, 'I will bring new people. You should be silent and not open your mouth. No one need know that you are mute.'

She whined. She was livid when he gestured to say that she was mute. But all her anger subsided with her whines.

He brought someone with him who looked like a respectable man. He grinned in front of the man and stooped low. Like a dog's eye on a bone, his eye was fixed on the man's wallet. One of the men who came was a true beast. His violent overtures hurt Kani. Unable to bear the pain, she wailed loudly, making her dumb noises, pushed him away with both her hands, and dropped him on to the floor. This led to an altercation. Her master beat her like a dog. She crumpled into a corner and sat there with a broken face. The man who had come went away in anger.

In the middle of the night, he lifted her from the floor and put her on a pallet. 'Did it hurt?' he asked. She didn't answer him. But her eyes betrayed bizarre emotions. The mean-minded fellow could not fathom that.

After that day, Kani became very gentle.

She did not love him in the least. She did not love anyone like she did her first love, the beggar with a stump for an arm.

Kani did not understand money. She did not know what her earnings were. Two saris, a blouse, a jumper, a tattered woollen ladies' overcoat for her nightly visits, some flowers for her hair and odorous oil to braid it with, a filling meal every day. The days passed thus.

Thank heavens she did not end up pregnant.

On some days, however, her grief would flow over. She would toss about where she lay. She would remember her village, the hut she was born in, the people who spoke her language, her first partner, the man with the stump for an arm. She would wail in grief. For two nights, her wailing would not stop. No customer would come her way.

One morning, at dawn, she bundled some foodstuffs and clothes into a knot and ran away. She reached the other end of the city and exited it.

~

She drifted into a village on the outskirts of the city. Her eyes met a pair of oxen and farmers busy in their tilling. She watched everything silently. It did not even occur to her that she had to comb her ruffled hair. Neither did she feel like looking at herself in her small, one-paisa mirror, nor did she feel like food.

The ground all around her was sprouting green after a recent shower of rain. Kani sat down on fresh grass, at a distance from the fields.

Her mind flooded with a hundred different memories from her childhood. Her face grew dark. Slowly, feeling drowsy, she lay there on the bare earth.

It was evening by the time she awoke to voices of farmer women nudging her. As darkness fell, the village appeared to be a scary place. She walked back to the city. At the very edge of the city was a school, deserted by the night. She found a place near the parapets and went to sleep.

~

At daybreak, she woke up and walked away, smoothening her rough hair and decorating herself with the knick-knacks which she carried with her.

After strolling around for a few hours, it seemed like she had gained some acquaintance with the place. She saw a vast field with grass sprouting all over, an intersection, a municipal fountain right at the centre, a statue of someone and a lone tall building at the far end.

Kani gave a few coins to a hawker selling groundnuts by the corner and bought some. Thus did she learn something about money, but the groundnuts hardly subdued her hunger.

At the fall of darkness, Kani came back to the intersection and sat in a corner. A lonesome lamp-post in the middle glowed faintly. A few who walked past turned to look at her. Some walked a few paces and then turned back to steal a glance.

A man who looked respectable walked past a second time, adjusting his glasses. Kani got up and walked away towards a tree, and some thin shrubbery. The man followed her with stealthy glances.

The next day Kani learnt that exchanging the piece of paper she had could fetch her snacks and a meal and also a few coins in return. How much and how exactly were matters beyond her.

From then on, it was a new routine. Mornings were spent in aimless strolls and in the evenings, an acquaintance or two by the intersection. And then by night in the shrubs on the green grass, dying a couple of times every day. Dying and coming back to life again.

Coming back to life to die the next evening.

Her days were spent in this manner.

She did not have a reckoning of the kinds of men who came to her. Drunkards, bastards, lost souls in search of clandestine joys, lecherous men who donned the cloak of respectability in the mornings, those who wanted to escape the banality of their homes and marriages. Were she not mute, she could have understood a thing or two about them and their worlds. But now these matters made little sense to her. She could have understood something of all this had she at least had a glimpse of their faces. But in the dark, faces were hardly visible.

She knew not whether these things were humane or beastly. Nor would she know of matters of love and lust. Whether they were men with sprouting moustaches, or men old and lame, made little difference to her. When her body was fatigued she would wail in pain. Her aches would send out strange noises of grief from within her.

What occurred in the minds of men who seek pleasure from a mute woman on the street was beyond her. Whatever happened, happened like clockwork. She was little more than a breathing machine.

~

The rain became heavy and there were no customers in sight. Slowly, her earnings dwindled. Kani grew frail and weak. She started walking up to people and seeking them out. Her cheeks dropped and her eyes grew vacant and dark. A fever was rising in her. She adorned herself more intensely to fight it off.

From a distance, with her woollen coat and flowers in her hair, she looked just about bearable. But if one were to see her up close, her eyes looked like they were dancing, like ghosts.

Some louts would come over to the school where she slept at night, but would not give her a paisa in return. She would pick a fight with them but they would pester her endlessly and rape her. Their rapacious laughs and beastly howls would make Kani shudder. When her protests became pointless, she would resign to her fate and submit to them.

Her fever increased. She felt a voice within her telling her not to take those baths at the lake. Before long, her skin was afflicted with a strange disease. The young Kani suffered. Her body began giving off a foul odour.

Kani changed her shelter. She walked towards a rundown hut a furlong away. There a middle-aged beggar had built for himself his own palace.

He fed her some gruel for three days.

She gaped at the sky through the holes in the thatched roof as she fell asleep. On the fourth day, the fever appeared to subside. She sat up. The beggar looked at her with desire. Her face did not betray a trace of emotion. She had become incapable of experiencing emotions a long while ago. He skipped his begging rounds for the day and stayed back with her. His diseased body seemed to be making good on all the desire it had missed out on.

In the evening, with her black overcoat upon her, Kani walked past the field and stood by its edge, where it was dark. She was feeling faint. The piece of land they once tilled, her mother, her father, the stump-armed lover, all of them walked past in a procession in her mind's eye. The brother who had left to become a coolie in Madras and the one who had left home in a fit of anger seemed to her to be hailing her from a distance. She was filled with grief.

Unable to stand for long, she collapsed upon the ground. In the distance, the groundnut-hawker's kerosene lamp glimmered and called out to her. But she did not have even a paisa. She wanted to snatch fistfuls of groundnuts and gobble them up. But she did not have the strength for it.

It was one in the night. Before long it turned half-past. Everyone who was strolling near the fountain left for their homes. Kani looked at each one of them with beseeching eyes.

A man stood there alone. He was heavily built and had a wicked glint in his eye. He gestured to her with his hands. Kani stood up with great effort and pulled herself behind him.

He seemed to be new to this. He pinned her just by the side of the shrubs. Kani tripped, and a guttural sound escaped her.

This irritated the man and he was quickly on his feet, brushing himself. He spat at her with scorn. Kani tried to sit up but she had no energy left.

He spat at her again and left without paying. Kani opened her mouth as if to wail loudly, but no sound emerged. She tried to stand up again but could not manage it.

He was walking away with quick strides. Finally, she managed to find her feet. She chased him like a mother would chase a villain stealing her child. She wailed in her hoarse voice and kicked up a fuss.

He was running away without paying her. She was beseeching him with her babble to not deceive her. She was crying out to him, saying, 'Do not cheat me of tomorrow's meal.'

He looked back at her with dread. Some people were still around. What if they heard? What if someone came up, tapped him on the shoulder and asked him to explain himself.

He stopped abruptly and returned. Clutching her throat, he pushed her to the ground and swore at her: 'Dirty bitch!' He kicked her in the stomach.

Kani collapsed in an instant. There were growls in her throat but they were not audible. There was still some breathing; slow, first, and then rare. Her final breaths were more laboured.

~

Everyone was on the move. No one had time to stop.

Someone said the municipal van would come by to pick up the corpse.

Up above in the skies, a vulture circled, and spiralled down.

Kani lay with her eyes open, as if keenly eyeing it. The vulture was slowly closing in to alight upon her—the last customer.

Translated from the Kannada by Ashwin Kumar

HEENG-KOCHURI

Bibhutibhushan Bandyopadhyay

We lived in a single room in Hari-babu's bamboo-and-tile house. Several families lived in the same building. One room was occupied by a bangle-seller and his wife. His name was Keshab. I addressed him as Keshab-kaka.

When water flowed in the pipes every morning, everyone would line up with their pitchers and bowls and cans and buckets near the tap, and quarrels would break out between the tenants.

My father would tell my mother, 'We can't possibly live here. These people behave like barbarians. We must move soon.'

I cannot say why we never moved. I think it must have been because we were poor, because my father had no money.

Across the road from our house was a rice warehouse, and next to it was a godown for gur, opposite which stood a municipality tap. A screaming and jostling crowd would collect water from this tap every day. I had even seen women fighting with one another.

Thus we spent a year in that house, from one June to another.

It was in June that we had left our village home. In the village, Kali and I had built a hut at the edge of the bamboo grove, next to a thorn apple bush. Kali, who was stronger than me, had carried several bundles of berry leaves and branches. What a perfect hut we had made, the two of us, just like a real house. That's what Kali would say. He had fixed an abandoned bird's nest to the thick branch of a tree. He had said that nocturnal woodpeckers or lapwings would lay eggs in that nest in the middle of August or on the moonlit nights of September.

It hadn't been possible for me to check on all this, for we had moved from the village in June to this house of bamboo and tiles.

I kept recalling the hut on the edge of the bamboo grove in the village, which Kali and I had built with so much care, and of the bird's nest fixed to the branch of the tree—had the woodpecker laid eggs in it on a moonlit September night?

This house in Calcutta was far too constricted for space, far too congested. I sat in the tin-covered verandah in front all morning, watching the neighbours line up for water, the gur being unloaded from a bullock-cart to the warehouse, a young wife gazing at the road, just like me, from the window of the two-storeyed house in the corner. Sometimes I bought chhatu at the Bihari man's shop on the main road at the head of our lane. The main road was full of vehicles. I had never seen a single horse-drawn carriage in our village. I could never have enough of seeing them go by, but my mother wouldn't allow me on the main road for fear that I would be run over.

A row of houses of bamboo and tiles, just like ours, stood a little further away, at the other end of the lane. I visited these houses sometimes. They were kept neat and clean and were well-appointed, with mirrors, dolls, glass showcases and pictures on the walls. Each of the rooms was occupied by a woman. I visited all of them—usually in the early evening, sometimes in the morning too.

One of the women in those houses was named Kusum. She loved me very much, and I loved her too. I spent much of my time in Kusum's room. She chatted with me and asked about our village. She belonged to a place called Bardhaman. But now she lived in this room.

Kusum said, 'I love you so much. You'll come every day, won't you?'

'I love you too. I do come every day.'

'Where is your village?'

'Ashshingri, in Jessore.'

'Is it your first time in Calcutta?'

'Yes.'

Kusum would dress up beautifully every evening, putting a teep on her forehead and some sort of flour-like powder on her face. She would do up her hair too—how well it suited her! But she wouldn't let me stay in her room at this time. She would say, 'Go home now, my babu will come.'

The first time I heard this I asked, 'Who's babu?'

'There's someone. You won't understand. Go home now.'

I would be upset. I would say, 'Let the babu come, I'll stay. What can the babu to do to me?'

'No, go away. You mustn't stay. Be a darling.'

'Who is this babu? Is he your brother?'

'You won't understand. Go home now.'

I was very curious to see who Kusum's babu was. Why did she tell me to go home?

I did see him one day. A portly man with long hair—he was holding a packet of food of some kind. At the shops they gave you food in packets like these, made with dried leaves. We didn't have leaves like these in our village; if you bought murki or jilipi at Hari's shop, he wrapped them in lotus leaves.

Unwrapping the packet, Kusum handed me a large kochuri, saying, 'Here you are, eat this on your way home.'

I bit into it, it was delicious. I had never eaten a kochuri like this in the village. The kochuris that Hari made were fried in oil and nowhere near as delectable.

Delighted, I said, 'Lovely! And what's this flavour?'

Kusum told me, 'It's heeng. This is a heeng-kochuri. Go home now.'

Kusum's babu said, 'Who is it?'

'The son of the tenants opposite the tap. Brahmins.'

Turning to me, Kusum's babu said, 'Go home, khoka, go home now.'

I thought of asking, why can't I stay, what's wrong with my staying? But when I looked at Kusum's babu, I didn't dare. He seemed a bad-tempered sort who might hit me. But since then, I waited as a rule till Kusum's babu arrived, greedy for my heeng-kochuri. Kusum would hand me two kochuris before anything else every day and say, 'Eat this on your way home.'

Kusum's babu would say, 'Oh, I forgot. I'd meant to get a couple of khasta goja for him. I'll bring them tomorrow, I promise.'

I wasn't afraid any more. I said, 'Don't forget, all right?'

Chortling, Kusum's babu said, 'I won't, I won't.'

Kusum said, 'Go home now, khoka.'

'I won't go now. Why can't I stay?'

Kusum's babu said something in response, I couldn't quite understand what. Kusum told him angrily, 'What a thing to say to a child!'

When I went home I asked my mother, 'Have you ever eaten a heeng-kochuri, Ma?'

'Why?'

'I have. So large, and it smells of heeng.'

'Where did you get it?'

'Kusum's babu brought some, he gave me one.'

'Naughty boy, haven't I told you not to go there? You mustn't.'

'Why not?'

'Because. You shouldn't be going there. They aren't good people.'

'No, Ma, Kusum is very nice. She loves me so much. She gives me heeng-kochuri every day.'

'Don't you show me your heeng-kochuri! Don't you get enough to eat at home? I'm warning you not to go there.'

I didn't go to Kusum's room at all for the next two or three days. But I couldn't stay away either. I went back, without telling my mother. Kusum asked, 'Why didn't you come?'

'My mother has warned me not to.'

'Then you'd better not come. She'll scold you.'

'That's why I didn't for two days.'

'But now you're here again.'

'Because I love you.'

'Oh, my darling. I hate it too when you don't come. I miss you so much.'

'So do I.'

'It's all my fate. I'm worried about your mother scolding you.'

'I shan't tell her. I miss you if I don't come. I'd better go now.'

'Come in the evening.'

'I will.'

~

Fulfilling our pact, I went to Kusum in the evening. When Kusum's babu arrived, he said, 'So here you are, chhokra. Why did you go missing these past couple of days? I'd brought khasta goja for you, but obviously your fate didn't mean for you to have any. Give him a couple of kochuris, will you?'

'Bring the goja tomorrow.'

'I shall, master Brahmin, glutton Brahmin. I'll bring amriti and jilipi too tomorrow. Ever tried an amriti?'

'No.'

'I'll bring some tomorrow, you must come.'

'But don't tell anyone. If my mother finds out she won't let me come.'

'Does your mother scold you for coming?'

'Hmm.'

Kusum intervened quickly, 'Never mind what he says. He's a little boy, don't take him seriously. Go home now, khoka. Here's your kochuri. Eat it on your way home.'

'No, I'll finish it here and have a glass of water, or my mother will find out.'

'I shan't give you water here. Drink at the tap by the road.'

Kusum's babu said, 'Why won't you give him a glass of water here? What harm will it do?'

Kusum told him harshly, 'Be quiet. I cannot serve a glass of water to a Brahmin's son. That's my punishment in this lifetime. It's bad enough that I give him food with my own hands.'

I was very upset with Kusum. Was I not good enough for her to give me a glass of water? As I was leaving, Kusum said again and again, 'Come tomorrow morning, all right?'

I didn't reply.

The next morning I found Kusum slicing vegetables. She said, 'Come, khoka.'

'I'm not talking to you.'

'What! Why? What have I done?'

'You said you couldn't give me a glass of water. You didn't, yesterday.'

'Is that all? Sit down, khoka. You won't understand. You belong to a Brahmin family—we can't serve you water. Understood? I'm making achaar, want some? It's not done yet. I've only just added the gur to the kul...'

And so Kusum and I were friends again. I forgot all my anger and hurt as soon as I was handed the kul-achaar. We sat and chatted for a long time. Then I went into Makhan's room, next to Kusum's. Hundreds of dolls adorned her room. On a wooden shelf lay apples and mangoes and litchis and many other amazing things all made of clay. A perfect apple! A perfect mango!

Makhan said, 'Come, khoka. Don't touch all those clay toys, sit down here. They'll break.'

'Why do you smoke?'

Makhan said with a smile, 'Listen to the boy! People smoke, don't they?'

'Do women smoke? My mother doesn't. My father does.'

'Listen to him. Those who smoke, do.'

'Kusum's babu will give me khasta goja.'

'Really? How nice.'

'Where's your babu?'

Makhan giggled, covering her mouth with the end of her sari.

'Hee hee, just listen to the boy, the things he says! Hee hee... Kusmi, come listen to what your boy's saying...'

Makhan seemed older than Kusum. Kusum was the most beautiful of them all. She addressed Makhan as didi.

Kusum came in and led me away to her room. She had told me not to go into anyone else's room. In truth I only went in the hope of getting something nice to eat. But I had no idea when the other women's babus could come. So disappointment awaited me in this respect. Taking me into her room, Kusum scolded me. She said, 'What do you have to talk about with them? You're a little boy, you're not allowed into the other room, stay here.'

'I want to go to Prabha...'

'Why? What for? Who knows what you'll say there. Silly boy. So greedy for food. Didn't I just give you kulchur?'

I said in a tone of pretended astonishment, 'I didn't ask for anything. Ask Prabha.'

'All right, no need to go to Prabha.'

'Can't I go just once? I'll be back in a moment.'

To tell the truth, the real attraction in Prabha's room was not so much food as it was a parrot.

The parrot would say, 'Ram Ram, who is it? Go away, kakima, kakima.' Whenever I entered, it would say, 'Who's there? Who's there?'

'My name is Basudeb.'

'Who's there? Who's there?'

I laughed. It was such fun listening to the parrot prattle. He sounded exactly like a human. 'Who's there? Who's there?'

Outside the room, Prabha asked, 'Who's that in my room?'

She was cooking. She came running with a ladle dripping dal. I asked with a smile, 'Are you going to beat me up?'

'Oh, it's the mad little Brahmin. I was wondering who it could be at this hour of the afternoon.'

'Don't you have any kulchur? Kusum gave me some. Delicious.'

'Kusum has a rich babu. I don't, do I? How do you expect me to make aamchur and kulchur?'

'Kusum's babu will give me a goja to eat.'

'And why not? He's dedicated that huge shop of his at the crossroads to Kusum. Never mind them. As they say, you're so vain, I could die...'

I told her apprehensively, 'Don't be angry with me, Prabha.'

'No, why should I be angry? Just sad, that's all. I'm a one-man whore too. We didn't just sail in here, you know. I left home at fifteen when my luck ran out.'

'Why did you leave home?'

'Why tell you all those sad tales? What will you make of them? Wait, my dal's burning. Words won't fill my stomach.'

'Should I go?'

'Come into the kitchen.'

Prabha was dark, quite plump, with a mole like a black hornet on her nose. She gave me hot jilipi and muri to eat one day. She didn't have too many things in her room, besides the pet parrot in the cage.

Prabha was cooking a broth with the chalta fruit. The chalta slices were being moistened in a marble cup. I hadn't tasted chalta in ages, not since we'd left our village. The trees lining the pond in the field would be bursting with ripe chalta at this time of the year.

I asked, 'Where did you get chalta, Prabha?'

'At the market. Where do you suppose?'

'They look delicious.'

Prabaha didn't reply. She went on cooking.

I said, 'Where are your parents?'

'This sinful mouth cannot answer.'

'Won't you go home?'

'What home?'

'Your home in the village?'

'I'll go home to hell.'

'Do you get kul in your village? We have so many kul trees.'

Prabha did not respond. She carried on cooking. A little later, she covered the clay oven on which she was cooking with an upturned bowl, made tea for herself and sipped it from a glass around which she had wrapped the end of her sari. She didn't ask me whether I'd like some. Not that I drank tea; I was only allowed the cream off the top.

Prabha began to tell me about the cows in her village home, how much milk they gave, and how the pond next to their house was full of fish. She would never see all this again.

Then Prabha did something extraordinary. She asked me, 'Want to have a little rice and chalta?'

I said apprehensively, 'I do. But Kusum mustn't find out.'

Prabha asked, laughing, 'Why are you so afraid of Kusum? What if she finds out? Eat now.'

I had barely mixed the chalta broth into the rice when I heard Kusum say, 'Is the little Brahmin with you, Prabha-di? I'd better send him home, he's been here a long time; he doesn't live here.'

I ran to a corner of the kitchen to hide, my hand still smeared with rice. Kusum entered before Prabha could respond and saw me. She said, 'What's this? Why are you in a corner? Are you hiding? Who's this rice for…'

Turning to Prabha in surprise, she said, 'He's a child, Prabha-di, not in his senses. But have you lost yours too? How could you serve him food?'

Subdued, Prabha said, 'He kept talking about the chalta, so I thought, a little rice with the…'

'No shame! Come with me, khoka. We already have a lifetime of punishment to deal with; I'm not going to increase my burden of sin by feeding a Brahmin boy. Come… Do you have food on your fingers? Have you been eating already?'

I answered shyly, 'No.'

'Come with me, let me rinse your hands…'

As Kusum was about to lead me out, Prabha said, 'Poor thing, you didn't even let him eat. He'd barely begun…'

'No, no need to eat. Come.'

Kusum proved stricter with me than even my mother. I had to abandon my meal and come away. Taking me to a corner of the yard and pouring water on my hands, she said, 'Why are you such a glutton, khoka? Don't you remember you're not allowed to eat there? Shame on you! I'll give you kochuri in the evening. Don't ever go in there to eat. You at least are a child, but she's not, how could she serve a Brahmin's son… Really, the things people do…'

Naturally Prabha couldn't hear any of this. She wasn't even nearby.

I said, 'Don't tell my mother, all right?'

'Can you imagine me telling your mother? I have better things to do.'

'She'll beat me up if you tell her.'

'You deserve it. That might stop you from being so greedy.'

When I returned home my mother asked, 'Where were you?'

'There, on the road.'

'You didn't go anywhere else, did you?'
'No.'

~

But one day I was caught. It was Kusum's fault. She told me, 'Come, khoka, let's go for a walk. Want to?'

It was late afternoon, not very sunny. When I saw we were crossing the tram lines, I said fearfully, 'My mother doesn't allow me to cross the main road. She's told me not to.'

'I'm with you, don't worry.'

Crossing the main road, we went a little further on and entered a slum of hovels. The houses stood on either side of a narrow lane. The building we entered was also full of women, without any men. One of the women said. 'Come, Kusmi, it's been so long. God, it's not like we don't have men-friends but does that mean you must forget us?'

With a glance at me she said, 'Who's this boy? He's very sweet.'

'He's from a Brahmin family. Lives in our lane. Follows me around.'

'How nice. Sit down, khoka.'

'The boy's a glutton. Give him food and he'll be happy.'

'Ah, but what do I offer you? I have kul-achaar, want some?'

Without a thought I blurted out, 'I love kul-achaar.'

Kusum snarled at me, 'Is there anything you don't love? So long as it's food. No, he has a cold, he mustn't have achaar. Never mind.'

I was heartbroken. Kusum didn't let me have the kulchur. Where was this cold of mine? I love kulchur so much.

After spending some time in this house, we went to another one. They, too, asked several questions about me. I was given homemade haalua in a bowl. Kusum didn't let me eat this either. Apparently I was suffering from indigestion.

Kusum escorted me back across the tram lines shortly before evening fell. A tram was approaching. I said, 'Wait, Kusum, I want to see the tram.'

'It's getting dark. Your mother will scold you.'

'Let her.'

'Oh, the boy's so bold.'

'Why did you say that, Kusum? Why didn't you let me have the kulchur? They wanted me to.'

'You're a child, what do you know? People have dangerous diseases in those neighbourhoods. You think I'll let anyone serve you food? You think you can eat anywhere you want to? You have no idea. Do you know what disease some of them might have?'

'What does "men-friend" mean, Kusum?'

'Nothing. Where did you hear it?'

'Weren't they telling you?'

'Let them. What's it to do with you? Such a naughty boy!'

Before sending me on my way, Kusum said, 'Come, he must have got the kochuri by now. I'll give you some.'

'Yes. I'm hungry.'

'Is there ever a time when you're not hungry? If I ever ran into your mother I'd ask her why her son is so greedy.'

'So what if I am? You'll give me the kochuri, won't you?'

'Come along.'

'Has he brought goja?'

'I don't know.'

'Will you give me goja tomorrow?'

'How dirty this lane is, my god!'

'Will you give me goja?'

'Yes, yes I will. Now just take the kochuri and leave me alone.'

That evening Kusum walked me to the municipality tap and left. I told my mother the truth. I'd been to Kusum's house, and she'd given me kochuri. My mother scolded me soundly and threatened to tie me up. She did tell my father at night, but he didn't seem to pay much attention.

~

I got a fever the next morning. I had to be in bed for four or five days. An ancient doctor examined me and prescribed medicines.

My bed was laid next to the window. One afternoon I discovered Kusum on the road, peering at the house opposite ours. Makhan was with her. She was standing two houses away.

I called out, 'Kusum...'

Turning round, Kusum saw me. Calling out to Makhan, she said, 'This house, didi, here...'

My mother was at the municipality tap. Kusum and Makhan came up to the window.

Kusum asked, 'What's the matter with you? Why haven't you come?'

Makhan said, 'Kusmi's dying of anxiety. What's happened to the boy, she keeps saying. So I said, let's go find out.'

I said, 'I've had a fever for five days now.'

Kusum asked, 'Where's your mother?'

'Go away, Kusum. If my mother sees you she won't let me visit you any more. I'll come as soon as I'm better. Go now.'

They left. But Kusum was back on the road the very next day. Very softly she said, 'Can I come?'

My mother wasn't home. I knew she was at Baidyanath's shop to measure out the dal. She had left a short while ago, telling me before she was going, 'Make sure the cat doesn't get chhoto-khoka's milk; I'm going to get some dal from Baidyanath's shop.'

Beckoning to Kusum, I said, 'Come.'

Standing outside my window, she said, 'How are you?'

'Much better. I can have rice tomorrow.'

'I brought a couple of oranges. Want them?'

'Quickly.'

'Don't forget to eat them.'

'I won't.'

'Come over when you're better.'

'I will.'

'Rice tomorrow?'

'My father said I can.'

'I'll come again tomorrow. All right?'

'Come. But don't come up to the window till I say so.'

'All right. I'll wait quietly on the road. Do you know how to whistle?'

'No. Come when I wave.'

Kusum came on schedule the next two afternoons. One day she brought Prabha along too because she wanted to see me. I shan't lie, Prabha gave me a couple of oranges too. I used to hide them beneath the pillow, and eat them when my mother wasn't in the room, tossing the pulp out through the window.

I went to Kusum's house twice after getting better.

Then something happened which led us to leave our house in Calcutta and go back to the village. One day, while my mother was opening a bottle of soda-water, a shard of glass went into her hand. There was blood everywhere, spurting out of her wrist. Everyone came running. Bipin-babu from the corner room put some sort of medicine on her arm and bandaged it. But her arm did not heal, getting worse by the day. She couldn't cook any more, and would cry in pain every night. The doctor visited regularly. My maternal uncles were well-off. When they came to know through a letter, one of them arrived and took all of us away to their house.

It was the middle of July. The taal had begun to ripen on the trees. There were many of these trees by a huge lake next to a field in the village where my maternal uncles lived. I remember picking up a ripe fruit from the ground the very first day.

My mother's arm healed here. In the middle of September we went to our own village. We couldn't go to Calcutta any more. My father also wound up the establishment there and came home.

~

A long thirty years later.

I lived in a boarding house in Calcutta, working as a clerk. My wife and children lived in the village. On a holiday, as I was chatting with my college friend Sripati, he said, 'Last evening, you know, while walking down Premchand Boral Street—painted faces on both sides—horrible!'

'I've seen them too. I have to take the same route. But I see them differently. I know them very well. I used to visit their homes quite often once upon a time.'

My friend exclaimed in surprise, 'You!'

'Yes, I! I swear!

'Rubbish, I don't believe it.'

'Very well, come with me. I'll prove it to you.'

About fifteen years ago I had found my way to Nandaram Sen Lane and visited Makhan at home. Neither Kusum nor Prabha was there. Makhan was the only one in the group still living in those houses.

I took Sripati to Nandaram Sen Lane. Makhan was still there. Her hair was quite grey, and she looked like a witch, with toothless gums.

When she saw me, Makhan said, 'Come in. How are you?'

'Do you recognize me?'

'Oh my God, how could I not? You grew up right in front of our eyes. By the way, I've tracked Kusum down.'

'Where? Where is she?'

'She works as a maid at a boarding house on Shobhabazar Street. The first building on the left. A dilapidated two-storeyed house next to the temple. They'd taken me to the temple the other day, that's how I found out.'

With Sripati in tow I found the boarding house. It wasn't evening yet. I asked the cook in the kitchen downstairs, 'Where's your maid?'

'She's gone to the market, sir, she'll be back soon. Why?'

'I have to talk to her. Her name is Kusum, isn't it?'

'Yes, sir.'

A little later a tall, thin woman—looking like a typical maid— entered through the front door and appeared in the kitchen. The cook said, 'These gentlemen are looking for you, Kusum.'

I stared at the maid in astonishment. Was this what the beautiful Kusum of my childhood had turned into? She may not have been as old as Makhan, but still, Kusum was an old woman now. She couldn't be described as anything but one. I remembered her face, but this aged woman had nothing in common with it. If the cook had not told us, I'd never have known it was the same Kusum.

Kusum looked at us in surprise too, asking, 'You're looking for me? Who sent you?'

'Makhan did.'

'Which Makhan?'

'Makhan, the landlady from Nandaram Lane.'

'I see. But why are you looking for me?'

'Come over there. There's something I have to tell you.'

'Let's go into the dining room.'

In the dining room I asked, 'Don't your recognize me, Kusum?'

'No, sir.'

'We used to live in Nandaram Sen Lane. I was eight. My parents were tenants at the barber's house. Remember?'

Smiling, Kusum said, 'I remember. So you're the mad little Brahmin? How you've grown! Are your parents alive?'

'No one's alive.'

'How many children?'

'Five.'

'Sit down, my dear, sit down.'

After we had chatted for a while, Kusum asked us to wait and disappeared somewhere. A little later she came in with two packets of food and handed them to us.

I hadn't remembered. But as I was about to eat, I did. Four large pieces of heeng-kochuri. At once I remembered Kusum's babu and the heeng-kochuri. I was reminded of the boy thirty years ago and his greed for kochuri. Kusum must have remembered. Or not—I didn't know. As I ate the kochuri, my mind took me across the dusty gap of thirty long years directly to the spot on Nandaram Lane next to the roadside municipality tap, in front of the gur warehouse, where Kusum was still a young woman of twenty-five, and her babu still came regularly with a packet of heeng-kochuri.

Translated from the Bangla by Arunava Sinha

THE HUNDRED-CANDLE-POWER BULB

Saadat Hasan Manto

He stood leaning against an electric pole in the square outside Kaisar Park where a few tongas awaited customers and pondered over the desolation that had overcome everything around him.

Until two years ago, this park had been a bustling, lively place; today it is a desolate wilderness. Where once men and women dressed in the most attractive fashionable clothes strutted about, today people dressed in abysmally dirty rags loiter about meaninglessly. There is a crowd in the market but it lacks colour and energy. The cement buildings that circle the market have lost their sheen; they gape at each other, open-mouthed and vacant-eyed, like widowed women.

He is amazed by this loss of colour. Where has the bride's vermilion disappeared? What happened to those lovely notes, those melodies that he had once heard here? It wasn't very long ago that he had last come here—after all, two years is not a very long time—when he had been enticed from Calcutta by a firm offering a better salary. How hard he had tried to rent a house in Kaisar Park and, despite a thousand entreaties, how unsuccessful he had been!

But as he can see, now any cobbler, barber or weaver who wished to move into these flats and rooms could simply move in and take possession.

Where once a film company had had a swanky office, stoves flickered. Where the city's smartest people once gathered, washermen now washed filthy laundry.

What a great revolution in a mere two years!

He was surprised, yes, but he was also aware of the context and background of this revolution. Newspapers, as well as friends who had stayed behind, had told him about the storm that had hit this city. Yet he wondered what a strange storm it must have been, for

61

it had sucked the colour and shine from buildings. Men had killed
men and debased women, but how had they managed to do the
same to timber-and-mortar buildings?

He had heard that women had been stripped naked in that
storm. Their breasts had been gouged out. Here, everything around
him seemed similarly naked and sexless.

He stood leaning against the electric pole, waiting for a friend
who was supposed to help him find a house to live in. The friend
had told him to wait outside Kaisar Park, near the tonga stand.

When he had come here two years ago, this had been a huge
tonga stand, the busiest and biggest in the city. The smartest and
most gaily decorated tongas were to be found here, because it was
here that the city offered every manner of delight. The best hotels
and restaurants were close by, along with the best tea, the finest
food and everything else besides. The city's biggest pimps and
agents were also to be found here. Money and drink flowed like
water because some of the biggest companies had their offices in
Kaisar Park.

He remembered having a good time here with his friend two
years ago. Every night he had had the prettiest girl beside him.
The war had made Scotch unavailable elsewhere, but here, a
dozen bottles could materialize within a minute.

The tongas still stood about, but now the pom-poms, the frills
and ribbons, the gleaming brass fittings were all gone. Perhaps
those, too, had taken wing and disappeared, along with everything
else.

He looked at his watch. Five o'clock. It was the month of
February, and the evening shadows had begun to lengthen. He
cursed his friend and was about to set off towards the desolate
hotel on his left to drink a cup of tea brewed, no doubt, from drain
water, when he heard someone call out softly. For a moment he
thought his friend had finally shown up, but when he turned
around he found a stranger standing in front of him. An ordinary-
looking man, dressed in a white cotton salwar which had no space
left for any more creases and a blue poplin shirt that was desperately
in need of a visit to the laundry.

He asked, 'Well, Brother, did you call me?'

The man answered softly, 'Yes.'

He took the man to be a refugee, probably asking for some money. 'What do you want?'

The man answered in the same soft tone, 'Nothing.' Then, coming a step closer, he whispered, 'Do you want something?'

'What?'

'A girl, maybe?' he said, and stepped back a little.

It was as though an arrow had pierced his chest. Look at him, even at a time like this, he is going about groping and preying on people's bodily hungers; a mad rage against all humanity overtook him. Overwhelmed by his feelings, he asked, 'Where is she?'

His tone did not seem very encouraging to the pimp. He stepped back a few paces and said, 'Never mind, you don't seem to need it very much.'

He stopped the pimp and asked, 'How can you tell? A man is always in need of that thing that you can provide—even when he is atop the scaffold waiting for the hangman's noose or on the smouldering funeral pyre…'

He was close to becoming a philosopher when he stopped and added, 'Look here, if it is somewhere close by, I am ready to come with you. I have asked a friend to meet me here.'

The pimp sidled up and said, 'It is right here, very close by.'

'Where?'

'There—in that building right across there.'

'There? In that big building?'

'Yes, sir.'

A shudder coursed through him, 'All right, then…' He pulled himself up and asked, 'Shall I come with you?'

'Please do, but I shall go first.' The pimp started to walk towards the building in front of them. Thinking countless self-loathing thoughts, he followed.

The building was barely a few feet away. The distance was covered in a matter of minutes. By now, both he and the pimp had entered the building which bore a battered weather-beaten board.

This building was more dilapidated than its neighbours—peeling plaster, gaping brickwork, broken pipes and heaps of rubbish all around.

Evening had fallen. As they crossed the threshold, it was dark inside. They crossed a wide courtyard and turned a corner. Here, construction had come to a standstill. Naked brickwork, heaps of hardened cement and mortar and small piles of gravel were scattered all about.

The pimp began to climb the half-finished stairs and turned to say, 'Please wait here. I won't be a minute.'

He stood, waiting. The pimp had disappeared. He raised his face to look at the top of the stairs where a bright light was visible.

Two minutes passed and he began to tiptoe up the stairs. At the top of the staircase he heard the pimp's voice, loud and harsh.

'Will you get up or not?'

A woman's voice answered, 'I told you, didn't I? Let me sleep.' Her voice sounded muffled, subdued.

The pimp's voice crackled, 'I said—get up! If you don't listen to me, I will...'

The woman's voice said, 'Kill me if you want, but I won't get up. For God's sake, have pity on me.'

The pimp wheedled, 'Get up, my love. Don't be so stubborn. Just think...what will we live on?'

The woman answered, 'Let the living go to hell! I'll die of hunger, if I must. Don't trouble me. I want to sleep.'

The pimp's voice hardened, 'So you won't get up? You bitch! You daughter of a sow!'

The woman began to shout, 'I won't get up...I won't get up...I won't get up...'

The pimp lowered his voice. 'Speak softly. Someone might hear...Come now, get up. You will get thirty or forty rupees.'

There was entreaty in the woman's voice now. 'Look! I am folding my hands before you... I have been awake for so long... I beg you, have pity on me. For God's sake have pity on me.'

'It's only for an hour or two... You can sleep later... Or else, I will have to be very stern with you.'

Silence reigned for a while. He took a few stealthy steps and peeped into the room from which bright light spilled out.

He saw a small room; a woman lay on the floor. Except for a few utensils scattered about, there was nothing else. The pimp sat beside the woman, pressing her legs. After a while he said, 'Come on now, get up. I swear upon God you will be back in an hour or two—you can sleep then.'

The woman jumped up like a rat that has been shown fire and screamed, 'All right, I am getting up!'

He stepped aside. Actually, he was a little scared. On tiptoe, he climbed down the stairs. He thought of running away—running away from this city, from this world itself. But where could he run to?

Then he thought: Who is this woman? Why is she being subjected to this cruelty? Who is the pimp? How is he related to the woman? And why do they live in that room lit with a bulb that is certainly not less than a hundred candle-power? How long have they been living here?

The light from that strong bulb still blinded him. He couldn't see anything around him. But he thought: How can anyone possibly sleep in that dazzling light? Why such a big bulb? Couldn't they have used a smaller bulb—of maybe fifteen or twenty candle-power?

As he stood, lost in thought, he heard a footfall. He turned around to see two shadows standing close beside him. One shadow, which belonged to the pimp, spoke up, 'See for yourself.'

He said, 'I have seen.'

'All right?'

'All right.'

'It'll cost you forty rupees.'

'Okay.'

'Give it to me now.'

By now he was no longer capable of rational thought. He thrust his hand in his pocket, pulled out a few notes and handed them to the pimp.

'Count them, how many are they?'

The rustling of currency notes could be heard.

The pimp said, 'There are fifty here.'

He said, 'Keep fifty, then.'

'Salaam, sahab.'

He thought of picking up a huge stone and hitting him on the head with it.

The pimp said, 'Take her. But please don't trouble her too much and please bring her back after an hour or two.'

'All right.'

He stepped out of that big building on whose front had once hung a board that he had read countless times.

A tonga stood outside. He began to move towards it, with the woman following.

Once again the pimp raised his hand to salaam. Once again, he was overcome with the urge to pick up a huge stone and hit him on the head with it.

The tonga started. It took him to a seedy little hotel nearby. Somehow, he pulled himself out of the anxiety that seized his brain and looked at the woman. She was wasted—from head to toe. Her eyelids were swollen. Her eyes were downcast. In fact, the entire upper part of her body was bent forward like a building that was about to topple over any second.

He said to her, 'Raise your head a bit.'

With a terrible start she said, 'What?'

'Nothing. All I said was: "Say something."'

Her eyes were bloodshot. They were red, as though someone had flung red-hot chillies into them. She remained quiet.

'What's your name?'

'Nothing at all.' Her tone burnt like acid.

'Where are you from?'

'Wherever you want me to be from.'

'Why are you so curt?'

By now the woman had woken up fully. She looked at him with her chilli-bright eyes and said, 'You get on with your job; I have to go.'

He said, 'Where to?'

The woman answered in a dry, couldn't-care-less tone, 'Where you got me from.'

'You can go now.'

'You do what you have to do, why are you troubling me?'

Filling his voice with all the compassion in his heart, he said, 'I am not troubling you. I sympathize with you.'

This infuriated her. 'I don't need a sympathizer.' And then, nearly shouting, she repeated, 'You get on with your job and let me go.'

He came close and attempted to pat her head, but she flung his hand away with a jerk.

'I tell you, don't trouble me. I have been awake for so many days. I have been awake ever since I have come here.'

From head to toe, he turned into a sympathizer.

'Go to sleep…right here.'

The woman's eyes became redder. In a sharp tone, she said, 'I haven't come here to sleep, this isn't my home.'

'Is that your home—where you have come from?'

The woman grew more agitated.'Uff! Stop this nonsense. I have no home. Why don't you get on with your job! Or else take me back and take your money from that…that…' And she bit back a terrible obscenity.

He thought it was futile talking to the woman while she was in that state, or even showing her any sympathy. So he said, 'Come, I will take you back.'

And he took her back to the big building.

The next day, sitting in a seedy hotel in Kaisar Park, he narrated the entire incident to his friend. The friend was suitably sympathetic. He expressed the deepest shock and disgust and asked, 'Was she young?'

He said, 'I don't know; I didn't really see her properly. All I could think was why didn't I pick up a stone and crush the pimp's head with it.'

The friend said, 'Truly, that would have been a great mercy.'

He couldn't sit in the hotel for very long with his friend. The previous day's incident weighed on his mind. So he finished his tea and took leave.

The friend walked towards the tonga stand. His eyes searched for the pimp but couldn't find him. It was past six. The big building loomed ahead, barely a few yards away. He walked towards it and soon he was inside it.

People milled past him, but he reached the stairs quite easily. He saw the light spilling down the staircase. He looked up and began to climb the stairs on tiptoe. For a few minutes he stood silently at the topmost stair. Dazzling bright light spilled out of the room, but there wasn't a sound to be heard. He crossed the landing. The door of the room was ajar. He looked around and peered into the room. Before he could spot the bulb, its piercing light jabbed at his eyes. He turned around to face the darkness outside and allow his eyes to get used to that dazzling light.

Once again he approached the door, but in such a way that he remained outside the piercing pool of light cast by the bulb. He peered within. He could see a woman lying on a mat. He craned forward for a closer look; she appeared to be asleep. A dupatta covered her face. Her chest rose and fell with her breaths. He stepped closer and nearly screamed. He controlled himself and saw—a short distance away from the woman, a man lay on the uncovered floor. His head was smashed to pieces. A blood-smeared brick lay close by. He saw everything in the blink of an eye and rushed towards the stairs. He slipped and fell several times but, heedless of his injuries, he tried his best to hold on to his senses. With great difficulty, he managed to reach home, but spent the night having the most terrifying nightmares.

Translated from the Urdu by Rakhshanda Jalil

RIVER OF FLESH

Kamleshwar

The doctor who examined Jugnu said that there were no traces of STDs, but there was definitely a hint of tuberculosis in her reports. She wrote out a prescription and advised nutritious meals.

The Committee had already put a ban on the profession and it worried them all; they were unable fathom the consequences. Medical check-ups had put an end to the works of many already. Those picked up by the pimp Ibrahim had 'passed'. Their tantrums therefore escalated and they smugly talked about their high lineage.

Ibrahim selected only the healthy girls, helping them to gradually settle in different parts of the city. He took care of them and regularly paid the different brothels they had been picked up from. Once, when Jugnu was worried, she had asked Ibrahim to settle her in one of his areas, but he had snubbed her saying, 'This is not marriage that I can fool the party once and forever. Whoever comes will see every inch of your body.'

That day, Jugnu had felt a pain in her heart for the first time. Was she now so worthless? The second blow came when Shahnaz, the woman next door, loudly abused her and gestured insultingly: 'Arre, Allah will show you the worst day of your life—when no man will even step onto your stairs.'

The entire mohalla was stirred by this incident. That curse was forbidden; no matter how bad one's situation was in this occupation, they still blessed each other, exclaiming: 'May your men live long,' and 'May God give men good jobs and strong thighs.'

It was on the same day that he had come for the first time, hesitantly. Fate had brought him. Clad in khaki pants and a blue shirt, he carried a sling bag in his hand. He had stubble and his facial hair was covered with a thin film of dust. Jugnu entered the room and sat on the bed. He kept standing there, confused about where to keep his bag. Jugnu unobtrusively took it and placed it on the headrest. Quietly, he sat next to Jugnu.

A few minutes passed before Jugnu said, 'Take off your shoes.'
A gush of odour filled the room when he took them off, the stench
similar to the odour that emanated from most men when they
removed their clothes, especially the clerk Mansoo, who always
visited her after eleven at night, and would sit on the bed rigidly
after he finished, because of his backache. Jugnu would then help
him to get up, and he would leave scratching his thighs, which
revolted her. Then there was Kanwarjeet, the hotel owner who
would not only stink, but would burp loudly after he finished.

The odour was now unbearable. 'Put them back on,' said
Jugnu.

He did so and sat down again. Jugnu was annoyed now. She
stared at him for a minute and said irritably, 'This is not a sitting
room; finish your job and leave.' He felt insulted and, to counter
that, mumbled, 'What is your name?'

'Jugnu.'

'Where do you come from?'

'Mind your own business.' She was annoyed again.

Like every other man, he asked, 'Do you like being in this
profession?'

'Yes. Don't you?' She lay down and pulled her sari up to her
thighs. He, too, lay by her side and timidly tried to put his hand
inside her blouse.

'It's better if you don't bother me. Why are you opening that?'
she snapped.

It was impossible for him to begin. Jugnu's face was covered in
a layer of cheap powder, the same powder had formed thin white
lines around her neck. There were dots of blood which had dried
on her lips. Earrings ogled like toad's eyes, her hair was drenched
with oil, the pillow was filthy and the bedsheet like crushed
jasmine. A peculiar odour filled the cramped room. In a corner, an
earthen pot of water was kept with a mug; in the same corner lay
some rags.

He kept lying on the bed and looked around. Behind Jugnu's
bed was a small almirah, its stone top marked by patches of oil. A

broken comb, a bottle of cheap nail polish and a few hairpins were scattered there. A few names and addresses were scribbled on the almirah door. In one corner, some film songbooks were stacked and false braids coiled like snakes lay beside them. The ambience of the room filled him with disgust. He placed his hand on Jugnu's naked thigh for some respite—it felt squidgy like stale fish, and rug-rough. From her half-naked body a pungent dairy odour emanated. As Jugnu removed his hand, it fell on the sheet beneath her thighs. The sheet felt wet.

'This is the time for making money—by now, four men could have enjoyed themselves and left.' Jugnu held him tightly in her arms.

When he sat up, Jugnu casually opened his bag and remarked, 'You carry a lot of money!' He presumed she had said this in order to extract extra money from him. For the first time, he looked at her attentively, and left quietly.

Jugnu always covered her head when on the street. She wanted to believe that she was not so cheap that men could comment on her as she passed by them. They would, in fact, look at her as if they all owned her equally. She often glanced at the men she knew well, and at those who visited her frequently like other customers. Then one day she saw him, the same man with a bag, wearing the same shirt. He was standing on the first floor of a building with his elbow resting on a windowsill and smoking a bidi. A red flag swaying on the top of the building cast a flickering shadow on his shoulders. She stopped to get her slippers fixed and assumed he had gone inside.

That night, he came. His eyes flickered with familiarity. He was not timid this time. Sitting on her bed Jugnu asked him, 'What do you do?'

'Nothing, I work among labourers.'

'Do some labour for me too, I'm also a labourer,' teased Jugnu.

'Aren't you late?' he enquired.

'I'm not feeling well today,' she answered lazily.

'What happened?'

'I have a pain in my lower back. My whole body is aching, I don't know why... Shall I call Tara? She will be very courteous, she's a very sensible woman.'

He turned down her offer. After sitting with her for a few minutes, he got up to leave and said, 'I came just like that.' Quietly climbing down the stairs in the darkness, he left. Jugnu silently stood at the window. She presumed that he would climb some other staircase. There was not much movement on the street at this hour, just a few men standing in groups in the distance. Some would occasionally climb one of the many stairs opening on to the street. She stared at the smoke wafting from a baker's chimney, and then her eyes followed him on the street. He had not stopped. Walking slowly, he had crossed the street and turned towards the main road—the road where he lived.

Jugnu was pleased. Returning to her bed, she lay down again, feeling happy.

The room was damp and stuffy. She had locked the door and was reading one of the film songbooks when, all at once, a knock sounded and Amma spoke: 'Jugnu beta, has that scoundrel passed out?'

'There's no one here, Amma!'

'Then come out onto the balcony, the breeze is lovely, dear. The street is also alive.'

Opening the door, Amma entered Jugnu's room. 'Are you feeling all right?'

'There's something wrong, Amma.'

'Drink a glass of milk, dear. There is still time, someone may come.'

She walked onto the balcony and Amma checked her temperature, noticing flabby tyres around her waist. 'You are ignoring your health. Look at this—you need exercise.' Hearing a loud noise from the next room, Amma walked toward it, mumbling, 'This bitch is never bridled without a ruckus, there will be murder in this room one day...'

This was routine. Amma always cursed Bilkis in this manner.

Bilkis claimed that no man could leave her room without a backache. She, too, enjoyed it. The moment men left her room, she would come to her door, clap loudly and taunt them: 'O Jubeda, look, Rustam retreats! His tall claims of power—*this* loser will sleep with a woman?' She would then clap loudly.

Irked, one of her customers once said, 'What nonsense is this?'

'You son of a sweeper, take this, and buy yourself some fresh cream!'

Insulted, he climbed down the stairs. The entire building remained in a constant state of terror because of Bilkis. No one knew when she would next pick a fight with her customers. Undeterred, she would gesture vulgarly and spit loudly, 'As if you all are sleeping with celibates!'

Whenever Bilkis saw Jugnu, she would taunt, 'You should sit at someone's house now.' But Jugnu never retorted, she never fought with anyone. She knew that Bilkis was loud-mouthed. She would not even spare Amma. But Amma always took care of her body and looks. Amma would always urge her, quite aggressively, to take care of her appearance: 'You are expanding like a buffalo, start wearing satin petticoats. Stop eating potatoes, you bitch.'

When she first noticed Jubeda's loose stomach, Amma brought her a belt, saying, 'Tie it during the day time and don't drink too much tea.' Amma bought fancy blouses of every size. She worried only about one thing: 'If it was in my control, I would freeze time for all of you.'

In the afternoons, Amma would affectionately wash one woman's hair, or press a sari for another. If it was spring, she would get their saris dyed bright yellow. She would never forget to get a scarf dyed for Fatte. She would celebrate both Eid and Bakr-Eid, as well as Holi and Diwali with much fervour. Sometimes, when she would think of Kamla, her eyes would moisten. 'A thousand wombs cannot bear a girl like her again. God had granted her such beauty, as if a mere touch would soil her radiant skin. Enmity among the affluent swallowed her. The scoundrels poisoned her—she writhed so much. Alas, I could not even take her to the hospital.'

Jugnu was sitting in the corridor, watching people walking on the street. Gradually, the crowd thinned. The flower- and gajra-sellers were packing up. She noticed that like every day Mannat had thrown a gajra through Kalawati's window and, as usual, she had smiled naughtily and cursed him. Banne walked straight up to Shehnaz's room with a crisp tahmad tied around his waist, wearing a net vest.

Half-crazy Chunnilal had spread his rag on the platform in front of Shankar's betel shop, and was sipping tea from a metal mug mumbling, 'You ruthless… Get your hands chopped the day you hum a wrong note! You callous… One day you'll come down here…here on this rag our nuptial night will be celebrated… You ruthless!'

Meanwhile, Jugnu thought she had seen the same blue-shirted man at the end of the street. Perhaps he was back, perhaps he too would climb one of the staircases. But it was a mere delusion. It was not him.

Many days later, he came again. Soon after entering Jugnu's room he lay down on her bed, yet he did not dare take off his shoes.

'Tell me your name at least,' Jugnu asked, lying down beside him.

'Madanlal. Why?'

'Just like that. You haven't been around?'

'I was in jail. Detention was going on, I went in due to that.'

'Why?'

'There was a strike…the owners got us arrested. We were released, but with much difficulty.'

'Are these strikes ever effective? Why did you do it?'

'They had dismissed us without prior notice. There were other reasons but you won't understand. May I take off my shoes?' Madanlal asked coyly.

'You may.'

The odour from his shoes and sweat-soaked socks did not bother her much today. She was gradually becoming familiar with the repulsive smell which now enveloped her and filled her body.

Madanlal left, but his stench remained. It was during those days, when Madanlal was around, that all of them had to visit the gynaecologist for their check-up. It was then that the doctor had said to Jugnu that while she had no venereal disease, traces of tuberculosis had been found.

Soon, Jugnu's coughing increased. She was frequently feverish. Amma had taken her to the hospital but her condition did not improve. Gradually, she became unfit for her profession. One day, she spat blood and Bilkis caused havoc, 'Throw her out of this place! We don't want to catch anything and die!' Amma scolded Bilkis for her harsh words but, deep down, she too had changed. In every possible way she suggested that Jugnu go elsewhere, for the sake of her health. If required, she could take some money, but under no circumstances should she ignore her health.

Jugnu had no idea where to go. She had no money. And whatever she could get hold of wouldn't last more than a few days. Eventually, she was admitted to a sanatorium and, slowly, her money disappeared. She had to stay there for four months, but she found no relief even after that. Although there was no restriction on her to not go out, she had visited Amma only a couple of times. Amma advised her, 'Don't disclose your whereabouts to anyone here. I've told them that you are visiting your sister in Rampur and will be back soon. But this wretched Inspector troubles me a lot, he thinks you have started sitting in some other place.'

She felt comforted when she caught a glimpse of affection in Amma's eyes. Amma, on the other hand, was distressed to see Jugnu's deteriorating condition. Indeed, her body appeared parched: she had lost hair and the glow had vanished from her face.

Jugnu was terrified to see her reflection in the mirror. Now what? How would she survive for the rest of her life? There was nothing left to count on, and she had no other skills.

Despite their profession being banned, there was a constant supply of new girls from Lucknow and Benares and these new girls had completely ruined the business. She had come to know that Shehnaz was struggling and Kalawati was destitute. She grew all the more depressed.

On her last visit, when she had asked Amma for some money, she had recounted her own woes—Amma's life was also crumbling. On her way back to the sanatorium, she glanced at the familiar faces around. She knew them; they were the same men who would frequent her room when she was in her prime.

When she saw Mansoo the clerk sitting in his shop, Jugnu was filled with revulsion—him on the bed, nursing his bad back, and leaving the room scratching his thighs.

Kanwarjeet, the hotel owner, was wearing a filthy pyjama and counting money at the counter; he always burped so disgustingly that it would make Jugnu nauseous.

Jugnu could not stay in the sanatorium for long. Eventually, she had to return, but she was very grateful to all those who helped her in her hour of need. She noted on the back of her prescription the amounts of money she had borrowed—she was neck-deep in debt. Kanwarjeet had given her forty-seven rupees as a great favour, while Mansoo had made her promise to return his money soon, as if his business would close down for want of twenty-five rupees.

The mechanic, Santram, had lent her twenty rupees before adding a cheap remark: 'One night for the interest accrued, agreed?' His vulgarity had instead made her aware that men still desired her, and that her body was not as worthless as she had thought.

In those days of need she had also met Madanlal and borrowed thirty rupees from him. He had said, 'This is part of a donation. Better you return it soon, as I do not have any savings to compensate for this.' There was such helplessness in his tone: he had chosen his words carefully to ensure that Jugnu did not misunderstand him. Before he left for the Party office he had also reminded her that he was not rich. Due to her dire need, Jugnu had to keep the money, though she felt awkward.

Since her return from the sanatorium, the police were also after her—they had not received their cut for the last seven months. In her building they had fixed different rates for different women.

Also, after returning to work, she felt very weak; her body

could not bear any strain. If a customer was more playful than usual, it would make her very uncomfortable. She would grow breathless in a few minutes, yet men would press upon her with all their weight.

Again and again, she felt like she used to feel in the beginning of her career—as if she was doing it for the first time.

She bought false hair for seven rupees from Kalawati, and also began padding her bra. It was cumbersome to wear the pads and take them out each time, but where she had always despised wearing a starched sari, the pads pleased her in the way that they made her look voluminous.

Despite these efforts, her earnings were not sufficient. A few nights would pass without customers, when she would lie alone on her bed contemplating the future and worrying about her deteriorating body. Impotent men annoyed her. They would bother her by digging into every inch of her flesh and waiting eternally to get aroused. They would run their hands all over her and make vulgar demands.

Jugnu preferred the men who came in like loaded guns—they would shoot and leave in minutes. They would neither make small talk nor bother her endlessly. Yet her income was not enough and her debts were not cleared. And while she had noted the details of her borrowings on the back of her prescription, there were never sufficient funds at hand to clear them off.

There was no alternative way to earn money, either. On her way to the local surgeon—for the recently erupted boil on the fold of her thighs—she crossed paths with Mansoo who said, 'It's been a few days now, and your business has also picked up well. I have taken a vow with the holy water of the Ganges that I'll never visit a brothel. See, I've even worn the tulsi weeds.'

Mansoo's claims made Jugnu laugh and he stared at her with wide eyes.

It wasn't easy for Jugnu to walk with the boil on her inner thigh. She was walking with her legs slightly spread—her gait was alluring to Mansoo. Where the street turned he whispered to her, 'So, you never told me when you are arranging it for?'

'If you have the courage, come and take it yourself!' she replied teasingly, hiding her helplessness. She was ashamed of her own retort, then realized there was nothing wrong with it—what is the use of so-called 'reputation' anyway? And why should she die with a burden of debt? Whatever could be returned was good.

The local surgeon told her that it would take a few days for the boil to come to a head and he gave her a bandage to cover it with. By the time she returned, it was afternoon and all the women were out on the verandah cleaning their teeth. This was the time when they would all sit together and begin their preparations for the evening.

Meanwhile, a group of young boys was crossing the street. They teased the women with vulgar gestures and enjoyed the abuses the women yelled about their fathers. These rogues would walk past every day, this was their regular amusement. Mature women would react to their obscene gestures by abusing their fathers, while the younger ones would just smile. At times, Hasan, Banwari or the cripple Matadin would chase the boys to the end of the street from where they would shout and make lewd gestures by raising their trousers or jerking their knees. This group used to come from the colony behind the mosque.

Afternoon was also the time when the women would interact among themselves and bitch about the others. Typically, their targets would be the girls who had moved to the elite parts of town, those who had been hand-picked by Ibrahim.

As dusk descended, the street would buzz with activity: flower-vendors would start their business, the betel-shop would be decked up, and a policeman would take his usual spot in front of Gafoor's shop—after his arrival, Gafoor could sell his bottles without any hitch.

Jugnu would remove her bandage in the evenings and do her make-up with disinterest. The boil had hardened and was very painful, but she still managed to entertain a few customers.

Sitting on her balcony, the thought of her future and her current physical condition filled Jugnu with fear. What would become of her? She would be dependent for every morsel of food. How would she survive like a lame mare? Was she destined to cover herself with a veil and sit on the steps of some mosque, begging in God's name? When her heart stirred with such thoughts, she considered consuming poison—like Akhtari, Bihabbon and Champa—or jumping into a river.

Hundreds of men came into her life, but none arrived with a shadow that could shelter her for the rest of her time on earth.

The familiar men were those she had borrowed money from, but there was no hope there, either. How could she trust them, when they would just vanish some day? With old age, men just leave. As their children grew they would stop coming to her. Men find myriad other sources of entertainment as the journey downhill begins. Then who would visit her? Not even those old familiar faces would appear on her horizon. How strange and secluded it would feel! And how painful it would be to live like that, so starkly different from the days gone by. Her only solace came from visits by those who had lent her money. She was expecting a visit from Mansoo as well. She was positive that he would come to ask for his money back and, indeed, he came.

The same familiar stink arrived. This time, Mansoo had come after eleven at night and just like always, he sat stone-stiff from the pain in his back after he was done. Jugnu also lay exhausted. The pressure on the boil had made her scream in pain. She had no stamina to get up and help Mansoo so that, as always, he could leave scratching his thighs.

When his stiff back eased a little, he told Jugnu, 'Do remember...'

Jugnu acknowledged that she did and helped him off the bed.

It was late in the night. Lying on her bed, Jugnu was staring at the walls of her room. There was nothing worth staring at, though. Dirty and ugly walls on which she had some day pasted pictures of film stars cut out from some old magazines. In a corner hung a string laden with bunches of old bangles, and an empty bottle of nail polish lay next to the wall on the floor.

An old quilt and a tin box were kept under her bed. In that box was a slip of paper; the letters on that slip had faded. It was now meaningless. The affinity was dead too. Who goes back into the past, and who calls out to one from there? The meandering stream of time flows between lives, ever-widening its flow and distancing the shores, apart and incomplete.

When she woke up in the morning she had a terrible body ache. The boil was unbearable too—her inner thigh was bursting with pain. With much effort she got ready for the evening, once again tying the bandage. In her room, she calculated her dues. She had marked each lender's visit on her almirah wall to remember how much had already been settled and for whom. Santram, the mechanic, had behaved very insolently. In lieu of twenty rupees he had already made four visits and, after the fifth one, when Jugnu had asked, 'Will you go without paying?' he had retorted, 'Why not?'

'The loan was settled last time,' Jugnu had replied, feebly yet clearly.

'One for the interest?' he sneered in a very demeaning tone. 'Money doesn't come for free, understand?' He climbed down the stairs and left without another word. Jugnu stared, numb and helpless. Unlike her friends, she could not pick fights with her customers. Nor could she shout at them; it was just not in her to insult men.

She owed the maximum amount to Kanwarjeet, he had visited only thrice—a total of fifteen rupees had been settled with him. Mansoo's twenty had been paid back too. Jugnu was slightly relieved about her debt issue, but suddenly she felt excruciating pain from the boil. She lay down with her legs spread apart.

There was a tap at the door and she saw Madanlal. For a moment she was annoyed to see him standing there. As if another usurious moneylender had appeared before her for recovery. Madanlal had not visited her for some time and his appearance at that moment did not please her. Helpless, she called him in; he entered and sat on the bed. He pushed his bag towards the headrest and Jugnu felt it gently—there were a few posters and a folded flag in it, plus a few old registers. She felt her heart palpitate in the anticipation that he might ask for hard cash. The pain from the boil was not subsiding either.

He was wearing the same old clothes and the same shoes. The stink of his sweat wafted into the room.

'You're here after a long time,' Jugnu somehow managed to say.

'May I take off my shoes?' Madanlal asked softly.

'You may...'

'Shall I close the door?'

'I'm in too much pain today, a boil has erupted on my inner thigh. I can lie straight but it's unbearable if I fold my legs.' Madanlal suddenly stopped unhooking his belt; he felt a little ashamed. Jugnu too felt strange, but he saved her from guilt. He talked on various topics but, throughout the conversation, Jugnu feared that he would eventually bring up the money she owed.

'All right then, I'll leave now.' Madanlal stood there with his bag. With an affectionate gaze he looked at Jugnu, as if parting with her distressed him. Jugnu could not ask him to stay, so she meekly brought up the dreaded topic: 'Your money...'

'That's not why I'm here,' said Madanlal, 'I came for you!'

The sweat under his armpits seemed blots of ink. With his moist hands he held Jugnu's hand and she felt the warmth and softness of his palms.

'I will come again,' he said as he left. Jugnu immediately rushed out to the balcony. She was repenting deep down that he had to return like that. She watched him. He crossed a couple of streets and then stopped. It was unbearable for Jugnu to see him stop there in the street. He looked up towards the balcony and climbed the stairs of the fifth house on the street. She somehow felt strangely afflicted. There was a shooting pain from the boil. Gradually, the burning subsided. If only she had asked him to stay, then he wouldn't have climbed that staircase—after all, he too had his needs. The pain was now bearable. He had gone back only because he cared for her suffering; the warmth of those moist palms had held no deception...

As she stood there, Kanwarjeet arrived. Jugnu felt as though an intruder had entered her home, but she managed to smile at him nonetheless.

Bilkis was standing in a corner talking to a large man while Jugnu quietly ushered Kanwarjeet in. She closed the door behind her and Kanwarjeet locked it.

'There's too much pain today, my boil has come to a head,' Jugnu tried to explain in a frustrated tone.

'Is it not gone yet?' asked Kanwarjeet.

'Hmmm, perhaps a day or two more,' Jugnu said in a pleading tone, hoping to be left alone.

'I'll not let you suffer the slightest bit, I will do it gently.' Kanwarjeet lay down on the bed.

'Tonight…' Jugnu started, but Kanwarjeet gently made her lie down next to him and said, 'I won't hurt you at all.'

Jugnu was utterly helpless now; she could not think of any way to make him understand. He placed his hands on her breasts. Slowly she changed sides, switched off the light, pulled the padding out of the bra and and placed them under the bed.

She tried a number of times to control her screaming and to stop Kanwarjeet. She was blinded by pain each time he put his full weight on her thighs. Kanwarjeet did stop a few times in between but, as if overpowered by some beastly instinct, his thrusts increased in force.

'Arre, stop it!' he shouted, pinning her down with force.

'Amma! He's killing me!' she screeched at the top of her voice as if someone was brutally murdering her. Then she squirmed and almost collapsed.

'Bitch!' Kanwarjeet panted as he sat up, exhausted.

Jugnu took a few minutes to gather herself. With the pain subsiding marginally, she could now move her limbs. She pulled out a cloth from beneath her pillow and switched on the light. Her thigh was soaked in the pus oozing from the boil, which had burst, and Kanwarjeet was sitting next to her, burping loudly as usual.

'See, it's gone,' he said as he stood up. Jugnu pulled her sari down to cover her thighs. 'Remember, this was the fourth visit,' he reminded her, opening the door to leave.

Jugnu pulled her sari up and wiped the pus. Suddenly she grew very restless. She called out to Fatte, who gave her water from the pot. Jugnu wiped the wound with a wet cloth saying, 'Look, Fatte, a man has just gone into Vimla's room. If he still hasn't left, call him here. He's wearing a blue shirt and carrying a bag.'

'Is he a customer?' Fatte asked.

'No, an acquaintance. Would you pour some more water?'

By the time Fatte came back with the water, Jugnu said pensively, 'Leave it, go and do your work. He said he'd come back some day...' She pressed the burst boil to release more pus and, with the pain, droplets of sweat flickered on her face.

Translated from the Hindi by Aradhana Pradhan

THE MURDER OF HONOUR

Premchand

I have read in stories and in history books the strangest and most interesting tales of the ups and downs of destiny. I have seen a king become a pauper and a pauper become a king, for destiny is a hidden secret. Women who roam the streets picking scraps have been known to sit on thrones of gold and those devotees of luxury at whose behest even destiny would bow down her head have, in their pride, fallen prey to crows and vultures. But nowhere is there an example of what befell me. Ah! When I remember those events my hair stands on end even today. And I am astonished. Why am I still alive and what for? Beauty is a source of desires. Did my heart not have desires but ah, the hands of a cruel fate wiped them out! How was I to know that the man who used to worship my every gesture and was ready to sacrifice all for me would one day humiliate and destroy me like this.

Today, it is three years since I first stepped into this house which at the time was like a garden in bloom. I was the nightingale of this garden, flying in the breeze, singing on the branches, sleeping on the blossoms. Sayeed was mine. I was his. Beside this marbled pond we played the chess of love. 'You are my life,' he would say. And I would answer, 'You are my dearest.' Our financial heritage was a grand one. There were no worries in our world, no sorrows in our life. For us life was physical bliss, one unending desire with the magic of spring in which wishes blossomed and happiness smiled. The world moved according to our wishes. The heavens blessed us and destiny was our companion.

One day Sayeed came to me and said, 'My life, I have come to you with a request. Be sure that the word of refusal does not come upon these smiling lips. I want to bequeath all my material possessions, all my property to you; for me, your love is enough. This is the biggest blessing for me; I want to erase my very identity. I wish to remain a mendicant at your doorstep. You become my Noor Jehan and I will become your Saleem, and in the cups of your coral-coloured palms I will spend my entire life.' My eyes filled with tears. Happiness reached its zenith and turned into teardrops.

~

But not even a year had passed and I noticed some change in Sayeed's behaviour. Between us there were no quarrels or ill feelings but now he was not Sayeed anymore. Even a moment's separation from me had been difficult for him but now he was missing night after night. His eyes lacked the earlier spark of love, and that thirst in his attitude was missing, as was the warmth of passion in his behaviour.

For a few days his coldness towards me made me cry endlessly. Memories of the love we had enjoyed tormented me. I had read that love was eternal. Did that source dry up so fast? Ah no, it was now nourishing some other garden. Eventually, I too began to avoid Sayeed. Not because I did not care but only because now I did not have the strength to look into his eyes. On just seeing him, thousands of miracles of love would come up before me and my eyes would fill with tears. My heart was still drawn towards him, sometimes involuntarily. I would yearn to fall at his feet and say, 'My dearest, why such cruelty? Why have you turned away from me? What wrong have I done?' But cursed be the pride that stood like a wall in my way. So much so that gradually jealousy took the place of love in my heart. Patience borne out of disappointment gave the heart satisfaction. For me, Sayeed was now a forgotten song of a spring that had passed. The passion in my heart turned cold. The candle of love was snuffed out. Not only this, even the respect I had for him left my heart. The man whose temple of love was impure certainly did not deserve that I pine and die for him.

One evening, as I lay on my bed reading a book, a beautiful woman entered my room. It seemed as if the room had been flooded with light. The incandescence of her beauty was such that it lit up the very walls with such lustre as though they had been freshly whitewashed. Her embellished beauty, her blooming flower-like attractive face, her seductive sweetness left such an awesome effect on me that I did not know how to praise her. My pride in my own beauty bit the dust. I was puzzled, who was this beautiful young creature and why had she come here? In spite of myself, I got up to ask her, when a smiling Sayeed entered the room. I understood then that this beautiful young woman was his beloved. My pride welled up within me. I did stand up holding my neck upright with dignity but my eyes flashed hate instead of awe at her resplendent beauty. Suddenly that young and beautiful woman was no longer the goddess of beauty but a poisonous snake who could bite with her venomous fangs. I sat down on my bed once more and opened the book in front of me. The young woman stood for a moment looking at my photographs and before leaving the room she looked at me once; her eyes were like smouldering coals. In their rays I glimpsed the redness of a violent revenge. A question arose within my heart—why had Sayeed brought her here? Was it to break my pride?

~

The property was in my name but that was just an illusion; Sayeed had full right over it. Even the servants thought of him as their master and often behaved disrespectfully with me. Patiently I was living the days of my life. When there were no hopes left in the heart, why feel pain?

It was the month of the monsoon, black clouds covered the skies and it was drizzling. Over the garden lay the darkness of jealousy and the fireflies on the seehas trees seemed as if they were sighing sparks of fire. For a long time I kept watching this drama of jealousy. The insects twinkled and extinguished, as if sporadic floods of light were being released. I also wanted to swing, and to sing. The weather leaves its magical effect even on hearts deadened with jealousy. In the garden was a circular bungalow. I went in and got a swing put in one of the rings in the verandah and began to swing myself. Today I realized that even in disappointment is a spiritual bliss which cannot be known to one who's every wish has been fulfilled. With relish I began singing the raag Malhaar— monsoon is a month of separation and sorrow. In the song, the saga of a broken heart is rendered in such sorrow-filled words that unheeded tears began falling from my eyes. All at once, I saw the light of a lantern approaching. Sayeed and the beautiful woman were walking in my direction. The beautiful woman came near me and said, 'A celebration of dance and song will be held here today, with rounds of drinking.'

I spoke in a tone laced with hatred, 'Congratulations.'

The beautiful woman went on, 'The raags Baramasa and Malhaar will be played; singers and musicians will be in attendance.'

'As you please,' I said.

The beautiful woman taunted, 'Your heart will tear apart with jealousy.'

Sayeed said to me, 'Zubeida, go to your room. She is not in her senses at the moment.'

The beautiful woman looked menacingly in my direction with reddened eyes and said, 'I don't regard you equal to even the dust of my feet.'

I could hold back no longer. Arrogantly I said, 'And what do I think of you? A bitch that goes about hungrily chewing the bones eaten and thrown away by others.'

Now even Sayeed's attitude changed. Staring at me with menacing eyes he said, 'Zubedia, what the devil has got into you?' Sayeed's words stung me. I was tormented. That those lips, from which I had always heard words of romance and love, should be spouting poison, and that too on an innocent! Had I become so worthless and disreputable that even a prostitute could provoke me and heap abuses? And I was forbidden to open my mouth! The fever that had been raging in my heart for a year now leapt up. I climbed down from the swing and looking at Sayeed with reproaching eyes said to him, 'You can decide for yourself whether the devil has got into me or you. Sayeed, till now I thought you were a decent and self-respecting man. That you could betray me I was aware of, but even in my dreams I had never thought that you are so devoid of self-respect that for the sake of a shameless prostitute you would humiliate me thus. God himself will avenge this.'

The beautiful woman said to me sharply, 'Did you call me a shameless woman?'

I replied, 'Without doubt, I say so.'

Sayeed, 'And I am shameless?'

I said, 'Without doubt! Not only shameless but pretentious, deceitful, sinner and everything else. These words are repulsive but still not enough to express my anger.'

I was still saying these things when suddenly Sayeed's tall, well-built servant caught hold of both my arms and in the wink of an eye the beautiful woman jerked down the ropes of the swing and tied me to an iron pillar in the verandah. At this time what thoughts raced through my heart I don't remember but darkness spread before my eyes. It seemed as if these three were not human beings but lords of death. In my heart fear had replaced anger. At this moment, even if some mighty other-worldly power had cut through the ropes that bound me and placed a sharp dagger in my hands, I would have done nothing but sat on the ground and shed tears over my humiliation and utter helplessness. It seemed to me that maybe the Almighty had sent this damnation down upon me. Maybe I was being punished for my lack of prayers and faith. I looked back to my past to find the wrong for which I was being punished thus. Leaving me in this state, the three of them went into the room. I thought my ordeal had ended but would they leave me tied like this? If the maids were to see me in this state what would they say? No, I was now no longer worthy of staying in this house. I was thinking of how to undo the ropes but sadly I did not know that the condition I was in at present was only a part of the mercilessness that lay ahead. I did not know until now how merciless and murderous that small-minded man was. I was debating with myself as to what extent was I responsible for this humiliation. If I had not replied to those heart-burning remarks by that beautiful woman, would this point have come? It would have come, certainly. That black snake had come with the intent to bite me; that is why she had begun speaking in such a painful manner. I should get angry and abuse her and give her the excuse to humiliate me.

It had begun to rain steadily and my body was drenched. There was utter darkness ahead. I was straining my ears to listen to the scheming going on inside but, due to the noise of the rain, could not hear their voices clearly. Meanwhile, the lantern again came into the verandah and the three dreadful faces once again stood before me. This time that blood-fairy held a thin stick in her hand and, looking at her, my blood froze. In her eyes was visible a bloodthirsty bestiality, a murderous madness. Fixing a mischievous look at me she said, 'Begum sahiba, I want to teach you such a lesson for your foul language that you will remember it for the rest of your life. And my teacher has told me that there is no other lesson which lasts longer than the one taught with a stick.'

Saying this, that tyrant hit me hard. I writhed with pain; it seemed as if someone had placed a spark of fire on my back. I couldn't hold back the thought that my parents had never hit me with even a twig made out of flowers. I started screaming and crying out aloud. Pride and shame vanished that moment. In the face of the frightening and crystal-clear reality of the stick all feelings simply disappeared. Those Hindu women who for the sake of their honour jump into the fire must have hearts made of iron. At this time the only thought in my heart was that I must somehow rid myself of this trouble. Sayeed was standing mute as a statue. I looked at him with beseeching eyes and with great humility said, 'Sayeed, for God's sake save me from this tyrant, I fall at your feet—you give me poison, cut my throat with a dagger but I do not have the strength to bear this torment. Remember those heart-to-heart talks; remember my love…for the sake of it save me at this time from this catastrophe. The Almighty shall reward you for this.'

Sayeed melted somewhat at these words. With fear in his eyes he looked at the beautiful woman and said, 'Zareena, let go now because I say so. For my sake, show mercy on her.'

Changing her attitude, Zareena said, 'For your sake I can do anything, but I can't tolerate abuses.'

Sayeed asked, 'But hasn't she received enough punishment for her abuses?'

Zareena answered, 'Indeed, you have placed a lot of worth on my honour! I have made queens pick up soiled basins; what does this Begum sahiba think? Even if I cut her up with a knife, it would not be punishment enough for her foul words.'

Sayeed, 'I can't watch this torture.'

'Then close your eyes.'

'Zareena, do not make me angry...forgive her now, I say.'

Zareena threw a scornful look at him, as though he was her slave. God knows what magical charm she had put on him that there was no feeling of family pride, status or even humanity left in him. May be she thought that he was not capable of a manly emotion like anger. Those who profess to understand appearances make such a mistake because one sees something on the inside while there is actually something else! Behind the veil of such beauty lay such mercilessness, such cruelty! Undoubtedly, beauty is the enemy of the art of studying appearances.

Zareena said, 'So now you have started feeling angry with me! Why not, after all, it is the Begum you have married. I am only a shameless bitch!'

'You make sarcastic remarks and I cannot see all this blood,' Sayeed replied.

'Then take this stick in your hand and hit her to the count of hundred. Your anger will subside; this is the only remedy.'

'Again that mockery,' said Sayeed.

'No, I never mock,' replied Zareena.

Sayeed stretched his hand forward to take the stick but no one knows what suspicion arose in Zareena, maybe she thought that he would break the stick and throw it away. She pulled back the stick and said, 'Oh, such dishonesty with me! Now see how deftly

I use my hands.' Saying this that merciless woman pounced upon me with endless lashes. Stiffening with pain, I cried out aloud. I'd fall at her feet, plead with her, apologize for my behaviour, shower blessings on her, swear by the saints and the Prophet but that murderer did not feel any mercy at all. Sayeed, like a wooden puppet, watched this spectacle and showed not the slightest remorse. Even my biggest enemy would have shown pity at my painful condition—my back had been ripped open and was blood-soaked, fresh wounds were being inflicted upon my body and every wound felt like a flame. I don't know how many lashes she inflicted on me, so much so that the stick, taking pity on me, split and broke. The wooden heart broke but the human heart did not melt.

~

After humiliating and destroying me thus the three devilish souls departed. Sayeed's servant undid my ropes as he walked away. Where could I go? Why would I step inside that house?

My entire body was like an open wound but the blisters on my heart were much more life-threatening. My heart was one large would; there was no space left for emotions. At that moment if I had seen a blind man fall into a well I would have laughed; I would have mocked an orphan's pitiful cries. A terrible revolution had taken place within me. I was not angry or sad, nor did I long for death, so much so that there was no desire to take revenge. The extreme nature of that utter humiliation had killed even the desire for vengeance. Although, had I wished, I could have trapped Sayeed legally, I could have made him beg for even a grain of food—but this insult, this gross humiliation, this debasement, was beyond the ken of revenge. Only one instinct remained and that was the sense of insult. I had been humiliated forever. Could this stain be somehow removed? Certainly not. Yes, it could be hidden and for that there was only one way—that I should fall into the black ditch of utter humiliation so that its pitch blackness would hide this dark stain. Was the wilderness not better than this house in whose foundations a gaping hole lay? In my sorry condition this argument took hold of me. I strengthened my resolve to complete my destruction, to further deepen my humiliation and further blacken my already blackened face. All night long I lay there, sometimes moaning with pain and sometimes lost in my thoughts. With every passing moment this terrible intention became stronger. Nobody in the house inquired after me. At the break of dawn I exited the garden. I don't know where my sense of shame disappeared. Would a person who has weathered a storm in the ocean be scared of lakes and ponds? I, who used to feel shy of the very walls of my home, was at this moment roaming about the streets of the town shamelessly. Not just any street but the ones where humiliation is regarded as a virtue, where no one laughs at anyone, where the bazaar of infamy is laid out, where modesty is sold and honour pillaged!

The third day after I walked out, I sat high atop a whorehouse, in a nice nook in the Bazaar of Beauty, surveying that market. It was evening, down below on the road was such a crowd of men that shoulder jostled shoulder. Today was the monsoon fair, people dressed in clean clothes moved in row upon row towards the river. The priceless commodities of our bazaar were also on display on the banks of the river. Somewhere there were beautiful women on swings, somewhere monsoon friendships, but to me it seemed that the view of this bazaar was most enjoyable from the river. It seemed as if all the roads of the town had been closed down, only this narrow lane was open and all eyes were fixed on the whorehouses only, as if the people on this street were not walking on the ground but wished to fly in the air. Yes indeed, I did not find educated people so bold. They too stared but through the corners of their eyes. Middle-aged men seemed the most unabashed. Maybe it was their intention to demonstrate the passion of youth. The bazaar was nothing but one long-drawn-out theatre; people would laugh and flirt, not for the sake of enjoyment but to attract the attention of the beautiful women. They faced one direction and looked in another. The street was a gathering of pimps and fakes.

Suddenly, Sayeed's phaeton came into view. I had often ridden in it. Sayeed was wearing good clothes and sitting stiffly. Such a handsome, attractive young man was not to be found in the entire town, masculinity dripped from his face and forehead. His eye rose once to my whorehouse and then fell. On his face spread a deathlike pallor as if some poisonous snake had bitten him. He said something to the coach-driver, and within moments the phaeton disappeared into thin air. Before this divinely satisfying happiness I experienced upon seeing him at this moment *that* body-numbing, near-fatal pain lost its reality. By humiliating myself I had humiliated him. This knife-edge was much sharper than the stick used to beat me. He dared not meet my eyes now. Yes, I had defeated him. I had thrown him into an emotional prison for life. To come out of this dark dungeon was impossible because he had immense pride in his family's status.

Next day at dawn, we heard the news that some killer had finished off Mirza Sayeed. His body was found in the same circular room of the same garden, with a bullet through his chest. At nine o'clock the second news was heard: Zareena too had been murdered by someone during the night. Her head had been severed from her body. Later investigations revealed that both these incidents were Sayeed's own doing. He first killed Zareena at her house and then came to his own house where he shot himself in the chest. This display of manly self-respect renewed Sayeed's love in my heart.

In the evening I reached my house. I had only been away for four days but it seemed as though I was returning after years. The atmosphere all around was of despair. As I set foot inside the house Sayeed's smiling face appeared unbidden before my eyes— the same manly beauty, the same handsomeness and the same attractive eyes. Unwittingly, my eyes filled with tears and a cold deep sigh rose from my heart. The grief was not why Sayeed had taken his life. Indeed, his criminal lack of sensitivity and running after beauty—for these two things I would never forgive him till my dying day. The grief was why had this madness consumed him

so? At present, going by the state of my heart I understand that in
a few days the wound inflicted by Sayeed's infidelity and
mercilessness will heal, the memory of my own humiliation too
shall probably be wiped out, but the imprint of the few days of his
love shall remain, and from now on only this shall support my life.

Translated from the Hindi by Anita Samkaria

ANCESTRY

Qurratulain Hyder

The large, damp washroom remained dimly lit even during the day. It had enormous brass urns, long-necked decanters, a raised bathtub, spherical pitchers, a bathing stool, a colourful soap dish, quantities of gram flour and specially prepared aromatic body washes. Also pumice stones, small spouted decanters, large decanters fitted with handles and covers, a load of dirty ghararas and dupattas hanging from a hook, saucers laden with dried fruit, hair cleansers, and a dark conglomeration of just about everything, much like the cave of Ali Baba and his forty thieves.

Occasionally, the same washroom served as a sanctuary for Chhammi Begum in her cheerless life. The closed window of the washroom with the green, painted glass overlooked the Chambeli Residence. Chhammi Begum had scratched off some of the green paint with her nail, so as to make it possible for her to peep out. She did this because her dearly loved cousin, Ajjoo Bhai, lived in the Chambeli Residence. For hours, she would gaze out, through the glass, at the residence across; perhaps with the same fervour as the emperor Shah Jahan would have gazed at the Taj Mahal from the confines of his lock-up.

This ancestral residence which belonged to a middling zamindar family had two sections. The mardana with dense chambeli—jasmine—bushes in the patio was identified as the Chambeli Residence. A tamarind tree provided dense shade in the inner courtyard of the zenana. Therefore, the entire mohalla referred to this part of the residence as the Tamarind Tree House. The wall dividing the two courtyards had a small doorway to provide an easy passage between the two homes.

Chhammi-bi's father and Ajjoo Bhai's father lived together. Soon after Chhammi-bi was born, her engagement to Ajjoo Bhai was decided. From the age of nine or ten, she was made to observe partial purdah from her betrothed. Ajjoo Bhai was incredibly good-looking and very mischievous. Being the only son of his parents and the only male heir to the property of both brothers, he was the apple of their eyes and was thoroughly pampered. He entertained himself with all manner of leisurely sports and pastimes, like flying kites and rearing pigeons. Nevertheless, his parents Bade Abba and Badi Amma felt quite certain that he would mend his ways once he was married.

Chhammi Begum had begun to look upon Ajjoo Bhai as her soulmate and spiritual guide ever since her earliest perceptions about matrimonial relations developed. She, too, was the only offspring of her parents and had been brought up with a great deal of indulgence. When a petulant, ill-humoured and irascible Chhammi Begum turned sixteen, the date for the marriage was fixed. Both families began to make elaborate preparations for the wedding when, all of a sudden, the dark shadow of death loomed large, turning the tables upon the happiness and contentment of the entire family.

That year, a cholera epidemic assailed Shahjahanpur and within fifteen days Chhammi Begum's Amma and Abba succumbed to it. Chhammi Begum felt as though the world had come to an end, but she sustained herself with the thought of her uncle and aunt's foster parentage. Above all, she would soon be married to Ajjoo Bhai. Having mourned for her parents for a sufficient time, Chhammi Begum once more began to nourish herself on colourful dreams about her future with Ajjoo Bhai.

The marriage had been postponed for a while but before Bade Abba could fix another date, he unexpectedly suffered a cardiac arrest and passed away.

No sooner had Bade Abba passed away than Ajjoo Bhai claimed that he would have to leave for Lucknow to clear up some cases in court. He took off with a few hangers-on. Now, only Badi Amma— who was absolutely distraught with sorrow—and Chhammi Begum remained in the Tamarind Tree House. The mardana became deserted and desolate. The porch continued to be watched over by the elderly employee, Dhammu Khan. Inside, Salamat Bua and her daughters continued to cook, even as they wept and blew their noses. Badi Amma sent for an elderly relative, Mullan Khan, to look after the house. He spread a rope cot in the verandah and began to live in it.

Ajjoo Bhai continued to stay in Lucknow. In every letter, he wrote to his Amma to say that the case had been deferred until a later date and that he would return in about a couple of months. After no less than six months, when he finally did return, Badi Amma put forward the suggestion of his marriage. Ajjoo Bhai replied that he could not think about marrying until the issues of the property had been resolved. It was then that Chhammi Begum sat on the heap of dirty clothes in a corner of the gloomy bathroom and began to cry softly.

By now, Chhammi Begum had turned nineteen. It seemed that Ajjoo Bhai had decided to continue living in Lucknow. People brought news that he was living a debauched life there. One could only wonder what further tricks Chhammi Begum's fate would play on her. One day, Badi Amma suffered a heart attack and she too passed away.

A shaken Chhammi Begum was left alone. The inner courtyard of the household became quiet. Only for the sake of security did the almost blind Mullan Mian move from the Chambeli Residence to the Tamarind Tree House. He remained in the verandah, coughing away to himself. Dhammu Khan coughed away at the entrance.

Ajjoo Bhai came home when his mother died. On the third day of her death, soon after the prayer service, he returned to Lucknow. Dear God! It was agonizing to think how he had abandoned Chhammi Begum when she most needed his support. When she thought about it, Chhammi Begum's heart broke in two. Each month, Ajjoo Bhai would mail a money-order of two hundred rupees from Lucknow and once in a while he would write to Mullan Khan to enquire about their welfare.

Mullan Khan's wife and daughter had arrived from Bareilly but, due to her nature, Chhammi Begum could not get along with

either of them. Having argued with her relatives through the day
or after getting exasperated without reason, Chhammi Begum
would retire to the washroom and weep. Or else she would gaze at
Chambeli House through the 'Shah Jahan' peep-hole. 'What sort
of a life is this?' she would muse. 'In one instant, I have everything
and, in another, everything is reduced to a cipher.' It seemed like
yesterday that the entire household was steeped in joy. Half-easy
chairs were laid out in the verandah. Armchairs sprawled in the
courtyard. The gas lamps shone with bright lights. Abba and Bade
Abba's friends would assemble. Now, mushairas were conducted;
now, the place resonated with qawwalis. When Ajjoo Bhai's friends
visited, he would come to the little doorway in the wall separating
the two households, clear his throat, and call out with appropriate
deference, 'Arrey bhai, Chhammi, can you send us some tea?'

Despite her sense of extreme hopelessness and helplessness,
Chhammi Begum felt certain that one day, Ajjoo would return
and once more the Chambeli Residence would come back to life.
Every Friday, she would go over to the men's quarters of the
house. Along with Dhammu Khan and Salamat Bua's daughters,
she would have the garden weeded and the shrubs pruned. The
cobwebs in the verandah would be cleared. The rooms within
were locked. She would peer into Abba, Bade Abba and Ajjoo's
rooms through the glass panes of the doors, shake her head, heave
bitter sighs and come away with a heavy heart.

Chhammi Begum turned thirty. Her hair greyed prematurely.
By now, she had given up looking after the chambeli garden. She
seemed to have lost interest in worldly matters, but her ill temper
and impatience remained unaffected; as a matter of fact, as she
grew older, they seemed to take a turn for the worse.

There was much that motivated Chhammi Begum's anger and
irritability. Her parents were pure-bred Rohilla Pathans. Her
ancestors had been bestowed with such diminutive titles as
zamindars of moderately substantial means. The entire family had
a fair and ruddy skin tone and like all Pathan families, this family,
too, was characterized by a strong inclination for self-reliance.

The disposition of the entire family towards uncontrollable anger was testimony to the fact that it had an unblemished lineage. The belief that the familial lineage and ancestral heritage should never be sullied led Chhammi Begum into a reclusive existence. She associated less frequently with the other women of the neighbourhood and began to wear white clothes like a widow, spending most of her time on a prayer mat. Often, in the quiet of hot afternoons, Salamat Bua would sit in the courtyard window and, chewing saffron-flavoured tobacco, would say to herself in a dreadful voice: 'The God Almighty decrees that he mocks at his creations only on two occasions—the first, when people try to hurt those whom he blesses with fortuity and the second when those whom he blights with misfortune try to rise above their lot—merely on these two occasions.' A terrified Chhammi Begum would scold her: 'Aye, Salamat Bua, do not speak of sinister things,' but an unfazed Salamat Bua would continue to babble on in the same strain.

~

It was a nauchandi Thursday in winter. Chhammi Begum was bathing. The smouldering coals under the bathtub had long turned to ash and Chhammi Begum shivered in the cold. As she quickly wrapped her hair in a towel and put on her wooden bathroom slippers, Salamat Bua's stupid granddaughter knocked noisily on the termite-eaten door of the washroom: 'Apa! Oh Apa! Hurry up and come out!'

'What is it, silly?' called back Chhammi Begum.

'Apa, there is a request from the Chambeli Residence to send three or four cups of tea—quickly.'

'What...what?' Chhammi could not believe her ears. She peeped through the 'Shah Jahan' peep-hole.

The gate leading out of the courtyard was open. Two horse carriages stood outside, while two or three roguish boys were unloading baggage. A dark-complexioned, sharp-featured woman, wearing a crimson georgette sari with a green Benarsee shawl wrapped round her, sat comfortably in an armchair on the verandah, carelessly shaking her legs and ringing the bell now and again to issue orders to the staff. A teenaged, tall and ill-mannered-looking girl, wearing a purple salwar-kameez and bearing a close resemblance to her mother, squatted on the floor, trying to open a suitcase. Just then Ajjoo Bhai—looking just as debonair and charming as ever—walked into the verandah from within. He bent over and said something to that scarlet witch, at which the women laughed out aloud. Dark clouds of despair gathered over Chhammi Begum's eyes. The already dark and shadowy bathroom was soon transformed into a blind alley. She steadied herself by hastily holding on to a peg, then wobbled out and fell motionless onto her bed in a trance.

It transpired that the courtesan Kallo had been living in the service of Ajjoo Bhai at his residence in Lucknow for years. Now he had married her by way of a proper nikah and brought her home as his lawfully wedded wife. Kallo had brought the girl Asharfi, wearing the chicory-coloured salwar-kameez, along with her. She had not been fathered by Ajjoo Bhai.

In the evening, Ajjoo Bhai entered the female quarters of the house unannounced, without requesting a purdah. Reaching the verandah, he called out: 'Arrey bhai Chhammo, come and meet your sister-in-law.'

Chhammi Begum shuddered. She got off the bed and wobbled into the washroom once more and locked herself in securely. Ajjoo Bhai stood a little guiltily under one of the archways of the verandah. Kallo stood behind him. For a few minutes, man and wife stood quietly like this, before returning to the Chambeli Residence.

From that day, Chhammi Begum's lifestyle suffered a radical change. All day long she read the Quran Sharif. For so many years Ajjoo had misled her, then he had married someone else. He had ruined her life. The marriage was an unbearable step in itself, but what was worse was that by marrying the courtesan Kallo-bai, Ajjoo had ruined the familial legacy. Chhammi Begum could never forgive him this crime. On several occasions, Kallo extended a friendly hand to Chhammi Begum. Often, she would come up to the little doorway between the two courtyards and call out softly: 'Bitiya, do let us know whether you need anything.' Whenever anything special was cooked, she would get the staff to send across a tray of the delectable preparations, but Chhammi Begum had given strict orders to Dhammu Khan that even if a fledgling strayed into her part of the house from the Chambeli Residence, he was to break its legs.

The month after Ajjoo Bhai returned home, he had Mullan Khan deliver the two hundred rupees that he had been sending all along from Lucknow. However, by now, everything had suffered change. Chhammi Begum paced over to the window and pitched a challenge: 'The deceased Juma Khan's daughter and the deceased Shabboo Khan's niece—may their souls rest in peace—will be damned if she accepts even a paisa sent over from a brothel. Mullan Khan, if you are a Pathan with a sense of propriety, go back immediately and return these two hundred rupees to the sender.' After her outburst, she shut the windows and secured them tightly with a large padlock.

In order to keep body and soul together, Chhammi Begum began to sell off her jewellery; when she had finished with that, she off-loaded the antique valuables in the house to flea-market dealers. But hunger is an enduring malady that requires prolonged treatment. Besides, Chhammi Begum had to feed Mullan Khan, Dhammu Khan and Salamat Bua as well as their families. She started an amateur school at home to teach the Quran Sharif and Urdu to little children. She also began to tailor clothes for people of the neighbourhood. The hard work caused her to fall ill and when her body was besieged with a high fever, Salamat Bua felt quite helpless and scolded her angrily: 'Bibi, would you rather die than submit to your lofty ideals of self-respect? What kind of wretched self-esteem is this?' But Chhammi Begum had already fallen into a deep stupor. Salamat ran across frantically to the Chambeli Residence.

Kallo immediately put on her burqa and made for the Tamarind
Tree House by way of the street outside. The doctor was called.
All night Kallo sat by her sister-in-law's side. Ajjoo Bhai came by
several times to visit his ailing cousin, but it seemed he still did not
have a sense of his unjust behaviour towards the miserable
Chhammi Begum. Perhaps Salamat Bua was right when she
claimed that that dark-skinned Kallo had surely cast a mysterious
spell on Ajjoo Bhai, to lure him to her.

No sooner did Chhammi Begum regain consciousness and
open her eyes than she beheld Kallo's face and became overcome
with uncontrollable despair and anger. Kallo felt intimidated by
this fury, characteristic of all Pathans. She promptly stood up and
returned to her own house.

Like most courtesans who marry and live as faithful wives,
Kallo was devoted to her husband. The desire closest to her heart
was that Chhammi Begum should accept her as the daughter-in-
law of the family and as her own sister-in-law, and permit her into
the Tamarind Tree Residence. Kallo's desire remained unfulfilled.

Ten years passed. Ajjoo Bhai felt concerned about Chhammi
Begum's marriage but by now she was middle-aged. Who would
marry her?

Chhammi Begum continued to observe strict purdah from him
and Kallo. She sustained herself by running a madrasah for young
girls. The country was partitioned, Shahjahanpur became deserted.
Most of the girls who studied at her madrasah migrated to Pakistan
with their parents. There was an acute shortage of food in Chhammi
Begum's residence. During this time Ajjoo Bhai visited Delhi on
an ill-fated errand and was killed in the sectarian violence. When
his body was brought home, a devastated Kallo was inconsolable.
She broke her bangles. She beat her arms, ringed with many
bangles, against the window separating the two courtyards until
they bled profusely. 'Bitiya! Bitiya! Open the door—haaye bitiya—
bitiya—arrey I have nowhere to go, no one to turn to!'

Chhammi Begum was sleeping soundly on the takht in the
verandah. Hearing Kallo's cries, she woke up, took a key hanging

from a tack in the wall, unfastened the lock and opened the door
to find Kallo standing there howling, looking like a witch with her
loosened hair all messed up. 'Oh my companion has been snatched
away. Haaye, bitiya, I have been widowed!' She approached
Chhammi and tried to put her hands upon her, but Chhammi
retreated, taking two steps back. She rubbed her sleepy eyes.
Then, all of a sudden, reality dawned upon her. She sat down by
the window, shocked, gathered her white dupatta over her mouth
and began to weep quietly. Still crying, she responded, 'Ari murdaar,
you have been widowed today, but I am the unfortunate one who
has always been a widow.' Kallo disappeared immediately after the
prayer service on the fortieth day of mourning for Ajjoo Bhai. No
one knew where she went off to. Her daughter Asharfi, whose
marriage Ajjoo Bhai, may his soul rest in peace, had had solemnized
with one of his sycophants, came down from Lucknow, gathered
up all the items in the house, loaded them onto two chakdas and
left. Chhammi Begum watched the comings and goings of the
ephemeral world through the scratched glass of the washroom
window.

The Chambeli Residence was taken over by the new
government's Custodian Bureau because Chhammi Begum was
unable to prove that Ajjoo Bhai had not migrated to Pakistan, but
had been killed in the sectarian violence. Like an aged spectre, she
remained in the Tamarind Tree House. Old age and starvation
preyed upon Mullan Khan and Dhammu Khan, while paralysis
struck Salamat Bua. Her daughters and sons-in-law migrated to
Pakistan. Chhammi Begum continued her occupation as a
seamstress to keep body and soul together. She was no longer
afraid to live alone in the house because by now, she had become
hoary and enjoyed a reputation as one of the venerable old ladies of
the mohalla.

After some time a Sikh doctor, a refugee, came to live in the
Chambeli Residence with his family. Sometimes the womenfolk
would come and sit by the window in the wall between the two
courtyards and, together, they and Chhammi Begum would

exchange notes about the joys and sorrows of their lives. The doctor saheb's daughter, Chiranjit, was married to a man in government service who lived in New Delhi. When she came home one day, she informed her mother that the Muslim wife of the executive officer under whom her husband served was in need of a lady teacher who could teach Urdu and the Quran Sharif to her children. 'I'm afraid to suggest this idea to Chhammi Khala, she might fly into a rage but why don't you talk to her about it?' she suggested.

The doctor saheb's wife mentioned this to Chhammi Begum. She reasoned with her, and put the hazards of her lonesome existence simply: 'Sister, how long will you deal with this economic hardship and loneliness all by yourself? Go to Delhi. You can live comfortably and respectably in Sabi-ud-din Saheb's house.'

Chhammi Begum's ill-temper had subsided a long while ago; her tantrums, tartness and fury had also abated. She considered that if she were to die tomorrow, there should be someone who could recite the Yaseen Sharif over her, in order to grant peace to her departing soul. To cut a long story short, Chhammi Begum put on her burqa and, carrying only a suitcase, a bedspread and her spouted decanter, left her now dilapidated house—she couldn't care less, because she had reached a stage where her only concern was forfeiture on the path of asceticism—to travel to Delhi by train. Since she had received Chiranjit Singh's letter, Begum Sabi-ud-din came to the railway station by car to meet Chhammi Begum. From that day, Chhammi Begum, the daughter of Juma Khan, zamindar of Shahjahanpur, began living as a housekeeper.

Chhammi Begum spent twelve years in Sabi-ud-din Saheb's house, wrapped up in a white dupatta, with her head covered right down to her forehead. The children she taught grew up. Having completed his BA, the elder son was sent to Pakistan to live with his paternal uncle. The younger daughter, too, went to Karachi. The youngest daughter was in college. Now, Begum Sabi-ud-din did not require the services of Chhammi Begum any longer. Sabi-ud-din Saheb was planning to return to his home town, Mirzapur, after his retirement. Before leaving, Begum Sabi-ud-din arranged for Chhammi Begum to live with her friend, Begum Rashid Ali. Rashid Ali Saheb was also a well-placed officer in the service of the government of India.

Chhammi Begum had lived very comfortably in Sabi-ud-din Saheb's residence. She had been given the respect due to an elderly member of the family. She had grown to love all three children dearly. She rarely got angry now; when she did, she would recall her vulnerability and compose herself. Those who used to fuss over her, smother her with affection, or put up with her tantrums had passed away. Sometimes she would think about Kallo and wonder about that wretched woman's whereabouts and well-being; perhaps she too was dead and gone. How should one put it? Life is so uncertain.

Begum Rashid Ali was quite different from Begum Sabi-ud-din. She was neither as compassionate nor as worldly-wise as her. Rather, she was more like the modern young women of today. Nevertheless, she took care of Chhammi Begum, giving her due respect. In her house too, Chhammi Begum lived like a member of the family. Rashid Ali took great care of her. Everyone was in awe of her unassailable countenance and her impressive lineage. Often, Begum Rashid would tell her women friends, 'Oh dear! Sometimes the most shattering transformations occur in people's lives. Have you heard the story of our mughlani? She belongs to such-and-such family from Shahjahanpur...' And the women would shake their heads, heave heavy sighs and go on to narrate similar, overwhelming accounts meant to impart a few life lessons.

Begum Rashid Ali's children were very young. They were looked after by an ayah from Hyderabad. Thus, Chhammi Begum became a housekeeper. Begum Rashid Ali was badly in need of Chhammi Begum's services: much of her own time was consumed by attending or throwing parties or visiting clubs and official functions.

Chhammi Begum spent five years in Rashid Ali's residence. When Rashid Saheb was to be transferred to Washington, Begum

Rashid Ali became concerned about relocating Chhammi Begum. One day, when she was attending one of her farewell lunches at the Raushan Ara Club, she advised Chhammi Begum to bring Munni to her by car.

Lunch was still underway when Chhammi Begum arrived at the Club. Holding Munni's hand, she began to stroll on the lawn. Chhammi Begum no longer observed purdah, she had started to wear saris. Who would recognize her in the wretched city of Delhi? On the verandah facing them, card games were being played. A fashionable, middle-aged lady who laughed loudly was continually engaged in a card game with about five or six men.

Having lived for seventeen years in New Delhi, Chhammi Begum had become accustomed to its so-called 'high society' as well as to contemporary Indian women and their radically modern ways, so she walked on, unfazed, along the lawns. A few minutes passed before the lady lifted her head and looked at Chhammi Begum attentively. She uttered something to a companion and Chhammi Begum saw one of the men stand up and take long strides towards her.

He came close and addressed her: 'Badi-bi, will you come this way?'

Chhammi Begum crossed over to the verandah. The unidentified lady enquired about the child's parents and her employers and went on to inform her that she was presently visiting Delhi, but her permanent residence was Mumbai. She added that she was on the lookout for a reliable, elderly lady who was willing to offer her services and asked whether Chhammi Begum could inform her if she knew of anyone. Chhammi Begum silently thanked the munificent God Almighty who makes arrangements for sustenance. She answered with a great deal of dignity that she would soon be relieved of her own services. 'My mistress will be coming out soon. You can have a word with her.' She stood waiting for Begum Rashid Ali on the verandah.

When Begum Rashid came out of the lunch-room, the unidentified lady stood up, introduced herself as Mrs Razia Bano, and spoke to her with regard to Chhammi Begum. Begum Rashid felt quite relieved and promised that before leaving for Washington, she would put Chhammi Begum on the train to Bombay. Razia Bano had already mentioned that she would be returning to Bombay that very evening. She wrote her address on a piece of paper and handed it over to Chhammi Begum. However, Begum Rashid asked with some degree of doubt: 'Will you travel such a long distance, Khala?' Chhammi Begum immediately nodded her head to indicate her willingness.

At this stage in life, Chhammi Begum did not feel the need to say no to anything. She did not even discuss her remuneration with Razia Bano; she had already fixed a sum for herself—forty rupees per month plus food. Forty rupees was more than sufficient for her personal requirements. She had always been provided clothes by her various employers. She had long since realized that a love of clothes and ornaments, material goods and property, the need for comradeship, kinship, love and affection are all meaningless, transient requirements that are liable to perish with time. She had detached herself from them.

As Begum Rashid Ali and Chhammi Begum started to leave the verandah, Razia Bano opened her purse, took out one hundred and fifty rupees, and handed them to Chhammi Begum. 'Travel and other miscellaneous expenses,' she said, a little nonchalantly. Begum Rashid Ali was taken by surprise by this generosity, but she knew that many wealthy women lived in Bombay. Chhammi Begum quietly put the money away in a pocket inside her sleeveless Nehru jacket. Life's little surprises failed to astonish her any more. Two days before Mr and Mrs Rashid Ali left for America, Chhammi Begum boarded the train for Bombay.

On reaching Bombay Central Railway Station, Chhammi Begum was perturbed by the hustle-bustle because, by now, she had grown accustomed to a quiet and peaceful life in the sprawling bungalows of New Delhi. Saying a short prayer, she walked out of the station, hired a coolie and got him to carry the tin travel case and the bedding roll wrapped in a durrie on his head. Carrying her spouted decanter, hand-fan and small betel-leaf box, she hailed a cab and told the Sardar taxi driver the address—Gulzar, Jordan Road. In a few minutes, the cab rolled into the portico of a tall and impressive new-fangled structure. Chhammi Begum paid off the elderly driver, who had been expressing his opinion on various aspects of the world in monologue fashion throughout the entire journey. Then, two smart young girls walked out of the elevator and got into the cab. The Sardarji resignedly set the meter of his taxi and drove out of the gate in silence. How very apathetic, organized and perfunctory life was in this city!

Once more, Chhammi Begum took out the crumpled slip of paper from the pocket of her jacket and squinted her eyes to confirm the address: eleventh floor, flat no. three. The bored-looking chowkidar got up from his stool and, without saying a word, conveyed her baggage into the elevator. Chhammi Begum was very nervous, but the chowkidar entered the elevator with her and silently accompanied her to the eleventh floor. Now, Chhammi Begum stood alone with her baggage in the enormous corridor. She caught sight of a door close by with the number three written above it. A metallic grille door was fixed over this door and secured with a padlock much like the door of a bank.

She rang the doorbell. After a few minutes, an elderly person opened the lid of the spy-hole in the grilled door and peeped out. Quite unexpectedly, Chhammi Begum was reminded of the glass window of her washroom in Tamarind Tree House, through which she had peeped out to behold that menacing-looking witch, dressed in red. Some time passed before both the doors were opened and an irritable-looking Gurkha stepped out. He stared at Chhammi Begum with cold, suspicious eyes. For a moment, she felt rather alarmed, but reminding herself that she was a Pathan, she lifted her chin and addressed him: 'Tell the Begum Saheb that Chhammi Begum has arrived from New Delhi.'

'I know. You have come from Delhi. Come in,' said the Gurkha drily. Stepping out, he picked up her tin box and bedding roll and Chhammi Begum followed him into the house. No sooner had she come in than he turned around and promptly bolted both the doors behind her. Now Chhammi Begum stood in a dimly lit, sophisticated drawing room. Neither Sabi-ud-din Saheb nor Rashid Ali Saheb's drawing rooms were as grand as this one. One wall was covered by a black curtain that had been drawn to one side, and Chhammi noticed that the wall was also fitted with a diminutive cinema screen. On the other side of the room was a bar.

Still holding her spouted decanter, her hand-fan and her betel-leaf box, Chhammi Begum enquired once more, 'Is the Begum Saheb in?'

'Memsaheb is asleep.'

'And the Saheb?' Before entering into service in any residence, she would shudder at the thought of being interviewed by the man of the house.

The Gurkha made no reply. Instead, he walked out of the drawing room towards a gallery. Chhammi Begum followed, looking around. On either side of the gallery were four doors, all of which were locked. This was a very spacious and luxuriously decorated flat. At the far end, on the right, was the kitchen and two small rooms for the servants, each provided with a balcony. Even the stairway leading up to the servants' quarters was secured with a security device from within. The Gurkha entered a small, clean, well-lit room, deposited her tin box and bedding-roll on the floor with a noisy thump and left without saying a word.

Chhammi Begum kept her betel-leaf box on a ledge in the built-in frame-work and cast a protracted look at her new residence, her new sanctuary. In one corner stood an iron bed: 'This will hurt a great deal,' she thought to herself. On the walls were pasted pictures of attractive film actresses. Perhaps this was the handiwork of some zealous domestic assistant who had occupied the room previously. It was very stuffy inside. When Chhammi Begum opened the window, she was surprised to behold the vast expanse of the sea right in front of her. The sea, rough and unpredictable, just like the events of her life. Never before had she seen this sight. She felt a sudden urge to prostrate herself before the maker of this infinite expanse who had brought her at such close quarters with the sea route to Mecca and Madina which lay at the far end. Now it would be possible for her to perform the holy pilgrimage of Hajj. She felt overwhelmed by these thoughts.

Attached to her room was a washroom for the support staff. Chhammi Begum opened her tin box, took out her clothes and entered the washroom. It stood in stark contrast to the large, spacious, dimly lit washroom of her ancestral home. Attempting to do so for years, she had finally been able to put aside all the comforts, the entourage of female attendants and the respectable women of straitened circumstances who waited on her, for man gradually becomes accustomed to the processes of change over the years, else he may cease to exist. Having bathed and changed into fresh clothes, she came into her room once more. Stillness seemed to have engulfed the entire house. The servants were away, the man of the house was probably at work, the children were at school and the Memsaheb was asleep. It was afternoon and Chhammi Begum felt an urge to have tea. All her life, she had had to put up with harsh realities—psychological and emotional conflicts which had honed her temper and reduced her to an old woman inclined to forget or overlook. Now, quite simply, she thought to herself, 'Let me go to the kitchen and make some tea.'

When she entered the vacant and quiet kitchen, she saw gas stoves which she did not know how to light. A little annoyed, she walked into the gallery. One of the four doors in it had been opened and an expensive-looking curtain sheltered the doorway. Hearing the patter of her footsteps, someone called out from within: 'Who is it?'

'Chhammi Begum—I have come from Delhi,' she replied with straightforwardness.

'Oh! Oh! You have arrived. Come—come in.'

She drew the curtain aside and entered. She stood in a most attractive, dream-like room with an American-style bed, face-to-face with Razia Bano who lay on it, partially awake, in a pink nylon nightdress, holding a cigarette between her fingers. Chhammi

Begum did not approve of her sheer attire at all, though she did not give voice to her disapproval. Instead, she thought to herself, 'Each one to himself. Perhaps these are the customs of the city.' Neither did she approve of the cigarette. Neither Begum Sabi-ud-din, nor Begum Rashid had smoked. Nevertheless, Chhammi Begum greeted her with indifference; 'As salaam alaikum.'

'Come in, Bua… Sit down,' she said, gesturing towards the floor.

Since setting out from her father and grandfather's residence in order to make an honest living, nobody had ever addressed her Chhammi Begum as 'Bua'. At Sabi-ud-din Saheb's residence and Rashid Saheb's residence, she had either been addressed a Chhammi Khala, or simply, Khala. Feigning indifference to Razia Bano's gesture—and quite conscious of her own status—Chhammi Begum sat at the edge of the divan.

Two telephones were positioned by Razia Bano's bedside, one red and the other white. The white one rang. Razia Bano lifted the receiver and spoke softly in English. She put out her hand and picked up a large and bulky notebook from the side table, wrote down something and replaced the receiver. Then, she picked up the receiver of the red telephone, dialled a number and spoke softly: 'Madho—number four—nine-thirty' and disconnected. Chhammi Begum sat through all this quietly, surveying the décor of the room: marble statues, huge portraits, a radiogram and a massive white wardrobe. Just then, a young and attractive girl wearing a negligee drew aside the curtain and entered the room. Someone opened one of the doors in the gallery. From within, a loud 'hi-fi' could be heard. The girl talked something over with Razia Bano and quickly marched out. The gallery door shut once more.

'By God's grace, how many children do you have?' enquired Chhammi Begum.

'I do not have children. These girls are my nieces. They live with me.' Razia Bano spoke briefly, before opening her enormous notebook once more.

'They must be studying in college.'

'Who?' asked Razia Bano absentmindedly.

'Your nieces.'

'Hmm!'

'By God's grace, is your husband a businessman?' Chhammi Begum believed that everyone in Bombay was a businessman.

'Hmm? What?' Razia Bano lifted her head from the notebook and asked exasperatedly. 'Husband? My husband is dead.'

'Surely we belong to Allah and to Him shall we return,' said Chhammi Begum inadvertently. For a few moments, may God forgive him, Chhammi Begum relived the pain of Ajjoo Bhai's death. Every time she heard of anybody's death, she would relive her own loss. Who could guess how Chhammi Begum had lived her dismal life, practising extreme self-control in the darkest hours of her existence? She had committed herself to passively accepting her lot and giving thanks for it.

Another young girl, dressed to kill in a churidar-pyjama, cavorted into the room. Razia Bano said something to her in English. The young girl ambled out in the same manner, smiling to herself. Now Razia Bano turned her attention towards Chhammi Begum who was yawning by now and craving for some tea. Razia Bano propped herself on a pillow placed under her elbow and began to speak: 'Bua.' Chhammi Begum shuddered once more. 'It is very good that you have come over to my place. I judged in the first instance I set eyes on you that you were miserable and needed support. Now, you should consider this house your own. It has been my desire for some time now that an elderly, respectable lady should read the Quran and offer namaz in my residence. For many years a lady belonging to Hyderabad did live with me. Last year, however, she left this place to perform the holy pilgrimage of Hajj and died while she was still there. Never mind...'

Razia Bano shifted her position and continued to talk. 'Now, Bua, I would like to share with you that the city of Bombay is surrogate to the ground where our actions shall be judged by our Creator on the Day of Judgment. All manner of people live here and all manner of things happen here too. You should never lend a patient ear to anyone, nor believe anything that is said to you. Keep to yourself and remain aloof. You can, however, keep a watchful eye on the kitchen. You may spend the rest of your time offering namaz and observing roza. It's time for you to rest and lead a comfortable life rather than working hard. Read the Quran Sharif and keep praying for my deliverance. We already have an ayah to look after these girls, my nieces' requirements. The cook's name is Ibrahim. The Gurkha is called Bishan Singh. My driver is Madho. Please do not get embroiled in anybody's personal affairs or quarrels.'

'I…' began Chhammi Begum, but Razia Bano cut her short.

'By the grace of God, I oversee a prosperous trade.' After a little deliberation, she went on to add, 'Are you familiar with the business of import and export?'

'Most certainly,' Chhammi Begum nodded. Sabi-ud-din Saheb was an officer in the Ministry of Trade and Commerce, and therefore, Chhammi Begum was not unfamiliar with such expressions. Chhammi Begum found Razia Bano to be a genteel and wise person and so very God-fearing; she forgave her the diaphanous night dress and the cigarette smoking.

'Despite being a woman, I deal in a thriving business, single-handedly. I have to meet with people of many different comportments. Besides, these girls—my nieces—are young and modern. Their friends also visit us, on and off. And the police have raided our residence on two occasions.'

'The police?' repeated a terrified Chhammi Begum.

Razia Bano broke into an amused laugh. 'You need not be afraid. In this city, a number of businessmen are forced to submit to the unreasonable demands of the police and the income tax officers. Over and above, I am a single woman; I have innumerable foes. Once, somebody lodged a complaint that I had not paid tax, that was enough to send the police over to my residence. So I've had a metal door fitted in addition to the wooden one. I must warn you to make sure you look through the peep-hole every time the doorbell rings. Always ascertain the identity of the caller before you open the door. Sometimes, even the policemen arrive unexpectedly, in plain clothes.'

But by now, due to her strenuous journey and her craving for some tea, Chhammi Begum was quite fatigued. Unable to bear waiting any longer, she stood up and addressed Razia Bano: 'Bibi, how does one light the burner of the gas stove?'

Razia Bano pressed an electric button placed by the side of her headrest. Within a minute the cook, Ibrahim, came to the door.

'Ibrahim, this is our new Bua. Will you quickly make her some tea?'

Chhammi Begum got up and followed Ibrahim into the kitchen.

~

With Zuhr, Asr and Maghrib namaaz complete, Chhammi Begum stood on the balcony, looking out once more. There was nothing to be done in the house. Razia Bano had gone out, bejewelled and dressed up in her finery. Lights burned in the rooms of two of her nieces; the third was not to be seen. Even the employees were out. This is why the bell rang several times before Chhammi Begum—accustomed to a practice acquired in New Delhi—bestirred herself and walked towards the drawing-room door to unfasten the lock. She hastily opened the inner door. The outer metallic door had been left ajar. In accordance with the warmth she had grown accustomed to displaying in Sabi-ud-din Saheb and Rashid Ali Saheb's residences, when she would usher guests into their homes graciously, Chhammi Begum held the inner door ajar and requested politely: 'Come in please.'

Two fat men from Marwar, and a heavily perfumed, apparently rich young man, entered the drawing room. The rich young man walked directly up to the bar. The two fat men sat themselves on the sofa with a thump. Often, people would visit Sabi-ud-din Saheb's residence in order to discuss business. However, Chhammi Begum was a little surprised to see the heavily perfumed young man. She consoled herself with the thought that perhaps these were the ways of this city. As she was still pondering whether to welcome her esteemed guests with tea or with water, the fat man wearing gold buttons and diamond rings inquired brusquely: 'Where is Madam?' Chhammi Begum knew well that in English, 'Madam' meant 'Begum'. She replied: 'Madam has gone out.'

'Where have the wretched chokri log gone?'

Chhammi Begum lost her temper. She knew too well that people from Bombay lacked refinement of speech, and that their demeanour was, by and large, impolite, but this sort of rudeness was quite unwarranted. She pursed her lips tightly and asked: 'Begum Saheb's nieces?' The door opened and Razia Bano entered the house. She told Chhammi Begum: 'Bua, you can go to your room and rest.'

'Yes,' Chhammi Begum replied, before walking down the gallery. As soon as she had walked past the room of one of Razia Bano's nieces, a young man came out and left.

In the sanctuary of her tiny room once more, Chhammi Begum spread out her prayer mat, and having performed her ablutions, offered Nafil prayers and thanked the Lord of Majesty and Bounty, her pure and immaculate Creator, who mocks His human beings only on two occasions. He who had upheld the respectability of her father and her grandfather and the honour of her illustrious ancestry, and who once more sustained her by means of nourishment from a respectable household that thrived on honourably received resources.

Translated from the Urdu by Fatima Rizvi

THE EMPTY BOX

Indira Goswami

Most people were usually asleep at this hour. Even those homeless beggars who had recently settled in the vicinity of the graveyard did not wake so early in the morning.

Some bulbuli birds had just begun to stir and chirp in the branches of the hizol tree in front of Toradoi's shack and, a few moments earlier, a line of small yellow-beaked cranes had flown noisily across the eastern horizon over the Brahmaputra River. An odd odour—a mix of the stench of burnt flesh and the fresh fragrance of small kagzi lemon flowers blowing in from somewhere—filled the area.

Toradoi walked out of her hovel and saw that Haibor, the man who sold firewood for pyres, was standing beneath the tree as usual. In the faint light of this early dawn, the thin legs protruding from his black half-pants stood out distinctly; his white teeth shone like pieces of chewed sugarcane.

She mumbled with displeasure on seeing him and rushed back indoors. What did she possess to make him stand there day in and day out, waiting as if to suck out her very bones? Some of the things he had said to her rang anew in her ears: 'That drunken driver of yours will not be out from jail for a long time yet. And who knows if he will be released at all? After all, he has knocked down and killed not one but two persons, and it has been proved that he was drunk when he was driving. But don't worry, I will help you. Keep your door open one night, just one night, and your two boys will not have to starve any more...'

It was due to this hope, of seeing her door open some night, that Haibor stood beneath the hizol tree every morning, long before other people woke up, when only the small birds sat on the branches chirping noisily among themselves.

After a little while, Toradoi walked out again and looked around. The man in the half-pants was gone. There were some people, here to furtively see the wooden box she had picked up from the graveyard, but Haibor, who supplied firewood for pyres, was not among them.

She peeped out to see if anyone was still loitering around, trying to get a glimpse of the box. What kind of people were these, she thought to herself. They were more like starving dogs that sniffed each other's bodies, trying to find out what they had eaten. They would not hesitate to snatch the very clothes off one's back and leave one naked.

When the zamindar of Chok Road had died a few days earlier, his body had been carried to the graveyard on his bed, which was made of the most expensive wood. And now Haladhar chowkidar slept on that same bed with his ugly wife. And that Sukura's wife, who earned her living chopping wood, now used the fine hookah she had picked up in the graveyard to smoke her tobacco. Someone had even found two gold rings lying among the charred remains of a well-to-do dead person! But no one had bothered to go and gape at those things. No one had been interested in seeing how the poverty-stricken Haladhar's hideous wife slept on the expensive wooden bed.

The hovels, sheds, shacks and other flimsy shelters made out of old corrugated sheets which had sprung up in the areas around the cemetery were full of such possessions, left by the relatives of the rich dead who had been cremated there. Many luxurious and showy objects, which had once been the pride and joy of some well-to-do family, now lay incongruously in the hut of some penniless beggar, grinning maliciously at their own social comedown! But there was no curiosity about these things. It seemed that these nasty people were intent only on maligning her and her black box.

Toradoi went into her hovel again and glanced at her two sons. They were sleeping soundly. Both of them were pitifully thin— their rib cages were so prominent that one could count their ribs. Their tattered half-pants hung down from their bloated lower abdomens, looking very much like the dried-up skins of goats hung up in a butcher's shop. And there, near them, was that wooden box. A youth seemed to stand inside it, the personification of a restless, youthful strength!

Toradoi touched the beautiful bakul flowers which had been carved into the wood, and the lovely flowers seemed to take on life and become real. She put her head down on the box and caressed the carvings with her cheeks. Then, she climbed into the open box and, as she had every night since she had brought it into her hut, she lay down inside it.

An unusual sensation of happiness flowed over her and under its overwhelming spell, she lay inside that large box for a long time, that coffin which someone had left behind after burning the dead body it carried. When she picked up that box from the graveyard, she had found some pieces of blood-stained ice in it. But she did not seem to remember that now. Toradoi could be heard sobbing from inside the box.

After some time, a police vehicle drove noisily past her shack. Indeed, the only cars that passed this way were the police vehicles. They came to make enquiries: were the 'handing-over certificates' of the person killed in the firing incident in order? Was it true that someone had come surreptitiously to bury an illegitimate child, without any certificate from the hospital? And so on and so forth. Also, the prostitutes from Satgaon flourished here. The more human flesh was burnt here, the hotter their own flesh and their animal instincts grew. Besides, there were so many unregistered corpses which were brought here to be cremated. These, and so many other such matters made the police vehicles come almost daily to this graveyard. They arrived, discussed the issue, quarrelled with the members of the 'smashan committee' and left.

Hearing the sound of the police Jonga, Toradoi sat up inside the coffin. How had she become so emotionally entangled in the box, she wondered? There were so many things, so many thoughts... Dear God, the box was strewn with vermilion and flowers. The previous night, she had brought out the blouse she had worn on her wedding day and put it on—it was the only piece of clothing she still possessed which was not tattered and torn. Then, in the dim light of the kerosene lamp, she had stood before her small mirror and carefully combed her hair, as carefully and eagerly as she had done on her wedding day ten years ago. As she combed her hair almost passionately, she hardly noticed that the comb often struck the bones of her shoulders and her neck. In the days gone by, when her body had been covered with soft, healthy flesh, she had not even known that she had bones in these locations. Now, people said, since she had come to live among the skeletons in the graveyard, she had turned into a skeleton.

This wooden box really was marvellous. Lying inside it, Toradoi felt as though she was sleeping with the lover she desired so passionately. Her hair, her hair oil and vermilion, all these were distinctly marked inside this box.

~

Could someone still be trying to peep inside to see what she was doing with the black box? Many people had been trying to see the box, and what she was doing with it, trying to peep through cracks in the door and window and the thin walls of her hut. She suspected that they had even told her two boys to keep a watch on her and her activities.

'Oh, how horrible,' she suspected them of saying, 'how could anyone sleep inside a coffin? Throw it away, get rid of it!'

Toradoi lay down inside the box again, and that feeling overwhelmed her, that unique sensation—the one she had never felt before!

All at once someone kicked heavily on her door and Toradoi jumped out of the box in alarm. She listened intently and knew that it was her brother, Someswar, who worked in the police force.

'Toradoi, Toradoi!' he called out. And as soon as she opened the door, a big man dressed in a police uniform walked in. He was a robust man, sporting a huge moustache, a pair of rough boots on his feet and a stout stick in his hands. He said, 'I have not been able to come and see you. But today I have been put on duty here, so I could. It seems that that loose woman from Satgaon has opened an office here! It really is scandalous, the way things are going! Religion and decency have disappeared. When Barua died the other day, his two sons came to this graveyard carrying their dead father. But while one of them, dressed only in a gamocha, was busy with the rituals for his dead father, the other one disappeared from the scene. He sneaked away to a prostitute's room without any of the others even being aware of it! These are the times we are living in!' He stopped talking and stared. Then he jumped back as though he had seen a poisonous snake. He kept staring in shocked surprise at the big black box in front of him.

He came close to the box and knocked on it with his stick. He even walked around it attentively, as though he was carrying out the ritualistic pradakshina. Then, kneeling down near it, he took out a handkerchief from his pocket and wiped his face. The man who had walked into the room in such a careless and pompous manner now looked like a defeated soldier. Glancing towards Toradoi, he asked in a small voice, 'Do you have any water in the house? Give me a glass.'

He gulped the water down at one go. Then, with his head bent low, he said, 'So, what I thought was right. This is that box. Yes, yes, it is the same coffin.' Suddenly lifting his head, and looking straight at her, he said, 'You worked in their house as their maidservant. When the young man's father, Thakur, lay ill, you helped them greatly, even washing his soiled clothes. Everyone knows that. And the son?'

Now this big, sturdy constable almost broke down weeping. He spoke in a broken and emotional voice, 'The young man had had an affair with you, did he not? At that time, he said he was determined to marry you. And the entire Thakur household was in a great turmoil over this. Ultimately came his transfer to Upper Assam, and this accident...'

Without any preamble, Toradoi suddenly asked him a question: 'What hit him?'

'A jeep,' Someswar replied. 'What a handsome man he was! I

removed the blood-stained pieces of ice with my own hands, and helped put his body on the funeral pyre. A young man's blood! These two hands of mine were absolutely—' Seeing Toradoi standing there stiffly like a statue, he could not finish the sentence. The big black box stood between them like a mysterious cavern.

Someswar stood up and in a rather dramatic manner, shouted, 'The days when a tea-garden sahib could marry Toradoi, the daughter of a coolie, are long past. That Jenkins Sahib, who dared to marry a coolie labourer's daughter, died a long time ago. The Thakur's younger son, Saru Bopai, said he would marry you, that he loved you with all his heart. But could he marry you? Could he take you out from this hovel and give you a place in their grand bungalow?'

Toradoi cried out in a heart-broken voice, 'Twelve years have gone by since that time. He did not marry all these years, because he could not marry me. Maybe he would not have married at all if he had lived.'

The big bossy constable stared at her as if he could not believe his ears. 'You fool!' he scolded. 'You were foolish enough to give everything a woman holds most dear all those years ago, and you still have not learnt anything. You are still a big fool. I am a policeman, and when I heard what you had done, I came prepared...'

Toradoi gazed helplessly at her elder brother. 'What is he saying? Dear God, what is he trying to say now?' she cried.

Someswar continued, 'Now, even after losing everything else, that man is trying to rob you of that which you have so long carried around with you as your most precious possession.'

In the meantime, the two boys had woken up and the three of them stared at Someswar.

'Oh God, what is he thinking of now?' thought Toradoi. 'What is he trying to say?' The poverty-stricken mother and her two starving sons looked like three spirits of the cemetery as they gazed at the well-fed man in front of them.

Someswar felt around in his pockets and the two small boys

thought that their uncle was about to give them some money—
like the other visitors often gave them. Like the man always
waiting under the hizol tree, who pushed coins into their hands
when no one was looking. This man was their own uncle, their
mother's brother, but he had not come to visit them, even when
their father was taken to prison.

Someswar got up and, taking out a bundle of letters from his
pocket, threw them in Toradoi's face. He said, 'These are the
invitation cards for his wedding. As I said, I came prepared when
I heard about your doings. See, he was not waiting for you, vowing
to marry no one but you. His wedding date was fixed, and even the
invitation cards had been printed. Read them, read these invitation
letters. He was on his way home for his wedding when the
accident took place…Read these letters, and pray for the peace of
his departed soul.'

As he stamped out of the room, his glance fell on Toradoi's
two sons, who were now holding on closely to her. Muttering to
himself, he put his hands inside his pockets, looking for coins to
give them. If he could have caught that loose woman who carried
on her trade even with people who came to cremate their dead, he
might have been able to make some money. Or even if he could
have caught that Haibor red-handed! That scoundrel sold cheap
wood, passing it off as expensive sal to the mourners coming to
burn their dead! Finding some loose coins, he handed a fistful of
them to his small nephews, then walked quickly out of the door.
The two half-starved boys, finding money in their hands, bolted
to the small shop outside.

Toradoi sat near the bundle of invitation letters. She felt them
with her hands, like the sons of the dead feel about in the ashes of
a funeral pyre for asthi, bone fragments left unburned. There was
no doubt, these were indeed wedding invitations.

~

For a long time after this, Toradoi did not come out of her hut.
Unable to bear the pangs of hunger, her two sons started to beg for

food from the people who came to the graveyard to cremate their dead. Someone even tied a gamocha around the younger boy's head, probably one which a bereaved had worn while performing the final rituals. The boys had picked up two liquor bottles from a heap of firewood and washed them. There was a well near the statue of Yama Devata riding on a buffalo. The boys scooped up water from this well in their bottles and drank that. The neighbours came to know what was happening. They knew that Toradoi did not bother to cook these days. She just sat in front of that huge box with its lid wide open, like the mouth of hell itself.

Haibor continued to wait for her beneath that tree every day.

Very early one morning, Toradoi and her sons were seen dragging the coffin out towards the graveyard. They dragged it to the place where, it was rumoured, someone had burned an illegitimate baby, without any 'handing-over' certificate from the hospital. There, Toradoi burned the box.

The small bulbuli birds woke up and started their noisy day. A bright red sun rose over the Brahmaputra river. The sun was surrounded by yellowish and light-brown clouds. It was not like an ordinary sun—it was more like the flushed face of a helpless prostitute—a face distorted with the fear and slander of having to spend a night with an unwanted man. The pale clouds seemed to lay bare the helplessness of that face, and at the same time, the readiness of the face to fight against her destiny…

The ashes of the burnt box lay scattered all around the graveyard, looking like the skin of a freshly slaughtered goat, spread out to dry in the morning sunlight.

The noise of the bulbuli birds on the branches of the hizol tree increased to a fever pitch.

Toradoi came out of her hut. No chador covered her body.

The surprising thing was that the man who always stood waiting for her beneath the tree was not there that day.

Toradoi walked further down—but the man was not there…

Translated from the Assamese by Gayatri Bhattacharyya

PONNAGARAM

Puthumaippithan

Have you heard of Ponnagaram, the golden city? You won't see anything there to compare with the dreams of the paurinakars, the narrators of the Puranas. People speak of merit gained through past deeds; here, you have to console yourself by hanging on to that philosophy and its truth. All the same, for the few human honey-bees who are obliged to live by increasing the profits of the few maharajas of this world, this is truly a city of gold.

That lane there, look, adjacent to the railway lines, and leading to the toddy depot; that's its main road. Four people can walk along comfortably upon it—provided no vehicle comes towards them. Branching off from it are several bends and curves. Like rabbit warrens.

Anyone who wishes to make a pilgrimage to this divine region had best come here when there is a fine rain drizzling and whining, for it is at its unsurpassable best then. Muddy puddles, all along the way. Bordering the road, there is the municipal Ganga—or rather, the Yamuna is the black river, isn't it? Beyond that, iron railings. Beyond that again, and at a height, the railway tracks.

On the other side, in rows, human cages. Yes, they're supposed to be dwellings.

Water taps? Yes, those are there. Electric lights? I can't remember. Isn't it enough to light ordinary oil lamps? When there is no moonlight or when the moon is waning, that is.

The children of Ponnagaram love playing at 'catching fish'. But how will fish be found in the municipality's holy waters? Occasionally, an over-ripe fruit or a stale vadai or some such thing is likely to come floating down from the homes of the rich. But that is a secret known only to the children of these parts.

Heaven knows what special delight there is in playing by the railway tracks. Of course, there is an iron fence. But can children understand the rule about not going beyond it? After all, they are not Glaxo or Mellins Food babies, are they, incapable of squeezing through the railings? And in any case, if they should 'go', the parents are only freed of some of their burden. It is their special joy to stand in a row chorusing, 'Good morni saar' to the product of the iron civilization as it steams past them. This is by way of their introduction to English education.

The place begins to come alive and is full of bustle only after five o'clock. It is from that moment that the women begin their work. Toddy carts arrive; women foregather to collect water. And collecting water there is like taking part in the Mahabharata war.

Hair, which had started to fade even in youth, is now as white as spun cotton. Young eyes, ruined. What else can you expect of eyes that watch the mechanical spindles at work day in and day out? Are eyes made of iron? And what about good health and the so-called beauty born of hard work? Good health indeed! Where does that come from? All bacteria, all poisonous viruses, cholera and such-like are produced and cultivated right here. All the same, where there is the will to survive, it will happen, somehow. In ancient stone-age times, man lived in a cave, along with lions and tigers; he killed them, they killed him in return. But did he lose his strength, refuse to procreate, become extinct? All life is one great hunt. So what?

A darkened string around the neck: the symbol of life's commitments. But nobody cares about it much in these parts. It's a different world here, Ayya, the virtues and dharmas that belong here have to be different, too.

Ammalu is a mill coolie. She can't be more than twenty, twenty-two years old. Her husband plies a jutka. He owns this jutka-cart. Five individuals make up the family: Ammalu, Murugesan her husband, his mother, his younger brother and his horse. Their daily meals, including the horse's, depend on the wages of two people. The house rent, the routine bribe to the police, the money for Murugesan's younger brother to smoke ganja on the sly—their wages have to cover all this. They are all occasional tipplers, certainly. How else could they forget their

hunger during the 'dull season'? Hunger, Ayya, hunger! You sing
with a great flourish, 'All else flies when hunger comes', but the
words don't actually touch you. If you were in their position for a
single day, those words and their meaning would rise out of your
very belly.

That day, Murugesan was in great spirits. He and his horse had
both drunk their fill and then set out upon a race. The cart turned
turtle and its axle broke. The horse was badly wounded. Murugesan
suffered severe bruising and internal injuries. When they brought
him home, he was totally unconscious. It was just as well that he
was drunk. At least he wasn't aware of his pain. Ammalu ground
up a poultice of sorts and applied it to the swellings. It was then
that he muttered something. He wanted some milk-gruel, he said.
There were two days to go before Ammalu would get her coolie
wages. What money was there in the house?

Ammalu comes to collect water.

It is pitch dark, According to the almanac, there should be a
moon tonight, but if it hides behind the clouds, what can the
municipality do about it?

There is the usual shouting and screaming. One way and
another, the water is collected. She turns to go home.

By the side of the lane lurks a man; he has had his eye on
Ammalu for some time.

They both disappear into the darkness. And Ammalu has
earned three-quarters of a rupee. Yes. So that she can give her
husband his milk-gruel.

You seem to go on and on about something called chastity.
Ayya, this is what it is like in Ponnagaram.

Translated from the Tamil by Lakshmi Holmström

GOD FORSAKEN

Siddique Alam

At the stroke of ten, the souls of the dead would descend from minarets, domes and parapets and take over every dark and dimly lit nook of the disused church. 'How are the human beings faring?' they would inquire of each other. If the goblins were unsightly, the witches were no less so, their long hair falling down to their hips. To them, this expression of solicitude seemed vastly amusing. 'Even after they are dead, these humans can't restrain themselves from back-biting,' they would whisper to each other. Their laughter would shake the old walls and columns. 'What else can be expected from humankind?' The witches were disgusted by the whole issue. They had looked at the world from every angle, weighed it and assessed it. They had escaped the countless spells and exorcisms of human beings, and endured much hatred. Besides the prejudice and the irrational fear of the humans, there was the unnecessary cruelty. The witches would often sit and squeeze and rub their sagging breasts and grind their teeth in frustration as they tried to shed a few tears. But they were unable to cry. It was the human beings who had a monopoly on tears. The human beings who had obscured the sky with their sighs, made the sea briny with their weeping. But that story is for a later telling.

~

The day Murli Naskar went completely insane, a bitch gave birth to its puppies in the backyard of his house. Once, Murli had tried to abuse this bitch. Murli had long hair and his family devoutly hoped and prayed for his death. Truth be told, Murli's only flaw was that you could expect the worst from him. For a little bit of cash, he let anyone use his body as a thoroughfare. Pick-pockets deposited their loot with him and prostitutes took him along when they visited VD clinics.

Ah, if only someone could have plumbed the depths of his

soul! He had grown weary of playing the part of husband for these disease-ridden cunts. He sincerely wanted a woman to carry his baby in her womb and go to a clinic with him, a regular clinic where a doctor with a stethoscope wound around his neck orders women to lie down on the examination table. Sure, these women were prostitutes by profession, they nevertheless disliked the probing fingers of men. Apart from God, if anyone else has a right to your soul it is a doctor. Once he gets a hold of you, even your body is no longer your own.

It was his love for education that drew Murli Naskar to Calcutta. His father and mother were not his natural parents. They had tried hard to rid themselves of the malignant growth that Murli Naskar was, through one dodge or another, and had finally succeeded. But, upon arrival in Calcutta, he quickly concluded that education was not the be-all and end-all in life. He had no funds for hostel expenses, textbooks or notebooks. It's quite possible that, like thousands of other boys, he too could have passed the Bachelor of Arts examination and got a clerical job, or found work as a schoolteacher and lived out his remaining years like a cowardly nincompoop. But Girja Shankar, a Sonagachi pimp, took him under his wing and saved him from such a pathetic existence. The two had met in a local train and, afterwards, Girja Shankar had brought Murli to Sonagachi and arranged for his upkeep in Mehndi Lakshmi's room. Exactly one week later, the cops picked up Girja Shankar and took him away. Girja Shankar used to collect a weekly 'take' from the whores for the police station in-charge, Gaya Prasad.

Mehndi Lakshmi told all this to Murli Naskar. Mehndi Lakshmi was getting on in years and rarely managed to snare a client. Even so, in the whole of Imam Baksh Lane, she was the most popular trick because she could play the role of an elderly aunt and also service clients. To atone for her sins, she had covered the four walls of her room with posters of gods and goddesses. Helping educated boys like Murli Naskar was her other hobby; so, with the help of a curtain she divided her room in two sections. In his part of the room, Murli Naskar would read the works of Nietzsche and Rajneesh Acharya. He would steal these books from a library in Gol Park and after he was done with them, he would sell them to a Sindhi bookseller in Free School Street who dealt in used books. In the other part of the room, Mehndi Lakshmi carried on her trade, cooked, read the Ramayan, or primped herself for her imaginary husband, Nawal Purohit.

'Nawal Purohit?' Murli would ask. 'If he is alive, how come he is not with you?'

'What the hell do you know?' Mehndi Lakshmi would respond. 'You've read a few books and now you fancy yourself a preacher? Eat your words, Murli. Not only is he alive but there is no finer carpenter in all of Mandir Haat.'

'How odd!' Murli Naskar would say.

Whatever he'd have read of Nietzsche would be scattered to the winds. All sort of thoughts would keep him brooding and scratching his head until it was time for Mehndi Lakshmi's clients. Then she would pull aside a corner of the curtain, flash a grin at him and say: 'Your eyes are getting tired, Murli. Perhaps you should go and watch TV for a while.'

Murli Naskar would gather his books and leave the room. And on occasions like these, he would be ensnared by the black-and-white TV that was on all the time at the cigarette-vendor's shop on the street corner. Here, all the over-age whores, the young women who were yet to get into the racket, defunct pimps and idling johns, would all cluster around in a motley crowd. Here, a cool breeze would course its way through the narrow alleys. People would spit or direct jets of betel-stained spittle at the walls. Or they would listen to the harangue of some petty politician. That is to say, here too, life would go on as it did on any other busy street. The only difference was that in respectable neighbourhoods people are acutely aware of their wickedness, but everyone had a clear conscience here. Everything was out in the open and the whores plied their trade diligently, like day-labourers. The pimps had their homes and families and the johns felt obliged to return to their world of respectability.

But Murli Naskar was a misfit here. So he took shelter in the students' politics of Surendar Nath College. He took up a political banner and flashed his dagger in the middle of tram tracks. He learned how to make bombs and, by cutting off the ear of a Congress Party minion, he made it possible for the man to gain fame as 'Earless Gopal'. And when it was time for the final exams, Murli took to sleeping late and long. Often Mehndi, unable to find another spot, would wrap herself around him and go to sleep. In a kind of a dream, Murli would keep pushing Mehndi away. But, after having serviced countless clients, Mehndi would not have the strength to respond. She wouldn't wake up until the sun had crept past the window, come around and fell on his face, heating it up. When she did wake up, she would feel sorry for Murli Naskar. She would make tea for him, hand him his toothbrush, and curse him.

'Did you come here to get an education or what? I thought I was atoning for my sins. Sins my ass. In the end, you too will turn out a pimp. Come on, Murli, hurry up. Finish your education and get lost. I have a lot of other matters to attend to.'

'Like what?'

'Don't you bother yourself with that! Just finish your education and get back to decent society. Many a dolled-up girl is waiting impatiently to bear your child.'

Murli would burst out laughing. Well, this is all right, he would think. When these whores don't hesitate to bear children, why should the girls from respectable families hold back? Respectable families—he chuckled again. These whores primp and preen too, hang icons of deities on their walls and celebrate marrying imaginary husbands. The only difference is that in respectable homes, where the woman is the wage-earner, it must be difficult to distinguish between the wife and the husband. Murli Naskar was disturbed by Karl Marx's theory on the concept of the absurd relationship between men and women. He understood prostitutes, but wives—what the hell! He felt sorry for them. For all that they do from dawn to dusk they never get even a fourth of a reward for their labours. In fact, they often don't even get enough to eat or to buy enough fabric to cover their nakedness.

The whores of Sonagachi would often tell the johns who took too long to finish: 'Hey! You think I'm your wife? Get lost, bum, it's time for me to meet other clients!'

But during moments of leisure, or when he was not mentally amidst this filthy lot, he would think: There must be some way to get away from all this. There were many ways out, and there was no one to stop him, but apart from this what other world was there, except the world of decent society, which seemed totally irrational to him.

One day he felt Christopher Columbus waking up inside him. But then he saw that decent society had its roots in the cops who stood near the tram tracks and took a weekly 'take' from the brothels, took snuff with pimps and joked and gossiped with whores. And beyond them were the shop-keepers, sitting with bored looks on their faces; or the businessmen, constantly devising means to launder their ill-gotten gains; or the governmental officials, who got fat on bribes, moved around in luxurious automobiles, installed air-conditioners in their homes and were adored by their wives as if they were glamourous movie stars. Or there were these schools and colleges which were no longer true to their charters.

That authentic city—where could it be? There must be a place where no one felt ashamed or embarrassed! Murli pondered this idea. And the inhabitants of this place—what would they be like? One thing was certain, it was sure to be a very interesting place and he lived in that dream.

But then in the end...all this talk is the stuff of fairy-tales, he would conclude. Okay, just imagine that we get there. In a few years won't we transform it into another Sonagachi? Won't it also become the centre of cold commerce, just like it is here? Will the politicians of that city be any different? Will its history be any different from the history we study in thick volumes?

'Murli Naskar, are you a Hindu?'

'Yes.'

'You lie. You keep a copy of the Quran with you.'

'I also have a Bible and the Bhagavad Gita.'

'Come on, pull down your pants and show us. This issue must be settled once and for all. I have a feeling you are a Muslim.'

'If I turn out to be a Muslim, it won't change your world or mine. But what made you think this? Lakshmi, it appears that you have taken to watching too much news on TV these days. Everywhere, politicians seem keen on using religion to prop up their political platforms.'

'Are you afraid?'

'Yes.'

'Of what?'

'If I knew, wouldn't I have tried to understand this fear, would I not have killed it?'

'Killed who?' Lakshmi's heart stood still.

Murli Naskar smiled. 'Mehndi, you've covered your walls with icons of gods and goddesses. Not one of them comes to your aid.'

'They sure do. Do you think at my age so many customers are falling from the sky? This is all due to the mercy of gods and goddesses.'

'I mean…' Murli admitted defeat and smiled. 'Right, I guess, you have a point.'

Then Mehndi Lakhsmi, flushed with her victory, went to the rooftop to spread her hair in the sunlight. 'This happened when I was a child,' she began. 'At that time, Sikka Aunty ruled the brothel. I used to go to school in a smart uniform and a red sash. My budding charms had already attracted two lovers, Billa and Tara.'

'Don't you need to explain at this point that you are a daughter of a whore?'

'That's there, certainly. Anyway, Billa and Tara were my lovers. Billa had a passion for dogs. He would steal dogs from Gailiff Street and gift them to me. They were very pretty dogs, with long hair or eyes like buttons. Some had no tails; others were so short that they looked as though their legs were buried in the ground below their knees. Tara never spoke much. He was Sikka Aunty's spy. He was also a police informer. One day Billa and Tara got into a knife fight. Then both of them disappeared. I had no idea where they went or where they are now.'

'This is a strange tale you're telling me. If I don't listen to it, curiosity makes me restless. If I listen to it, it makes no sense.'

'What?'

'I mean, it's a good story but you seem to enter it a bit too early.'

'Get away, Murli, my life is full of stories. Not like yours where there are only books and books and books. Once a Gujarati trader got all worked up and wanted to take me to Mumbai. I was very young at the time. I asked him what made Mumbai so special. He said, there is the sea there. I said, what else besides the sea? Tall buildings. What else besides tall buildings? The film-city. So I asked him, does it have places like Sonagachi? He said, even better places. For instance, I asked. He said: Muhammad Ali Road. Then why don't you go pick up a Mehndi Lakshmi from there, you jerk. After that he complained bitterly to Sikka Aunty about my behaviour and turned her against me. She kicked me out of my quarters. Later, Sikka Aunty begged me to come back. But by then, my fortunes had improved and I was doing very well on my own.'

Murli Naskar spent much of his time on the rooftop, sitting on a crumbling parapet, practising Indian film songs on his mouth organ. A client of Mehndi Lakshmi's had forgotten this mouth organ in her bed. When he wearied of the instrument, he would sit and look at the endless array of dilapidated buildings that stretched as far as the horizon. On all the rooftops prostitutes were taking baths, washing clothes, cooking, dandling babies and drying their hair in the sunlight. Down below, God's creation was living out its life. Above, the sky which God had made, in which people had stuck paper kites here and there. And it looked as though the earth and all its ruinous structures were suspended from their strings.

He would say to himself: Why am I here? Then he would sigh:

What great achievement could I have laid claim to if I weren't here? Then he would turn and address Mehndi Lakshmi: 'Well, Lakshmi, if I went away like Billa and Tara, would you miss me?'

'You aren't my Billa and you aren't my Tara. What does it matter whether I miss you or not?'

'That's why I can't come to any sort of decision. I feel that at least there should be somebody who will worry about me.'

And on that day Murli Naskar thought: I need a new personality. He began to grow a moustache. But in this matter too, he needed someone's advice. Girja Shankar? He no longer enjoyed the sort of relationship with Girja Shankar that he once used to have. Girja Shankar had married a whore from Chuna Gali, built an illegal hut under Bridge Number Three on Convent Road and was busy raising kids. He had also established a tea-shop near Thieves' Turning where idlers hung out to exchange gossip.

One day he saw Murli Naskar, grinned, and told him to sit down on a wooden bench. 'Who told you to grow a moustache? You don't look too bad with it. But who told you to grow one?'

'My heart.'

'You should listen to your heart. I listened to my heart and now, look, I have three kids and this tea-shop isn't so bad, is it? But my wife is ill and every second month she is in bad shape.'

'What kind of illness?'

'The kind that women get. Don't ask me to explain. It's not proper to talk about these things. All I know is that right now I'm not doing too well but, at the same time, I am not doing too badly either.'

'Do you have any regrets, Girja?'

'I couldn't say. All I know is that whenever a man tries to change, he ends up becoming the same person.'

On his way back, Murli stopped to piss near the gate of an abandoned church. When he pulled up the zipper his penis got caught in the metal teeth. He screamed in agony and tears sprang to his eyes. He pulled up the zipper with great care and sat down with his back against the tottering gate. Smarting under the pain he breathed hard. He dried his tears and waited for the pain to subside. He could feel spasms as if someone were pinching his sensitive skin again and again. After a short while, he felt better and mustered the courage to examine his injury. Was he bleeding? He looked at the gate. A heavy chain secured it. But some of the lower bars had been pushed apart to create an opening. A man could wriggle through with some effort; a dog could, quite easily. Murli went inside the compound and, standing behind a wall, he slowly slid down his zipper. In one place, the teeth had left tiny cuts. Small drops of blood oozed. He pulled up the zipper once again, walked across a terrace, past a gazebo and sat down under a small tree and lowered his head. Most of the glass panes of the church windows were obscured by dirt and dust, but were still intact. One side of the wooden entryway had broken off and fallen inwards. People had doubtless figured out a use for it. From this angle, nothing of the inside of the church could be seen. But on the left, corkscrew stairs went up towards a tower. From even where he stood, Murli could smell the stench of bat shit inside.

Later, when Murli met Girja Shankar at his tea-shop, Girja looked pale. He had shaved his head. He was running a high temperature.

'You should go to Campbell Hospital,' Murli advised. 'It is near Sealdah station.'

'I have been there. They did a blood test. I will get the report tomorrow,' he said, taking a sip of tea that Sia Dullari had brought.

Just by looking at Sia Dullari you could not tell that she used to prostitute herself in Chuna Gali. After giving birth to three kids one after the other, her body had become wide and heavy. She still put on lots of make-up and also worshipped regularly at a temple. Their unlawful hut stood a hand's breadth away from the railway line. In the front yard of the hut, a sacred flag fluttered atop a thin bamboo pole. On it, Hanuman was depicted flying across the sky with a mace in one hand and a mountain in the other. Every ten minutes the local train went by on the tracks, making the little hut shake to its foundations. The three kids grew up crawling about on metal tracks.

'Your earlier profession, it seems to me, was better,' Murli Naskar said. 'And you've completely ruined the woman you have married.'

'Then you go and become a pimp,' Girja Shankar responded angrily. 'You don't understand these matters. Go, and become a middleman for some whore, Murli. Apart from this, not even God has a use for you.'

'The tea was quite good,' Murli said. 'It's just that I tend to blurt out whatever is in my heart. I have what they call "verbal diarrhoea".'

'What? What?' both husband and wife exclaimed in unison.

'Let it go,' Murli Naskar said. 'When I come next time, I will bring chocolates for the kiddies.'

'And if you come without chocolate after that, the kiddies will think less of you.' Girja laughed and started to cough. 'Don't fall into this trap, Murli. Raising children is not an easy task. And children are of no use. When they are old enough, they vanish into their own world, just as we did.'

The following week, when Murli Shankar arrived at Girja Shankar's teashop, it wasn't there. The hut next to the railway line had also been demolished. He inquired about Girja Shankar from the people in the neighbourhood but nobody seemed to know anything. In fact, nothing remained of the hutments that had bordered the railway line except an abandoned railway yard and some broken columns and canopies. Murli returned home, munching chocolates and casting grim glances at the urban mess of Kolkata. He related this strange and unbelievable story to Mehndi Lakshmi.

'Girja might have shifted location,' Mehndi Lakshmi said, directing a stream of betel-stained spit at the wall. 'Girja is very clever. He got hold of Sia Dullari, the most beautiful whore of Chuna Gali.'

'He looked quite ill, Mehndi.'

'Why didn't you tell me this before? Did you check at the hospital?'

'I'm afraid that was my one oversight,' Murli said, rising. 'I'm sure I will discover something at Campbell Hospital.' But hundreds of people were admitted to and thousands discharged from this huge hospital. Finding out about Girja Shankar was a monumental task. Murli wandered through the corridors of the hospital which reeked of medicinal odours. Then, an intelligent guard told him about the hospital morgue. But there was no record of Girja even in the morgue.

'I still say Girja Shankar has shifted somewhere else,' Mehndi Lakshmi said. 'The man who has a beautiful wife should keep moving. Remember what they say: the poor man's wife belongs to the whole neighbourhood.'

'Enough, Mehndi. You're getting senile,' Murli said. 'I can't imagine what sort of pleasure any of your clients might get out of you.'

'Clients bring their own enjoyment.' Mehndi smiled, displaying her betel-stained teeth. 'We merely provide the means.'

'You're right,' Murli said. 'I never looked at the matter from this angle.'

And from that day onwards, he started looking at the people who came into the street with keener interest. It was true—a fact—that people brought their own enjoyment with them. With hungry eyes and slobbering mouths, like vultures they inspected the decked-out harlots who lined the street on either side. These people—young, old, married, bachelors—if he started roaming the streets of this district he would recognize thousands of them. But what would he gain from that? Could he change his world or theirs? Gradually, he took to keeping company with the pimps Lala, Rahim, Baghicha, Gulab Chand.

'The chicks of Kangan Kota are worth looking at.' Lala was talking about a village in Chhattisgarh. 'Not softies like these city girls. Their bodies feel as firm as pomegranates to the touch. But those bitches don't want to come to Kolkata.'

'The girls from Bangladesh have ruined the trade, damn them,' Baghicha said as he snorted some snuff. 'Look, you guys, how young the girls who are arriving nowadays are. Hey, Gulab,' he said, 'remember that girl from Loreto who used to come here, I don't see her any more, what was her name?'

'She must have gotten married.' Rahim laughed boisterously. His teeth were turning yellow. The pimps were chatting amiably but also keeping a sharp eye on people entering the lane.

One day, Mehndi Lakshmi sent someone to fetch Murli from this spot. A dwarfish, elderly man was waiting for him.

'Sia Dullari,' said Mehndi, flashing betel-stained teeth. 'She is waiting for you in Chuna Gali.'

'What is this about?' Murli asked the short guy who was slurping the tea that Mehndi Lakshmi had prepared for him.

'I don't know anything.'

He was also a pimp, obviously.

'Sia Dullari has sent you a message. Okay, my dear, do remember me if any need should arise. My name is Hari Nath.'

After Hari Nath had left, Mehndi Lakshmi asked Murli, 'Will you go to Chuna Gali?'

'No.'

'Any reason?'

'Why should I have to give you reasons? I just don't want to go.'

But he had told Mehndi Lakshmi a lie. As soon as he got a chance, he went straight to Chuna Gali.

He found Sia Dullari on the fourth floor of a building with her three children. She was nursing her youngest child. When she saw Murli, she covered her big breasts with the end of her sari.

'Where is Girja, Sia?' Murli said, accepting a proffered stool. He had no affection for Chuna Gali. From the adjacent streets the nasty effluvia of raw hides flowed through the air, laden with germs.

'How should I know?' Sia replied. 'He just vanished one day. All you men are like that.'

Murli knew that she was lying. For the first time, he assessed Sia Dullari from head to toe. Although she no longer had the figure she used to, after her return to Chuna Gali something of what she had lost was coming back.

Murli took a deep breath. 'Have you started taking on clients?'

'Not yet,' Sia Dullari said. Then she made a sign for him to close the door. 'I need a man.'

'What about that Hari Nath fellow? He wasn't half bad.'

'No,' Sia Dullari said. 'I need a new man.'

To lighten the serious mood, Murli said, 'Nowadays, the johns find whores all by themselves. They bring very powerful eyeglasses.'

'I cannot go and stand in the street,' Sia Dullari said. 'I have three children.'

'Why don't you place them in the orphanage?'

'Why don't you carry them there yourself?'

Murli saw that Sia's eyes were wet with tears.

'If you go soft like this, you won't be able to exist,' Murli said with a laugh. 'I don't promise anything, but I have an old regard for Girja Shankar. Once, Girja had mockingly told me to take up pimping. And now his wife is urging me on to the same path.'

'All paths in life are alike,' Sia Dullari said, wiping her tears with the hem of her sari. 'In one place one thing is good, and in another place, a different one. But all in all, it is all the same.'

'I've never read this in any book.'

'Learn it from Sia Dullari,' she said, placing the child on a cot and starting to comb her hair. With Murli looking on, she changed her sari, put on make-up and then posed like a model, her right hand on her hip. Murli's throat went dry. Sia Dullari was really quite beautiful. He turned away.

'Why don't you look at me?' he heard Sia say. 'Don't I please you?'

'Ask your clients.'

'I'm asking you.'

'Not me.'

'Then I will have to ask the clients,' Sia said, smiling. 'Murli, I have heard a lot about you from Girja and you are not one bit less than what he described. You are worse than a pimp.'

~

It was a difficult task to arrange clients for Sia—most wanted young girls. But he noticed that the customers who came to her once, returned again and again. Mehndi Lakhsmi heard about his new job only when he told her.

'A pimp! You, Murli!' she exclaimed. 'Oh god, I had such dreams for you.'

'You are such a dreamer,' Murli said, laughing. 'And that is a bad habit.'

Within six months, Sia Dullari had a flourishing trade. Many of her old customers returned. Many among them had become prominent names in the business world.

When Murli returned to Mehndi one midnight all worn out and tired, she gave him a tongue-lashing. 'I can smell cheap booze on you, Murli,' she yelled. 'That witch Sia is ruining you.'

'Go ahead, abuse me,' Murli responded drunkenly. 'But keep in mind, she is the sunflower of Chuna Gali.'

'And what am I? Nothing?' Mehndi growled.

'You are an old pot, Mehndi. With nothing but ashes inside.'

Then she took a slipper and attacked him. He dodged and ducked around doorways and ran up stairs as he endured the walloping. The other whores laughed merrily, thoroughly enjoying the commotion. And when both of them had worn themselves out, Murli placed his head on Mehndi's breasts and said, 'I'm famished, Mehndi and it seems there is a kind of emptiness everywhere. Perhaps a little food might be able to fill this emptiness.'

Mehndi warmed up something for him to eat.

~

Over the last three days, Sia Dullari had not entertained a single client. She had also changed her abode. Now she had a TV and a refrigerator in her room. She had also engaged a nursemaid who looked after the children. She had started to teach herself how to use a sewing machine. A bearded maulvi with a skullcap came to teach her how to sew.

'Sia?'

'Yes.'

'May I ask you something?'

'No.'

Murli scratched his head and tried to dip his nose into a book.

'What are you trying to say?' Sia said and stopped her sewing machine.

'What finally happened to Girja?'

'I told you, I don't know.'

'You don't want to tell me.'

'Aren't things moving along without Girja?'

The machine started to move: clackety-clack-clack.

'It's very strange.'

Murli got up suddenly and stood behind Sia and started to caress her soft, delicate neck.

'What do you want?' Sia moved away from him and shot him an angry look.

'You look nice and fresh today. I can also feel the need for a woman.'

Sia jumped up. 'Get away! How dare you touch me!'

'Why not?' Murli was bewildered. 'And if you think I want free service, you're wrong. I am ready to pay.'

'Murli, I am warning you. You better not come near me.' She grabbed a heavy, cast-iron pan from the stove.

'Incredible!' Murli said, flinging up his hands in a gesture of defeat accepted. 'Who the hell are you? A whore for hire.'

'Yes, but not for everyone.'

'I'm quitting. Find yourself another pimp.'

He heard Sia sob as he turned to leave.

'Murli, I don't know what happened to Girja. He contracted a horrible disease.'

Murli stopped and looked at her. The tears were spoiling Sia's mascara.

'As soon as he got the report on his blood analysis, the cops arrested him,' she said. 'The cops also came after me, but I grabbed the kids and ran.'

'Is Girja still in prison?'

'He ran away from the hospital and killed himself. He threw

himself under a train on the Iron Bridge and got chopped up.'

Murli's head began to swim and his blood ran cold. He sat down on Sia's bed.

'And you, Sia? Do you also have this disease?'

'I don't know. I've never had myself checked.'

'You don't let me near you. Something's wrong.'

'I don't have the time to get into a long discussion with you.'

Sia sat down at her sewing machine: clackety-clack-clack.

'Possibly you are of no more use to me. Go. I'll find another man.'

He heard her words rise coldly above the noise of the machine.

~

Mehndi was happy to have Murli back. She lovingly ran her fingers over his new books. But Murli had become irritable and had fallen abnormally silent.

'Sia kicked you out,' Mehndi chirped cheerily.

'Drop it, Mehndi,' Murli said. After that Mehndi never brought up the Sia business again.

~

The sound of the azaan echoed loudly in all the rooms within the dense network of tottering houses. Murli was standing near the crumbling parapet on the rooftop, looking at flocks of kite-hawks and crows in the sky. Occasionally, he would put the mouth organ to his lips but then forget to play it. Down below in the street, the crowd of customers was getting bigger and bigger. He spat and plunged his fingers into his dense hair.

Mor Bibi, the whore from Murshidabad, was placing a soot mark on her son's forehead to ward off evil spirits.

'Why don't you get married, Murli?' she asked.

'Who will marry me, Mor Bibi?'

'Who won't?'

'What sort of a reply is this?' Murli said, staring into the depths of the sky where the clouds were stained with a rosy hue. 'Wonder if any good will come of that,' he said to himself and went down the stairs and stepped into the lane where a bitch was moaning in labour. Some kids had formed a circle around it and were watching silently.

'Get away! Go to your homes,' he yelled at the kids and chased them away. He then raced to Chuna Gali as fast as he could. Sia did not show any surprise when she saw him.

'Sia, you have to stop your whoring,' Murli said. 'I intend to marry you.'

'And look, I am dying to marry you.'

'In any case, you have to stop this racket. You can't go around spreading disease.'

'Who told you I am sick? And who will feed us?' Sia said with a smile. 'Sia Dullari's pimp?'

'Yes,' Murli said. 'I will raise your kids. Get you tested.'

For a second or two, Sia said nothing.

Then as if she had become hysterical, she screamed, 'Get away from me! I don't want to set eyes on you! Go away! Go away! Go away!'

In her madness, she didn't see the gleam of the dagger that Murli held in his right hand.

~

The news of Murli Naskar's insanity spread like wildfire all over Sonagachi. Mehndi Lakshmi had picked up the newly born pups and was busy taking care of them. When she heard about what had happened, she ran to him but he refused to recognize her. A few uniformed policemen came after him because he had been accused of murdering Sia Dullari in Chuna Gali. The cops caught him with the help of some other pimps but after some months he was back. He made a shelter for himself under the balcony of Mehndi Lakshmi's house. With his long matted hair and unkempt beard, Murli Naskar had the visage of someone who was about to be crucified.

Most of the time, he sat with his back to the wall and yelled at those who walked by: 'Stay away from it. Stay away from it. It is full of stinging scorpions.'

Mehndi sent all his books to him in the hope that they would help him recover his memory. But the books stayed where they were. He never even opened them. Then, one day he collected them and flung into an open drain.

'Stay away from them,' he said to a beggar who was shitting on the edge of the drain and watching him curiously with his one good eye. 'These aren't good for you. They are full of wriggling scorpions.'

~

Inside the church, the spirits of the dead were running for the exit.

Girja Shankar held up a hand to stop them. 'It is Sia,' he said. 'Stay away, all of you.' But the spirits kept leaving.

The ghost of Sia Dullari was walking on top of a narrow wall with her hair all spread around her. 'Look at me,' she said. 'See what I have learned.'

She was naked and beautiful and had green eyes and milk was oozing from her breasts and she refused to recognize Girja. Girja tried to scratch out her eyes with his long fingernails.

'Why?' Sia protested.

But Girja had already plucked out one eye. The other eye showed no concern and kept winking at him.

'Why did you leave my children?'

'They are happier without us,' Sia's spirit responded. 'And Murli has committed suicide. He is probably on the roof at this moment.'

All the spirits hastened to the roof. The sky was full of stars and Murli was bent over a book near a parapet in their light.

He saw them and snorted contemptuously and gestured towards the city which was bathed in the dim starlight.

'Doesn't this city make you want to vomit?'

'What about you?' the spirits asked.

'Shut up!' Murli said and took out a mouth organ and began to play. The sound spread over the brightly lit roads of the city like some invisible ghost. But people, busy with their daily chores, paid no attention. They had more important matters to attend to.

Translated from the Urdu by Javaid Qazi

MARKET PRICE

Nabendu Ghosh

'Goodness gracious me! What a scare you gave me!' Chhaya turned her face away in simulated anger.

'What's there to be scared of?' Balram smiled. 'I walked in to see you sitting quietly by the stove, lost in thought. All I did was ask, "What's bothering you?"—albeit in a fabricated baritone. Is that all it takes to scare you? You jumped out of your skin, almost dropped the vessel on the stove. What a courageous woman I'm living with!'

'Okay, I'm a coward. Won't you be scared if, in an unknown city, you hear a strange voice speaking in a false manner?' Chhaya sat down next to the clay stove. This time she was truly put out.

The glow from the dying embers of the stove turned her face red. Beads of perspiration gathered on her forehead. They added to the natural appeal she held for Balram. He smiled as he bent forward to place before her the groceries he'd got from the market.

'All right, it's my fault. But don't look the other way, will you?' Balram pleaded. Chhaya didn't speak a word. 'Oh Chhayarani—'

Chhaya turned her face further away.

Balram moved closer to her and started reciting lines from a play:

'Why be petulant, darling? Why this pout?
Why the film of tears in your eyes?
Why this frozen eloquence?
Why penalize my small offence
With rigid rejection?'

Chhaya could no longer retain her stern composure—she dissolved into peals of laughter. 'Jatra again! Oh dear—'

'But you have to admit I have good taste. Here's the entire market at your feet: rohu, potatoes, tomatoes, cucumber, beans, chillies, lemon—'

'Enough! I can see for myself. You've ensured that you are made permanent in this role of marketing manager.'

'Let me assure you, my lady, even if I lose this job I won't let go of such a pretty mistress!'

'My god! What a shameless bazaar sarkar I have on my staff,' Chhaya giggled.

'Honestly, my knuckles are aching from carrying your shopping bag,' Balram cribbed as he stretched out on the cot. 'Can't do without a cup of tea, Chhayarani!'

'Of course! I'll get it right away.' Chhaya smiled. 'But can we finish accounting first?'

In a half-lying posture, Balram lit a cigarette. 'Prices have gone up,' he said, blowing smoke. 'Potatoes—eight annas, six annas for the cauliflower, fish is three rupees fifty paisa a kilo, rice is twenty-seven rupees a quintal...'

'Oh god! Spiralling up with each passing day!'

'Sure it will. Aren't we a "developing" nation?'

'Developing nation? How?'

'Economics is just a notch above your head, pretty woman. Development means more money in people's pockets, and more money means higher prices—'

'Maybe.' Chhaya shrugged. 'But if prices go up at this rate, human life will become dirt cheap—'

'So what if it gets cheaper? Development is important. Therein lies the greatness of our nation—it doesn't lose sleep over the value of a few expendable men.'

'Get lost! Your words don't make any sense to me.'

'Why bother! There's enough time left for you to digest economics. For now, a fine cup of tea for me will suffice, beauty.'

Wearing an insincere frown, Chhaya got busy with the kettle. Then she sorted out the vegetables and washed the fish fillets. A child's cry wafted in from the next door. A Hindi film song was playing somewhere in the lane. A couple of sparrows had turned her window sill into their playground.

'These fillets—how much are they, 250 grams?' Chhaya inquired.

Balram laughed aloud. 'That's what I told the fishmonger. "Be kind—instead of charging me for half a kilo tell me this is only 250 gms." But she just didn't agree—'

'Oh, so you've branded me a fishmonger!' Chhaya chuckled. Then turning serious, she said, 'But in earnest, how will people survive? My mother used to say, after her marriage, when she first came to my father's village—you do remember, don't you?—this was Gorajapur in Jessore district—a two-seer rohu would cost three, four annas. If that wasn't to your liking, just lower a net into the pond and haul a catch of three or four fish. Choose one, and let the others go...'

Balram leaned on a pillow and fixed Chhaya with his gaze. She had already finished her bath. Her tresses, still wet, were tied in a loose knot at the end. A red line of alta added grace to her feet. Her longish, berry-shaped face wasn't exactly perfect. Nevertheless, it had something very appealing about it. Her well-formed body, too, was an intoxicant. Poor lady, Balram let out a deep sigh and focused on her words. This very Chhaya was initially so tongue-tied! And now, her happiness spilled over in words. Like one step leading on to another, one thought lead her on to another chain of thoughts, and then on to something else altogether.

'Did I tell you? This happened when the daughter of Bhattacharjee, the village priest, was to be married off. He came and requested my grandpa to fish out a one-mone rohu from the pond. The old man just gifted him that fish. Some days back I ran into a grandson of that same daughter of Bhattacharjee. He narrated the incident to me. In the course of our conversation he said...'

'Chhaya—'

'What?'

'The kettle's whistling away.'

'Oh god, yes!' Chhaya hurried to make the tea, handed the cup to Balram and went back to her cooking.

Balram cast a glance around the room. A single room with an adjoining verandah: even in this narrow lane of Kashi it cost twenty rupees a month by way of rent. Quite an ordinary room but

Chhaya's magic touch had transformed it into a tiny haven of peace. It had been about five months since they had set up this establishment, but already it held every household item one would need. A wooden charpoy, a cane chair, two moras, mattress, pillows, mosquito net, cooking utensils, cups, saucers, glasses— nothing was lacking.

Balram's gaze returned to Chhaya. Again she was lost in her own thoughts. 'What are you thinking of, Chhayarani?'

A wan smile flitted over her face. 'Nothing…' She turned her face away from him.

'That's a lie. Thinking of home, are you?'

'No, no.'

'Come here.'

Chhaya smiled as she moved up to Balram.

'Tell me…'

Chhaya sat down next to him.

'Come closer.'

'No, I must return to my cooking.'

'Yes, I know that, but tell me what's on your mind.'

'Nothing special, I was only thinking that all we need now is a job for you. We could then move elsewhere. This neighbourhood isn't very homely.'

'Why? Has anyone made any unseemly remark?'

'No, why should they? But the other day that lady from No. 4 commented, "The two of you lovebirds make me green with envy."'

Balram smiled. 'What's bad about that?'

Chhaya pulled a face. 'It's so dark, you don't even get a glimpse of the sky.'

'Poor soul,' Balram thought to himself. 'The caged bird now wants a touch of the sky once again.'

'All right,' he spoke aloud, 'we'll move house.'

Chhaya suddenly placed her head on his chest and said, 'But when will you get to know about the job? It's been a week since…'

A cloud fell over Balram's face. He thought for a while before replying, 'We must wait for another fortnight. You don't land jobs overnight.'

'That's very true,' Chhaya immediately responded. 'Now we are provided for about a month, and still have a hundred and fifty rupees, right?'

Balram nodded his head.

'Oh god! That burnt smell...' Chhaya jumped up and rushed towards the stove, picked up the ladle and stirred the vegetables in the pan. 'You...make me forget everything...' she kept stirring. After a while she again looked towards Balram. He was quietly lying on the cot.

'Are you sleeping?'

'Na-ah,' Balram opened his eyes.

'Then? Lost in thought?' Chhaya walked up to the bed and sat near his feet.

'Again you've moved away from the stove? Want to serve cinders for lunch?'

'Oh dear, the gentleman is upset, I can see.' She tickled him under his feet. 'Please don't be in a rage, my lord!'

Balram didn't smile.

Chhaya frowned as she inched closer to him. 'Will you swear upon me and tell me—'

'Tell you what?'

'What's bothering you?'

'Must you know everything?'

'Yes, I must.'

'No—'

'I must—or else...'

At this Balram turned to face Chhaya. 'It's this job I met those people about last week.'

'What about it?'

'They're demanding a thousand rupees for it. That's essentially to soften the head clerk. The job's not mine yet because I haven't come up with the money. Otherwise I would've got the job that very day.'

'A thousand rupees!' Chhaya's face lost its colour. 'And if you can't pay the amount?'

'No job then. It'll go to one of the others waiting with the money. I've sought a fortnight's time. Let me see what I can do.'

'Where will you arrange it from?'

'Don't know.' Balram sat up. 'Might have to steal or loot somebody.'

'Don't talk rubbish!' Chhaya raised her voice.

A hush fell upon the tiny room. Outside, a cow rushed down the gully. 'Run, run,' some coarse voices chased the cow. The sparrows perched on the window hadn't stopped chirping.

'Don't worry,' Chhaya said soothingly.

'What should I do then?' Balram's lips curved in a crooked smile.

'I still have my necklace, a pair of bangles, earrings and the wedding ring,' Chhaya spoke softly. 'Let's go and sell them.'

'What are you saying, Chhaya?'

'Precisely what I ought to. You get me a new set once you get the job. How can I be happy until I flaunt some jewellery gifted by you?'

'Just shut up! Don't ever speak such words, Chhaya, there's no question of selling your stree dhan,' Balram turned his face away putting an end to the conversation.

Chhaya had no more words to offer. She knew Balram better than to speak when he was upset. But why couldn't he understand? They simply couldn't carry on without a job. Chhaya broke into tears. Her muffled cry drew Balram's attention. 'What's the matter?'

Chhaya looked away.

Balram moved up to her. 'Don't cry, Chhaya.'

'Don't speak with me!'

'Why don't you let me bear the burden of worry?'

'Is your problem different from mine? Have you thought about how to keep the kitchen fire going without a salary? Those pieces of gold won't fill my belly—' Chhaya succumbed to a fresh round of tears.

'Arre...there she goes again.' This time Balram started singing out his plea:

'Don't, dearest, don't
Shed any more tears—
They'll cause a flood
That might sink my heart...
Creation, even.
Your tears, dearest of mine,
Aren't raindrops
They're liquid fire...'

Chhaya smiled through her tears. Almost as if the sun broke through rain clouds.

'Get lost! Your dramatics only make me angry.'

'Why? Is it bad to be an actor?'

'You first answer me—'

'Answer what?'

'As if you don't know! I'm talking about the jewellery.'

'Look here, Chhaya—'

'No, I'll start banging my head against the wall. This job is a must for us.'

'As you wish, then—' Balram again turned his face away.

At once Chhaya spread out her arms to hold Balram in an embrace. 'My precious!'

'But Chhaya,' Balram wiped the tears off her cheeks.

Unhesitatingly, Chhaya shut him off with a kiss. 'No more ifs and buts,' she added busily. 'This very afternoon the two of us will go out. We'll sell off the jewellery so that you can confirm the job tomorrow itself. Is that clear?' Chhaya didn't give Balram a chance to react. 'Not a word more,' she said firmly. 'After selling off the gold we will go on a tour of the town. Then we'll go for a movie. Tonight we'll dine out. I won't listen to any objection. We'll do as I tell you. Now hurry up and finish your bath...quick!'

Like an obedient child, Balram stood up. He surrendered himself completely to Chhaya's whims. A strange game was

signalled by the shut door in this sunless bylane of Kashi. The
name of the game was love: when Balram came out of his bath,
Chhaya took it upon herself to brush his hair. When they sat
down to lunch, one fed the other. Instead of a siesta, Balram chose
to entertain Chhaya with choicest dialogues from the Jatras he'd
watched or acted in, and she evinced her delight by repeatedly
burying her face in his chest.

The housewife next door may've been listening in. She
may've heard some of the lines but she surely couldn't witness this
with her own eyes. The only voyeurs who could not be barred out
of the door or window were the sparrows—they kept up their
chirpy commentary even as they got busy trying to build a love
nest of their own in one corner of the air-vent high above the
window.

As soon as the lazy afternoon rolled into evening, Chhaya
commanded Balram to get dressed. She, too, dressed up for the
outing. There was admiration for each other in their gaze. Chhaya
sat on the floor to open her trunk and fished out her jewellery box.
She placed it in a canvas bag and covered it with a scarf. She
stepped out of their quarters, locked the door and strode up to
keep pace with Balram.

'Why go around the market with so much gold?' Balram tried
to protest.

'Shhh! Just walk with me in silence.'

'Okay, thy wish…' Balram smiled.

When Chhaya was locking up her quarters, the sickly seven-
year-old boy next door called out, 'Maa!'

'What's it?' a rough voice floated out from inside.

'Come and take a look!'

'Quick!' Chhaya whispered. 'In no time she'll be at the door.'
Before she could step into the lane, the mother of five was at the
door. In long strides Chhaya and Balram covered the distance up
to the main road. 'Oof,' Chhaya heaved a sigh of relief, 'there she
was before one could say "presto". Are we some kind of museum
piece?'

'Let them ogle—what's the harm?' Balram was willing to be charitable.

'Never—' Chhaya retorted. 'She's such a jealous female—she can't bear to see me happy.'

They were on the main road now. The late-January sun was already setting in the horizon. They hailed a tonga and arrived at the market. A couple of hours later, with eleven hundred rupees in their pocket, they sat down on the wooden bench of a tea-stall and ordered a tea each.

'Don't grieve over the jewellery,' Chhaya tried to console Balram. 'We'll get new ones made.'

They finished their tea and made their way to a Hollywood movie. They had dinner in a nice hotel. When they returned to their room at night, the clock struck ten.

The sound of the door opening automated the seven-year-old to whine: 'Maa, come sharp! They're back.'

'Quick!' Chhaya hurried Balram indoors. 'Hasten up.'

Before she could step inside, Lady Nextdoor was back at her watch. 'Witch!' Chhaya hissed, leaning against the wall.

'Chhee! Shame on you—' Balram didn't sound too pleased.

The minute he lit a matchstick to light up the lamp, Chhaya blew it off.

'What's wrong with you?'

'Shhh! I want to say something to you.'

'Sure—but do we need the darkness for that?'

'Yes, I can't say what I want to tell you except in the dark. Come closer to me. Where's your ear?' she groped in the dark.

Balram could feel her feverish breath as she whispered into his ears. Then she peacefully rested her head on his shoulder.

'Let go of me. I must light the lamp,' he wriggled.

'No. Why aren't you saying something?'

'I will. Let me first light the lamp, sweetie—'

As soon as Chhaya let go of him, Balram lit the lamp. Chhaya went and sat down on the bed. Balram walked up to her and held her in a fixed gaze. A smile kept playing on his lips.

'Don't—look—that way. I feel shy—embarrassed.'
'Chhayarani…'
'Yes?'

'You're the hue that colours spring,
The rainbow ribbon for the clouds
You put to shame the full moon
Oh lotus-bodied.
My heart quivers every time
My eyes stray to your face.'

'Ummm,' Chhaya gurgled.
'What's it?' Balram was puzzled.
'Acting like the hero of the film we saw today, aren't you?'
'Of course. I'll caress you all night.'
Chhaya moved a lock of hair from Balram's forehead. Peering
into his eyes, she cooed—'I'm so happy today! Just wrap up the
job, then we can move to another mohalla. But I'm warning you, it
must have two bedrooms. You're looking at a salary of two hundred
and fifty a month. Surely we can afford thirty rupees for a two-
room setup. Thirty for room rent, a hundred and fifty for household
expenses, another ten to twenty rupees for the new member who'll
join us… Even so, a saving of forty to fifty rupees shouldn't be
difficult, right? What do you say, can't we?'
Balram nodded his assent. 'Yes, we can… Rather, we'll have to.
Shit!'
'What?'
'Must rush rightaway. I forgot to pick up cigarettes from the
paan shop. I'll get it from the one at the end of this lane…' Balram
opened the door and went out humming to himself.
Chhaya closed the door after him. On the verge of changing
into her night clothes, she stopped before the mirror. No, she
won't change: she'll spend this magical night in this cheerful
Santipuri sari. Tonight is for celebrating. Ishh! She should have
picked up some flowers. 'Forgetful, you!' she said to her reflection
in the mirror. Never mind: she has a bottle of French perfume—

she'll spray some of that on herself. Even better—she'll spray some on Balram too.

Chhaya succumbed to day-dreaming as she lay waiting for Balram. Could she imagine such happiness even a few months ago?

Chhaya had accompanied her mother when she made her way to Calcutta after the Partition. She was married into a decently middle-class family. Her husband had a steady job in a factory nearby. But before she could notch up two years of married life, her husband died of small-pox. Her mother couldn't reconcile herself to Chhaya's widowhood: she too, bought a ticket to heaven. With the little treasure trove left by her mother and her husband, and the uninhibited appeal of her uncontrollable youth, she was reduced to a slave in her brother-in-law's household. An aunt-in-law was her worst enemy. A couple of years down, her brother-in-law audaciously turned down every marriage proposal and started eyeing her greedily. Every time he spoke to her, his words were lined with double entendre. Initially, Chhaya ignored his overtures. When she openly objected to his advances, her aunt-in-law uttered a single word: 'Whore!'

At this juncture a Jatra group put up a performance in their para. *Kurukshetra*—the play was titled. Chhaya watched Balram enact the role of Arjun. She was charmed. She was not oblivious to all that has been drilled into every Hindu widow down the centuries—but why had the words lost their edge? From the neighbourhood gossip Chhaya gleaned that Balram lived close by and, at that point of time, was unemployed.

One day she ran into Balram. Noting the deep curiosity in her eyes, Balram followed her to her doorstep. Then on, every single afternoon, when the aunt-in-law was enjoying her siesta and the brother-in-law was away at work, Chhaya would stand at her window—and find Balram keeping a watch. At first, Chhaya would shut the window. Later, she would leave it open.

One afternoon, from his post outside her window, Balram smiled at her. Another day, Chhaya smiled back. Some days later, on the pretext of going to the Kalighat temple, Chhaya met him at Maidan. They spoke and they spoke. After listening to her story, he proposed marriage. He urged her to elope with him. After a lot of conflict, and when she could no longer ward off her greedy brother-in-law's overtures, she resolved to join Balram. Yes, by now she too was feverishly anticipating the hour of their union. So one afternoon, when she stepped out ostensibly to buy some household item, she took with her a bag containing some saris and her jewellery.

Once they arrived in Kashi, they spent a month in a hotel. In the meantime they rented this place and moved in. They also quietly exchanged garlands in front of some gods. A local Brahmin Balram had arranged was the sole witness to this marriage.

Six months had elapsed since that day. Every effort to get a job that has so far eluded them will come to fruition now. Oh Lord Vishwanath of Kashi, please take mercy on us! Since she met Balram, Chhaya has found a new meaning in life. Her Balram is Charm personified. But why is he taking so long to buy a cigarette? Must have struck up an adda with some stranger at the paan shop. Don't we know how he loves to chat with his friends!

Whose footfall was that in the lane? Chhaya peeped out of the door. No, it isn't him. Chhaya ruminated for a while, then put the latch on the door. Let him come back—she'll teach him a lesson. She'll simply keep him waiting at the door. Balram will have to play out the 'Maan Bhanjan' sequence in the Radha-Krishna Jatra where He pleads guilty to Her and urges Her to relent and make love to Him.

Chhaya smiled to herself. She brought out the bottle of perfume from her chest. The tiny room was redolent with the heady scent that percolated into her consciousness and piqued her desire for his tight embrace. She sharpened the enticement in her eyes with a fresh coat of kajal. Balram doesn't quite know the magnetic power of her sexuality...

~

At that very moment Balram is at the Kashi station. He's bought a ticket to Kolkata, looked around him to check if he recognized anyone, then lit a cigarette. Walking towards platform number four in order to board the last train to Mughalsarai, he kept planning his next move. Kolkata would be the best place to hide in. It's easy to be anonymous amidst hundreds of thousands. He felt the inner pocket of his coat. Aah, the sweet sensation of currency notes! Eleven hundred rupees, almost. Enough to sustain him for the next few months. By then he would work out a new arrangement. Given the hard times we're going through, it was impossible to carry on an affair for longer than six months. The exchange of garlands? Huh! A mere ritual, a game of sorts, nothing more.

But Balram isn't heartless. He's left Chhaya with nearly a hundred and fifty rupees—and an enviable storehouse of sexuality. Surely her youth won't evaporate overnight, like camphor. Besides, he's leaving her in Kashi, the city of Lord Shiva. It's a holy city where thousands descend every single day for pilgrimage. The complex network of narrow dingy lanes...

Balram comes to a halt on platform number four. The signal is down, emitting a green light made hazy by the misty winter. Letting out a mouthful of smoke that lost its way in the darkness of the January night, Balram lets out a deep sigh. Poor Chhaya! Such a sweet soul, she was. And so pretty. He was sorry to abandon the curious warmth of her firm, youthful body. His only consolation is that she'll stay on in his memories. The memories of intimate nights and playful days.

And Chhaya, too, won't easily forget him. The memory of Teenkari Das, a.k.a Balram Chowdhury who charmed her as Arjun, will grow day by day inside her womb. It will continue to grow after it comes out of her womb. It will continue to grow and gnaw at her soul until her last breath. No, Chhaya will not forget Balram, even if he forgets her.

Translated from the Bangla by Ratnottama Sengupta

COMING?

Khurshid Akram

'Coming?'

The word was familiar to me. I recognized the voice. As the rosy sunset faded into a smoky evening, the water of the Hooghly River took on the colour of molten copper. Before me, the Howrah Bridge, behind me the Hooghly Bridge, looking like a slender eel, and a clear sky, a pleasant breeze. After many years, I was here, experiencing this breeze again with pleasure. Over the past eight years, not a single evening had given me the peacefulness of this atmosphere, this breeze. Returning to Calcutta now after many years, I was reminded of how often I would get nostalgic for just this breeze. No one was with me right then. No friend or companion. They were all busy.

But I am not alone; I am never alone in this city. The very air of this town recognizes me. I am a part of the dust and debris of this place. I am intimate with the pathways of this town. At any time, at any place, I feel a sense of belonging here. With every object, I feel a sort of kinship. I enter a lane of Shyam Bazaar for the first time. But at first sight, it seems to me that it is the same as I remember. On seeing a bus conductor in Muttya Burj, I think I have seen him somewhere. Is there anything that I am unfamiliar with? I can look at the rear of a double-decker bus and tell you whether it is going to Khizrpur or Gol Park. If a function is taking place in Rabindra Sadan, I can tell you whether the people gathered there have come to see a theatrical production or an exhibition of paintings.

All of Calcutta is in the palm of my hand. In fact, one could say that the city is like the lines of my hand. I have stayed away for the last eight years. But what of that? I recognize the birds of this city, I know its every sound. With eyes closed I can tell whether this noisy crowd of spectators is in the Mohan Bagan ground or the Mohammedan ground. All the comings and goings, all the hullaballoo, all the noises, every outburst is well known to me. This word, 'Coming?', that I heard just now, I have heard it countless times before. In Calcutta square; behind Victoria; above the Metro tram; in Curzon Park; in the shadow of the wall of Governor's House; wherever city administrators have not provided adequate street-lighting. Wherever there was darkness, I have heard this sound, like the whirring of cockroaches. At the young age of nineteen, when I first heard this word, how scared I was! The way children are disgusted or frightened by the sight of a cockroach. I wonder why they are so fearful.

Hey! What's this? A lot of people are milling about. Prostitutes are plying their trade quite openly. Run away from here, run as fast as you can. What if someone recognizes you? I left the darkness and ran towards the light, but even then my anxiety did not leave me. In front of me, the shops of Grand Arcade were bathed in light. There were hordes of people around. But I felt as though I were completely alone. Even in these brightly lit surroundings, I felt insecure, as though I had lost my physical self in the darkness. Quickly, I entered a restaurant and downed a couple of glasses of water. Bring me more water, fellow, my throat is bone dry.

Afterwards, it all changed. I got older and the city taught me many things. For instance, that I should not be afraid of such things. They are ordinary matters. A shortcut runs through the middle of this dark area. People have worn away a footpath over this grass. In the darkness, the path glimmers dimly. As soon as you step on to this pathway, it leads you on, showing you the way, as it were. Anyone who wants to can follow it. No harm in that. But on either side of this path is darkness. And from the darkness, the word: 'Coming?'

How I laughed on hearing this word! Was this what had frightened me so much? There is nothing to it! When a fearless child picks up a cockroach by its antennae and the other children say, hey, there is no reason to be afraid of this, it can't do anything, it doesn't bite, it doesn't sting. Dangling in the air, the cockroach just wants to get away. When it is let go, it quickly makes for some dark corner and hides. Free at last!

By now I had become quite bold. Whenever we would feel like taking an idle walk with friends, we would end up in the darkness.

'Want to come?'

'Want to sit?'

'Sure, I'll sit. Listen, come here. How old are you?'

'You want to marry me? Why do you want to know my age? If you want to sit, then come along.'

'We'll see. Come, give us a sweet kiss.'

'Come with me and we can kiss.'

'Okay. But why is your back dripping with sweat?'

'Hey! Get your hands off me. You can't touch me without paying in advance.'

'Okay, okay, tell me how much do you want? If you won't tell me how old you are, at least tell me your rate.'

'Fifteen rupees for each guy.'

'Hell! So much money at your age? How about three rupees for each one?'

'Go fuck your mother for three rupees! Bastards! I'm trying to make a living here and these sons-of-whores are clowning around.' She kept hurling abuse. We laughed and laughed until our stomachs ached.

Once again, I stopped in my tracks when I heard the familiar words. In front of Outram Wharf, on the pavement next to the open space in front of Fort William, those words are pretty normal. I stood still and my eyes met the gaze of a young girl standing behind a tree. She looked fifteen or sixteen. Nearby were other trees, and behind each tree...

Across the sky, flocks of birds were returning to their roosts. Near the Circular train stop, office workers were waiting to make their homeward journey. Exactly at this moment, when the workday business of the city was being wound up, another class of workers was setting up shop.

In the darkness.

'Coming?'

I felt bad when I saw this underage girl. Who had brought her to this darkness? I thought I should ask her. 'Mother, at this glorious age, who has brought you to this darkness? Go, go back to your house. All this is wicked.' Doesn't she know evil? If she has come to this spot, she must know what is good and what is bad. Had she been home, her father might have said to her: 'It is getting dark. Switch on the light.' Had she been home, she would know only good. At her age, all girls know the sweet taste of goodness. But if she is here, then she most certainly knows what wickedness is. As I pondered this, it occurred to me that I should ask her: 'Mother, you've come to know evil, but what is the sweetness of good like? Do you remember its taste?'

I turned away without saying anything. The slightest turn was difficult. After I had taken a few steps, I felt as though the breeze had stopped blowing and breathing had become painful. My lungs are not so weak that just a few steps can make me breathless. I'm not that old. I can run, touch Howrah Bridge, and return again in a single breath. The way water is held behind a barrage, the wind seemed to be held back just like that. Suddenly, something went by, touching my hair. It was as though the restless wind was eager to kiss my face, anxious to enter my chest. I took a powerful breath. Ah! The evening air of Calcutta. This breeze, this evening, this river—it makes me nostalgic.

It feels good to walk. After eight years I am walking on this path again. It's easy. Walking from the house to the office, from the office to the house, I don't have to think. I climb the stairs to my house with ease. I won't have to ask anyone, 'Is this the way to Akashvani offices, sir?' The floodlights of Eden Garden stadium had turned night into day. A day-and-night cricket match was being played. The one-hundredth championship of the Bengal Cricket Association. I heard that the Indian batsmen were thrashing the South African bowlers. This is in the semi-finals. Then who could beat the Indian team in the finals, besides Pakistan? But they aren't in this tournament. Even if they had been, the screams of the spectators would have broken Imran Khan's spine. Don't they know these playing grounds are in Calcutta? A roar of approval rose from the spectators. This has to be a sixer. We want victory. India's victory. Long live India.

Here, the Mohan Bagan club is lit up with a dazzle of lights all over. This year there has been no end to the victories achieved by Mohan Bagan. They were champions, but then they won the shield. After that the DCM Cup, then the Russian Cup and also the Federation Cup. This meant that for one year Mohan Bagan was the football champion of India. Long live Mohan Bagan! This is Calcutta's victory over all Indian football teams. One ought to say this is Bengal's victory. Long live Bengal!

Akashvani building, Governor's House, the Assembly chambers, the thirty-foot statue of Netaji, all were aglow with light. Wherever the bus stops or halts. By this I mean at the regular stops and also at the traffic lights. At these places people waited for buses to take them home. This is one of Calcutta's wonders. The drivers here don't move according to traffic regulations. The people here don't think of the main road as anything more than a lane in any neighbourhood. It is such a busy road, but no one stops. Anyone who has to cross the street signals oncoming cars with his hands and crosses over. As if it were the driver's responsibility to watch out for pedestrians. A wonder, yes, but this is also the custom of Calcutta. This won't be seen in any other big city. Blessed Calcutta!

At the traffic lights where Reed Road turns away from Assembly House, many people wait for buses. Light falls on their faces, on their clothes, on their feet. I'm just loitering. This gleaming road, this brightness, and spectators screaming at every run in the last overs of the inning: many people are fated to experience this sort of happiness in life. Many people have seen it. The glow of the thousands of bulbs that has flooded the stadium, making night into day, would also reveal a needle in the nearby streets. Many people have seen this. This is my Calcutta. Why shouldn't my chest swell with pride? When my chest swelled with pride, many odd ideas came to mind. For instance, I thought I would go and see Reed Road. Does Calcutta's most beautiful road still retain its dreamy beauty? I've seen Delhi's Rajpath Road, and Bombay's

Marine Drive. When compared with these, Reed Road is perhaps even more impressive.

When I got near the crowd, I stopped in my tracks. Are all these people, these women, waiting for a bus? No. One, two, three, four, five—they are not waiting for a bus. They are simply waiting. In spite of the roar of traffic, in spite of the fact that they do not speak, I hear the quavering sound of their voices: 'Coming?' 'You want to sit?'

Their lips do not move but under the bright lights their eyes are speaking.

'Coming?'

When I was a kid, on blisteringly hot afternoons, I would take a shiny mirror and flash it at the bats hiding in the hollow bamboos that supported a thatched roof, forcing the bats to take flight. Seeing them flap around blindly in the bright light of day, I would clap my hands gleefully till they glowed red. In exactly the same way, the bat hidden within my darkness began to flutter and flap when those women turned their bright eyes upon me. Mercifully, amongst all the people gathered there, not one has the power to see this bat, otherwise they would clap their hands and laugh at me. The business that was conducted in darkness is now being carried on under bright lights. Can anyone contradict me?

The women are simply waiting for buses. They are housewives, waiting for a bus. If anyone can prove that I am a liar, I will quit my job and sit in front of Kali Ghat temple or Maula Aziz Ali's tomb with a begging bowl. I recognize them. I know them well. Hey, where's the difficulty? If I didn't recognize them, I too, would have assumed they were housewives, exactly what all the others believe. They comb out their hair and put it up most modestly. They take up the loose ends of their sarees, gather them around their hips and throw them over their left shoulders in the exact manner in which all Bengali women wear their sarees. There is no difference between them and housewives. The only difference is that housewives are actually waiting for buses, but these women await something else.

How come they are standing here? Don't they feel ashamed under these bright lights? Is there no dark zone left in the world? I felt like telling them, let the lights go out. It was as if they had come to know what was in my heart. They said: 'Listen, today this place is all lit up. It isn't like this normally. Had you come a couple of days ago, you would have found that this place was not so brightly lit and if you come a couple of days from now you will not find it brightly lit either. These flood-lights are a vanity of the rich folk. This is our permanent place. Where else could we go, if we were to leave this spot?'

Stay where you are, ladies, stay where you are—you misunderstood me. All I wanted to say was that your business ought be conducted in darkness, not under bright lights. In another few days will you come here and stand stark naked? Don't you have any sense of modesty, any decency? Don't you have any regard for the institutions for the advancement of Bengali women?

We do, sir. We feel very embarrassed. Come and see us in our homes. We are also women. But out of twenty-four hours, if we don't spend four hours in this business then we won't even get a morsel of stale bread to eat. In these four hours we are not ashamed of darkness or of light. Nor do we discriminate between a lad, a youngster, a mature fellow or an old dodderer. Nor do we concern ourselves with the One who sits above.

Where was my respectability? Where was the Reed Road of my dreams? I felt as though I could not see anything any more. All I wanted to do was to cross the road. Then, having crossed this one, cross another. Having crossed it, across the tram line, I saw the statue of Mahatma Gandhi. The area was quite well-lit. The statue was covered with bird-shit from head to toe. I jumped over the railing and went in. I had walked a great distance. I had walked an exceedingly long way. I had no other choice except to sit down. Many years ago, I had sat here with four friends and raised quite a rackus.

The four of us had pooled our money and bought a new Zenit camera. This goes back to the days when the Zenit camera carried the 'Made in USSR' stamp. We put a new roll of film in the camera and set forth on the first day of January to take photographs of the heart of our Calcutta: I mean the most important sites of Dharamtala. We shot different types of photographs from different angles. That day we took many photos of Mahatma Gandhi's statue. In one, of the Chirji International Center, the Tata building could be seen in the background. Another one had the Eden Gardens stadium behind. Anyone unfamiliar with it can be shown this Eden. Behind it the Hooghly River, and beyond it the Howrah Bridge. Across the bridge was the Howrah station. You can catch a train from the station and go to Bihar. Then stop in Bihar and visit Jhumri Talya. Another trick photo made it look as though I had one hand on Mahatma Gandhi's shoulder and another on his walking stick. One could interpret this photo to mean that he would never walk alone. I am ready to walk with him. The others were very impressed by this photograph.

'Hey, buddy, what technique did you use in taking this photo?'

'Don't ask me. Apart from my skill as a photographer, there is this camera. It's Russian, not a cheap toy. It was purchased in Fancy Market—totally genuine.'

We continued to show this photo to everyone for a long time. I have no idea who has this photo now, I don't have it; I very much doubt it anyway. At certain times, some objects are extremely precious, but later you don't have space for them. Love letters, for instance.

As I got up from there, I decided to head for a restaurant on Park Street, freshen up and have a cup of coffee. So that's what I did. If I met someone, then maybe I'd head to a bar. Ahead of me was a long, empty path. At the far end, the turning for Park Street with very few people on the pavement. The road packed with cars. I was walking slowly. I was in no hurry. I was like a tourist in my own city. I had only gone a few feet when I noticed an elderly woman coming towards me. She must have been a hundred yards or so away from me. I got the feeling that she wasn't in any hurry either. She didn't have to keep to any important appointment. Like me.

The cool evening air. Dark clouds starting to hide the sky: this is Calcutta. When will the moon rise? When will the clouds part? I had no idea. It is possible that in a little while the breeze will stop. Then it will feel as though you are in a pressure cooker. It seemed to me that the woman was looking in my direction. Perhaps, but only casually. It is possible that precisely at this hour, her son was also wandering about the city, like me. Did thoughts like these make her focus on me? No. She was staring at me. With eyes full of hope. What sort of hope? She didn't look like a vagrant. Got it. Now she will come close to me. She will pretend to cry and say, 'Son, my husband is in the hospital. He has blood cancer. Help me pay for his treatment. I am not asking for alms. My son, please help me. May you gain an even higher position in your career, may your wife and children always enjoy good health.'

If not this, then she might say, 'Sir, the factory where my husband works has shut down due to a strike. The workers have been locked out. May God keep you safe, son, I have to marry off a daughter. The ceremony is next week. I'm a poor widow. Please help me. Or I will be dishonoured...'

I know. I know. All these con-games. I know them well. Since Calcutta came into existence, similar con-games have been played.

And people who a have bit too much of the mothering instinct and lack street smarts fall into these snares and reach into their pockets. They hope God will reward them for this virtuous act. The con-artist turns and laughs. You stupid man! You live in Calcutta? Then he salutes the sky with the money in his hand. God, had you not created idiots in this world, we would have starved to death. I've seen this and more, in this city. No matter. I've not forgotten. Let her come near me. I won't give her even a paisa. I don't expect any rewards for my good deeds and certainly not for this sort of good deed.

Between us now the distance is vastly reduced. From the way she looks, and judging from what she is wearing, she appears to be a typical lower-middle-class woman of Calcutta. So this means that my first impression of her was correct. Now she will come to me and begin her tale of woe. I won't give her a paisa, but I will most certainly hear her out. Let's see what sorts of stories these new con-artists are coming up with. Something fresh or the same old stuff. The same old tune that was being played when Adam and Eve walked the earth. My daughter, my honour...

She stopped in front of me. I waited calmly. Then, suddenly, I saw the gleam in her eyes and the bat hidden inside me started to flap and flutter.

I know those eyes. No, no, no, it is not like that. Not at her age, those eyes. The flash of those eyes kept on agitating the bat inside. Speak. Say something, woman. You want to say something, don't you? Do speak. You will not return empty-handed. My throat is bone dry. I cannot move my feet. For the love of God, start your tale of woe. I will definitely give you something. You will not go back empty-handed. Speak.

She came close and, gesturing towards the darkness on the right, said: 'Coming?'

Translated from the Urdu by Javaid Qazi

KALINDI

Manisha Kulshreshtha

In a crush of rickshaws, the one I am on, though slow, still crawls on. The crowd is so dense that it feels as if shoulders will rub themselves raw. The rickshaws are getting entangled with each other. The mass of people seems to have increased in number. I am returning to that alley which used to be so well-known because of the women who once lived there, and probably do even to this day. The women whose bodies were available to all and whose musk drew men from far and wide. Truck-drivers who brought goods into Mumbai; labourers from remote states who come to the city looking for employment, having left their families behind; workers; lower-middle-class men who have long lost interest in their wives—this street perennially swarms with unfamiliar faces. At any given hour, on any given day, these faces seem to be clamouring for something. Time holds no significance for them. These faces are always tormented with a hunger that can never be fulfilled.

The place I was headed to was a three-storey yellow building—somewhat dilapidated and with a crumbling roof. Unsavoury practices ran rampant in this area. Many families were involved in all sorts of activities—good and bad. Bootleggers, petty smugglers, drug-dealers, movie extras, bar- and orchestra- dancers. There were also women who were openly involved in the flesh trade. Those who quietly, away from the eyes of their children, and with the consent of their fathers or husbands, exchanged bodily pleasures for money with which to run their houses. Very little money; a mere pittance!

There was a series of these yellow buildings. In front of them were the pimps (mostly the husbands or lovers of these women) and the customers who were haggling over the women's bodies. The rooms were deep and dark, smelling damp and foul. The women, waiting for their customers. In the shadows cast by those yellow buildings, fear and terror quivered. Knives often flashed. Rapes were common too.

Sometimes I'm astonished to think how easily I could have become hooked on to drugs there. Or I could have become a plaything of some paedophilic man or woman. A sensual woman like Durga might have entrapped me or the lap games which David likes to play could have destroyed me. Like the other children of the chawl I, too, was easy prey.

Jamuna, who was well aware of what went on there, would use her sixth sense to warn me: don't sit with this person, don't talk to that one, dare you go to that one's room, dare you play with that one. Yet I still relive those frightening thoughts: if such a thing had happened, how would it have been like? I receive a pleasure-infused pain from such reminiscences. I scratch the itchy, innermost recesses of my being till I bleed. A sweet pain; a sweet pleasure.

The word 'customer' was a dreaded one for all children my age who lived on that street. A vampire who would throttle women. Once in his grasp, women would scream. A vampire who, if he didn't turn up, the rotis in the house would run out; and if the rotis didn't run out, there would be no vegetables or curry to eat them with. There were great legends associated with this term. The first time I heard the word, apart from me, no other child found anything odd about it. We were all playing in the balcony of the building at about half-past-ten one night when Chhotu Dalal came up to us and said, 'Bastards, is this the time to play? Even opium has no effect on you anymore. Go and sleep. This is the time for customers.'

I had never seen a customer. Once, returning from school I saw her quickly push a man from the room. I asked, 'Was he a customer?' She merely stared at me in astonishment and sank on to the bed without giving me food; I remained hungry till evening. I just sat flipping through a photo-album, kept in her trunk, and looked at the photographs which had yellowed with age. All the faces were strangers to me. In one picture was a group of women; one of them was her mother. In one torn photograph, I could make her out and half the arm of some other person.

She was different from the other women of the alley. She was like those women who live life on their own terms, whether they are right or wrong. Thus, it didn't matter that she was uneducated. Even when I was a child, I was pleased by how determined, how strong she was. In front of people she would remain quiet but would talk nineteen to the dozen when alone. She would express her fears which I, like a brave lad, would try to alleviate. Her chief battles were with her daily needs. She would take on and quit all kinds of jobs. Sometimes she would go from door to door, selling soap. At times she would stay up late, stitching falls on to the hems of saris. At other times, she would work as a masseuse.

She did not understand the value of the sense of wholeness which she had given up to life. She recognized her gnawed-and-slashed wholeness only when it was being gnawed or slashed at. Exactly when this process of gnawing and slashing began is a mere blur in her memory.

Now she is abed. She lies facing me but cannot meet my eyes. I plumb the inner recesses of my mind and dig deep to examine the roots of the unbreakable bond that I share with this woman. I stare fixedly outside the window; the ancient trees sway their branches restlessly. Their green leaves have taken on a slaty colour from the dust and the smoke. Their roots want to break through the coal-tar covering of the street to breathe; underground, there is no moisture, no fertility. Just thirsty sand. The trees are in a strange condition, and wonder how they came reach this place. When they first raised their heads as seedlings, this place used to be the entrance to a jungle. Now, there are crowds everywhere, teeming marketplaces and mazes of alleys. Nauseated by the stench from the surroundings, I look at her. Her being, slashed and gnawed, and her will to live flash across her forehead.

This woman was alive in my dreams, in my childhood. There is a difference of merely fifteen years in our ages. When I was a child, she was only a teenager. The road to school would become fragrant with her chatter. And for the two miles to school she would carry my bag. I used to tell her that I, too, like the other children of the chawl, would attend the nearby government school; I wouldn't have to walk so much then. 'You are different from the others. And see, so am I.'

The road, crowded and full of smoke, would turn into a jungle filled with wild flowers. She would turn back before we reached the school. I would shout, 'Come up to the gate at least.' She would refuse with a growl, 'Don't I have other things to do?' Her soft face would harden.

Throughout my childhood I admired this woman. She was a fairy to me, whether in a cheap nylon sari or a cotton salwar-kameez. I admired her swarthy complexion, her curly hair, the dark circles under her eyes, her muscular back, her uncovered legs, her raised collarbone—everything.

Later, however, everything about her began angering me. After dropping me off to school, I didn't know where she would vanish. She had stopped selling soap or giving massages to the women in the brothel. When I returned from school, I would never find her in her room. In the evening, she would hear me scream in anger, and would soak up my childish, teary display of rage with her smiles. She would hand me a cup of milk and a bun and look at me lovingly. She had started staying very happy.

By the time I was fifteen years old, I had begun to understand most things; in fact, almost everything. The 'English' school I attended, and my upbringing in this environment, was hollowing out a great void of confusion within. I was in a deep dilemma, and there was no telling how my personality was forming or breaking down inside me. Fighting with someone at school I would let loose the most vulgar language I had heard from women of the chawl, for which I would be beaten by the master for physical training. Speaking to the boys in the chawl, I would suddenly break into English and be laughed at. Here, in the chawl, were perennial lessons about the body and its secrets—which reached even up to her room on the second floor—among women roaming about in their petticoats and on the stairs which always stank faintly for urine. The sounds and smells of sex, the abuses, left me more or less numb.

One day, as we lay in the dimly lit room, staring at shadows as they formed and disintegrated in the corners, she said to me, 'I know that nowadays all sorts of questions are arising in your mind. Come, ask me about everything that has been bothering you.'

I stayed silent for a long time. Then I took the one question which had gnawed up half my soul and decided to cast it out of the hole within my heart which it had burrowed into.

'Were you ever married?'

'No.'

'You will tell me the truth, won't you?'

'Yes.'

'Swear?'

'Yes, I swear.'

'Swear by me.'

'Are you crazy? A swear is a swear.'

'Then swear by me.'

'Okay, I swear by you.'

'If you did not get married then where did I come from?'

'The same way all other people arrive.'

'Then I too am a child of some customer.'

'That is not true. No.'

'You promised to tell me the truth.'

'You will not understand.'

'I understand everything.'

'No, you don't.'

'I knew that you wouldn't tell me. That you'd go back on your promise.'

'I am speaking the truth. Really, I am. You do have a father. His name is written in your school register. He left me. Don't you dare take his name now! You ask these questions because you study in this English-medium school. If you'd been studying in the local government school you would not have asked me these questions. You would have quietly tried to understand these things yourself.'

After learning the truth, I wanted to run away from that

building full of prostitutes, pimps and the dancing women who worked in bars and orchestras.

'Jamuna, let's go and live somewhere else.'

'How will we pay the rent?'

'How do you pay for this room? I can live in a small hut with mud walls, but not this place.'

'I do not pay rent for this room. It is my mother's, she bought it.'

'But you told me that your house is somewhere in distant Ratnagiri. Where you have mango orchards.'

'Yes, that's right. She was a prostitute. She bought this. Your father's house is in Ratnagiri.'

'And now you too have started this…' Her eyes again took on a stony expression and she started to hit her head against the wall. Slowly at first, then harder and harder. I was disgusted with the drama.

That day, too, she went mad when she heard me use the word 'customer'. Trying to play innocent. All the children on the street talk about 'customers' day and night, no woman ever says anything to them. And her? She and her drama!

From that day onwards I stopped saying anything to her or asking her anything. My suspicion turned into conviction: after dropping me off at school, she went off to her business. How could she pay my 'English'-school fees if she wasn't in that business? I was sure that as she read stories of fairies to me at night, she would give me opium. Her purse was always full of wads of ten-rupee notes. Now she also owned a bank pass book.

~

One day, halfway to school, I turned back. I put my bag on a table in a cheap hotel in front of the yellow building and sat there. I saw that she was wearing a sari. Her hair was open and adorned with chrysanthemums. She held a purse. I just had to find out where she went. Shattering all illusions, I'd let my feet slip and fall headlong into the abyss.

I left my school bag on the table and followed her. Street after street. Crossroads and turns. Over unpaved paths and railway lines. Then, the 9.15 local. I boarded the train without having bought a ticket. I thought she saw me but she turned her face away. I hid behind a fat man. I got off at the same station as she did. She began walking again and I, following, was irritated: how much further? Then she turned into a building which looked like a church. While the security guard was inspecting a visitor's pass, I slipped in through the wicket gate.

I found myself in a large, well-maintained garden with a massive building on the grounds, of red and yellow stone. Massive pillars, expansive arches, tall doors. Everything open and vast. The air: clean and scented. I forgot everything and my heart was filled with joy. Compared to the stinking hell where I lived, this was heaven. I would have stood there longer, soaking in the beauty, but she had slipped into the maze of corridors within the building. Where there were massive halls. Men in white. Clean, beautiful women and students—both boys and girls—entered and exited. Does she work here? Or some relative of hers?

She entered one of the halls off the corridor but immediately turned back. At once, I hid behind a white pillar. She was heading towards the same pillar. 'Did she see me?' My heart leaped into my mouth. My breathing had still not steadied after all the running and the walking. I caught another glimpse of her: she seemed a little sad, but peaceful. Just before the pillar, she pushed open a large door and entered a room. I heaved a sigh of relief and stepped out from my hiding place. I was now absolutely alone there, amidst the drifting leaves and in the cool emptiness. I looked around me. On both sides of the corridor hung paintings. Strange paintings. Green cows and purple mountains. Groups of emaciated, half-naked men, bent over in fields—hordes of women. Faces—some laughing, some teary—painted on to red flowers on trees. What sort of pictures were these, grotesque and frightening? Suddenly, I heard the shuffling of numerous feet. Some talk, some laughter. I jumped on to the lawns from the corridor.

It had been over fifteen minutes since she had entered that room. I didn't take my eyes off that door. All at once, fear began to burrow into my stomach. I felt the small tremors in my stomach which are the harbingers of a full-blown panic attack. What would I do if she got lost in these corridors and these massive rooms? She'd go home, unaware I was in the building; she would look for me there and here I would be, lost in these utterly alien surroundings. The way back, the train station—I knew nothing of them. I had never travelled beyond Ghatkopar.

If she had a job there, she would return the next day surely. And what if she didn't have a job here but had merely come on an errand, what would I do then? I felt that I may be fifteen years old, but was still a child. The boys of the chawl were right to tease me that I was still a breast-feeding baby, and still hung on to her sari-pallu. My palms were clammy with sweat. Hunger burned my stomach. My eyes stung with tears. A fierce insecurity filled my heart. I wanted to ask the chaprasi sitting next to the gate if he knew Jamuna Bai Salunke. But what if he caught hold of me and asked, 'How did you get in?'

I nervously walked on the grass alongside the corridor. Ahead, the corridor ended and the windows began. One after the other, I climbed up on to the slim ledges beneath each window and shuffled along, peering in. Some windows were curtained, others not. Some of the large rooms were full of paintings, with boys and girls making more. Large and small sculptures in a few rooms; some people building strange-looking objects from wood and iron. There were huge lights and cameras. The terror within me was now turning into curiosity. I was now hopeful of finding her.

I stopped dead at one window. The room was empty, and the curtains were drawn aside. There were paintings of nude men and women on the wall. Men and women—some young, some old, some very old. I was stunned. By then, I had seen books with pictures of nude women—such books were easily available in the chawl. White, beautiful, naked—sexy women. What nonsense was this? Some had stony faces. Some bodies slouched over.

Women with drooping breasts and massive buttocks. I was beginning to feel disgust. Then, a group of boys and girls entered the room and, behind them, *she*. I felt like calling out to her. But, by then, she had climbed on to a table. I was shocked. Where was her sari? What was this towelling robe she was wearing? Would she now start teaching these boys and girls dressed thus? A bearded man lay on his stomach on the table, his legs folded, and lifted his hip in the air. He then got off and took a seat on a round table. The boys and girls took seats alongside the table. She was on the other long table... Where was she? Who was this naked woman lying on the table, her hip lifted into the air?

I became numb. What was all this? I jumped, lifeless, from the ledge. I lay for some time, unable to comprehend what was going on. What sort of profession was this? Those prostitutes, the white nude women in those books—was there any difference between them and her body's naked display?

Then I ran over a long, grassy field, jumped over a wall and came away from that place. Finding a spot to hide from the security guard, I waited for her. After about two hours she came out of the building and began walking. After a while, she turned and looked behind. I listlessly slid behind a tree, then started walking again, tired but now alert. I reached home two hours after her, having wandered aimlessly like a tramp, very hungry and burdened with numerous questions.

Those naked, wet images of hers remained entwined with questions for a number of years before drying up and shedding with age. Perhaps a few still exist: green, fresh. I mean, she could have done something else, could she not? Did she have to be nude? She still works there. Says she will do it until she is pensioned off. That she will stay here. I know she is stubborn.

My gaze falls on a new web of wrinkles on her face. Enmeshed in that web are the broken wings of many old dreams. Her eyes are closed. Today, when I see the web of wrinkles on her face, I wonder: Was she really so smart? Was it wise to have to have remained safe, with her values intact, like the tongue behind the barrier of thirty-two teeth? She kept fleeing from me all her life, desperate to hide the naked images of her existence from me—was that wise?

~

Is he any less stubborn?

Even though the Professor-saheb phoned him, he did not come to the art college. I knew he wouldn't come; there are many ghosts there, hiding behind pillars and upon tables, which will scare him. This afternoon I fell unconscious while posing. Perhaps I kept my knees bent for too long, and my blood stopped circulating properly. A doctor was summoned and I was given two injections. I was also given a bottle of glucose intravenously. The college arranged for an ambulance to bring me here. But he didn't come then, and it is only now that he has. He knows I am still modelling for artists. Professor-saheb says, 'Anyone can paint a young and beautiful body. The real artist is the one who can capture the beauty of the fine lines of age on face.' Perhaps that is an excuse. It isn't easy to get hold of young models; in this major art college, in this big city, we are just six models, including permanent ones and those on contract. And there are so many departments too: sculpture, photography, abstract, contemporary, mural.

He has become thin. Why has he grown a beard? He does not talk. He sits quietly, not saying a word. He doesn't even want to make eye contact with me. Why should I be bothered? Let it be. He stares at the trees outside. If he wants to sit quietly like this, why does he bother to come at all? He can enquire about my welfare over the phone. But he is still attached to me. Luckily, he has stopped saying, 'Come with me.' I don't want to go there, to that society. My mother was immersed in this society, from her head down to her toes. To uproot myself utterly from this society, I exposed my roots and roamed everywhere, forever being insulted, forever shrivelling and drying up. And he…he too remained in limbo, a Trishanku suspended between heaven and earth. Now, his children should breathe freely, untrammelled, in that society.

Which is why I do not want to go there, dragging my exposed, fungus-infested roots along.

He has come here after so many days. He must be thinking that I have come far, hiding my naked truths from him, and he must think that I do not want to meet his eye. It is when you do not meet my eye that I look away. You, who slipped out from between my thighs in the seventh month, would I be shy with *you*?

I am cleverer than you think. I let the truths about me be revealed to you after hiding them for many days, and when I was sure that your curiosity about me could not be contained any longer. I allowed you to delude yourself into thinking that I had no idea that you knew the truth. You can now think whatever you want: that having disrobed myself, I put on a show of purity in this settlement of prostitutes. I am aware that you know every truth of mine. Be it pure or not. You had every right to know, from the moment you took your first breath, after you slipped out from between my thighs and into a pool of blood.

I don't know if I was wrong to hide things from him but I did certainly strive more than my mother ever did. If a customer arrived after we returned from school she would simply say, 'Deepu, Laali, get under the bed.' Crouched there, we would finish our homework.

I could see all sorts of marks on my mother's body. Ash-grey marks from lit cigarettes, purple and blue brusies—they would frighten me very much. I would be very angry with my mother. Why couldn't she wash dishes or take up a job cleaning houses? Why did she allow herself to be trampled upon by men for a few rupees? She had even begun to hope that I would follow suit.

My mother withdrew me from school when I was in eighth grade and began thinking of making me an expensive 'call girl'. She had even discussed this with a broker. I didn't want to become a prostitute, cheap or expensive. I ran away with a taxi-driver. He spoke of undying love. He said, 'I have a house in Ratnagiri, it has fields and some mango trees.' What he didn't tell me was that he already had another wife. One day he cast me out, an unborn child in my womb. Then, I didn't know that society beyond these yellow houses was another world altogether.

After I left, so did my brother Deepu. He became a truck-driver's helper and ran away, never to return. My mother's anger knew no bounds. Both of her children, because of whom she had allowed herself to be trampled upon, had run away. She turned all of her anger upon me. No sooner had I entered the room than she beat me up, like one thrashes laundry. So much, that I began to bleed profusely and gave birth to my son in the seventh month of pregnancy. By then, mother wasn't keeping well, and customers avoided her. I took to massaging the much-kneaded bodies of prostitutes for five rupees a massage. Then, mother died.

I was alone. Pimps started making the rounds of my room.

Then, along with my childhood friend Jolly, I took on the job of a salesgirl. I sold everything—Surf, soap, kitchenware. One day, she took me to the art college. Earlier we used to be paid by the sitting. Sixty rupees per sitting. After doing this for seven years, I got a job as a permanent model at the art college; I have been working there for seventeen years now.

The first time, I felt a great deal of shame. But Jolly explained that there was nothing wrong with the job. 'This is good but definitely a little bold, Jamuna. I have done this for many years. Now I am planning to get married to Moses from the bakery. His family will not accept my modelling, so I am keeping you there as my replacement.'

I had never taken off my clothes, even while bathing in the sack-curtained bathroom of the chawl, so how could I in front of these boys and girls? I didn't know what they were thinking, but there was never a look of cheap curiosity on their faces. They seemed to be waiting patiently. I stepped out of my towelling robe with the firm belief that this was perhaps a little better than becoming a prostitute.

Earlier, at the students' request I would strike difficult poses, thinking, No matter, this too. In two minutes I would realize what a difficult ask this was: my body would be stiff for a full fifteen minutes and in constant pain. I'd have to hold my breath for the entire quarter hour. After each fifteen-minute session I got a ten-minute break and, after every half-an-hour, a cup of tea. Later, I was able to demonstrate easy poses in which I could sit or lie down for fifteen to twenty minutes. I also learnt how to control the urge to scratch—the mind can get used to anything. I never look at my pictures. Mostly, they are very ugly.

Sometimes, on humid days, the heat from numerous lights would make me sweat, which would accumulate under my breasts, flow down my stomach and settle between my thighs. Once, I happened to glance at the canvas a student was painting and saw that he had painted the sweat as it slipped down from the breasts to the stomach. When he saw me looking at him, he smiled sweetly. It reminded me of *him*. On coming back from school, he would smile sweetly like this upon seeing me. If I was not home when he reached, he would sulk all day.

In all my time at the college, there was only one painting of me which I liked. Eight foot high. The expanse of the body, a light purple; the swell of the breasts and buttocks, pink. Hair yellow, streaked with blue waves. Massive eyes, like those of a temple goddess. To me it seemed as if this was not the image of a tired, stiffened me, with gooseflesh on my skin from the cold. This was someone else. It was Professor Mohnish who had painted that canvas. He said, 'Jamuna, do you know? Your complexion is not wheatish or brown, it is purplish. I have never used such strong colours before. Today, when I opened the windows with the lights turned off, and saw you in natural light, I picked up these colours for the first time. I have never used the brush to make slanting strokes but today, when I saw the shape of your body, I was compelled to do so.'

The professor received some big award for that painting and it was published in a book along with his photograph. He showed it to me. 'Look, your picture has been published in *Art Today*. I have titled this painting "Kalindi". Here, read your name, Kalindi: it means Jamuna, Jamuna Salunke.' Then he forced me to accept one thousand rupees as a token of appreciation. He said, 'A live model is the true basis of any masterpiece by an artist. But they don't get the respect due to them.'

While addressing every new batch of students, the professor would say, 'They are not fashion models. Nor are they contestants from a beauty pageant. They are ordinary people, male and female, of all sizes, shapes and ages, who help us create realistic art. Here, nudity has no meaning. When you are engrossed in the nuances of the art—light and shade, cuts and corners, the technicalities involved—you are just thinking about your work, not about the nudity of these models. They are not made to sit here to exhibit their nudity; they are "super professionals". Thanks to them, you are able to see the proper shape of a human body, the shape that is not clear through clothes. Here, it is important that you are able to view the different dimensions of the flexible muscles of the body, in a state of stress or relaxation. Like I said earlier, nude modelling is not an easy job. They have to work hard and concentrate to give a good pose. Legs become numb in twenty minutes, hip bones start aching, and veins become knotted.'

How I wish I could have taped this conversation and made my son listen to it, who had seen me posing that day through the open window, on the very day that this masterpiece was being painted. A purple-tinted Jamuna.

Yes, I saw him that day. Climbing into the local train. I knew that he would have no money on him, which is why I didn't take a rickshaw from the station after getting off the train. I walked instead. I was determined to give him all the answers to his questions without saying anything. So when the professor spoke about painting in natural light, I quietly agreed. I even saw him from the corner of my eye. His face turned red, then purple, and, finally, black. Then he jumped down from the window.

That day, when he came home, I ordered kadhai chicken and rotis from the nearby hotel after many days. Perhaps his hunger was keen and his anger without sting. He ate quietly. After eating he sat chewing on his lips in anger.

He was washing his hands when I asked him, 'You didn't go to school?'

'Of course I did.'

I wanted to say: 'You followed me today! I saw you getting off the local train. You think you are smart. What do you think of yourself? Did you think the security guard would let you enter just like that?'

But I couldn't, because he would have a counter question: 'Then why didn't you take me with you?' What would I say then? Yes, I would say, 'That's my profession.'

'A filthy profession,' he'd say, 'quit it.'

My reply: 'There is no such thing as a bad or a good profession. I only know that these art students need me. Because of what I do, they learn. There, nobody looks at me in a lewd manner. I am not going to leave this job. I get seven thousand rupees a month for it.'

I stayed silent. In silence, I gathered the dishes and washed them. He kept cracking his knuckles. Look, even today he is cracking his knuckles. How many times have I told him not to!

'Do you want to break your fingers?' I glare at him. He laughs. The laughter of his childhood.

'Quit this profession now.'

'Yes, I will. I will be retiring soon.'

'Do you need money?'

'I have enough now. I will ask when I need. What about you? How's everything with you?'

'Fine.'

'What about your job?'

'I changed it.'

'You don't take photographs anymore?'

'I do. But not of earthquakes and bomb blasts. Newspapers pay very little, even for photographs of people soaked in blood.'

'Then?'

'Then what? After the children, my expenses have mounted. A one-room house wouldn't do. So I started my own freelance work, in many places at the same time.'

'That's why you have become so thin. One should work only as much as one can endure.'

'I cannot live there in the same way I used to here. I manage to earn more money now. I work in advertising too, taking photographs of models. Recently, I also held an exhibition of my photographs. It was reviewed in a magazine.'

'In *Art Today*! "Divine Nudity"?'

'How do you know?'

I closed my eyes. I knew his arrogance had leaked out from within him and had left him deflated.

Translated from the Hindi by Bushra Alvi Razzack

A PROSTITUTE'S LETTER: TO PANDIT JAWAHARLAL NEHRU AND QAID-E-AZAM JINNAH

Krishan Chander

I hope that you have never before received a letter from a prostitute. I also hope that you have never seen my face, nor the face of any other woman of my area for that matter. I understand the degree of repulsion that you might feel at my attempt at writing a letter to you, that too, such an open letter! But what am I to do? The conditions are such and the demand from these two girls is so strong that I cannot stop myself. I am not writing this willingly. These two girls—Bela and Batul—have persuaded me to do so. So please forgive me, a fallen woman, my audacity in writing to you. I beg for pardon from your generous heart. If you find any objectionable comments in my letter, please do forgive me, and consider it a result merely of my helplessness.

Why are Bela and Batul persuading me to write to you? Who are these two girls and why is their demand so strident? Before answering these questions, I wish to tell you something about myself. Don't worry, I am not going to reveal the history of my disgusting life. I am also not going to tell you how and under which circumstances I became a prostitute. I am not going to take advantage of any sober sentiment to plead for false mercy. I don't intend to fabricate an untruthful saga of love in front of my sympathizers. The purpose behind the writing of this letter is not to expose the details of a prostitute's work. I don't want to say anything in my defence; I merely want to tell you a few things about myself that could impact the future of Bela and Batul.

Undoubtedly, you would have been to Bombay at various times. Jinnah sahib would have seen much of the city. But why would you have seen our bazaar? I live in a bazaar known as Faras Road; it is situated between Grant Road and Madanpura. On the other side of Grant Road is Lamington Road, Para House,

Chowpati, Marine Drive and Fort. These areas are contained within the vicinity of the civilized classes of Bombay. Across Madanpura is where the poor classes live. Faras Road sits in between them—so that the rich as well as the poor are equally benefited. But Faras Road is much closer to Madanpura, because the distance between a destitute and a prostitute is always small.

This bazaar is not beautiful, neither are its occupants. The middle of the bazaar is filled with the continuous noise of the tram and large numbers of stray dogs, loafers, dandies, wastrels and professional criminals can be found roaming about its streets. The lame or the handicapped, the wastrels, the hooligans, cocaine-addicts and pickpockets, those with chronic diseases, the gonorrhoea-ridden bald men—all enjoy a free run of the market. There are filthy hotels, countless flies buzzing on the litter spread over damp footpaths, large warehouses of wood and coal, professional pimps and vendors of stale garlands, owners of old and decaying film magazines, sellers of sex manuals such as *Kokashastra* and of naked and obscene photographs, Chinese and Muslim barbers and abusive, langot-clad wrestlers. All the garbage of our society can be found on Faras Road.

It should be obvious that you won't be visiting Faras Road; no decent man would even look in this direction. The civilized class lives across Grant Road and the elite live in Malabar Hills. Once, I passed by Jinnah sahib's bungalow and offered my salaam there, bending low; Batul was also with me. I could never explain adequately to you the extent of the gratitude that Batul has for you, Jinnah sahib. If there is anyone she likes after Allah and His Messenger, it is only you. She has put your photograph in a locket that she keeps near her heart. This is not an act with evil intentions. Batul is only eleven years old. She is just a small girl, though the occupants of Faras Road harbour bad intentions for her. Well, I will talk about that later.

This is Faras Road, where I live. My shop is at the corner of the dark street, near the Chinese barber's salon at the west end of the road. People don't usually recognize it as a shop, but you are an intelligent man, what can I hide from you? I will merely say that my shop is there, and I do business in the same way as a merchant, vegetable-seller, fruit-seller, hotel-owner, motor-mechanic, cinema-owner, cloth-retailer or shopkeeper might. And as in every business, apart from making profit, the businessman desires to make his customer happy. My business, too, follows the same rule. The only difference is that I don't do black marketing; otherwise, there would be no difference between me and other businessmen.

This shop is not in a good location. People stumble and fall at night and even during the day. In this dark street, people are robbed of their money, alcoholics vomit after getting drunk and the abuse all around is generous. Trivial arguments become big disputes. Murders have become routine. At every moment, life is under threat.

I am not a rich prostitute and I cannot afford to live on Pali Hill, or in a bungalow at the Worli seashore. I am merely an ordinary prostitute. I have seen all of India and have had a variety of experiences in the company of many people from diverse backgrounds. But, for ten years now I have been in the same shop, on the same Faras Road, in this same city: Bombay. I get six thousand rupees as pagri rent for my shop, though the neighbourhood is not very good. The atmosphere is contemptible, surrounded by sludge and waste dumps, where diseased dogs are ready to chase and bite anxious customers. Still, I get my six thousand rupees as pagri rent.

My one-storeyed house has two rooms. The front room is my drawing room. I sing, dance and entertain my customers here. The back room is used as a kitchen and bathroom, as well as the bedroom. In one corner is a tap, a stove and utensils; and in the other is a big bed, beneath which is one small bed. Under the small bed, trunks full of my clothes are stored. The front room has electricity but the back room remains in utter darkness. The owner of the house has not got it whitewashed for a long time, and he is not in the mood to do so any time soon either. Who has such leisure? The entire night I sing and dance, and during the day I sleep here, resting my head on a pillow.

I have given the back room to Bela and Batul. Often, when the customers go there to freshen up, Bela and Batul stare at them with wide open eyes. My letter, as well as their eyes, speaks of the same concerns. If they were not with me now, this sinful woman would not have had the courage to commit this folly. I know that the world will laugh at me. I know that this letter might not even reach you. But I am helpless. I will write this letter as Bela and Batul want me to.

Perhaps you might be thinking that Bela and Batul are my daughters. No. This is not true; I have no children. I bought both girls from the bazaar. During the days when Hindu–Muslim riots were at their peak, and human blood was flowing like water on the streets of Grant Road, Faras Road and Madanpura, I purchased Bela for three hundred rupees from a Muslim pimp. He had brought Bela from Delhi. Bela's parents lived in the street in front of Poonch House, Rawalpindi. Her family was middle class; decency and simplicity flowed in their blood. Bela was their only daughter. She was only in the fourth standard when Muslims massacred Hindus in Rawalpindi on 12 July.

Bela was returning from school. She saw a big crowd in front of her house and the houses of other Hindus. Weapon-carrying rioters were taking women and children out of their houses and killing them on the road. They were shouting 'Allahu Akbar!' Bela saw her father being killed and witnessed her mother dying with her own eyes. The cruel Muslims chopped off her mother's breasts. The same breasts from which a mother, regardless of whether she is Hindu, Muslim, Sikh or Jew feeds her child and brings a new chapter of creation into the vastness of the world. Those same milk-filled breasts were gouged out by people who shouted 'Allahu Akbar'. Has anyone ever committed such atrocities on any humans before? Some ignorance has filled their souls with dark ink. I have read the Holy Quran and I understand that whatever happened to Bela's parents in Rawalpindi is not taught by Islam. It was neither

humanity, nor enmity, nor revenge. It was such an act of brutality,
cowardliness, cruelty and Satanism, that it emerged from the chest
of darkness and stained even the last ray of hope.

Bela is with me now. Before, she was with a bearded Muslim
pimp and prior to that, a Muslim pimp from Delhi. Bela was
merely twelve years old when she was in the fourth standard. If she
were still in her own house, she would have been promoted to the
fifth standard. She would have grown up, and her parents would
have married her to a sober man from a poor family. She would
have led a normal life. She would have loved her husband and
children and would have loved the little happiness of her own
home. But this delicate bud was marred by an untimely bruise.
Bela no longer looks like a twelve-year-old girl. Even at this
tender age, she appears to have aged beyond her years.

Qaid-e-Aazam sahib, if you could see the fear in her eyes, the
indifference she has for humanity and the blood that runs in her
veins or her thirst for death, then you would understand her
condition. You are an intelligent man. You will only have seen
innocent women from elite Hindu and Muslim families. Perhaps
you understand that innocence has no religion. It is the
responsibility of all of humanity and the possession of the entire
world. The God of each and every religion will never forgive the
person who brings it to an end.

Batul and Bela live here as sisters, but they are not biologically
related. Batul is a Muslim girl and Bela was born into a Hindu
family. Today, they both live in a brothel on Faras Road. Bela
comes from Rawalpindi and Batul is the daughter of a Khan from
a small village, Khem Kiran, in Jalandhar. Batul's father had seven
daughters: three were married and four remained spinsters. Batul's
father was an ordinary farmer in Khem Kiran. Though poor, he
was a man of repute who had lived there for years.

In this village of Jats, there were only two or three Pathan
families. Panditji, you can guess their suppression and their plight.
Though they were Muslims, they were not allowed to build a
masjid in their own village. Instead, they would offer their prayers
quietly in their houses, as they had been doing ever since Maharaja

Ranjit Singh had been enthroned. Not a single Muslim has ever given a call for prayer in this village. Though they had the Islamic faith in their hearts, the conditions were extremely difficult and they were kept silenced by the burden of old traditions and customs.

Batul was the youngest daughter of her father, and also the one closest to him. She was extremely pretty; in fact, she was so beautiful that even a single touch would stain her beauty. Panditji, you are of Kashmiri descent yourself, and being an artist you understand the real meaning of beauty. Now, this beauty has so merged with my filth that it will be difficult for me to find a sober man who can recognize her worth. Amongst this filth you would see old and decaying Marwaris, contractors with big, dense moustaches and black-marketers with evil intentions. Batul is illiterate and she has only heard the name of Jinnah sahib. In her innocence, taking Pakistan to be a kind of drama, she too shouted slogans of 'Inquilab zindabad'. She is merely eleven years old.

Illiterate Batul came to live with me recently. A Hindu pimp brought her to me, and I bought her for five hundred rupees. I have no idea where she was before she came here. Yes, the lady doctor has said so many things about her—you might go mad if I tell you everything. Batul is not in a sound state of mind. Her father was murdered brutally by the Jats. The killing has shattered the six-thousand-year-old history of Hindu civilization, and human barbarity has appeared in a cruel state before everyone. First, the Jaats plucked out his eyes and then urinated in his mouth. They slit his throat and then cut his body and took out his intestines. They also raped his married daughters. Rehana, Gulwarkhas, Marjana and Sosan Begum were raped, one by one, in front of their father's corpse. Sisters and mothers were raped by men to whom they had once sung lullabies or had lowered their heads in front of, out of modesty, piousness and shyness.

The Hindu religion has lost its reverence and has destroyed its ethos and customs. Today, silence prevails; each and every verse of the Granth Sahib is ashamed and every verse of the Gita is injured. Who can talk about the artistry of Ajanta in front of me now? Who can tell me about the writings of Ashoka? Who can sing in

praise of the sculptor of Ellora? On the helpless chewed-up lips of
Batul, in the teeth-marks of brutes and demons on her arms, in
her disfigured limbs, lies the death of your Ajanta, the funeral of
your Ellora, and the shroud of your civilized society. Come, come,
I will show you the beauty that once Batul was. I will show you the
unburied living corpse that Batul now is.

I have said so many things because of my overwhelming
sentiments. I shouldn't have done so. You might feel offended by
it. Perhaps, until now, nobody would have told you such things.
You may not be able to do anything for us at all. But since both
India and Pakistan have gained independence, perhaps even a
prostitute now has the right to ask a question to her leaders: What
will happen to Bela and Batul?

Bela and Batul are not only two girls, but two communities and
two civilizations. They are temple and mosque. Batul now lives in
the house of a prostitute who conducts her business near the
Chinese barbershop. Neither Bela nor Batul enjoy this. I have
bought them. If I wished, I could force them into this business,
but I will not do what Rawalpindi and Jalandhar did to them.

Until now, I have kept them distanced from the world of Faras
Road, but when my clients go to my back room to wash their
hands and legs, Bela and Batul's eyes communicate something to
me. I cannot tolerate that gaze. I cannot even communicate their
message to you properly. Why don't you comprehend the message
in their eyes for yourself? Panditji, I wish for you to adopt Batul as
your daughter and Jinnah sahib, I want you to adopt Bela as your
daughter. Please take them away from the clutches of Faras Road.
Take them to your homes; listen to the pleas of lakhs of souls. The
same plea echoes from Noakhali to Rawalpindi and from Bharatpur
to Bombay.

Is this plea inaudible in government houses? Will you not
listen to our voice?

Yours sincerely,

A Prostitute of Faras Road

Translated from the Urdu by Haris Qadeer

THE KEPT WOMAN

Subodh Ghose

The sound of footsteps on the staircase was muffled by the laughter and voices of men and women. A forceful knock announced that the visitors were at the door. 'Anybody in?' a male voice floated into the room.

Inside the room Prasad sat up, startled. The room was in a mess, so were his thoughts. He could not decide what to do. Then, in a hushed tone, he said, 'Just the thing I was afraid of! Come, Lata, get up quickly!'

Lata turned her face away. 'Why bother me? I don't care for any of them!'

She continued to lie against the bolster and concentrated on her cigarette. A bottle of whisky stood on the table by the bed, a corkscrew by its side. The silk sari was hanging loosely at her waist. Night had been just ushered in by the lamps.

'That's not fair, darling! Please, quickly rearrange the room!' Prasad pleaded. 'What's wrong with that? It is not that I alone will stand to gain—you will also earn their respect. Come on! Time's short, they're waiting outside.'

Lata sat up. Prasad whisked away the bottle inside the cupboard. He took the paintings off the wall and pushed them under the bed. Then he looked around for any tell-tale signs of aiyyashi. Yes, the curtain with the naked figures embroidered on it was still dancing in the wind. He pulled it down, rolled it into a bundle and tossed it under the bed.

Prasad: 'Rush!'

Lata: 'Ugh! I can't stand this hypocrisy. I don't feel like dancing to your tune. Throughout the day I must be restrained, I can't even laugh out loud because your "respectability" must be protected in front of the servants. If I have to put up an act round the clock, why should I do it here? If I did it in a theatre I'd make some money!'

The more anxious Prasad got with every passing second, the more she showed her indifference through heartless sloth. Prasad stood by helplessly, his look entreating her to help him out of the situation at hand. Lata tickled his chin and broke into a smile. 'Gentleman, if you are so frightened of losing your dignity, why keep a woman? You can't have your cake and eat it too!'

She took out a towel and a sari from the cupboard and left the room. Prasad sighed with relief and walked towards the door. As he opened it, a group of four middle-aged and young men walked in, accompanied by seven young ladies and matrons with children. 'Namaskar!' Prasad welcomed them.

Nice people, these. Etiquette did not weigh heavy on their behaviour. They weren't bogged down by the formalities of first-time visitors. They all took seats of their own accord. The women took a mat from one corner of the room, spread it out on the floor and made themselves at home.

An elderly man looked towards a young man and said, 'Now put forth your complaint, Ranjit.'

'Yes, I do have a complaint against you, sir,' Ranjit said to Prasad. 'Like you, we are all here on a holiday. It's just the few of us here; you don't come across so many Bengalis in this town. We're trying to enlarge our group—and you're avoiding us!'

'Yes,' Prasad was shamefaced. 'I have rather kept to myself!'

'Dada,' Abha took the lead from amongst the women and addressed her brother, 'isn't this unfair? You've already enrolled a new member in your team—what about us?'

'Wait a while, please.' Prasad smiled shyly. 'She'll join us any minute.'

As if on cue, Lata entered the room. She was dressed in a broad-bordered Tangail saree. She stopped short on seeing the aged Rakhal Babu and pulled her pallu in a ghunghat over her head. The parting of her hair was painted red with sindoor, she sported a big tika on her forehead and her feet were adorned with alta. One look at her and Prasad's clouded visage brightened up. He started speaking freely.

Abha tried to seat Lata next to her on the mat. Instead, Lata led all the women into her room. The group split into two and each had its fill of chatter and laughter. The children started quarrelling and, in trying to stop them, the elders added to the racket. For the first time in the six weeks that they had been here the isolated bungalow in Barakar Colony seemed to come alive.

Lata got busy trying to cook up some snacks to go with the tea. 'Why bother, Boudi?' the other ladies protested, 'plain tea will do! Forget the snacks.'

'But what about the kids? I can't serve them tea!' Then she added with a show of temper, 'Just look at the gentleman there! Engrossed in talking with no care in the world! Shouldn't he at least think of asking whether I need any help or not?'

The womenfolk broke into laughter. 'Jealous, aren't you, that he can chat without a care!'

Abha suddenly walked up to the drawing room and said to Prasad of her own volition, 'Boudi is very angry with you. There are things to be done, and you're simply not interested!'

Prasad: 'Why, what's the matter?'

Abha: 'Come and find out for yourself.'

Lata was waiting in the corridor, and as soon as Prasad stepped in, she whispered to him, 'I can make the tea, but what can I serve the little ones? Why don't you get some sweets?'

'Boudi,' Abha and another young lady who overheard her said, 'you're being extremely formal!'

'Will it do if I open the can of biscuits?' Prasad asked, then added, 'Of course, I don't mind going to the bazaar...'

'Oh yes, I'd completely forgotten the biscuits,' Lata said. 'Right, they'll do fine.'

The can was empty when the party got up to leave at ten. Before that, Prasad had to entertain his guests with a song—the esraj hiding behind a cover had given away his talent to the guests.

Rakhal Babu picked up his shawl and wrapped it around himself. His wife tried to cover the marks of beriberi with the shoes on her swollen feet. Tarak Babu lit another cheroot and started tapping the ground with his cane. Excepting Abha, all the other ladies were his nieces. Of the kids, some were Rakhal Babu's grandchildren, some Harish Babu's. This last babu and his wife were missing from the group this evening because he'd had a fresh attack of gout.

Rakhal Babu: 'Well, you may have some peace now!'

But another quarter of an hour passed by in exchanging pleasantries before they finally bade goodbye. Prasad saw them off to the gate.

'At last!' he exclaimed, as he brought the whisky out of the cupboard. Lata was exhausted and lay down on the bed. 'Hey, what's this love? Don't be a spoil-sport!' Prasad urged, his voice throbbing with excitement.

Lata didn't respond in any manner whatsoever. When Prasad tried to pull her towards himself she snapped, 'Don't be lewd!'

'All right, all right, I won't be. But you get rid of this silly dress while I fix a peg for each of us…'

'Why are you being so crude?' Lata's voice was harsh. 'Nothing will vanish into thin air…'

She went into the other room, took off her sari, wiped off the sindoor and washed off the alta. She removed every trace of the impersonator—the housewife who had come out into the open that evening. Then she put on a filmsy nightie and returned to the drawing room.

'Lovely! This is what suits you best,' Prasad gushed.

Unmoved, as though she'd not heard him, she picked up the cigarettes, walked to the window and stood looking out of it. A row of dim lights twinkled in the distance. Everything else was wrapped in darkness. The putrid stench from the garbage under a nearby tree filled the air. Lata took long drags on her cigarette.

Suddenly Prasad became aware that Lata had been keeping away from him. He turned around to look at her. Already on his second glass, he started mumbling: 'Well, all right, keep standing there. Please yourself! But I must admit, you are a born actress! All the people who'd descended on us—you fooled all of them! Thank you very much, darling! You saved my honour. I'll give you a handsome baksheesh. And next year we will go to Kashmir! But...you dared to say I'm vulgar! You harlot—you called me a lech! I'll skin you alive...'

Roaring in anger, he struck the table and it toppled over.

'Why this sudden show of temper?' Lata asked in a quiet but firm voice. 'Sit down quietly.'

But Prasad couldn't contain himself: he kept flaring up intermittently. Lata knew the perfect remedy for his temper—if only she were to stretch out on the bed and fling her legs across his lap, tease him or sing a line of an erotic song, his anger would evaporate. Prasad glared at Lata for a while and barked: 'You will do just as I tell you, and stay just as I keep you.'

Lata: 'All right.'

Prasad: 'Why all these nakhras? You are only a kept—a concubine!'

'Yes, I do know that.'

'You are not fit even to be Abha's slave!'

Lata suddenly felt licked by a tongue of flame. All this while she had kept her cool, thinking it was the senseless talk of a drunken frenzy. But these last words revealed a glimpse of the truth.

She walked up to Prasad and stood towering over him, her eyes a pool of fire. Hours seemed to pass in the next few moments before she spoke. 'I have no reason to remain tied to you. I'll return to Tarakeshwar tomorrow.'

She went into her room and bolted the door.

Later, in the middle of the night, he knocked on her door. He had come out of his drunken stupor and regained his usual caution. He knew her well enough to realize that rousing her ire would not do him any good. She lived a life of sin. Reputation, fame, status—these ideas were alien to her. She couldn't care less for Prasad's respectability. If she decided to reveal her identity before departing from this town, what could stop her? The only gain would be the stigma that would be attached to his name thereafter.

'Lata!' he pleaded, standing outside her room, 'please don't be angry with me. I won't sleep until you say you've forgiven me. You can't leave me and go away just like that! I won't budge from here until you say you won't leave me...'

The pleas were reinforced by repeated knocks on the door. 'All right!' Lata finally gave in. 'I won't go,' she said in a quiet voice. 'Have your dinner and go to sleep.'

~

'Chachi!' The voice is Vikram's, the youngest child of the subedar. The whirr of his top can be heard from time to time. 'Seven already!' thought Prasad. This child has been a regular visitor every morning. He will have tea and biscuits with Lata, then go out to build a mud castle under the papaya tree in the garden, raze it to the ground with a branch, and then go home.

The events of the previous evening crowded back into his mind. Lying in bed, Prasad could make out that Lata was already up and getting dressed. Then she opened the door and went out the verandah. 'Come in, Vikram,' he heard her say.

'How much longer do you want to sleep, Chachi?' Vikram's voice was accusatory.

Prasad knows everything that was happening outside. Mahaveer, the servant, is already busy sweeping the courtyard. Later, he will bring tea for Prasad. That will set in motion the routine which has become a way of life in this house. Like an efficient housewife, Lata will supervise all the servants at work. She will dole out the day's rations, then have a bath and go to the temple. Only after that will she have her breakfast. In this make-believe household, this routine will be followed thoroughly and devotedly. It is not inspired by love or attachment; it is a mechanical process that works on its own momentum. Prasad has to put up with this affliction like a passenger squashed in a second-class compartment, until the day reaches its destination—the evening. Only then does Lata become her own self again.

After Vikram leaves, in comes the Lala's wife with her tale of woe and misery. The Lala's son-in-law is out of job, and the daughter has no end of suffering. Listening to her, Lata's face wears a pained expression, as though she is moved by the recital.

But this morning all these actions seemed to Prasad a mean act of deception. If such a big lie could be passed for truth, then the difference between day and night could be wiped out too!

Rakhal Babu's bearer came with a letter: 'Prasad Babu, will you please send Lata around to our house this evening? She will have dinner with us. Affectionately, Uncle.'

Prasad read the note with displeasure gnawing at him. He grew worried, apprehensive. He couldn't decide what to do. As he lifted the curtain, he could see Lata sifting through the rice.

This morning she, too, was not in her usual frame of mind. She could not put her finger on what bothered her. It had never happened before. A man would abuse her and get away with it? No, not even a zamindar's son had such courage. Lata was amazed at her own reaction. Today she did not, in the least, feel any inclination to make an issue out of the previous night's incident.

It did not take her long to recognize that it was not out of fear but out of a weakness. But why? Why this weakness?

Brooding over the evening's events she once again became fiercely angry. He wants to get rid of me? Well, let him do so! That Marwari seth would only be too glad of the chance! But, before she went away, she would have to teach this man a lesson of such sound wisdom that he would never dare to misbehave with a prostitute in future.

'Lata—'

At the sound of his voice, her heart missed a beat. As he came forward, she bent forward and tried to sift through the rice with deeper concentration.

'Rakhal Babu has invited you for dinner tonight. Will you go?'

Lata looked at him. The cloud of apprehension lifted from his face. 'All right. But there shouldn't be any scene.'

~

The change of scene heralds a change of act. It is as amazing as it
is complicated. Not only Lata, Prasad, too, has emerged from his
shell and is busy socializing. Most of his evenings are now spent in
the drawing room of Abha's bungalow. Lata takes turns in going
to Rakhal Babu's, Tarak Babu's and Harish Babu's. There are the
Subedar's and Lala's as well. The only house she hasn't been able
to visit is Abha's. She has been invited twice. But on both the
occasions she suddenly started feeling unwell soon after she received
the invitation: once she had fever, the other time she had a terrible
headache.

Prasad sounds genuinely happy. 'Say, I must compliment you!
Everybody is so highly impressed, they are all singing your praises!
Oh, what a superb piece of deception!'

Lata can respond with only a wan smile.

'Just see to it that it doesn't cross the bounds of credence,'
Prasad adds.

'And what if it does? It will only boost your image.'

'My, the things that are happening! Do you even stop to think
what would happen if you were recognized?'

'Whatever will happen to me? I will go back to where I came
from.'

Prasad is suddenly depressed. He becomes anxious, then
mumbles unmindfully, 'True, it wouldn't matter to you in any
way, but…'

~

Abha came to Prasad's bungalow on two other evenings. She
talked to Lata, but it lacked the spontaneity of the first day's
conversations. Nor could Lata respond normally. The schism
grew with every meeting between them. Their exchanges were
frequently interspersed with awkward silences. Lata served tea,
which Abha politely declined. Lata could not bring herself to
request her to drink it. The tea was left alone and went cold.

Left by themselves, Prasad and Lata could see the distance
which had opened up between them and which stared them in

their faces. The exchanges between them had progressively lessened. Frequently, returning home after a walk, Lata would find Prasad gone. Often, coming home at night, Prasad would find Lata asleep.

Predictably, Lata figured in the gossip sessions at the ladies' get-togethers. Masima would remark: 'She's a quiet sort.'

Tarak Babu's nieces would put in unanimously: 'She's really a very nice person. Abha has no business talking against her.'

Masima would demand, 'Why, what does she hold against Lata?'

Mamata would reply, 'She says Lata is an uneducated, illiterate country bum.'

'What does Abha think of herself?' Masima inexplicably got very angry. 'Is she an exceptionally intelligent pundit? Shame on her! A woman whose husband dies within two months of marriage, what good is her learning? Is she going to wear it around her neck like a mangalsutra? Isn't she ashamed to even talk about it?'

Nibha and Prabha burst out laughing. They failed to find a reason for this outburst against Abha, except that Masima herself happened to be a countrybred!

Lalaji's wife had stopped by to visit Lata. She took her to her room since Prasad and Abha were engrossed in a conversation in the drawing room. Prasad made no effort to lower his voice even when he talked of things that turned Abha ashen. She frowned as she said, looking towards the door, 'Aren't you scared of anything, Prasad Babu?'

A while later, the two were seen going out for a stroll. Lalaji's wife gaped at Lata in wonder, then asked, 'Who is that hussy? I don't like her coquetry. I think you ought to be more strict.'

'If I am faithful, then my husband would be so too,' Lata replied. 'No one can take him away from me.'

'Well, that is true,' the Lala's wife conceded, rather unwillingly. But to her own self Lata's words sounded hollow and ironical. She couldn't help laughing to herself.

~

Prabha's husband had come and they were both going back that day. Both Prasad and Lata had been invited to join them for lunch. Lata joined the other young ladies in teasing and ragging the jijaji. When taking leave, Prabha's husband bowed to touch Lata's feet.

Prasad was peeved. On their way home he remarked, 'You are crossing all bounds of decency.'

Lata did not respond either way.

Prasad continued: 'You, of course, don't care. It's me who'll be held responsible for this sinful deception.'

Lata could have consoled herself if she could bring herself to believe what Prasad said. If all the sins of her life with him made his life accursed, then she could in fact rejoice. But how could it be so? She did not believe that she would be exempted of the responsibility. It was treachery to deceive those who love and trust us. Wasn't she a partner in this treacherous act? Her heart grew heavy with misgivings. But even as he condemned herself, she could not help laughing at Prasad's unease.

Back in the bungalow, Prasad once again tried to talk about the incident. 'I've been noticing that these days you've been acting like a housewife even when there's nobody around. Why do you do that?'

'But you don't ask me to join you in the evenings any more—'

'So what? I'll ask you when I need you. But why did you give up smoking? You don't have to change your way of life, or put up with any inconvenience.'

'There is no need to advise me either. I'll live the way I want to.'

Prasad felt insulted by this haughty reply, but he could neither disregard it nor say anything against it.

Lata had actually become very careless. She felt pity for Abha: if Abha was content to steal a fake coin, well, let her. Nobody could deprive Lata of what she had come to treasure—her popularity. No, not even Prasad had the power to do so. She alone could damage it in any measure.

Lata would not object if the rest of her life passed in this manner. So what if, under the cover of marital understanding and social acceptance, she led an empty, hollow life? Their household was a living example of a palace built on quicksand.

~

Prasad had left for Abha's as soon as he learnt in the morning about her sickness, and returned only in the evening, when Lata had come back from her walk. Abha had fever accompanied by hysterical fits of tears. Ranjit was worried because though she had fever before, she had never had any of these fits.

Prasad was also worried. He helplessly paced the room. He felt that he had become the victim of a practical joke he had tried to play on others.

For the first time since that day at Prabha's, Prasad talked to Lata. 'You are crossing every limit of tolerance, Lata. How dare you say things about Abha?'

'Say things about her? I have never even mentioned her to anybody!'

'That is another way of condemning a person.' Prasad was not worked up or excited as he said this—his tone was calm and collected, like that of a judge passing a sentence.

'Well, what do you plan to do about it?'

'I don't want to let you go on with this impersonation,' Prasad continued. 'You've done enough, and you've done it pretty well. But think about yourself; how long can you go on in this manner? How will this benefit you?'

Lata kept quiet. Prasad spoke in a firmer voice: 'Besides, if anybody comes to know your reality, what will happen to me? I can't just sit idly while you hold my reputation, dignity and status at ransom. I can't think of subordinating all my desires to your whims for the fear of being exposed.'

Lata gazed fixedly at the table-lamp. She could probably give a sharp rejoinder to all these allegations. But she couldn't argue rationally. Neither her education nor her situation permitted her to do so.

'You must leave,' Prasad intoned.

Lata became stiff.

'I will give you your due sum and some more.'

Lata turned her face away. 'And then? How am I to live thereafter?' she asked feebly.

Prasad lost his temper. 'Is that my concern? Did you concern yourself with my problems? Have you forgotten the row you created on the first day when you had to cook? You left for the station with all your luggage, and I had to plead with a whore!'

Not a word of this accusation was false—there was no scope for denial anywhere. It was all a part of their history, built on facts.

Prasad cooled down soon enough. 'I don't need you any more,' he said. 'I am not in the frame of mind that made me bring you here.' His voice dipped as he continued: 'Honestly, I can't stand it any more. You ought to understand, Lata!'

The words sounded like the moaning of a man in great suffering. Lata could only respond: 'You are serious? I have to go?'

'Yes, definitely. I'm only thinking of whom to send you back with.'

'You don't have to worry about that,' Lata stood up screaming. 'I can take care of myself. If anybody inquires, just cook up a story. Tell them an uncle had come to fetch me. I'll leave at dawn.' And she dashed out of the room.

~

Just the night.

Whether she falls asleep or stays awake, it will pass. She must leave early, very early. Before Vikram comes. But she must have her revenge before she leaves.

She was sitting on the floor of the verandah, very still. The vadi were still out in the open: the dew would spoil them. The pickles ought to be stored away too. But she did not feel the inclination to move.

Lata thought to herself: He's scared. He's afraid of the consequences if anybody learns about Lata. What if Masima comes to know? What if Tarak Kaka or Harish Mama learnt that I am not Lata, I am Champabai of Tarakeshwar. What if I reveal my true identity? Poor man, what'll happen to his bloated dignity?

But that's impossible. No! She just could not have her revenge in this manner. Let Lata live on in the memory of all these people, with all the glory and affection she had gained for herself!

Lata could very well see the direction in which the gentleman Prasad's affections were flowing. She could well imagine the day, a year or two later maybe, when the widowed Abha would come to this bungalow, her forehead adorned with sindoor, the room resounding with the music of her bangles.

What is he doing? Why is the light still on in his room? Probably reading. Has he changed? How about putting him to the test? If she went into his room in her negligee, her hair let down, her eyes lined with surma, a glass of whisky in hand, she could easily gauge the strength of his determination to give her up.

Chhee!

She probably wouldn't have felt miserable if she still had the inclination to do these things. But she couldn't even think of touching him, let alone give herself up to him. Never in her life had she felt so degraded—no, not even when she catered to the perversions of some of her lecherous customers.

Perhaps if she dulled her sensitivity with some whisky, the act would not seem so abhorrent. But the thought of drinking whisky itself repulsed her.

All her weapons seemed to have lost their edge. She had become defenceless simply by hankering for the glory accorded to a false image! She had come to care too much for this image she had herself built, with a ghunghat, sindoor, bangles... No, she couldn't destroy the illusion. She wouldn't even try to wreck it— she was hopelessly in love with it.

She wiped the tears from her eyes. Yes, she would go. But she must not leave without avenging herself. In the silence of the night she kept thinking about that moment.

Champabai will spit out her hatred for this respectable

gentleman-in-love with abuses directed at him and his forefathers. Thanks to his upbringing, he cannot retaliate in equal measure or reply in the same manner. All he can do is listen in stunned silence and squirm under the impact of the insult. She will derive at least some satisfaction from this sight.

~

In his room, Prasad suddenly shut his book and sat up anxiously. A wounded serpent goes away, but returns to avenge itself. He was seized by a fear. He ought not to rouse her wrath. Instead, he should try to placate her before she left.

He took out a bundle of notes from the drawer and went to Lata.

'Please take this. You are not angry with me, Lata, are you?'

Lata held out her hand and accepted the notes without uttering a single word.

'You are not angry, Lata, are you?' Prasad repeated himself. 'Why don't you say something, Lata?'

She looked at him. Her eyes, burning with the light from the lamp, gleamed eerily, reminding him of a serpent peering at an enemy from the darkness of its hole. Frightened, he called out in a hoarse voice—'Lata! I haven't done you any harm.'

It was probably to protect her eyes from the glare of the lamp that Lata pulled the ghunghat even lower in front of her face. To avenge herself against an insignificant, despicable man, she could not tear apart the guise of the ideal housewife; Lata, who had won the love and praise of one and all the members of Barakar Colony. The concubine Lata could not become the harlot Champabai of Tarakeshwar even in the seclusion of the bungalow in the dead of night. Like an insulted, hurt wife, she could only sigh and say, 'No, why would you harm me? It's Abha Thakurji who has brought me to this destitute condition!'

Translated from the Bangla by Ratnottama Sengupta

THE HOUSEWIFE

Ismat Chughtai

The day Mirza's new maid Lajo arrived, the entire neighbourhood rose up in an uproar. The sweeper, who used to vanish after casually flicking his broom about, now swept the floor to bits. The milkman, who liberally added water, began supplying milk thick as clotted cream.

Whose wishful thinking was it that they gave her the name 'Lajo'? Lajo was far from being demure and coy. Who gave birth to her, and where, was a mystery. She had survived on the streets on hand-outs from people, and had learnt to grab for herself that which she could not beg for. When she reached puberty, her body became her greatest asset. In the company of street boys of her age, she gained knowledge of the deepest secrets of nature and soon became the proverbial cow-camel without a nose-ring. Lajo was unused to bargaining and scheming. If she received something, great. If not, she could work on credit. And if no credit was available, she didn't mind offering charity either.

'You! Don't you feel ashamed?' people would ask her.

'I do,' she would reply shamelessly.

'You will repent one day,' they would say.

Lajo remained unconcerned. She was used to words both harsh and sweet. She had an innocent face, naturally kohl-lined eyes, small teeth and a sweet complexion. She had an intoxicating, alluring gait which could leave onlookers tongue-tied and starry-eyed.

Mirza was a bachelor, tired of cooking for himself. His small grocery shop—which he called General Store—left him no time. He could not visit his hometown to get himself married. At times, his business would run so perilously close to ruin that it would seem as if his belongings would be auctioned off. At times, trade boomed, and he barely had time to lift his head, let alone think about getting married.

Bakshi had met Lajo at a bus stop. His wife was then heavily pregnant and they needed a maid. Once the baby was born, he beat her up and kicked her out. Lajo was accustomed to being beaten up and cast out, but it was Bakshi who had become addicted to her. But he had a new job by then, overseas, and thought, Why not leave her at Mirza's house? Mirza debases himself with prostitutes, let him enjoy this treat for free.

'God forbid! I will not allow lowly women inside my house!' Mirza replied angrily.

'Oh quit it Mian, let her stay. She will do all the work,' Bakshi said.

'No! Why are you leaving me with this nuisance? Why don't you take her with you?'

'I have only a ticket only for myself, not for the entire clan.'

In the meanwhile, however, Lajo had hitched her skirt up high and had started working in the kitchen. She was walking around with a broom tied to a long pole. When Bakshi informed her of Mirza's refusal, she took no notice of it. She issued instructions on how the pots were to be arranged on the shelves and left for the tap outside to fetch water.

'If you want, I will take you back home.'

'Scat! Are you my husband that you will take me home? You mind your affairs, I will manage the Mian on my own.'

Bakshi showered the choicest abuse upon Lajo, and asked her why she was being a pricey bitch. In return, Lajo heaped worse abuses on Bakshi and singed him so badly that even a lout like him broke out in a sweat of embarrassment.

After Bakshi left, Mirza felt such awkwardness that he left for the mosque. Sitting there, he regretted this nuisance, for not only would she mean extra expense, she would also steal from him. When he returned home after the evening maghrib namaaz, Mirza was shocked. It seemed as if his dear dead mother had come back to life, for the house was spick and span, the earthen water pot was covered with a shining bowl and the lantern was sparkling clean.

'Mian, should I lay out the meal?' Lajo was a worldly-wise woman.

'Meal?'

'It is ready. I will make hot rotis—take a seat.' Without waiting for a reply, she went into the kitchen.

It was his mother who had last cooked him spinach and potato curry and daal tempered with cumin and onion. Mirza choked up.

'Where did you get the money from?' he asked.

'I borrowed from the shopkeeper.'

'I will pay you your return fare.'

'Return?'

'Yes. I cannot afford...'

'Who is asking for a salary?'

'But...'

'Are the chillies in the food excessive?' Lajo enquired as she placed a roti on a platter, as if ending the discussion.

He felt like saying yes, damn woman, it *is* too hot, but Lajo was busily bringing him hot rotis, as if someone was preparing them in advance in the kitchen.

I will settle this in the morning...Thinking this, Mirza retired to his room. For the first time in his life, a woman was asleep in his house. He was tired and soon dozed off.

The following morning, when Mirza broached the topic of her going back, Lajo declared: 'No Mian, I am not leaving.'

'But...'

'Did you not like the food I cooked?'

'It is not that.'

'Did I not clean the house?'

'All that is fine, but...'

'Then what is wrong?' Lajo got angry.

Lajo had given her heart away at first sight. Not to Mirza but to his house. Any house that had no woman belonged to her. A man does not own his house, he is just a guest in it. Bakshi, that maggoty kebab! He had kept her in a separate room, that too a buffalo-shed which belonged to Nandi, the potter. The buffalo was long dead, but had left behind a stench which entered Lajo's very veins. To say nothing of Bakshi and his airs. Here, she was the queen of the household.

Mirza was a consummate idiot; this Lajo had understood immediately upon meeting him. He was a genuine guest in his own house. He'd come in quietly and eat whatever she would lay out in front of him. On his way out he'd give her money; he quizzed Lajo on expenses a few times but was soon satisfied that she did not cheat him. He would leave in the morning and return by evening.

Lajo would set the house in order and then bathe in the courtyard. Sometimes, she would visit Ramu's grandmother in the neighbourhood. Ramu worked in Mirza's shop; he had taken a shine to Lajo. He was barely thirteen or fourteen. A face full of pimples. He had fallen into bad company. It was he who had revealed that Mirza often visited prostitutes.

Lajo was hurt. Useless expense, she thought. Those women are all dacoits! After all, what was she for? Till date, wherever she had stayed, she had performed all her duties diligently. It had been a week since Lajo had arrived, and she had never been so insulted anywhere else. She held a large-hearted view of the man-woman relationship. Love, for her, was the only beautiful experience. She had gained an early exposure to love, but she had not had the guidance of an elder, a mother or a grandmother, to tutor her in its finer nuances. In this matter, Lajo was like the neighbourhood queen-cat which claims the affection of the tomcat as a matter of right.

She had other offers, but she considered herself Mirza's maid. She refused all overtures, lest Mirza be mocked.

Mirza was a block of ice on the outside but, inside him a volcano raged. He would deliberately stay away from home. His heart was in the grip of a strange confusion. The neighbourhood Romeos, too, were partly responsible for his condition. For, everywhere, Lajo was the topic of discussion. Today, she scratched the face of the milkman; yesterday, she threw cow-dung on the paan-seller's face! Wherever she would go, men would rush after her, their hearts laid out on their hands. If the schoolmaster met her in some lane, he would insist on lecturing her. Even the mullah of the mosque, hearing the sound of her bangles, would recite the verses meant to ward off evil spirits.

Mirza entered the house a little irritated. Lajo had just had a bath. Her wet hair was spread out over her her shoulders, her face was flushed from blowing into kitchen fire. The smoke had left her teary-eyed. Seeing Mirza at this unexpected hour, she grimaced. Mirza stuttered, and kept himself from falling over. He finished his meal, keeping his head lowered, and left for the mosque. His heart, however, was at home. He wondered why he suddenly missed home. When he returned, Lajo was quarrelling with someone at the door. Seeing Mirza, the man left.

'Who was he…?' he enquired like a distrustful husband.

'Raghuwa.'

'Raghuwa?' The man had supplied Mirza with milk for years but he didn't know his name.

'The milkman.'

'Should I refill the hookah, Mian?' Lajo tried to change the subject.

'No, what was he saying?'

'He was asking how much milk he should bring.'

'What did you say?'

'I said, die, why don't you? Bring as much as you do daily.'

'Then…?' Mirza began to smoulder.

'Then I said, Bastard, give that milk to your mother…that cow-buffalo!'

'Damned scoundrel! He is a bastard. Stop taking milk from him. I will fetch it on my way back from the store.'

Later, after dinner, Mirza put on a starched kurta and stuck a wad of perfumed cotton wool behind his ear. Taking his stick, he left the house with a flourish. Lajo burnt with jealousy—like a well-done kebab. She stood by meekly, like a devout wife, inwardly cursing the prostitute.

The prostitute was busy finalizing a deal with another customer. Mirza became angry and went off to the Lala's shop to wait. By the time he came home fuming, having discussed politics and

increasing prices, it was eleven at night. There was a carafé of
water kept next to his bed but he did not notice it. He stomped
into the kitchen and drank cold water from the earthen pot kept
there. But the fire within leapt ever higher.

Lajo's blemishless golden leg was visible from the door. She
turned awkwardly; her bangles clinked. Her leg stretched out even
further. Mirza downed one more glass of water. Muttering, he
went back to his own bed.

Turning and tossing bruised his body. The water he kept
drinking filled out his stomach like a drum. From behind the
door, the leg enticed him even more. An unknown fear began
choking him. She was sure to raise hell, the loudmouth, but
Shaitan himself was at his back, egging him on. By now, he had
walked many miles from his bed to the kitchen. He was exhausted.

Then, a very innocent thought reared its head in his mind. If
he were to cover Lajo's leg, surely he would not feel so thirsty. As
soon as this thought spread its hood, it brought back his confidence.
But if she were to wake up, what would she make of his actions?
But if one must save oneself, risks have to be undertaken.

Quietly placing his shoes under the cot, he crept forward with
bated breath. He pinched the hem of her skirt and pulled it down.
Soon, he regretted his action—what if the poor soul felt hot.
Confused, Mirza stood nervously; then, placing a stone over his
heart, he turned around.

His nervous feet had barely taken him to the doorsill when all
hell broke loose. Lajo, turning on her side, caught hold of him.
Mirza was dumbstruck. In all his years no one had taken such
liberties with Mirza. Lajo stripped him of his shame even as he
kept up a steady protest.

In the morning Mirza was shy, like a newly wed bride. Lajo,
the chest-thumping victor, hummed a tune even as she poured a
thick layer of ghee on the paranthas. Her eyes revealed nothing of
the tumult of the previous night. Sticking to routine, she sat in the
doorway waving the flies away. Mirza feared that Lajo had gotten
a hold of his finger; she would now demand his entire arm.

In the afternoon, when Lajo brought Mirza's lunch to the store, there was a spring in her gait. On seeing Lajo, people would generally stop by to enquire prices. Frequently, they'd be forced to buy things. Lajo would quickly pack the goods, including coquetry and smiles with every sale. Thus, she would sell in a short while what Mirza would take an entire day to sell. That day, this fact was annoying him immensely.

Soon, however, Mirza acquired prosperity fit for a king. He put on weight and his complexion cleared. People knew why and flared up in envy. Mirza's madness, too, increased by the day. The more Lajo served him, the more his thirst for her increased. In his heart he began to fear the world. He now had first-hand, heady experience of Lajo's wantonness. Whenever she would bring lunch, an earthquake would hit the entire market. Mirza's blood would boil whenever she would arrive—snapping her fingers at someone, swaying her hips, cursing, abusing, jeering and showing her thumb to everyone.

He would say, 'Don't bring me food here.'

'Why?' Lajo's face would fall.

She would go mad sitting home alone all day. The market was colourful; a place of laughter and fun.

On the days Lajo stayed home, all manner of doubts would rise in Mirza's heart. Wonder what she is up to, he would think. He would return home at odd hours to check on her. She would immediately insist upon relaxing him, and taking care of his fatigue. Who wouldn't be afraid of such an artful woman?

One day, on one such surprise visit, he found Lajo arguing with a scrap-dealer, and the scrap-dealer standing with a grin on his face, looking as if he were drinking glass after glass of sweet sherbet. When he saw Mirza, he fled. But Mirza caught hold of the man and administered two tight slaps and one kick.

'What was the matter?' Mirza's nostrils flared.

'Corpse! He was offering ten annas per seer for the scrap. I told him to sell it to his mother. Bastard!'

The going rate was eight annas per seer.

'Who told you to sell it?' Mirza muttered, stretching out his leg to untie his shoelaces.

It was when Mirza saw Lajo playing kabaddi with the boys of the street that his anger knew no bounds. Her long skirt rode up as she ran about. And while the children were engrossed in the game, their fathers were enjoying the free show. Each one of them had earlier attempted to entice Lajo with offers of a kotha—a room—which she had rejected.

Mirza walked past, his head bowed in shame. The men mocked him. 'Look how angry he is, as if she were his lawfully wedded wife.'

Lajo had become a problem for Mirza. Just the thought that he would be separated from her was enough to make him break out in a cold sweat. His mind was not on his store at all. He was tormented by the thought that her mouth would water at some exceptionally juicy offer and she would leave him.

'Mian, why don't you marry her?' Miran Mian suggested after hearing Mirza's problem.

'God forbid! The nikah is a sacred rite. How can it be associated with a prostitute like her? She has flounced her skirt everywhere, how can she be a bride now?'

But when he came home and didn't find Lajo there, he panicked. The Lala had been sniffing around for many days and it was no secret that he had publicly said, 'Forget a kotha, she can have a bungalow if she desires one.' Even Miran Mian, who claimed to be his friend, had made secret overtures.

Mirza was sitting, agitated, when Lajo walked in. She had been with Ramu's grandmother who needed a back massage. That day, Mirza decided: he would marry Lajo, whether it brought shame to his family or not.

'Why, Mian?' Lajo was bewildered by Mirza's proposal.

'Why? Are you interested in someone else?' Mirza asked angrily.

'Thoo…thoo! Why should I be interested in anyone else?'

'That Rao, the one who promises you a bungalow…'

'I wouldn't even spit on his bungalow. I hit him on the face with a shoe!'

'So then...?'

But Lajo could not explain to Mirza that there was no need for a nikah. She was his and would always remain his. What had she done that he felt the need for a wedding? A master such as Mirza could only be found after gaining merit over many rebirths. Lajo had faced terrible times and to her Mirza was an angel. All her lovers would eventually turn into her masters, and would then beat her.

Mirza had never touched her, even with a stick made out of flowers, and he loved her deeply. He had even provided her with two sets of clothes and gifted her ornaments—made out of pure gold, which no one in the last seven generations of her family had seen.

He told Ramu's grandmother of his intention, and even she was shocked.

'Mian, why do you want to tie a bell round your neck? Is the bitch acting pricey? Give her a good thumping and she will come right back on track. When a shoe-beating is the solution, why a nikah?'

But Mirza was hell-bent—if she is mine, she must accept a nikah.

'Why, is religion coming in the way?' Ramu's grandmother asked Lajo.

'No, mother, that is not the problem. I have always considered him mine.'

Lajo was exceedingly sweet-natured. She could take a momentary customer and serve him as she would a husband. She never held back anything from any of her lovers. She gave with all her heart and took to her heart's content. But Mirza was special—only her heart knew what joy it was to give him love, and to snatch it from him. Before him, others were stubborn dogs. She was quite aware of her reality—the nikah is the privilege of virgins and she could not remember a time when she was one. She was unworthy of becoming a bride.

She begged and pleaded with Mirza, but he was adamant.

214 River of Flesh

Once an auspicious date was identified, they were married soon after the night-time namaaz of Isha. The entire mohalla was excited. Women and girls sang wedding songs to the accompaniment of dhols. Some joined the wedding from the bride's side while others appointed themselves the bridegroom's party. Mirza obliged everyone, happily doling out money to all. Lajo—now Kaneez Fatima—was duly married to Mirza Irfan Beg.

~

Mirza banned the skirt and got a tight-fitting pyjama and kurta made. Kaneez Fatima, however, was used to room between her legs. Two pyjama sleeves, and fabric between the legs, are sheer torture. She would miss no opportunity to take it off. She had taken off her pyjama, hung it on a clothesline, and was dropping the skirt over her head when Mirza walked in. Instead of stopping the skirt at her waist, she let it fall down to her ankles.

'God forbid!' Mirza cursed, and threw a sheet over Lajo. Mirza lectured to her at length but Lajo could not understand what her fault was. These were the things which would infuriate Mirza no end. Mirza then tossed the perfectly good skirt into the hearth.

He left the house muttering under his breath and Lajo was left sitting there like a thief. Throwing off the sheet she examined herself—had she contracted leprosy? She kept weeping even as she bathed under the tap. Mithwa, the son of the reed-maker, would often watch her bathe from atop a nearby roof while pretending to fly his kite. But that day she was so sad that she did not show him a thumb of derision, she did not threaten him with a shoe, nor did she run off inside. She only covered herself with the sheet.

She placed a stone over her heart and pulled on the accursed pyjama—as tight as the Shaitan's innards. And, worse, the drawstring slipped out. She shouted with all her might until Billo arrived and the drawstring was threaded.

'Wonder whose idea of a joke this pyjama was, good only to slide over a gun. Untie…re-tie…each time one goes to the toilet.'

When Mirza came home from the store, the string had slipped out again. Lajo was trying to pull it out with a finger. Mirza's heart welled up with love. Kissing her, he sat her on his lap. The errant drawstring was found after a great deal of effort. After that, she did not begrudge the pyjama anymore.

Now another problem emerged. The qualities which were once Lajo's attractions became shamelessness in Mirza's bride. The flourishes of street women do not suit respectable ladies. Lajo could not become the ideal bride that Mirza would beg love from. That one would shy away and the other would pursue. That one would be pretend-angry, the other would make amends. Lajo was a stone from the streets. It was not in her to become a delicate flower and adorn the marital bed. Mirza, however, bridled the wildness within Lajo with incessant nagging and scolding.

Mirza was very satisfied with himself for having transformed Lajo into a decent, respectable lady. It was another matter that he was now in no hurry to get home. Like other husbands, he would spend time with friends so that no one could call him hen-pecked. It is easy for a man to cater to the fancies of a beloved, but very cumbersome to obey the dictates of a wife.

To make up for his absence at home, Mirza suggested a maid, but Lajo's eyes became bloodshot at the suggestion. She knew Mirza was visiting prostitutes again; all the men of the neighbourhood did. However, inside her house, she would not tolerate any interference. No one could lay a finger on her shining utensils or enter her kitchen. She was willing to share Mirza but not his house, for here she reigned supreme.

Soon, it was as if Mirza had installed Lajo in his house and completely forgotten about her. Weeks would pass with mere grunts of acknowledgement. As long as she was his mistress, everybody noticed her. Once she settled down into a respectable man's house, however, she became a mother, a sister and a daughter. No one bothered to peep within from beyond the curtain any longer except Mithwa, the reed-weaver's son. He alone kept his infatuation smouldering and continued to fly kites atop the neighbouring roof. After Mirza would leave, Lajo would finish her chores and bathe under the tap, which had been installed for privacy. And, by now, Lajo had stopped looking up at the top of the building.

~

It was a Dussehra night, and Mirza had been out partying with friends. He had returned in the morning and had then hurriedly left for the store after having bathed and changed into clean clothes. Lajo was already angry when her eyes went up to the terrace; or maybe it was that Mithwa's gaze carried daggers that day. They pierced her drenched body. The boy lost a kite-fight for the first time in many days. As the severed kite floated away, its trailing cord touched her back. Lajo whimpered and—unknowingly or on purpose, it is impossible to say—rushed off inside without covering herself with a sheet. Lightning flashed, and struck the terrace. The she realized that she had left the tap running and immediately raced back.

After this, whenever Lajo would pull aside the front-door curtain to order food from the sweetmeat shop, she would always see Mithwa nearby.

'Oye Mithwa! Why do you keep loitering about? Go get me some kachori. And have a lot of chillies added to the chutney.'

Mithwa was stirred more than ever before. If by chance he missed being on the terrace at bath time, he would get up with a jolt. The love which Lajo had shared extravagantly and with both her hands all her life was also available for Mithwa. If Mirza missed a meal, she would hardly throw the food away. A needy man could always eat it. And there was no one needier than Mithwa.

Having fettered her with marriage, Mirza imagined that he had made Lajo a housewife. Had he not witnessed the scene with his own eyes, he would have never believed it. When Lajo saw Mirza in the doorway she burst into laughter. She never imagined that Mirza would be so offended. But Mithwa recognized his rage and, picking up his dhoti, ran, not stopping until he had crossed three whole villages.

Mirza beat Lajo so hard that, had she not been tempered by the hot and cold of the world, she would have died. Soon the entire locality was abuzz with the news that Mirza had caught his wife red-handed with Mithwa and had consigned them both to the depths of hell. Mirza was shamed. He and his family had lost their honour. People gathered in hordes to witness the drama. They were all disappointed to find out that Mithwa had escaped and the wife had been beaten to within an inch of her life. 'But she will live, Ramu's grandmother will pull her through.'

One would think that after being beaten so mercilessly by Mirza, Lajo would hate the very sight of him. God forbid, the opposite happened! The beating cemented her love, more than the nikah had. On regaining consciousness, she enquired about Mirza's well-being. All her previous masters would eventually become her lovers. After such an honour, there could be no question of a salary. And the beatings gratis. Until now, Mirza had never hit her, even with a stick made out of flowers. Her earlier masters would share her with their friends. Mirza considered her his property, and staked uncontested claim upon her. As far as she was concerned, this was high respect. She may not have been in use, yet she was still so dear to him. Mirza's pain took precedence over her injuries. Everyone advised her to flee if she valued her life, but she refused.

It was Miran Mian who was holding back Mirza. Mirza could see no way out: he had to murder Lajo, and chop off her nose and hair. He had been dishonoured, and she had survived. How would he face the world now?

'You want to be hanged for killing a whore?'

'I don't care'

'Just divorce her and end the matter,' Miran Mian counselled. 'Had she been from a respectable family, things would have been different.'

Mirza immediately divorced Lajo and sent the thirty-two rupees of her mehr along with her clothes and belongings to Ramu's grandmother. When Lajo heard about the divorce she felt relieved, as if a great load had been lifted off her head. She just did not like marriage. All this had happened because of it, now it was at an end.

'Is Mian annoyed?' she enquired of Ramu's grandmother.

'I don't want to see you. Blacken your face and leave.'

News of Mirza's divorce sped all over the entire mohalla. Immediately, the Lala sent a message: 'The bungalow is ready.'

Lajo had her reply conveyed: 'Keep your mother in it.'

Of the thirty-two rupees she had received as the refunded mehr, she handed over ten to Ramo's grandmother as boarding and lodging charges. She sold the tight pyjama to Shakoora's daughter-in-law for a pittance. In fifteen days she was left with nothing, like dust had fallen away from her. It was as if the beating had renewed her. Her gait had a new spring in it. When she stepped out to buy paan, or to visit the sweetmeats shop, the lanes would come alive. Mirza would seethe with envy.

One day she was at the paan-seller's, arguing with him over a few grains of cardamom. The paan-seller was enjoying himself. Mirza walked past with lowered gaze.

Miran Mian tried to reason with Mirza. 'My dear sir, you are now obsessing about her. What she does now is none of your business; you have given her a divorce. What relationship do you have with her now?'

Mirza lost his temper. 'She used to be my wife. How can I tolerate it?'

'So what? She is not your wife now. In fact, she was never your wife.'

'What about the nikah?'

'Absolutely illegal.'

'You mean that…'

'It never happened, brother! Who knows whose illegitimate child she is? And a nikah with a bastard cannot be held legitimate.'

'So the nikah never happened?'

'Not at all.'

Later, a mullah also certified that nikah with a bastard is invalid.

'Then my honour is intact, too.' Mirza smiled. A great weight had been lifted off his head.

'Of course.'

'This is a strange business. Then there was no divorce either.'

'Brother, when no nikah took place, how can there be a divorce?'

'The thirty-two rupees of mehr were given without any reason.' Mirza began to regret his loss.

Soon, the news that Mirza had had no nikah, and no divorce either, started capering around in the mohalla. Of course, he lost the thirty-two rupees.

On hearing this good news, Lajo broke into a dance. A load slipped off her chest. The nikah and the talaaq were both nightmares, and had ended.

She was most happy to know that Mian had not been disgraced. She would have been gutted if Mirza would have had to bear loss of face. What a boon it was to be a bastard—it had saved the situation. God forbid, had she been a legitimate child, all would have been lost.

She was feeling stifled in Ramu's grandmother's house. Never before in her life had she had the chance to reign over a household. She was worried for the house. For fear of theft, Mirza would not have got the house swept. Trash must be piling up inside, she thought.

Mirza was leaving for the store when Lajo blocked his way.

'So Mian, should I join work from tomorrow?' she teased.

'God forbid!' Mirza kept his head lowered and strode off. Inwardly, he thought, I'll have to keep a maid, why not this accursed wench. After all, the matter has been cleared up.

Lajo did not wait for the following day. Hopping across terraces, she jumped into the house and, hitching her skirt up high, began work.

When Mirza came home in the evening he felt as though his

dear dead mother had come back to life. The house was clean, the
delicate fragrances of sandalwood and frankincense wafted through
the rooms, the water-pot was clean, and covered with a bowl
scrubbed to a high shine—his heart filled with pleasure. He ate
dinner in silence. As befitted her position, Lajo sat in the doorway
with a punkah in hand.

Later that night, after Lajo had stretched out in the kitchen,
Mirza suffered a severe attack of thirst. Ignoring his heart, he kept
tossing and turning about, listening to the tinkle of her bangles.

Mirza's heart was telling him that he had treated her quite
unmercifully.

'God forbid…!' He leapt out of bed with a start and gathered
the housewife into his arms.

Translated from the Urdu by Sameena Hasan Siddiqui

ROLL OF THE DICE

Nayana Addarkar

When the lights on the railway overbridge came on, some activity began in the hutments below the bridge. Women began to drag themselves out of the occasional hut, getting ready to deck themselves up for the night ahead. Stretching her arms and legs and yawning, Zaitun too got up from the bedding she shared with her child. Drawing the comb perfunctorily over her hair, she unravelled her soiled sari, dusted it and draped it neatly back onto herself. Barring this saree that she was wearing, she had nothing better to wear. Hussain had given her this sari. But scoundrel that he was, he'd taken everything else from her when he vanished.

'Chal bé harami! Time for work,' muttered Zaitun, lifting Hamid from the ragged old bedcover that he lay on. She couldn't help laughing at herself mirthlessly. How soon the jargon of the place had got into her, and the booze too! Stepping out from the hovel, she groped inside her blouse and fished out a crumpled ten-rupee note that was tucked in there. She walked on, and stopped at the old railway station.

Seeing Zaitun, a man holding on to his lungi moved towards her. Coming closer, he began to pet little Hamid who was cradled in her arms. Shoving the man aside, she confronted him, 'Hey you, mother-fucker! You think this is your mother's shop that you want to fondle for free, you bastard!' As the man shamelessly continued his antics, Zaitun chased him away angrily and came out of the station, irritated. Crossing the road, she went straight to Jose's bar. Taking out the tenner, she took the glass of liquor Jose held out and poured it down her throat. Wiping her lips on her sleeve, she came out and stood leaning against the compound wall. She put Hamid on a rag at her feet.

About ten minutes went by. She saw a young man glancing hesitantly at her. Gauging a potential customer, she beckoned him with her eyes and, lifting Hamid, Zaitun walked towards the back of the nearby chapel. The place was deserted. Glancing around nervously, the youth began to follow her slowly. He has the urge and also the shame! Zaitun began to laugh at the thought. Back home, Hussain used to take her behind the dargah to the hill. At that time, she too would go fearfully and bashfully. Whispering sweet nothings, he would playfully caress and fondle her, undressing her piece by piece, and introducing her to hitherto unknown levels of pleasure. She never knew when she got hooked. But the realization that the games had led to a swelling belly ended up with her being abandoned in Goa.

Her reverie was broken by the youth who was timidly pawing at her boobs. Perhaps he was nervous because it was his first encounter. Zaitun helpfully tried to encourage him, but beyond fondling her, the young man did not seem to proceed. Zaitun was irritated. The shot of liquor on an empty stomach had begun to hit her. She was also apprehensive that after a while Hamid would start crying for his milk.

When the young man kept touching her, Zaitum stood up. Saying, 'What's up, you want it for free?' she draped her sari back.

'How much?' the young man asked tremulously, opening his purse. From it, bulging with notes, he pulled out fifty rupees and held the note out to Zaitun. It was the first time that Zaitun was making fifty rupees, and that too for mere foreplay. Otherwise, just a fiver or a tenner from drunks was all the business that she would get. Zaitun's eyes glistened at the sight of the note. If she could make money like this, she would even be able to go back to her village. Hastily, grabbing the money and the youth's hand, she pointed to a half-constructed old building beyond the alley. 'It will be better there... And bring another fifty rupees. Come up to the top at eleven. You'll come, won't you?' said Zaitun, playfully tapping the young man's cheek. She lifted Hamid up and quickly walked through the lane. Going back to the bar, she downed a glass of liquor. She then went to a roadside eatery and ordered: 'Get a plate of mutton.' The owner raised his eyebrows. Normally, it was just half-plate rice-curry or bhaji-pao—how come a mutton plate today? 'You have the money?' he demanded.

'Why are you asking? Haven't I always paid you? Khali-pili bakwas!' Saying this, she put Hamid to her breast. Hearing Zaitun's words which had begun to slur, the man gauged that she must have caught hold of a gullible guy. He brought her her order.

Zaitun gulped down the mutton and went back to the half-built building. By now, most of the shops had closed. The people in the nearby buildings had gone to sleep. Taking the sleeping Hamid, Zaitun walked up the steps. The young man of a while ago was sitting at the top of the building. He had removed his clothes and placed them against the wall, neatly folded. By the faint light of the bulb in the verandah of the flat in the next building, Zaitun could make out the wallet, which he had kept on top of the clothes. Looking at it brought back the longing to go home. Feasting her eyes on the purse, she placed the sleeping Hamid next to the clothes. Quickly removing her sari, she lay down on her back. The hesitant youth of a while ago now loomed confidently over her. She caught the stink of booze. Saala piyela hai!

Zaitun began to kiss his face. Probably his first time. He began to fondle her body feverishly. She remembered Hussain. He too used to maul her excitedly. At first, in the bushes behind the dargah and later, in the house itself, when her mistress was away. But when the vomiting began, her employer was stunned. She dreaded that it was Hussain, her son, who was responsible. She had not imagined such an outcome. She'd brought the girl from an orphanage in Miraj, after paying them off, to work as her maid. Now Zaitun could end up as her daughter-in-law! The mistress herself hatched a plan. She sent the girl with Hussain to Goa. Hussain took her around and showed her several places in Goa. A couple of days later, he woke her up from her slumber in the wee hours. Telling her that they had a train to catch to go back home, he took her to the station. Not a soul could be seen on the platform. Making Zaitun lie down on a bench, he sat by her side. Zaitun fell into a deep sleep. When she woke up, she found with a shock that she was alone. Even her bag was not there. In a frenzy,

Zaitun walked all over the station in search of Hussain. But Hussain was nowhere to be found. The realization sank in slowly—she had been duped.

Hauling her pregnant belly, she had trudged to shops and houses looking for work. But nobody would employ her. Finally, pangs of hunger gnawing at her, she had made her way to the old railway station. As she staggered along, a guy waved ten rupees at her and beckoned her by crooking his finger. For the first time, Zaitun sold herself to satisfy her hunger. Later on, it became a routine. Hamid was now almost four months old. Just as she was recovering from the pangs of childbirth, she had to get back to work in order to feed two mouths. Drunkards were not particular about the body—a whore in any state would do, as long as they could satisfy themselves.

Hamid began to cry. Zaitun became alert. The young man's foot had hit the child. 'Enough now, Baba has woken up.' But the youth was now thoroughly aroused. He did not allow Zaitun to get up. Pinning her down, he continued his noisy frenzy. Hussain too used to shriek loudly and go on and on. Zaitun tried to push the young man away from her. The youth, who was building to his climax, felt cheated. Stretching his leg, he angrily aimed a kick at Hamid. The child went into a paroxysm of screams. Zaitun's maternal instincts were instantly provoked. In a fit of anger, she pushed the man with all her strength and stood up. Grabbing him, she lifted him up and smacked him across the face. But the young man was still highly aroused. He began to push Zaitun down again. Angrily, Zaitun shoved him. The young man stumbled against the low parapet of the balcony and, unable to keep his balance, he toppled over, landing with a faint thud on the ground below. The bulb of the balcony in the next building had been switched off by now. Zaitun quickly turned back. Feverishly, she lifted her baby. Scooping up the young man's purse, she hurriedly strode through the back alleys. Deciding that any bus leaving at dawn would take her back home, she began walking hurriedly towards the bus stand.

In the morning, while Zaitun was riding the bus on her way home, the police were conducting the panchanama of the naked body of a young man who had fallen from the balcony of a building on Station Road.

Translated from the Konkani by Xavier Cota

THE LETTERS

Modhurima Sinha

Leela looked at the papers which had cascaded down, spilling out of the ornate old box with the ivory lid. She bent down and picked out one sheet. A letter. A love letter. A love letter from her father—Gourishankar. A love letter from her father to...some Nuzhat Begum. With trembling feet, Leela sat on her haunches and picked up a few more. An hour passed and Leela was immersed in the letters written by her father to the unknown Nuzhat Begum. In some letters he addressed her as Nuzhat Jaan. Outside, the clouds smeared the courtyard of Gouri Mahal with dark shadows. The low rumbling of thunder made her look up from the letters. The windows were open and the gathering storm was gaining momentum in leaps and bounds. Whistling winds cut through the thunder and made Leela jump up to shut the windows. The old letters scattered. She collected the letters strewn around the closed room and sat on the four-poster bed.

The letters were all written by her father to an unknown woman, who sang beautifully, he said. But why were the letters in this house? Such passionate letters, so much poetry, from her father. This seemed to be a different man. What was Baba like? Leela tried to remember her father at his worst, at his best. She had lost her mother at the age of two and hardly remembered her. A vague, blurry image of being picked up and a faint smell of some unknown oil—or was it shampoo? Very often, she felt she had just imagined it. Baba never remarried. She recalled how the family pressured her father from time to time to remarry, as she grew up. Gourishankar always smiled and said, 'There are so many of you. Leela will be fine.' There were her relatives, of course, and Leela enjoyed being with her kaka, kaki, grandmother, and cousins. The courtyard and Thakur Dalan were full of games. Hide and seek, kumir danga, kho kho. Her cousin Rimi and she would take their dolls and play on the Thakur Dalan behind the pillars. She did miss not having her mother. But Baba was a good father and spent a lot of time with her. At night he slept with her on the same bed till she turned ten. Leela loved the room that was hers and over the years grew attached to every corner of that room. Even when her father died a few years ago, she took comfort from that room.

But she had never guessed that he had had a lover. Nobody in the family had told her either. Or didn't they know? He was always so full of life. Leela remembered him staying at home, always, on her mother's birthday. He would feed a hundred children on that day. A huge meal with pulao, mutton curry, rabri. Didn't he love her? Why didn't he remarry? Who was Nuzhat Jaan? She rustled up a small storm, looking for an envelope in that box. There was none. No address. Leela got up and walked out into the balcony. It was raining now. She looked unfocused at the courtyard below. Who could she ask? And now, when the whole family was divided.

Gouri Mahal was being sold. After her father's death, her kaka and pishi had decided to sell it. Leela fought for the house, the beautiful mansion, but the majority wanted it sold. Her cousins, all friends once upon a time, disagreed with her. When it came to money, they all wanted money. Hardly anyone had any sentiments. Some of the old servants were upset. But kaka and his three children called the house a white elephant and wanted to get rid of it. Leela requested them to find a hotel chain or some heritage association to save the house from being broken down. But the family was in a hurry. The first buyer with a serious price won the deal. They told her that she would be rich too. But Leela didn't care. Her job as a journalist excited her. Her father had left her enough funds. She was alone in the world, she realized. Her last boyfriend was selfish and harboured ancient concepts regarding women. Narrow. There were marriage proposals every day but she didn't want to marry anyone. The promise of great wealth and her lineage had suitors lined up. Leela hugged the pillar and walked across to the other side.

She found Jamuna-di in the kitchen. Jamuna-di was old and crumbling. Jamuna-di looked like she had been in this house for

the entire one hundred and fifty years of its existence. Gouri
Mahal, with its elegant Doric pillars, carved walls, marble staircases,
coloured chandeliers, was now finally crumbling. Kaka wasted his
life and had never worked it seems. Baba worked in the family
bookshop. But when he died, that was sold. Who was reading any
more? Leela looked at her cell phone with disgust. She too was a
slave to her phone. She looked at Jamuna-di, who was cooking
baigun. Leela hated baigun.

Leela sat next to Jamuna-di on the floor in the old, withered
kitchen with smoky walls and asked her, 'Jamuna-di, who is
Nuzhat Begum?' Jamuna-di looked at her, startled. Her eyes woke
up from their usual slumber and in the shock of the moment the
kadhai with baigun and aloo crashed to the floor. Nobody had
heard, it seemed. Leela helped her and said, 'What happened
Jamuna-di?' She washed the vegetables and set up the kadhai on
the gas for her. 'Jamuna-di. I know. Please don't hide things from
me. I need to know.'

Jamuna-di looked at her sadly. 'Ke bollo tomay? Everyone had
promised never to tell you.'

'Jamuna-di,' explained Leela, 'I found letters. This house will
die soon. Before we move, I was cleaning out the cupboards. In
Baba's almirah, which I hadn't touched from the time he left us, I
found a box full of letters. That's how I know.' Jamuna-di stared in
incomprehension. The stillness in the kitchen was tangible. Far
away, a koel called desperately. It was spring.

'She wrote letters to him? He kept them?' she asked, half-
afraid, half-curious.

'No,' said Leela. 'These are letters written by him to her in
beautiful Bengali. Baba's handwriting is so beautiful, Jamuna-di.'

Jamuna-di stared. 'He wrote letters to her? Then they should
be with her. Why are they here? In Bengali? How would she read
them?'

It was Leela's turn to stare, 'Keno?'

'She was from Lucknow. And spoke Urdu. Bangla was not her
language.'

Leela was silent for a long time. 'Jamuna-di, you seem to know a lot. I need more details.'

It was difficult getting anything out from an old traditional retainer like Jamuna-di. These loyalists are rare today. But Jamuna-di's ultimate loyalty lay with Leela, whom she had almost brought up. Once they vacated Gouri Mahal, Jamuna-di would come with Leela to her new flat in South Kolkata. So Jamuna-di gave her the details that she knew.

~

Leela stood in an unknown street in north Kolkata, in front of a small building with a few flats. She had gone through hell and fire and finally extracted the location and address from Jamuna-di, whose husband had known the place. Jamuna-di's husband, Kartik-da, was Leela's father's right-hand man. Kartik-da had died along with Leela's father in the car accident a few years ago.

Leela rang the bell with clammy hands. Was she alive? What if she were dead?

~

Nuzhat Begum and Leela stood in front of the Thakur Dalan. Nuzhat Begum, graceful, beautiful, definitely old, but dignified. Beside her stood Leela in her fragrant youth, hair tied up in a ponytail. They both just stared at the Dalan silently. Leela felt a pressure on her hands. She looked sideways. Nuzhat Begum had tears in her eyes. 'Your father spoke about this so often. He loved this house, you know?'

Leela smiled and took her upstairs. Nuzhat Begum went all over the house. Every room, corridor, different staircases. She walked through the broad verandahs, with the grills and the trellis. She heard the plump pigeons coo seductively. The baithak-khana smelt of mothballs. Leela opened up the tall shuttered windows, and the dusty mirrors trembled in expectation. Nuzhat Begum looked up at the chandeliers. They glittered in hope. She looked at the framed portraits and stopped in front of one of Leela's parents. She knew this was the woman whom Gourishankar had lost. The woman whose place she had never been able to take. Leela came

and stood beside her. The two women looked into each other's
eyes searching for an unknown message. A hesitant cough. They
both looked at the last door. Jamuna-di stood, all huddled in her
white sari with a black border.

Leela told her it was Jamuna-di. Nuzhat Begum walked towards
her and held her hands. 'I knew your husband Kartik-bhai so well,'
she said in Hindi. 'He was a wonderful man. You know Jamuna-
apa, Kartik-bhai made my home for me. He decorated the flat
when Gouri brought me away from that hell I lived in. He was a
brave man, Gouri. Imagine, thirty-two years ago, he gave me a
home. A tawaif who was not that young any more. And your
Kartik dressed it up for me. In that building, Jamuna-apa, the few
families who lived did not protest, because they did not know for a
long time. When they found out, only one protested. And Kartik-
bhai slapped him. For me. Imagine! Actually, that house belonged
to Gouri. He gifted it to me legally. So the other tenants said
nothing. We lived peacefully. Gouri came almost every day. When
he couldn't, Kartik would come. He would buy my rice, dal, ghee,
flowers… I never had to go out. Kartik-bhai was like Mohan-
chacha who had brought me from Lucknow to Kolkata many
years ago.' She stopped, embarrassed, shy, but never awkward.

Leela drew her away from the door and sat her down on a sofa.
It creaked noisily. Jamuna-di sat at their feet. It seemed to Leela,
Nuzhat Begum always belonged to this space. She seemed
comfortable and strangely detached, simultaneously. They all
looked up as a young boy came in with a tray. There were sweets
and samosas on the plate. A glass of water. 'Thank you Jamuna-
di,' said Leela. Jamuna-di was crying quietly. Nuzhat Begum
touched her arm softly and said, 'Kya Jamuna-apa, Kartik yaad aa
gaye?' Jamuna-di broke down on Nuzhat Begum's lap and cried
convulsively. These unknown memories of her husband had stirred
her beyond anything she had ever known. Nuzhat Begum put her
right hand on Jamuna-di's head and spoke.

'Gouri gave me the house after your mother passed away.' She
looked at Leela. 'Your abba was a great human being.'

Leela looked up. 'I know. He always tried… And now I know him better because of those letters.'

'Can I see them?" asked Nuzhat Begum.

Leela went out and returned in a few minutes with the box of letters. She handed them over to Nuzhat Begum. Leela watched her open letter after letter and fold them back.

'Can you read them?'

Nuzhat Begum smiled, and then giggled like a teenager. 'Nahi. I cannot read Bengali. So Gouri would write them, read them out to me and take them back. He would explain. I did learn to understand Bengali slowly because of my long association with him.'

'You never wrote a letter to him?'

Nuzhat Begum looked up. 'Many. In Urdu. Then I explained them to him and kept them in one box.'

'You still have them?'

'Yes.'

'But when I sang, he understood everything. Your father understood music. He bought me a television.'

'Sing please,' said Leela.

Nuzhat Begum sang.

Jamnuna-di lifted her head and heard.

Leela pulled her knees to her chin and heard.

Curious disapproving family members peeped from the door, and they heard.

When she was leaving, Leela gave her the letters. She stood looking down at the courtyard. 'This beautiful home will be brought down?'

Leela just nodded silently.

~

Leela leaned forward and hugged her. Nuzhat Begum held her for a while. As she moved away, Leela held her back and smelt her hair. She looked at her questioningly. 'What is this smell? I know it.'

Nuzhat Begum took her hand out of Leela's grasp and said, 'Gouri gave me this oil after your mother passed away. He asked me to use it always. And I do, to this day.'

THE PROSTITUTE

J. P. Das

After winding up his day's work, Pramod returned to his hotel in the evening. He had won the day, for he had managed to get orders from a number of offices for the equipment his company sold. Of course, he had to resort to underhand methods like bribes, lies and flattery for that. His long years of experience had taught him that bribery was a sure-fire method in business; once money changes hands it is as though an unwritten deed of contract is signed between the man who gives and the man who takes the bribe. Thereafter, it is smooth sailing all the way. In other methods there is considerable loss of time, and success, too, is not assured.

He sat down on a chair and made a mental summing up of the day's proceedings. He had spent much less money than he had budgeted for. He decided to keep the balance amount with himself, without returning it to the company. He was not at all worried over this lapse on his part. What worried him was his tacit consent to helping a rival company during his talk with them. It pricked his conscience a little.

While sipping tea, he decided not to give it any more thought. His day had passed smoothly and he wanted to enjoy his last night in that city. The following day, in the morning, he would have to go to the market to purchase things ordered by his wife and children. At midday he would board the train for home. Having decided on the next day's programme, he took out a slim notebook containing telephone numbers. The numbers of ministers, officers and other powerful persons featured in it, but there was also a special page which contained some mysterious numbers furnished by his friends from time to time. Pramod dialled the first number on this page. From the other side came a man's voice on the line, 'Who do you want?'

'Kamla Devi,' replied Pramod.

'What's your name?' asked the man.

'Vinod. Vinod Sharma,' said Pramod.

'Okay. Please be on the line for a while.'

Pramod waited; when no one spoke for two minutes he was about to cut the line, but the man's voice came again, 'No. There's no Kamla Devi here.' Without waiting for Pramod to say anything, the man replaced the receiver. Pramod swore under his breath and dialled the next number. There was no response. He tried to remember who had given him that number so that he could curse him. But he could not remember his name, even after straining his memory. Then he bypassed all the other numbers and came to the last one. A female voice came on the line, 'Who do you want?'

'I want Vimla Devi,' replied Pramod.

'Vimla does not stay here nowadays.'

Pramod had thought that the woman would hang up immediately, but she did not. That encouraged him. 'A friend of mine has given me your number,' he said.

'Who was it?' asked the woman.

'Shankar. Shankar Gupta of Kanpur,' replied Pramod, concocting a false name and address.

'Hmmm...'

Pramod understood that things were going right and so he ventured, 'I want to come to your place in the evening.'

'Did you say Shankar Gupta of Kanpur? Okay,' responded the woman. Pramod collected the address and said that he would come around half-past eight.

He took his bath, dressed and found that he still had time to spare. To while away the time, he ordered soda and, taking out a bottle of whisky, placed it on the table. Since the soda was delayed, he thought he could talk to the representative of the rival company over the telephone. He dialled his number but, as soon as he dialled the number, he changed his mind; he would rather talk with him in the morning. But by then the telephone on the other side had started ringing and Pramod wished the gentleman were not at home. But he was home and he picked up the receiver.

'I think I should meet you once again before I leave this place,' said Pramod.

'I, too, wanted to look you up. We've a lot of work with you,' responded the man.

Just then his soda came and, without thinking, Pramod suggested, 'It'd be nice if you could drop in for a drink with me.' Immediately, he regretted his impulsive invitation and hoped that the man would not accept it. But he agreed instantly.

To retrieve the situation, somehow, Pramod said, 'Okay, I am going out on some work and will be back between nine to nine-thirty. Please come around that time.' After saying this he was afraid that the man might even agree to that. So without allowing him to respond he butted in, 'I think that'll be too late for you. Isn't it? Well, let's settle it this way. I shall come again in a week's time. We'll certainly meet then. We'll have a programme for the entire evening.'

'That would be all right. Please keep in mind the talk I had with you this morning. All your conditions are acceptable to us,' said the man.

'Certainly, certainly,' responded Pramod and replaced the receiver.

He resolved not to extend such hasty invitations in future. But he had work with that man and although he knew that he was betraying the secrets of his own company, he also knew that it was an extremely lucrative deal for him.

He decided not to give it any more thought and concentrated on his drink. But he could not get rid of the thought of the lucrative and unscrupulous deal offered by the man that morning. He made a mental estimate of his monthly gain from the deal and how he would spend that money for his family. Drinks, coupled with thoughts of the hefty pecuniary gain, thrilled him no end and he got ready to proceed to the address which he had obtained over the telephone.

He had a lot of money in his briefcase and he did not consider it safe to leave it in his hotel room. He also did not know whether his destination was a safe place or not. He decided to keep the currency notes in his inner pocket—but there was not enough space. Finally, he put the money in the briefcase and, as an afterthought, also put in the whisky bottle, which was half-empty. Then he came out of the hotel carrying the briefcase, hailed a cab and gave the driver the address. He arrived there just at half-past eight and gave himself a pat on his back for being so punctual despite his busy schedule.

The place was dark and depressing. A frail, sickly man, convulsed with coughs, sat on the verandah and added to the gloom of the house. On seeing Pramod approach he stood up, bobbed a courtesy and offered him a chair. After Pramod took the chair he said, 'You have to wait a while, there are other people inside.' Pramod got irritated on hearing this and looked at the man with disdain, without trying to hide his irritation. But the man was a cool customer, he ignored Pramod's irritation and said, 'The other gentleman will come out any moment now. Shall I call for some tea?'

'No,' shot back Pramod.

'Have you come here earlier?' asked the man, trying to be friendly.

'Yes, but a long time ago.'

'If it was more than a year back, I was not here then. I came here only last March. I am not keeping well here in this city.'

Pramod did not allow him to be friendly any more and irritably cut him short. 'How long do I have to wait here?'

'Not long. He'll come out any moment. By the way, do you know any of the girls here?'

'It has been so long now that I don't remember the names. How much money…'

'You'll give the money to the girl inside. Please go to Radha. She's a very sober girl. I'm sure you will like her.'

Just then, two men came out of the house and hurriedly left without looking up. Seized by a paroxysm of coughing, the sickly man went inside, signalling to Pramod to wait. Pramod cursed the man under his breath and decided not to visit again. He wanted to treat the man shabbily but the man was so calm and sober that it was not possible to misbehave with him. After some time, the man came out, took Pramod inside and directed him to a room.

Pramod was happy to find the room quite bright, and everything neat and clean. The girl who stood leaning against the bedpost appeared pretty and educated, too. Having learnt from his previous experiences, Pramod kept the briefcase on a table and sat on the bed. Then he began taking off his shoes. The girl, who was till then only quietly smiling at him, moved the shoes to one side and sat near him.

'What's your name?' asked Pramod.

'Radha,' she replied.

'Is Radha your real name?'

'No, my name was Khshyanaprabha. But since it was quite a tongue-twister, I changed it to Radha.'

'How long have you been here?'

'For the last six months.'

All lies, thought Pramod. Radha, Khshyanaprabha, six months—all lies! Then he thought he should strike the bargain soon. When the girl asked for a sum less than he had expected, Pramod anticipated some sort of a catch. Therefore, to clarify the matter, he asked, 'Besides this, do I have to pay anyone anything?'

'That's up to you.'

'Shall I give the money now or…later?'

'As you wish.'

Pramod remembered that all his money was in the briefcase. He should have taken out some money and kept it in his pocket, he thought. He took off his wrist watch and, on the pretext of placing it on the table, examined whether the briefcase was properly locked; it was. He was now on the lookout for an opportunity to take some money out from it.

He came on to the bed and took Radha in his arms. While fondling her, he asked, 'Is any drink available here?'

'It has to be ordered from outside. What do you want?'

Pramod asked her the cost of various drinks and then said, 'It's very costly.'

'That's right. Since all the shops would have downed their shutters by now, the drink has to be procured from some illegal vendor. That's why it's so costly.' Pramod thought, if only Radha would go out of the room for a while, he could take out some money and the half-empty bottle from the briefcase. He would have to offer drinks to the girl, too. She might drink like a fish. In that case, what would be his total expenses for the evening along with the taxi-fare...? He calculated. Not much. Besides, once the deal with the rival company is struck, he wouldn't feel the pinch of such paltry expenses, he reflected happily.

'That's why I have brought along a bottle,' said Pramod.

'Shall I call for soda?' asked Radha.

Although he wanted soda in order to make Radha go out of the room for a while, he said, 'No. A little warm water will do.'

'Please wait. I shall arrange it.'

As soon as she went out of the room, Pramod opened the briefcase, brought out the bottle and took out some money from the bundles of notes inside it. Then he locked the briefcase, placed the key in a secret pocket in his trousers, and heaved a sigh of relief. 'Who knows what'll happen in a place like this,' he thought.

When Radha came back with some warm water, just to test her, Pramod called her Khshyanaprabha. She gave a start and placing the glass of warm water on the table stood looking at him. A thin mist of sadness spread across her face. In a voice heavy with emotion she said, 'After a long time someone called me by my old name. I felt very happy, I felt sad, too. Please always call me by this name.'

'Keep that false love to yourself. As if I am coming to you every day,' Pramod said to himself. But aloud he said, 'I like you a lot.'

When Radha took the bottle from his hand and poured him a glass, Pramod thought that the girl would swig down the whole bottle. But when she prepared only one glass, Pramod asked her why she did not take some for herself.

'I don't drink,' replied the girl.

'You have to drink with me,' Pramod insisted.

'I tasted it once. Didn't like it.'

'I won't drink if you do not drink,' said Pramod, caressing her.

'All right. Give me just a few drops.'

Pramod made a glass for her. When Radha took the glass from his hand he thought that she was only shamming abstinence. Radha touched the glass with her lips only once and after Pramod had finished drinking, she poured everything into his glass.

'Let me give you the money now,' said Pramod.

'Why're you worried about it? It can wait. Please relax and finish your glass. Shall I order something for you to eat?' Pramod thought it was another trick of hers to extract money from him.

'No, not necessary,' he said.

'You've not told me your name,' said Radha.

It was not safe to give one's name and address to such women, thought Pramod. He was going to say 'Vinod Sharma' when his eyes fell on the first letter of his name tattooed on his arm. Though Radha was not likely to see it, Pramod said, 'My name is Prakash.'

'Do you live in the city?' asked the girl.

'No. I've come here from outside. I come here often.'

Then Pramod took off his shirt, brought out the notes from his pocket, counted them a couple of times and handed them over to Radha. She placed them on the table and said, 'Let me switch off the light now.' Pramod nodded.

Pramod woke up to the darkness inside the room. He saw the watch. It was eleven-thirty. All of a sudden, fear gripped him. It seemed as if the briefcase, packed with all that money, was not there. But once his eyes got used to the darkness he saw that the briefcase was still on the table. Radha was sleeping by his side. On seeing him awake, she got up and switched on the light. Pramod put on his clothes, checked the money in the briefcase, and kept the bottle in it. When he was leaving the room, Radha said with sleep-laden eyes, 'Please come again.'

He squeezed her shoulder a little and said, 'Sure, my dear Khshyanaprabha.'

The sickly man was dozing in his chair outside. On seeing Pramod come out of the house, he stood up and asked, 'Was everything all right? Didn't I tell you that Radha is a nice girl?' Pramod could guess that the man was out to touch him for some money so, without allowing him to continue his conversation, he cut him short, 'Go and get a cab for me.'

After going into his hotel room, Pramod first opened the briefcase and counted the money. Everything was all right. There was no more sleep in his eyes and he decided to write the report of the day's work for his company. While writing the report, he thought about the conditions on which he would work for the rival company. Just then, he recalled Radha, and he remembered her as a good-natured girl. But he immediately corrected himself—how can one, whose character is bad, be of a good nature?

Translated from the Odia by Bibhuti Mishra

THE SHAH'S HARLOT

Amrita Pritam

No one called her Neelam, she was the Shah's harlot to everyone.

Neelam blossomed into youth in a courtesan tenement of Lahore's Hira Mandi. A Sardar from a princely state performed ritually removed her nose-ring and deflowered her for a sum of full five thousand rupees. Then one day she left the cheap tenement of Hira Mandi and moved to Falleti's, the most expensive hotel in town. Although she had not moved away from Lahore the whole town seemed to have forgotten her original name overnight and started referring to her as the Shah's harlot.

She was known for her mellifluous voice. No singing girl could render Mirza as well as her. Although people had forgotten her name, no one had forgotten her voice. Every home with a gramophone was sure to have her records. At any get-together there were always requests for her record to be played over and again.

Her relationship with the Shah was no secret and his family knew of it. Not only did they know of it, they had also accepted it. Though when the Shah's son, who was to be married now, was still a baby, the Shahni had threatened to take poison and kill herself. But the Shah, clasping a necklace of the purest of pearls on his wife's neck, told her: 'Shahni! She is lucky for your household. I know a gem when I see it. Haven't you heard of the qualities of the neelam. It can make or mar someone. This neelam has made me. Ever since I took her, even the mud that I touch turns into gold.'

'But she will ruin the home one day. We will be left with nothing,' the Shahni, swallowing the pain that rose in her heart, tried to counter his argument.

But the adamant Shah said, 'On the other hand I am scared. One can never tell with these harlots. If someone else lures her away, our fate may be marred forever.'

The Shahni could say nothing more and left everything to time. But time did not move on for many years to come. True enough, more wealth came into Shah's hands in comparison to what he spent on Neelam. Earlier, he had a small shop in the city but now his was the largest showroom, with cast-iron railings. Not just his house, he owned the entire colony which was rented out to well-off tenants. And the Shahni did not let go of the keys to the lockers of her home.

Long ago while locking the box with the gold coins, the Shahni had told her husband, 'Keep her in the hotel if you will or build a Taj Mahal for her, but she must never enter my home. I do not wish to see her.' True to her word, the Shahni had not seen her till date. When she said this her elder boy was still in school. Now he was to be married but she had not allowed even Neelam's records to enter her home, nor could anyone talk of her. Although her sons had heard her records all over the bazaar and also heard innumerable people referring to her as 'the Shah's harlot'.

The elder son's marriage had been fixed. Tailors and embroiderers were sitting in the house for the past four months. One would be embellishing a suit with gold, another with silver, yet another would bespangle dresses and edge dupattas with golden trimmings. The Shahni's was flush with money—she would take out a pouch full of rupees, spend it, and return to the locker to fill it again.

The Shah's friends insisted that they wanted to hear the harlot sing at the boy's wedding. They put the proposal forward with tact, 'Shahji, many singing and dancing girls are available but you must make sure that your melody queen comes, even if she sings just a verse of Mirza.'

Falleti's was not just any other hotel. Only the Britishers would stay there. It had not only single and double rooms but also suites of three big rooms. Neelam lived in one such suite. The Shah thought he would humour his friends by organizing an evening of music in her suite.

'That would be like going to a house of entertainment,' a friend

objected and everyone joined him, saying, 'no Shahji, only you
have the right to go there. We have never said anything before for
so many years. She is all yours. But we want to celebrate our
nephew's wedding so in the true feudal tradition; you must call her
home, the home of our sister-in-law...'

The proposal appealed to the Shah. It was wise not to take his
friends to Neelam's abode although he had learnt that one or two
aristocrats were visiting her in his absence. He also wanted Neelam
to see the grandeur of his home. But afraid of the Shahni, he was
not conceding to the request of his friends.

Well, two of his friends found a way out and approached the
Shahni, 'Bhabhi, won't you arrange an evening of music for the
boy's wedding? We don't want to miss out on any ceremony. The
Shah wants to arrange a get-together at Neelam's place. It is all
right but thousands of rupees will be wasted on it. After all you
have to take care; he has already spent enough on the harlot. Be
wise and call her to sing here one evening. We will enjoy the music
and a lot of money will be saved.'

First the Shahni resisted, 'I do not wish to see the harlot.'
However, the friends persisted, 'This here is your empire. She will
come as a servant obeying your orders. It will be her humiliation
not yours. She will be just another entertainer.'

The Shahni finally saw the merit of the case but she laid down
the rules, 'Liquor will not be served. Everyone will sit as they
would in a decent home. You men can join us. She will just come,
sing and leave. I will give here the four patasas that I will be giving
to other girls who come to sing the wedding songs.'

'That is exactly what we want,' the Shah's friends flattered.
'You have saved this home with your wisdom, otherwise God
knows what may have happened?'

And the harlot came. The Shahni had sent her personal carriage
to fetch her. The home was full of relatives and friends. White
sheets had been spread out in the big room with big round
cushions and a dholaki was placed right in the middle. The
women of the home started singing the wedding songs.

As the carriage stopped outside the house, many eager women ran towards the windows and the staircase to catch a glimpse of the woman they had all heard about but had never seen.

'It is an ill omen to leave the song unfinished,' the Shahni scolded. But she found her own voice weak, as though her heart was sinking. She walked slowly to the front door. She rearranged the borders of her sari as though seeking courage from its auspicious pink colour to face the other woman.

There was Neelam! She was resplendent in a shimmering green garara trimmed with gold and a bright red shirt. A green silk dupatta was draped on her head and trailed down by her feet. She seemed to be twinkling and the Shahni felt that the shimmering green of her attire had spread itself out in the doorway.

Then her green glass bangles tinkled and the Shahni saw a fair hand rise up in a salaam of greeting. A musical voice spoke out, 'Many congratulations Shahni. Many congratulations to you.'

She was a dainty little thing. The Shahni pointed towards the round cushion and asked her to sit down and doing so she felt that her raised fleshy arm looked very unsightly.

In one corner of the room, the Shah was sitting with his friends. The delicate darling glanced at them, gave her stylish salaam and sat pretty by the cushion. Her glass bangles tinkled again. The Shahni looked once again at those arms bedecked with green glass bangles. Then she spontaneously moved her gaze to her own gold bracelets.

The whole room was bedazzled. All eyes were looking in one direction, even the Shahni's, but she was annoyed at the other admiring stares. She wanted to scold everyone again and ask the women to continue with the wedding songs. But she could not find her voice. Others too seemed to have lost their voices. She started looking at the dholaki in the middle of the room and wanted beat it hard to break the stunned silence.

She who had caused the silence broke it too. She said, 'First of all I will sing a ghodhi, all right Shahni?' And, looking at the Shahni, she started to sing:

Nikki-nikki bundi nikeya meen ve ware
Teri maan ve suhagan tere shagan kare
(Tiny droplets, my young one, come down in rain
As your lucky mother performs the sacred ritual)

Hearing the song, the Shahni felt a little at ease because she was the mother and was being sung about. Her husband was only her's and only she had the right to perform the rituals.

Smiling, the Shahni sat right in front of the woman who was singing through the rites and rituals of her son's marriage.

The ghodhi ended and conversation returned to the room. The women wanted a dholaki song and the men wanted to hear the verses of Mirza.

The singer paid no heed to the request from the menfolk and put her knee on the dholaki. The Shahni was pleased with the fact that instead of pandering to the men, Neelam was fulfilling the requests of the women.

Some women did not know of Neelam. They were asking one another about her. The Shahni heard whispers, 'She is the one, the Shah's harlot.' Even though they had whispered softly, the words were piercing the Shahni's ears—the Shah's harlot, the Shah's harlot—and her face went pale again.

The beat of the dholaki got louder as did the singer's voice:

Soohe ve cheere waalea main kehani aan…
(I call out to you the red-turbaned one…)

The Shahni's heart sank. God forbid! The red-turbaned one was her son and today he was to mount a horse to bring home a bride.

There was no end to the requests. One song would end and another would start. The singer would oblige the women in one song and the men in the other. Every now and then she would say, 'Let someone else sing now, give me a breather.' But who had the courage to sing in front of her. Singing came to her naturally and her voice was so melodious. She too was saying this just for effect because when one song ended, she would start the next one.

It was all right as far as the wedding songs went but once she started singing verses by Mirza in her mellifluous voice, even the breeze stopped blowing to listen to her. The men in the room froze. The Shahni started feeling uneasy. She glanced at the Shah. He was a statue like the others but the Shahni felt he had turned to stone.

The Shahni panicked. She felt that if she lost this moment then she would be reduced to a clay statue forever. She had to do something, something to prove her existence.

It was late in the evening, and the function was coming to a close.

The Shahni had said that she would distribute only patasas but once the singing ended, tea and delicious savouries were served generously. The Shahni took a rolled hundred-rupee note in her hand, touched it to her son's head and then gave it to the one who was known as the Shah's harlot.

'Let it be Shahni. I already live on your morsels,' she said and laughed. Her laughter twinkled as did her silence.

The Shahni's face went white. She felt that the Shah's harlot, that wretch, had belittled her by openly referring to her liaison with her husband. However, she took quick control of the situation. Pressing the note firmly in the other woman's hand she said, 'You will always take from the Shah, but when will you have the chance to take something from me? Come, keep this today.'

The Shah's harlot, accepting the note, seemed most humbled. The auspicious pink colour of the Shahni's sari had spread itself all over the room.

Translated from the Punjabi by Nirupama Dutt

NOTES ON CONTRIBUTORS

A. P. Ashwin Kumar teaches in Tumkur University, Tumakuru, India, where he edits the research journal *Pragmata*. He has a PhD from Manipal University in Cultural Studies and is a bi-directional academic and literary translator working in English and Kannada.

Anita Samkaria is Associate Professor of English at Satyawati College, University of Delhi. She is also the coordinator of the Family Counselling Centre in her college, which works towards creating awareness about gender issues and women's empowerment. Her areas of interest include translation and gender studies.

Amrita Pritam, a prominent writer and poet in Punjabi and Hindi, is widely acclaimed as the leading poet of the Punjabi language in the twentieth century. She is most remembered for her poignant elegy, *Ajj aakhaan Waris Shah nu (Today I Invoke Waris Shah)*, which addresses the eighteenth-century Punjabi poet in anguish, asking him to condemn the massacres that occurred during the Partition of India. As a novelist, her most noted work was *Pinjar* which movingly chronicles the plight of women, as well as the Partition riots. Pritam lived both in India and Pakistan.

Aradhana Pradhan is a PhD Research Scholar associated with the Department of English, Jamia Millia Islamia, New Delhi. Her field of research is women studies and Indian cinema post-Independence. She holds a Diplom de Langue in French and Zertifikat zum Berufsdeutsch in German. A freelance teacher of English, she has taught at Sardar Patel Vidyalaya and Jamia Secondary School, among others. She recently launched Masi Inc., a literary event company, as Founder-Director and is also the Co-Founder-Director of the Patna Literature Festival. She works as a freelance translator and web content developer for Indian art and craft sites.

Arunava Sinha translates classic, modern and contemporary Bengali fiction and non-fiction into English. Thirty-one of his translations have been published so far. Twice the winner of the Crossword translation award, for Sankar's *Chowringhee* (2007) and Anita Agnihotri's *Seventeen* (2011), respectively, and the winner of the Muse India translation award (2013) for Buddhadeva Bose's *When the Time Is Right*, he has also been shortlisted for The Independent Foreign Fiction prize (2009) for his translation of *Chowringhee*. Besides India, his translations have been published in the UK and the US in English, and in several European and Asian countries through further translation. He was born and grew up in Kolkata, and lives and writes in New Delhi.

Baburao Bagul was a radical Dalit thinker, poet and writer from Maharashtra, whose writing was among the first wave of modern Dalit voices. His first collection of stories, *Jewhan Mi Jaat Chorli Hoti* (The Time I Concealed My Caste) shook up Marathi literature's ideas at the time with its raw description of the lives of the marginalized and oppressed. His second collection *Maran Swasta Hot Ahe* (Death Is Becoming Cheap) established him firmly as a leading writer of fiction. His was a new and powerful voice that inspired later generations of Dalit writers and feminists.

Bibhuti Mishra was a short-story writer and freelance journalist who lived in Bhubaneswar. He was a regular contributor to Odia journals and translated from Odia into English.

Bibhutibhushan Bandyopadhyay was one of the leading writers of modern Bengali literature, with sixteen novels and more than two hundred short stories to his credit. His writing has been praised for its poetic sensibility, intimately tied with a detailed depiction of life in the deeply stratified and exploitative society of rural Bengal. His autobiographical novel *Pather Panchali* was later adapted, along with the sequel *Aparajito*, into the Apu Trilogy by filmmaker Satyajit Ray. Bandyopadhyay was posthumously awarded the Rabindra Puraskar, West Bengal's most prestigious literary prize.

Bushra Alvi Razzack is a freelance writer and editor. She writes on society and culture, translates literary works from Urdu and Hindi to English, and has also taught English in India, Saudi Arabia and the United Arab Emirates. Many of her poems have appeared in various anthologies. Her first book, a collection of her poetry and other writings, will soon be published.

Fatima Rizvi teaches literature in the Department of English and Modern European Languages at the University of Lucknow. Her areas of interest include postcolonial literature and literature in translation. Her academic papers have been published in journals of national and international repute and in collections of critical essays. She translates from Urdu and Hindi into English. She is on the board of the Centre for Cultural Texts, Records and Translation of Indian Literatures, a project sponsored by the government of Uttar Pradesh under the Centre of Excellence scheme.

Gayatri Bhattacharyya was born and brought up in Shillong, and studied in Shillong and Guwahati. She went on to retire as Professor of English from Gauhati University. She now uses her time to translate books and short stories from Assamese to English. Nine of her translated books and anthologies have so far been published by Sahitya Akademi, Rupa Publications, Zubaan Books and Vitasta Publishers, among others.

Haris Qadeer is an Assistant Professor at the Department of English, University of Delhi. He earned his doctoral degree from Aligarh Muslim University. He was awarded the University gold medal for his MA (English). His academic papers have been published in journals of national and international repute. His areas of interest include writings by Indian Muslim women, South Asian literature in English and Urdu literature in Hindi/English translations. He translates from Urdu/Hindi to English.

Indira Goswami was a celebrated Assamese writer, poet, professor and scholar who worked passionately to bring about change in the lives of the marginalized and overlooked. She is equally known for her efforts to broker peace between the ULFA and the Indian government, as she is for her poetic and vivid writing on topics as diverse as the plight of widows in Vrindavan, animal sacrifice at the Kamakhya temple, secessionism in the Northeast, and the 1984 anti-Sikh riots. She won numerous awards and honours during her lifetime, including the Jnanpith and the Sahitya Akademi Awards. The government of Assam awarded her the Assam Ratna posthumously.

Ismat Chughtai, considered the grand dame of Urdu fiction, was known for her indomitable spirit and fierce feminist ideology. Her short stories and screenplays, along with those of Rashid Jahan, Wajida Tabassum and Qurratulain Hyder created a revolutionary feminist politics and aesthetics in twentieth-century Urdu literature. In her trademark outspoken yet home-grown style of writing, she explored feminine sexuality, middle-class gentility, and other evolving conflicts in modern India, while resolutely refusing to bow to conventional norms. She remains a relevant and electric voice even today.

J. P. Das is a well-known Odia poet, playwright and fiction writer. Several collections of his short stories have been translated into English, and he is also the author of a widely acclaimed historical novel, *Desh Kaal Patra* (*A Time Elsewhere*). His plays have been translated into and performed in many languages. An art historian, his scholarly works on Odishan art include *Puri Paintings* and *Chitra Pothi*. He currently lives and works in New Delhi.

Javaid Qazi was born in Pakistan in 1947 and has been in love with the English language since as far back as he can remember. At the age of twenty-one, he moved to the US where he completed a doctorate in English Literature. He believes in style, in variety and in providing the reader with an interesting experience. He loves travel, speaks French, Italian and Urdu and lives in San Jose, California with his wife and cat and where he continues to write, read and struggle to create literature that reflects a true image of the world that he inhabits, but also a world lit up by the prismatic colours of his imagination.

Kamala Das was a major Indian poet and writer in English as well as in Malayalam. Her candid treatment of female sexuality infuses her writing with power, whether in her explicit and unflinching autobiography or the more literary elements of her poetry and fiction. She was nominated for the Nobel Prize in Literature, and is the recipient of a slew of Indian literary awards, including the Sahitya Akademi Award, as well as the Asian Poetry Prize.

Kamleshwar was an eminent Hindi writer from Uttar Pradesh, who became a part of Hindi literature's post-Independence 'Nayi Kahani' movement. His works depict the trials and tribulations of a fast-changing society, groping for new values in the face of the collapse of the old value system. He wrote about the woes of contemporary society, which he saw as being in the grip of excessive materialism. He also carved out a niche for himself in scriptwriting for Hindi movies, and for television, and as the editor of the Hindi dailies, *Dainik Jagran* and *Dainik Bhaskar*.

Khurshid Akram was born and brought up in Calcutta and belongs to the generation of Urdu writers which came to the fore during the 1990s. He has a volume each of short stories (*Ek Ghair Mashroot Muafinama*), poetry (*Pichhli Peet ke Kaaraney*), and criticism (*Andaz-e-Nazar Mera*), along with published work in these genres in various magazines, journals and anthologies. He has also translated four books into Urdu from Hindi, Bangla and English, as well as created a compilation (*Jadeed Hindi Shairi*) of Hindi poems. Akram was the editor of the prestigious Urdu literary monthly *Aajkal* and currently works as a Senior News Editor in All India Radio.

Krishan Chander was a prolific writer of satirical short stories in Hindi and Urdu, as well as a well-known screenplay writer. He also wrote over twenty novels and radio plays. His writing addresses social and political themes such as the partition of Kashmir, the Partition of India and Pakistan, and the Bengal famine, and is known for its fundamental humanism and idealistic approach. He was a dedicated member of the Progressive Writers' Association and an ardent socialist. His short story 'Annadata' was made into the film *Dharti ke Lal* by K. A. Abbas.

Lakshmi Holmström is an Indian-born British writer, literary critic and translator of Tamil fiction into English. Her most prominent works have been her translations of short stories and novels of contemporary writers in Tamil, including Mauni, Ashokamitran, Sundara Ramasami, C. S. Lakshmi, Bama and Imayam. She is the Founder-Trustee of SALIDAA (South Asian Diaspora Literature and Arts Archive), an organization which archives the works of British writers and artists of South Asian origin. She currently lives in the UK. She was appointed Member of the Order of the British Empire (MBE) in the 2011 New Year Honours for her services to literature.

Manisha Kulshreshtha is a well-known Hindi fiction writer, born and brought up in Rajasthan. She has published six short-story collections and three novels. Her first published novel, *Shigaf* (*The Slit*), based on Kashmir, is written in the unusual form of a blog and was shortlisted for the Gitanjali Indo-French Jury Prize in 2012. A Kathak dancer herself, she recently published a novel based on dance and ancient views of Indian feminism, titled *Panchkanya*.

Modhurima Sinha completed her schooling from Loreto House, Calcutta, and received a masters degree in English Literature from Presidency College, Calcutta, before becoming a journalist and dabbling in advertising and photography. She has authored *Call of the Real*, a book on Bengal's contemporary master painters, published by MAPIN. She has also worked with noted American photographer Laura McPhee for many years, and has assisted film-maker Aparna Sen. *The Third Eye*, a short film directed by her, has recently travelled to many film festivals across the world. Sinha is married, has a son, and enjoys balancing her family with her job at the Taj in Calcutta while pursuing her creative dreams.

Nabendu Ghosh was a legendary writer who shot into eminence in Bengali literature with his novel *Daak Diye Jaai* about the Quit India movement in 1942. His subjects were rooted in realism, and his language refashioned the prevalent aesthetic modes of expression. He continued to write short stories and novels even after he moved to Bombay where he created classic movie scripts like *Parineeta, Devdas, Yahudi, Sujata, Bandini, Aar Paar, Teesri Kasam* and *Abhimaan*. Later, Ghosh directed the National Award-winning film *Trishagni*, as well as *Netraheen Sakshi* and *Ladkiyaan*.

Nayana Addarkar is a front-ranking Konkani writer of poems, short fiction, skits, humour, and children's stories. She is also a translator and has several publications to her credit.

Niranjana was one of the foremost progressive voices in Kannada literature. He was a prolific writer, journalist, pamphleteer and freedom fighter, as well as a member of the Communist Party. His first novel, *Vimochane* (1953), blazed a new trail in Kannada writing, while *Mrutyunjaya* (1976), his most famous novel, won Karnataka's Jnanpith Prize. Niranjana also edited and was the main translator of *Vishwa Katha Kosha*, an ambitious multi-volume collection of short stories from around the world in Kannada translation. He was married to Anupama Niranjana, a well-known Kannada writer and medical doctor.

Nirupama Dutt is Chandigarh's homegrown poet, journalist, literary and art critic and translator of many seasons who has written and edited several books. She writes in both Punjabi and English. She received the Punjabi Akademi Award for her anthology of poems, *Ik Nadi Sanwali Jahi* (A River Somewhat Dark). Her poetry anthologies have also come out in English and Hindi. Her translations include *Stories of the Soil* (a translated collection of forty-one stories from Punjabi), *Poet of the Revolution* (translation of the memoirs and poetry of Lal Singh Dil), *Pluto Poems* (short poems by Gulzar) and *The Last Weave*, (the Kabir poems by Yatindra Mishra). At present she is translating three novellas by Amrita Pritam and working on a novel of her own.

Premchand is one of the most celebrated writers of the Indian subcontinent, and is the father of the Hindustani short-story genre. His works include more than a dozen novels, about two hundred and fifty short stories, several essays and the translations of a number of literary works into Hindi. He was one of the first Hindi authors to prominently turn towards realism and social commentary in his writing, favouring a rational approach to the problems besetting the poor.

Puthumaippithan was one of the most influential and revolutionary writers of Tamil fiction. His works were marked by social satire, progressive thinking and outspoken criticism of accepted conventions because of which he faced extreme hostility from critics during his lifetime. His writing unflinchingly addressed conflicts between emotion and reason, the hypocrisies of religion, particularly as brought out in rituals and caste practices, as well as the oppression of women. Over the past sixty years, his works have become foundational texts of contemporary Tamil literature, and have been nationalized by the Tamil Nadu government.

Qurratulain Hyder was one of the most influential voices in Urdu fiction, known for her warmth and candidness in articulating her innermost feelings and ideals. She personified independence in thought, both ideologically as well as in her depiction of social class and milieu. Her widely read novel, *Aag ka Dariya* (*River of Fire*) has been compared to Gabriel Garcia Marquez's *One Hundred Years of Solitude* for its depth and breadth of writing. Hyder won the Jnanpith and Sahitya Akademi Awards, and was also awarded the Padma Bhushan, India's highest civilian honour.

Rakhshanda Jalil is a well-known Indian writer, critic and literary historian. She is best known for her acclaimed book on Delhi's lesser-known monuments, *Invisible City: The Hidden Monuments of India* and a well-received collection of short stories, *Release and Other Stories*. Her PhD on the Progressive Writers' Movement as reflected in Urdu Literature was published by Oxford University Press as *Liking Progress, Loving Change* in 2014. She runs an organization called Hindustani Awaaz, devoted to the popularization of Hindi-Urdu literature and culture.

Ratnottama Sengupta, a senior journalist, has been writing for newspapers and journals, participating in discussions on electronic media, teaching mass communication, writing books on cinema and art, programming film festivals and curating art exhibitions. Daughter of Nabendu Ghosh, a leading name in Bengali literature and legendary screen playwright-director, she has written on Hindi films for the *Encyclopaedia Britannica*, been a member of the Central Board of Film Certification, served on the National Film Awards jury and has herself won a National Award. Currently the editor of CineBengal.com and the former arts editor at the *Times of India,* she is also a member of the selection committee of the Kolkata International Film Festival, the International Film Festival of India, and serves on the script committee for the National Film Development Corporation of India.

Saadat Hasan Manto was an Urdu writer, playwright and author, who is considered to have written some of the greatest short stories in contemporary South Asia. He was a journalist, essayist, radio playwright and screenwriter in Bombay, before migrating to Lahore after the Partition of India. His writing vividly chronicled the chaos that prevailed during and after Partition. Manto also wrote unflinchingly about women's exploitation and sexuality, which caused many of his short stories to be mired in controversy and obscenity trials.

Sameena Hasan Siddiqui is presently Director, Centre for the Study of Comparative Religion and Civilizations, Jamia Millia Islamia, New Delhi. She has taught at Delhi University, and is a historian specializing in socio-cultural conditions of medieval India with particular interest in Sufi studies. Her published work includes *Khadang-e-Ghadar: Politics, Ethics and Change*, as well as three scholarly books on the Sufi dargah and on medieval India. She has authored many well-researched articles on Nizamuddin Auliya and judicial land records. She is at present working on deconstructing identities and interplay of region and religion in North India between the eighth and fifteenth centuries.

Shanta Gokhale is a novelist, translator, columnist and cultural critic. Amongst the many books and plays written her, she has two award-winning novels, *Rita Welinkar* and *Tya Varshi*, both written originally in Marathi and translated by her into English. She has also penned a critical history of Marathi drama, *Playwright at the Centre*.

Siddique Alam, a novelist, short-story writer, playwright and poet, was born in Purulia in 1952. He has published three collections of short stories, one novel, and a collection of poems. His new novel *Chini Kothi* (*Chinese Mansion*) and his translation of J. M. Coetzee's *Waiting for the Barbarians* are in press. One of the finest voices in contemporary Urdu fiction, Alam is known for the elements of magic realism that he introduced to the fabric of the genre. He is also known as an incisive critic, and for his use of innovative and experimental methods as a playwright.

Subodh Ghosh was a renowned Bengali author, who wrote some of the best-known and most widely read stories in Bengali literature. He also worked as a circus clown, bus conductor, sweeper, and for many years, as a journalist with *Ananda Bazaar Patrika*. His writing brings legendary love stories to life, delicately explores interpersonal relationships, and conjures up a bygone way of Adivasi life. Many of his stories have been recreated on screen by directors like Bimal Roy (*Sujata, Anjangarh*), Tapan Sinha (*Jatugriha*), Mrinal Sen (*Ek Adhuri Kahani*, based on 'Gotranter'), Ritwik Ghatak (*Ajantrik*), Gulzar (*Ijaazat*, based on 'Jatugriho') and Basu Chatterjee (*Chitchor*, based on 'Chittachakor').

Xavier Cota translates literature, mainly stories in Konkani, into English. His translated fiction and other articles have appeared in *The Week, Gentleman's World, Katha Prize Stories*, Sahitya Akademi publications, *Mainstream* as well as in local papers in Goa. He won the 2005 Katha Award for Translation. His translated publications of Damodar Mauzo's Konkani works include *These Are My Children*, a collection of stories published by Katha; *Tsunami Simon*, a novel published by Ponytale Books; and *Teresa's Man and Other Stories* from Goa, published by Rupa Publications India. He also translates legal documents from Portuguese to English. Cota, who earlier worked with a bank, lives in Betalbatim, Goa, where he is the convenor of the village forum, working for advocacy of civic and consumer rights.

ACKNOWLEDGEMENTS

This anthology has been made possible because of Juanita Kakoty, whose meticulous follow-up resulted in a final manuscript.

Anurag Basnet of Speaking Tiger made the delicate edits needed for some of the more idiomatic translations and nudged us towards a story hunt across India. The twelve languages represented in this anthology owe a great deal to his perseverance.

Tinku Khanna's passion and commitment helped me stay the course and bring the anthology out, five years after Rakhshanda Jalil first thought of it.

I am grateful to Ravi Singh for his understanding of the importance of such an anthology, and to Kanishka Gupta, of Writer's Side, who performed the matchmaking between editor and publisher.

Indu Chandrasekhar, Kannan Sundaram, Anurag Chaturvedi, Jerry Pinto and Sujata Prasad, who pointed me to stories.

I am grateful to all copyright holders for permission to reprint copyrighted material. Shobha Bagul for allowing us to use her father Baburao Bagul's story, Tejaswini Niranjana for allowing us to use her father Niranjana's story, Jayasuriya Das for permitting the use of his mother Kamala Das's 'A Doll for the Child Prostitute', Arunava Sinha for permitting the use of his translation of 'Heeng-Kochuri' by Bibhutibhushan Bandyopadhyay, Lakshmi Holmström for allowing us to reprint her translation of Puthumaippithan's 'Ponagaram', Anita Samkaria for permitting the use of her translation of 'The Murder of Honour' by Premchand, Nirupama Dutt for her translation of 'The Shah's Harlot' by Amrita Pritam, Aradhana Pradhan for her translation of 'River of Flesh' by Kamleshwar, Rakhshanda Jalil for her translation of 'The Hundred Candle-Power Bulb' by Manto, Shanta Gokhale for 'Woman of the Street' by Baburao Bagul, Ashwin Kumar for his translation of 'The Last Customer' by Niranjana, Fatima Rizvi for her translation

...estry' by Qurratulain Hyder, Gayatri Bhattacharya for her ...slation of 'The Empty Box' by Indira Goswami, Javaid Qazi .or his translations of 'God Forsaken' and 'Coming?' by Siddique Alam and Khurshid Akram, respectively, Ratnottama Sengupta for the translated pieces 'Market Price' by Nabendu Ghosh and 'The Concubine' by Subodh Ghosh, Xavier Cota for 'Roll of the Dice' by Nayana Addarkar, Haris Qadeer for his translation of 'A Prostitute's Letter: For Pandit Jawaharlal Nehru and Qaid-e-Aazam Jinnah' by Krishna Chander, and Sameena Hasan Siddiqui for her translation of 'The Housewife' by Ismat Chugtai. We are also immensely grateful to Khurshid Akram for permitting us the use of his story 'Coming?', as translated by Javaid Qazi; J. P. Das for his story 'The Prostitute', as translated by Bibhuti Mishra; Siddique Alam for 'God Forsaken' as translated by Javaid Kazi; Manisha Kulshreshtha for 'Kalindi' as translated by Bushra Alvi Razzack, and to Modhurima Sinha for her story 'The Letters'.

A big thank you to my patient husband Sunil Narula and parents Vidyasagar and Rajni Gupta for sitting through interrupted conversations and meals as I found a new story to include or rushed off to edit an old one. And, finally, to Gloria Steinem for her encouragement and to Mahasweta Devi for taking up the pen after months to write something for the book.